PENGUIN BOOKS

COMBUSTION

Steve Worland has worked extensively in film and television in Australia and the USA. He has written scripts for Working Title and Icon Productions, worked in script development for James Cameron's *Lightstorm* and wrote Fox Searchlight's *Bootmen*, which won five Australian Film Institute awards. Steve also wrote the action-comedy telemovie *Hard Knox*, episodes of the television series *Big Sky* and the Saturn award-winning *Farscape*. He is the author of the action-adventure novel *Velocity* and is currently writing his third book.

You can connect with Steve at steveworland.com, facebook.com/StevenWorland and twitter.com/StevenWorland

T0342581

STEVE WORLAND

COMBUSTION

PENGUIN BOOKS

PENGUIN BOOKS

Published by the Penguin Group
Penguin Group (Australia)
707 Collins Street, Melbourne, Victoria 3008, Australia
(a division of Penguin Australia Pty Ltd)
Penguin Group (USA) Inc.
375 Hudson Street, New York, New York 10014, USA
Penguin Group (Canada)
90 Eglinton Avenue East, Suite 700, Toronto, Canada ON M4P 2Y3
(a division of Penguin Canada Books Inc.)
Penguin Books Ltd
80 Strand, London WC2R 0RL England
Penguin Ireland
25 St Stephen's Green, Dublin 2, Ireland
(a division of Penguin Books Ltd)
Penguin Books India Pvt Ltd
11 Community Centre, Panchsheel Park, New Delhi 110 017, India
Penguin Group (NZ)
67 Apollo Drive, Rosedale, Auckland 0632, New Zealand
(a division of Penguin New Zealand Pty Ltd)
Penguin Books (South Africa) (Pty) Ltd
Rosebank Office Park, Block D, 181 Jan Smuts Avenue, Parktown North,
Johannesburg 2196, South Africa
Penguin (Beijing) Ltd
7F, Tower B, Jiaming Center, 27 East Third Ring Road North, Chaoyang District,
Beijing 100020, China

Penguin Books Ltd, Registered Offices: 80 Strand, London WC2R 0RL, England

First published by Penguin Group (Australia), 2013
This edition published by Penguin Group (Australia), 2014

1 3 5 7 9 10 8 6 4 2

Text copyright © Steve Worland 2013

The moral right of the author has been asserted

Cover design by Adam Laszczuk © Penguin Group (Australia)
Text design by Sam Jayaweera © Penguin Group (Australia)
Cover photographs: Road: Andy Ennis/Alamy; Cars: Stars and Stripes/Alamy; Explosion: Shutterstock
Printed and bound in Australia by Griffin Press,
an accredited ISO AS/NZS 14001 Environmental Management Systems printer.

National Library of Australia
Cataloguing-in-Publication data:

Worland, Steve, author.
Combustion / Steve Worland.
9780143567011 (paperback)
Australian fiction.

A823.4

penguin.com.au

PROLOGUE

Boom.

Corey Purchase watches the football leave Pete Roland's boot. He's marked a thousand kicks from this guy over the years, but their speed *always* surprises him. Without exception the ball arrives earlier than Corey expects, even when he expects it to arrive early.

Bloody hell, it's quick.

The football spirals through the night sky like a laser-guided missile and again Corey is surprised. It's not only super *fast* but super *accurate*. The fifteen-year-old reaches out, extends his hands –

Bam. It lands right on his fingertips.

Whoa! Corey missteps and the football slides out of his grasp, hits the grass, bounces up. He drags it back to his chest and clamps it there.

What the hell was that?

It felt like the ground moved under him. He ignores it and swings towards the goalposts. He needs to come up with something and he needs to do it fast. There's fifteen seconds left on the clock, if that. Only a goal and six points will win this game.

The goalposts are fifty metres to the left, at a sharp angle to his current position. None of his teammates are free so a kick to the goal square is too risky. Instead, he steps left and goes himself. The five-hundred-strong crowd who pack the old wooden grandstand at Burra High School rise as one.

He bounces the football, runs hard.

Fifty metres becomes thirty-five.

The crowd roars.

Out of the corner of his eye he sees a defender sprint across the field to cut him off. The guy trips, falls, crashes to the ground.

Too bad, so sad.

Corey bounces the football again, keeps running.

Thirty-five metres becomes twenty-five.

Corey loses his balance again – then instantly regains it.

What on earth was that?

He can't worry about it. The goalposts are right there. They're still on an angle but much closer, just twenty metres away. He steps right, drops the football, swings his right foot and unleashes a thunderbolt.

Boom. The football soars between the uprights.

Goal! The crowd goes nuts.

And the siren sounds.

Game over.

Corey punches the air then turns to the grandstand, searches for Roberta. She always sits in the middle at the back so she has a bird's-eye view –

Crack. The wooden structure shudders violently, then lurches to the left.

'What was that —'

The ground beneath Corey rises sharply. 'Hey!' He's thrown off balance, crashes to the turf, can smell the freshly cut grass. He scrambles to his feet but the ground shakes with a fierce lateral movement and it's impossible to stay upright. He's tossed to the ground again.

Earthquake.

Corey looks up. Wood shatters and bolts snap on the grandstand. Parents, teachers and students rush to the exits, create a bottleneck in both aisles. The structure tilts wildly as the ground splits underneath the left side and swallows the cement foundation.

'Jesus.'

Where's Roberta?

Corey scans the panicked faces in the grandstand. *There!* Exactly where he thought she'd be, in the middle at the rear. She grasps the back railing, hasn't followed the mass of people who surge towards the exits.

He must help her. He rises to his feet. It's difficult to stay balanced but he drives himself forward, slow at first – then faster – then faster still. He sprints towards the grandstand forty metres away. He has no idea what he'll do when he gets there, he just knows he must get there.

Screams fill the air as Corey reaches the right side of the heaving structure and circles around to the back. He looks up, locks eyes with Roberta, her face a portrait of terror. 'Hold on!'

How does he fix this? He searches the grandstand, looks for a way up to her. There must be a route – he just can't find it. It's happening too fast.

The shuddering intensifies. The chasm widens and the left side of the grandstand tips over at an even steeper angle, slides into the widening fissure like it's being swallowed whole. Roberta holds on to the railing.

He'll catch her. Yes. That's what he'll do. He rushes forward –

The earth tears and rises in front of him, pitches him to the ground. He looks up. The railing Roberta still holds is wrenched from its moorings. She hangs in the air for a terrible moment – then silently falls into the chasm.

'No!' Corey finds his feet and sprints towards it, to grab her and pull her out.

Crack. The left side of the grandstand collapses – and drops into the chasm after her.

The shaking stops. Corey runs to the mound of debris.

There's nothing he can do. He drops to his knees, stricken.

The fifth of March, 1997.

The Burra earthquake occurs between the Para and Eden-Burnside fault lines, one hundred and sixty kilometres north of Adelaide. It registers 5.0 on the Richter scale and claims the lives of three people, including Roberta Purchase, Corey's mother, three days before his sixteenth birthday.

1

'Won't be long now.'

From his position on the overpass, Zac Bunsen stares down the desolate 110 Freeway through miniature Nikon binoculars. Traffic is light and the moon is high as it illuminates the sprawling City of Angels before him.

A winner in the genetic lottery, the thirty-nine-year-old resembles Brad Pitt's better looking cousin. Dressed in black, he checks his Patek Philippe Nautilus again, then adjusts the volume on his iPhone and returns it to his jacket pocket.

He's not listening to music through his headset. Back in 2004, researchers at the University of Bonn developed a microphone that captured soundwaves inaudible to the human ear. The researchers trapped the ethylene gas released when the stem of a plant was cut, then bombarded it with calibrated laser beams, causing it to vibrate, which produced a soundwave that was recorded by the new microphone. The more a plant was cut, the louder the sound.

At first Bunsen found the recordings unbearable to hear. They sounded like screams of torture. Then he realised that's what they were – an audible representation of the pain human beings have inflicted on the natural world for centuries. So now he listens to them when he needs to pump himself up, like a boxer listening to 'Eye of the Tiger' before the big fight. He's listened to them a lot recently, in preparation for the biggest fight of his life – a fight that begins tonight.

He looks through the binoculars again and picks up three dark shapes on the freeway. They're distant but move towards him fast. He pockets the binoculars and kills the sound in his headset: 'We are live.'

Two men stand beside him on the overpass: his second in command, the weather-beaten head of security, Kilroy Jones, with the unapologetically long, grey ponytail, and the fresh-faced Jacob Ryan, with the severe buzz cut. Like Bunsen they are both dressed in black, and wear backpacks and miniature headsets.

Bunsen can see the dark shapes clearly now. Three vehicles drive in convoy. A black sedan leads a large, tall, dark blue van, which is followed by another black sedan. They move quickly: five hundred metres and closing.

Bunsen turns to the others. 'Ready?'

They nod. They've trained long and hard for this moment. They know exactly what must be done. As one they step up to the guardrail.

Bunsen takes a breath. He remembers the lyric of a song his mother loved back in the day: 'You've gotta be cruel to be kind.' For Bunsen this is the beginning of cruel. Kind will come later, but only after he has been very, very cruel.

The vehicles are right there.

'Go.'

The three men step off the overpass.

Thump, thump, thump. They hit the roof of the van five metres below and move with purpose. Kilroy kneels, pulls off his backpack and draws out a pneumatic rivet gun attached to a small compressed air cylinder. Jacob pivots to the front of the van and swings down to the cabin. Bunsen turns to the rear of the vehicle and takes in the sedan that follows close behind. He extracts two half-metre lengths of pipe from his backpack and slides them together with a sharp clack.

The two uniformed men inside the sedan stare up at him, astonished. Then the passenger frantically draws a pistol and rolls down his window.

Bunsen fires the RPG-7 grenade launcher.

Boom. The warhead slams into the bonnet of the sedan and the engine detonates, lifts the vehicle a metre off the road. It hangs in the air for a frozen moment, then drops back down with a snap-crunch. The left front wheel separates from the chassis, the axle stub digs into the tarmac and the sedan flips, lands on its roof and slides to the side of the freeway.

Bunsen turns to see Jacob drop to the driver's front step, draw a 9mm pistol and fire into the cabin twice. He yanks the door open, drags the driver's limp body onto the street, then slides behind the wheel. His voice buzzes in Bunsen's headset: 'I'm in.'

'Roger that.' Bunsen reloads the RPG-7 and fires at the vehicle in front.

Boom. The grenade enters the sedan through the rear window and explodes. The burning car veers hard left then ploughs into the guardrail.

Bunsen is pleased. In under a minute they have taken control of the van and both its escorts have been neutralised. He glances at Kilroy. The old man works fast, uses the rivet gun expertly. 'How long?'

'Almost there.'

Jacob's voice rattles in Bunsen's ears again. 'Company ahead.'

Bunsen turns. A pair of police cruisers speed along the freeway towards them, lights flashing.

Sirens. Bunsen looks over his shoulder and his eyes find another pair of police cruisers advancing from the rear. Seven hundred metres away and closing fast.

They're surrounded.

Bunsen barks into his headset: 'Send in the Tyrannosaur.'

To the left a piercing banshee scream cuts across the landscape as a giant black beast rises from beside the freeway. It pivots and thumps towards the van, low and fast, its ear-splitting howl fused with a ground-shaking throb that blots out all trace of the police sirens.

Bunsen watches the S64 Erickson Air-Crane Heavy Lift helicopter hover overhead, twin Pratt & Whitney turbines driving gigantic twenty-metre-long rotor blades that buffet the van with the turbulence of a Category 7 hurricane.

Four hooks swing on chains from beneath the giant chopper. Bunsen and Kilroy each grab two and latch them to the metal hoops the old man just riveted to the van's roof.

'Go!' Bunsen shouts into his headset and there's an almighty jolt. The van is yanked off the road and hoisted into the sky like a child's toy. Bunsen looks down at the gobsmacked police officers as they watch the van soar overhead.

The Tyrannosaur is at three thousand feet within a minute. A rope ladder is attached to one of the chains. Kilroy grabs it and climbs towards the rear-facing cabin behind the cockpit. He moves fast for a guy pushing sixty. Next, Jacob clambers onto the roof and follows Kilroy up the ladder.

Bunsen's about to do the same when he notices blinking lights five hundred metres to the right. He turns and takes in the sleek silhouette of a Bell JetRanger helicopter.

A Los Angeles Police Department JetRanger helicopter.

And everything had been going so well.

The Tyrannosaur may have a 2600-gallon water-bombing capability, may be able to lift five tonnes, but it's not fast. It can't outrun a JetRanger and doesn't have its range. The JetRanger will be able to follow it for as long as it needs, then identify where it lands. And unless the JetRanger moves closer, the RPG-7 is of no use, its effective range barely two hundred metres.

Damn it.

There's only one thing to do. Bunsen crouches at the back of the van and looks over the edge at the rear roller door. It is padlocked. He draws a 9mm pistol from his jacket, aims, blows off the lock with the first shot, grabs the door, rolls it up, lowers himself over the edge and swings inside.

He lands in front of four olive-green cases that are strapped down and look like oversized coffins, each three metres long by half a metre wide.

They are the reason for tonight's mission.

Bunsen lays the RPG-7 on the floor and kneels beside the second case along. He unlatches the heavy lid, pushes it open, looks inside – and smiles.

A BLU-116.

He unclips the case so both sides and both ends lie flat against the floor then works the BLU-116's control panel, hears a high-pitched whir as it spins to life, then speaks into his headset: 'Enrico, swing me round.'

'Roger that.' In the Tyrannosaur's cockpit, the stocky pilot plays the controls. The big chopper pivots gracefully.

Bunsen stares out the van's rear opening, waits for the moment.

The blinking lights of the JetRanger glide into view, silhouetted against the black sky, still following five hundred metres behind.

'That's it.' The Tyrannosaur stops turning.

Bunsen works the BLU-116's control panel again.

Boom. Its rocket motor fires.

The two-and-a-half-metre-long missile takes two seconds to cross the black sky and reach its target.

Ka-boom. The JetRanger explodes in a vivid white-orange fireball that momentarily lights up the city.

The BLU-116 Bunker Buster, with a weight of almost a tonne, including 110 kilograms of PBXN high explosive, was designed to destroy hard targets through the deep penetration of rock or cement. It was too much weapon for the job of taking out a single JetRanger but that was all Bunsen had on hand so he had to use it. Fortunately, he has three more BLUs, which will be enough for what comes next. This shipment had been on route from the manufacturer in Pasadena to the Los Angeles Air Force base in El Segundo, for deployment in the Middle East. Bunsen will deploy the remaining weapons in a place far removed from the mountains of Afghanistan.

'Okay, take us home.'

The Tyrannosaur, so named by Bunsen for its sinister dark colour and hulking shape, swings around and resumes its course.

Bunsen watches the JetRanger's burning debris drift and flutter to the ground, then climbs to the van's roof, then the Tyrannosaur's cabin, pushing against the savage rotor wash as he goes.

Phase One has been a success. He observes the lines of traffic that crisscross the city below, the lights of countless vehicles blinking in the darkness. California has more cars per capita than any place on the planet – the state profoundly influences the worldwide automotive industry in every conceivable way, from vehicle design to road safety legislation – and yet, of all those motor vehicles Bunsen can see below, he knows that less than one per cent are pure electric, with no exhaust emissions. *Less than one per cent.* That's why he's doing what he's doing. To increase that one per cent, and put a halt to the greenhouse gases that choke and smother this planet.

Bunsen reaches the Tyrannosaur's cockpit, climbs in and buckles up. He will stop at nothing, use everything at his disposal, including the vast fortune he inherited, to reach his goal. He's glad he's finally found a purpose for the money. To him it represents nothing but the frivolous waste of his father's intellect: a life spent writing television shows, *bad sitcoms* no less, disposable entertainment forgotten the moment they aired.

Bunsen will not make the same mistake. His work will never be forgotten. He will spend his father's money, every last dollar if necessary, to change this world for the better – or he will die trying.

2

'Throttling engines to fifty per cent.'

Judd Bell stares out of the rectangular portal and takes in the rust-red surface below. The landscape reminds him of the Central Australian desert he knows so well, though he's a long way from the Northern Territory today. He is, in fact, two thousand feet above the surface of Mars in the Orion Multi-Purpose Crew Vehicle. In front of him a Heads Up Display (HUD) projects an outline of the spacecraft's descent trajectory onto the portal's glass. He peers through it, scans the dark red planet for the landing point.

'I see it.' It's a kilometre in the distance. He works the hand controller and fires the manoeuvring thrusters, pushes Orion towards the spot. 'Sixteen hundred feet, down seventy.'

The astronaut's mouth is dry. Apart from that he feels good, considering he's spent seven months with five other astronauts sardined into a spacecraft the size of a small condominium. He's sure his current goodwill is the result of the pure oxygen being pumped into his bubble helmet, which is also the reason for his dry mouth.

An alarm sounds in his headset. Judd's eyes don't move from the portal as he speaks into his helmet's microphone: 'What's that?'

The question is directed at Delroy 'Del' Tennison, the thin, balding copilot standing beside Judd and studying a bank of LED screens and gauges. The Florida native references a screen as he kills the piercing drone. 'Program alarm eleven-oh-seven.'

'Why?' Judd knows that alarm has something to do with the landing computer being overwhelmed with data but he doesn't know how serious it is. It's Del's job to find out. He manages Orion's systems, Judd just flies it.

'On it.' Del's eyes flick between three LED screens, searching for an answer.

Judd breathes in and focuses on the Marscape below. He caresses the controller and eases the spacecraft onwards. Orion is similar to the Lunar Module that landed on the Moon – except it's five times larger and carries three times as many people. Shaped like a short, fat bullet it has four levels housing crew quarters, scientific equipment and supplies for a month-long stay on the red planet. On the top level is the flight deck, where Judd and Del currently stand, side by side, strapped into harnesses. Behind them are their four crewmates, suited, helmeted and belted into their chairs. They sit silently. At this point theirs is a watching brief.

Judd focuses on the HUD for a moment then surveys the deep-red surface below. 'Thousand feet, down fifty.' Through the low light he can see the landing point clearly for the first time.

It's not good. At all.

His feeling of goodwill vanishes. This mission has been a long time coming, the culmination of a billion man-hours of concerted effort and a trillion dollars of taxpayers' money, all to have the onboard computer direct the spacecraft to a landing point slap-bang in the middle of a crater the size of Yankee Stadium.

It's not a big crater by Martian standards but it's big enough, with sides so steep a landing is impossible – Orion would simply slide to the bottom of the incline as soon as it touched down. To ice the cake this crater is both filled with *and* surrounded by boulders which range in size from medicine ball to Cadillac Eldorado. It would only take a small rock snagging one of Orion's four spindly landing legs to damage the ship irreparably. Then the crew, unable to leave the planet, would spend the rest of their truncated lives staring up at a distant blue speck wishing they'd never dreamed of visiting the stars when they were children.

'Not liking the look of this.' Judd keeps his voice even, doesn't want the words that reach Mission Control in two minutes to scare the cattle. Not that it matters. In two minutes this will be over and there's nothing the gang in Houston can do about it. They have no control over this craft. They're too far away.

Judd works the hand controller, pivots the ship and takes a look at his surroundings. He needs to find somewhere else to land that's about the size of two tennis courts side by side. There's nowhere obvious; boulders dot the landscape. He sets Orion on a course to cross the crater.

Judd's more concerned than fearful. He had, for a long time, been fearful, but that passed after he saved the space shuttle *Atlantis* off the north coast of Australia. Of course, he isn't flying a shuttle today so that's part of the reason, too. He hadn't trusted the shuttle but he trusts Orion. It is a brand-new piece of equipment, specifically designed and purpose built for the task of interplanetary travel, without the Nixonian budget cuts and cobbled-together Frankenstein design that compromised the shuttle.

The alarm trills in Judd's ear again. Del kills the noise and pre-empts Judd's question. 'I'm looking for it.'

'Seven-eighty, down twenty-five.' Judd searches the landscape as Orion clears Yankee crater. There are boulders everywhere and still no place level enough to put down. He works the hand controller again, slows the rate of descent. 'How's fuel?'

'Eleven per cent.'

He's used too much gas tooling around, avoiding Yankee crater then looking for a level spot. Judd doesn't say anything but he wants to swear. Instead of dropping the f-bomb he says: 'Okay. Four-fifty feet down sixty.' He scans the scenery again. There must be somewhere he can land this bucket.

'There.' He sees a spot. It's not too far away, looks wide enough, without too many rocks, and it's level. He works the thrusters, angles Orion towards it. 'Got an answer on that alarm?'

'Still looking into it —'

The ship shudders and the HUD projection flickers, then disappears from the portal's glass. 'I've lost Heads Up.'

Del's voice is panicked. 'Guidance computer is down.'

'Guess we got an answer on that alarm. Go with the back-up.'

Del works the touchscreen in front of him, reads the news, his voice incredulous: 'They're both rebooting. It'll take two minutes.'

'This is over in one.' Judd breathes out, really wanting to swear now. He knows what he must do. Without height or speed information he's going to have to seat-of-the-pants it. 'Going visual.'

'Commander!' Del's stunned voice is an octave higher than usual. That one word tells Judd everything the forty-two-year-old is thinking, which is: 'Dude! No. We abort-to-orbit. You don't land on Mars without a guidance computer.'

Abort-to-orbit is a last resort as far as Judd's concerned. The guidance computers may have failed but Judd trusts this machine. All those dollars and man-hours demand that he parks this sucker safely in the Martian dust and mankind can finally say it has reached the planets. 'How's fuel?'

'Descent quantity.'

'Okay.' It means Judd has ninety seconds to land the spacecraft – *minus* the twenty per cent he must save in case he needs to twist the red abort-to-orbit handle by his left hand if something unforeseen happens. He has seventy-two seconds and counting.

Judd pushes Orion towards the only landing area that looks remotely suitable. He estimates his height at three hundred feet. 'Give me remaining fuel time minus abort.'

'Fifty-seven seconds.'

Orion drops towards Mars. Judd scans his chosen landing spot and realises it's nowhere near as good as it looked from a distance. It's actually *terrible* and is littered with rocks. They're not as large as the boulders surrounding Yankee crater but they're big enough to be a problem if the metre-wide footpad at the end of one of the landing legs was to come down on one at an awkward angle. The legs have two metres of suspension play built into them but that won't do any good if the footpad is destroyed and the spacecraft tips on its side.

'Come on.' This planet is really starting to piss him off. It's the damn low light: it's playing tricks on him. Because Mars is so far from the sun it's cloaked in a dull gloom that Judd's eyes are taking their sweet time getting accustomed to.

'Thirty-eight seconds.'

Judd drops Orion lower as he watches the LED screen beside the portal, which shows him an image of the ground directly below. The engine's quiet whisper is the only sound, telling him to *hurry up* and find a spot *now*. He searches. Where? Where the hell is it? Where is *my* spot? There *must* be a spot.

There isn't one. The lower they drop the worse it looks.

'Twenty-six seconds.' Judd can hear Del's concern. They'd never been this low on fuel in a simulation.

'There!'

He sees it. A clear, flat section of dust to the right. There are a few smaller rocks but it's not too bad. That's what it's come down too: *not too bad*. It'll have to do. He eases Orion towards the area, keeps his eyes on the LED screen and the landing spot that's *not too bad*. He's thirty feet from the surface.

A large shape looms from the left. Judd glimpses it. 'What's that–?'

The screen turns red and he loses sight of it as thrust from the engine hits the planet's surface and kicks up a cloud of dust. It obscures the camera's view of the ground, then the portal, cuts off Judd's only reference points.

He's flying blind.

'Twelve seconds.' Del's voice is thin as a reed.

Judd plays the hand controller, holds Orion in place as his left hand lightly touches the red abort-to-orbit handle. If he turns it to the right the engine will fire at full power for eighteen seconds – and he'll have seven months to think about his failure on the way home.

He needs a moment to think. What was that shape? Was it a boulder he hadn't noticed or a shadow? He didn't see it on the way in, but this damn planet is so dark.

Shadow or boulder?

'Five seconds.' Del sounds like he's about to be sick.

Boulder or shadow?

Judd makes a decision.

The spacecraft drops onto the planet.

'Contact.' Del's voice wavers as he confirms the probes under the footpads have touched *something*.

'Shutdown.' Judd presses the engine stop button. The quiet whisper disappears and Orion settles onto Mars. He can feel the four landing legs compress under thirty tonnes of spacecraft. He awaits the sound of cracking metal, or the sensation of a tilting horizon as a landing leg snags on a boulder he's not sure is there.

A long moment passes.

No one breathes.

There's no cracking or tilting – because there's no boulder. It was a shadow. Orion's shadow.

Judd turns to Del with a grin. 'Well, that was seven months of boredom followed by seventy seconds of terror.'

Del nods, too drained to speak.

Judd does it for him. 'Let's get outside.'

Orion's hatch swings open and Judd steps out – onto the wrought-iron catwalk beside the towering High Fidelity Orion Landing Simulator (OLS) in Building Five at Johnson Space Center (JSC). It was built two years ago for NASA by Lockheed-Martin, at a cost of two hundred and sixty million dollars, and replaced both shuttle simulators.

Until the first flight to Mars lifts off in September 2020, Judd expects to spend thousands of hours training in the OLS. And he's more than happy to do it, as every time he flies a successful sim it increases his chances of piloting one of the five planned Mars missions. He's the only one of the training astronauts to have successfully landed the simulator on the Martian surface more than once, including his partner, Rhonda Jacolby, who is tipped to be FOM (First On Mars). He's sure his success in the sim is annoying the hell out of her but so far she's done a bang-up job of not letting it show.

Judd looks at the row of technicians who sit in the glass control room above the simulator. 'Thanks, guys. Almost got us with that reboot.'

One of the technicians grins down at him: 'Yeah, well, you gotta be cruel to be kind.'

Cruel to be kind. It's true. There's nothing to be gained by going easy on a pilot. Not with six lives and a trillion bucks on the line. The techs had to throw everything at them. Judd even added his own pressure as he imagined the four other crew members strapped in behind him on the flight deck, lives that will be in his hands if he makes the landing for real.

He pulls off his helmet and runs a hand through his crew cut. He feels pretty good for thirty-nine, though recently he has needed to watch his weight, which has been both an annoying and disheartening reminder of impending middle age. He's tall, so he can get away with a little extra around the mid-section, but still, he must stay away from the damn Krispy Kremes. They are his crack. Unfortunately he only has to *look* at one of those glazed donuts and he puts on five pounds.

He clunks down the metal stairs to ground level. Del follows behind, claps him on the back. 'That was pretty damn cool.'

'Thanks, man.'

'Wouldn't expect anything else from one of the four.' Del walks on. 'See you at the debrief.'

'Will do.' Almost a year later and the *Atlantis* 4 are still a big deal. Judd, Rhonda, his Australian mate Corey Purchase and his old friend, launch director Severson Burke – the four people who saved the hijacked shuttle *Atlantis* and prevented the detonation of a radioactive dirty bomb in Virginia – are regarded as bona fide, *genuine* heroes, a title Judd feels uncomfortable with. Of course, he hasn't told anyone he feels 'uncomfortable' because then he'd have to explain why, and he has no interest in doing that. Ever.

He hasn't even told Rhonda.

A buzz in his pocket. He fishes out his iPhone. Speak of the Devil. Rhonda Jacolby. His beloved. She's in Wisconsin at the moment, checking out a prospective contractor for the Orion's launch system. He picks up. 'Yaallow.'

'Hey.'

'Hey yourself.'

'I have like fifteen seconds before I have another meeting – oh God it's so boring it makes my mouth numb just talking about it. So, how did it go?'

He knows she's asking about the sim run he just completed. 'It came and it went.'

'You nailed it, didn't you?'

'Booyah!' He's happier about it than he realised.

'Baby.' He can hear that she's genuinely thrilled for him.

'They threw in a double guidance computer reboot during the descent phase.'

'That's not a good way to land.'

'It's not landing, it's guessing.'

He can hear her smile. 'Congrats. You're the only one to land it three times.'

'Yes indeed.' He doesn't want to make too much of it. He knows how disappointed she is to have made only one successful landing. 'So, how's it going up there?'

'Errr.' The sound is an exhausted breath released through clenched teeth.

'That good?'

'Omigod.'

'It'll be over soon.'

'I am really looking forward to the Beverly Wilshire.'

'Me too.'

'Okay, gotta jump. The meeting's about to start.'

There's a pregnant pause. He waits for it. A little sugar. Just a taste.

'Okay, I'll see you in LA, biatch.'

'Don't be late, mofo.'

They hang up.

She didn't say it. She went with her usual, the jokey 'biatch' instead of 'love you', and he replied in kind, with the ever reliable 'mofo'. He thought that because she was on the other side of the country it might be different this time, but no, she didn't say it so he didn't say it either.

This last year their relationship has gone from strength to strength, though he would like a little more sugar. And by 'sugar' he's not talking about anything related to their physical relationship, which has always been stridently expansive (words that perfectly describe it yet make no actual sense). When he went 'lovey-dovey' (*her* term), by bringing her flowers or holding her hand or expressing heartfelt sentiment, she'd either shut him down or make fun. He likes a bit of the 'lovey-dovey' or 'sugar' (his term) occasionally, but, for some reason, it just doesn't fly with her. She is the least sentimental person he has ever met, man, woman or child, so a month ago he stopped saying 'love you' at the end of phone calls, or before they fell asleep, or as they left for work. It's not a huge deal in the scheme of the world, but he misses it.

He will see her tomorrow when the *Atlantis* 4 all meet in Los Angeles to announce the *Atlantis* 4 movie. Yes, Twentieth Century Fox has bought the *Atlantis* 4's life rights and is fast-tracking the film to be a 'tentpole' next summer. It starts shooting in a week so Fox wants them in town for a round of press engagements and has comped them an all-expenses-paid weekend at the Beverly Wilshire, hence her excitement at the prospect of a luxurious stay at one of the world's great hotels.

Judd is looking forward to seeing Corey in LA. He's talked to the Aussie on the phone while he's been on his eight-month 'hitch around America' tour, but it isn't quite the same. Judd missed him more than he'd imagined, guesses it had something to do with having shared an experience no one else could understand.

Judd pushes through a side door, steps into the warm afternoon and pauses as he takes in the vivid Texas sky. It's so blue it hurts his eyes, a thin white contrail from a passenger jet its only blemish. Since the *Atlantis* hijacking he's really tried to stop and smell the roses. His life is so hectic that it's easy to miss the little things, like this perfect sky. Looking at it makes his heart sing, makes him appreciate that he's part of a larger universe with endless possibilities just waiting to be explored.

He glances at his Omega Ploprof. He must get cracking. The debrief starts in ten minutes, then he needs to head home, pack for the weekend, finish his report on Orion's landing software, attempt to read the *Atlantis 4* screenplay then get a good night's sleep before arriving at the airport bright and early tomorrow morning. He must remember to reserve row 56, seat A online tonight, and pack his baseball cap, his headphones and mirror-lensed sunglasses. He'll definitely need them for the flight west.

3

'Seen but not heard. This is very important so let me be perfectly clear. Seen. But. Not. Heard. Okay?' Corey Purchase sits behind the wheel of a convertible BMW M3 and stares at the passenger in the seat beside him. 'Don't give me that face. I can't have you screwing this up. *Seen but not heard.* Are we clear?'

The recipient of the lecture is not a recalcitrant child or a sulky teen, but a strikingly ugly canine named Spike. He's a white blue heeler who looks like he's been used as a canvas by a naughty toddler with a tin of navy blue paint.

He barks.

'Okay. Good.' With a nod the lanky, thirty-one-year-old Australian turns and studies the house on the opposite side of the street. It's bigger than he expected. Much bigger.

Spike barks.

'Yeah, only one person lives here.'

Another bark.

'I guess you could call it a McMansion.'

And another bark.

'Yes, it would have been more impressive to turn up in a chopper than a borrowed car, but unless you have a stash of money squirreled away that I'm unware of, then we don't have the dosh to be renting aircraft for the evening, okay?'

Money's only half the story, though. The truth is that since the destruction of his Huey Loach helicopter (may it rest in pieces at the bottom of the Pacific Ocean), Corey has been, for the first time in his life, a bit gun-shy about flying, which he's kept quiet from everyone, including the mutt to his right.

Maybe it was the sheer number of life and death situations he'd been through in Central Australia with Judd in that Loach, but Corey is more than happy not to be airborne at the moment. It's one of the reasons he spent the better part of the last year hitchhiking around America. The trip had been excellent and they'd seen a lot of the States – and he hadn't needed to fly once.

The journey had been a success in a different, unexpected way too. At one point or another it had been covered by every major media outlet and blogger, his trip plastered all over the Tweeters and the Facebooks or whatever they were called. That a bona fide hero, a member of the *Atlantis* 4 no less, a man who had helped save tens of thousands of lives, had taken the time to see the real America in such a low-key way greatly endeared him to the general public. He'd stumbled upon a phenomenon that occurred to a select number of Australian men who had ventured stateside over the years. Whether it was Errol Flynn, Paul Hogan, Steve Irwin, Hugh Jackman or Keith Urban, Americans occasionally liked to add a laconic, rough-and-tumble, hail-fellow-well-met Aussie bloke to their cultural mix – and now Corey Purchase is one of them.

The astonishing result of this, and what will pay Corey more money than he's earned, in total, *ever*, is the *Atlantis* 4 movie that Twentieth Century Fox is about to make. And that is a very good thing because, as of this moment, one Corey J. Purchase has nothing but the dog, his blue jeans, a couple of navy Bonds T-shirts, his Justin boots and the not so princely sum of $1217 in savings.

He's so broke he can't even afford to run a mobile phone – and you really need a mobile phone in LA. When he first arrived in the City of Angels he hadn't expected to stay long, two weeks at most, enough to finalise the Fox deal with his agent Matty Bowen, who graciously lent him this Bimmer for his stay, then continue his trip around America.

Then he met her.

The front door to the McMansion swings open and Corey sees her, silhouetted against the warm glow inside.

Lola Jacklin.

Even from a distance of thirty metres she takes his breath away. Corey felt it the moment he walked into the sprawling Beverly Hills office on his first day in Los Angeles and shook her hand. She is a partner at Bowen & Associates, the agency that represents the *Atlantis* 4.

The twenty-eight-year-old is whip smart and knowledgeable about subjects that Corey does not have the first clue, like the entertainment business and world politics and the fate of art in movies. She is, on the other hand, *not* well versed in the subjects Corey knows a lot about, like Central Australia and moving cattle with helicopters and saving space shuttles. So, whenever they're together she's fascinated by his stories, is quick to laugh at his jokes (even if they're lame), and has a ready smile that seems to indicate she enjoys his company. He certainly enjoys *her* company, is both enlightened and delighted by the sprawling scope of her thoughts, which cover everything from what is happening in 'town', as everyone who works in the LA entertainment business seems to call the city, to the fate of the planet. That she has a light southern drawl, is slight and willowy with long dark hair, and has the angular features he finds so appealing is a bonus but makes no difference to the depth of his feelings for her.

There's just the one problem.

If she is 'the one', how does he tell her that he can understand everything his dog says? In the past that conversation with prospective girlfriends has immediately and irrevocably destroyed the budding relationship, so this time he's decided that honesty is *not* the best policy, at least not yet. He's going to hide the crazy, at least until the appetizer, then break it to her slow. That's why he's been telling Spike he's to be seen but not heard. Corey won't respond to any questions from the animal during this, their third date.

Spike barks.

'Taking my shirt off will *not* make her like me more.'

Another bark.

'Well, if I did it would have to be in a natural, organic way and not just out of the blue. Anyhow, I have a plan so shhh!' Corey takes a deep breath, opens the door, steps out of the BMW, then turns back to the dog with a firm whisper: '*Seen but not heard.*'

Lola watches Corey lope across the street towards her, that crooked grin on his face and that sparkle in his eye. It's amazing. He's *always* happy, like he doesn't have a care in the world. They embrace and suddenly everything she's been rehearsing this afternoon is that much harder to say.

She slides into the passenger seat, excited to be sitting beside this funny, strapping Australian man she met four weeks ago. She notices the dog in the back seat. 'Hello there.'

Spike barks.

'That's Spike. He's just along for the ride. To be seen but not heard. If his grotesque appearance is too disturbing, I find that it helps to squint when you look at him. If you do it just right he can almost appear homely.'

She laughs and pats Spike's head. 'Oh no, you're beautiful.'

'On the inside.' Corey nods at Lola's waist. 'Belt up.'

She fastens her seatbelt as he twists the V8 to life and hits the gas. The BMW pulls away from the kerb.

Lola glances at the Australian. She feels something in her chest whenever she's with him, felt it the first moment they were introduced at the B&A office. She's not even sure what the feeling is; it's like shortness of breath combined with indigestion, but in a nice way. It makes what she has to do tonight so difficult. She should have done it on the phone when he rang to confirm the date, but she chickened out. *Chickened out!* The woman regarded as one of the best closers in town, nicknamed, she thought a tad unfairly, *Bitchkrieg* by the studios. Truth is, she wanted to have one more night out with the chopper pilot because he's so much fun. She'll do what she has to do later – there's no need to spoil the whole evening.

The sun dips beneath the horizon as they hit the freeway and Lola stares out the windscreen at the twinkling lights of her adopted city. Ever since she was a little girl, when *Doc Hollywood*, a mildly successful early nineties Michael J. Fox movie, came to shoot in her hometown, she'd caught the movie bug and wanted to live in LA. The fact that she now represents the *Back to the Future* star only underscores how stellar her trajectory from that tiny southern backwater to the top tier of the entertainment industry has been.

Corey takes in the glorious sunset before them, then glances at Lola. 'So, I've been working on a pitch – a movie pitch.'

Lola turns to him. 'Really? Excellent.'

'Well, you know, being here these last few weeks got my creative juices flowing. Well, maybe they're not *creative*, but something's definitely flowing.'

'What's the idea? Pitch it.'

'It's just a thought at the moment.'

'Well, turn it into an idea.'

'You really want to do this on a night off?'

'There are no nights off. Let's hear it.'

'Okay, but you have to be brutally honest. If it's terrible, it's terrible, okay?'

'If it's terrible, it's terrible.'

'Okay.' He takes a breath, a little nervous. 'I'm starting now: Hello, Ms Studio Executive Lady, how are you today?' He speaks in a stiff, formal voice.

'Very well. Thanks for coming in.'

'No, thank you, my lady – I don't know why I'm speaking in an olde English accent but I'll push on, shall I?'

She does her best cockney British accent: 'I prefer the Aussie accent myself, guv'nor, but, yes, let's push on.'

That puts him at ease. 'Okay, continuing.' He takes a breath. 'Now, let me ask you a very important question: which do you prefer, vampires or zombies?'

'Vampires.'

'Ba-baum. *Family Feud* sound for wrong answer. The correct choice is both.'

'Both?'

'Exactly! You mash them together and get *Zompire*, the first movie to feature a vampire zombie as the main character. He's undead, *twice*. People have always loved vampires and now they love zombies so it only makes sense to combine them in an irresistible collision of blood-sucking flesh-eating. That's all I've got so far.'

Lola nods. 'Not bad. "He's undead – *twice*" is a good tag line.'

'Great.' He nods happily, then: 'What's a tag line?'

'You know, the slogan on a movie poster.'

'Oh. Of course. Right. So the idea's not a complete shocker?'

'It's good, but if you want to take it to a studio you'll need to think up an exciting plot that you can explain in twenty-five words or less, create vivid characters who grow and change over the course of that story, and create a compelling mythology that explains how and why Zompires exist. Also, consider what the subtext of the story is.'

'I've never really understood what subtext is.'

'It's the underlying meaning of the film. Also, is there a love story? Where is it set? And when? Who's the bad guy? You always need an interesting bad guy with a believable motivation. Is it a comedy or a drama? The title *Zompire* almost makes it sound like a comedy, but if, for example, it's called *VZ*, shorthand for the vampire-zombie hybrid, suddenly it seems more serious. On a poster I can see the V in blood red and the Z in raggedy grey. It's intriguing, and graphically they're strong letters.'

Corey studies her. 'Now I know why you've got such a big house. You're good at this.'

'Well, yeah, it's my business and I've had a lot of practice and I love movies. So, the takeaway is this: if you want people to take it seriously you need to flesh it out, no pun. Even little things, like is there a hero car of some kind?'

'Hero car?'

'You know, like the Tumbler from *Batman Begins*, or the Millennium Falcon from *Star Wars*, or the Minis in *The Italian Job*. It doesn't have to be a car, just some sort of groovy transportation.'

It makes perfect sense to him. 'Of course.'

'And think about who could be in it. Makes it easier when you're pitching a studio if they have an actor in mind for the lead role.'

He raises his hand. 'Oh! I know who'd be great. That guy,

the one in the tights —' He can't quite place the name. 'You know, that movie about the bloke who turns into a tornado —'

'*The Blue Cyclone*.'

'*The Blue Cyclone*! Yeah! Him. That guy. What's his name? Steve . . .'

'Scott. Scott Ford.'

'That's it. Scott! I guess everyone wants him in their movie.'

'Oh. Well, yeah, they do. He's, you know, a big star.' She takes a moment, then gestures to the road ahead. 'So, where are we going?'

'Nearly there.'

Lola's flustered. When Corey mentioned Scott Ford she had to change the subject. *Oh man.* It's not like she's doing anything wrong being here, but, gee, it sure feels like it. She needs to deal with this ASAP.

'Ta-da. We're here.' Corey's voice pulls her from her thoughts as he directs the BMW onto a patch of grass that overlooks a deserted beach.

She looks around. 'Malibu?'

'Yep, not far from Bowen's place. I walk down here at night sometimes, look out at the ocean.'

In fact, the house where Corey's been staying, which belongs to Matty Bowen, Corey's agent and Lola's boss, is just up the beach a little way, in case they want to 'repair for a nightcap', as it were. Not that Corey's expecting any 'repairing' or 'nightcap' activity. So far the relationship has been completely chaste, not even a kiss – though he's hoping that might change tonight. He has a plan. It's not a particularly sophisticated plan, in fact it could be described as both rudimentary *and* amateurish, but it's all he's got and he's gonna take it to the hoop.

They climb out of the car and Corey pulls a small wicker picnic hamper and a tartan blanket from the boot. He wanted the evening to be just right so he thought a hand-packed picnic was the way to go. He'd raided Bowen's enormous fridge for supplies.

Lola's impressed. 'Thought of everything.'

They head towards a grassy knoll that overlooks the beach, the moonlight showing the way. Spike gallops ahead.

Corey stops at the spot where that moonlight glistens on the ocean at just the right angle, puts down the hamper and turns to Lola. She smiles and he realises this is it – *this* is the moment. Yes, he knows the night is young and he's going early but it feels right.

She tilts her head. 'What?'

'If you don't mind, I thought we could —' He steps closer. '—dance.'

'Oh, God. Okay. I have to tell you I don't do much of that. It's like I'm from that town in *Footloose*.'

He grins and takes her left hand in his, places his other hand on her waist and moves her in time to the rolling surf. He can see she's surprised, but, he's almost certain, delighted too. Their eyes meet.

Time slows.

She smiles and he takes in her beaming face. He can't believe it. The moonlight, the beach, the dancing – it's working! Maybe his unsophisticated plan isn't so rudimentary and amateurish after all. He leans down to kiss her. She hesitates for a moment then rises up on her toes to meet him – then turns away.

Time speeds up.

'I'm-seeing-someone-I'm-so-sorry.' She blurts it out as one word.

Corey lets her go and steps back, shocked. 'Oh. I didn't, I had no — I mean I would never —'

'I-met-him-just-before-I-met-you.' That sounds like one word too.

'Right. Well, that's a bit embarrassing – for me.'

'No, no, it's not. I should have said something earlier.'

Corey is stunned. And sad. And yes, embarrassed. He rarely gets embarrassed but he's definitely feeling it now. So he doesn't just stand there like some fool who tried to kiss a girl and somehow screwed it up, he flaps out the blanket to lay it on the grass – then stops, mid-flap, his heart not in it. 'Can I ask a question?'

Lola really doesn't want him to. She can't remember the last time someone asked her a question she didn't already know the answer to. She likes to be prepared yet has no idea what the Australian is about to say. 'Sure.'

'If you have a boyfriend, why are we here?'

She takes a breath, studies the tartan blanket in his hand. It's easier than looking into his blue eyes. 'Because you're a funny, unique guy and I enjoy your company and I hope we can be friends.'

Hope we can be friends. It sounds so lame. As soon as she says it it's like the air shifts somehow, even though there isn't a breath of wind. He doesn't say a word but he doesn't have to. His response is all in his expression, the look of disappointment he's trying to mask with that crooked grin she likes so much. She can see the smile is no longer genuine but forced, and that's the saddest part of this whole sorry episode.

'Can I ask one more question?'

She really doesn't want him to. 'Of course.'

'Who's your boyfriend?' Then quickly: 'You don't have to tell me.'

She hesitates for a moment, then says: 'Scott Ford.'

'The Blue Cyclone guy? With the tights?'

She nods.

Corey is visibly surprised. Even if you don't know who Scott Ford is you still know who Scott Ford is. He is currently *People* magazine's Sexiest Man Alive, has that classic, square-jawed American face, matched with the chiselled physique of a Greek god. He's also a bona fide international movie star, with over four billion in world-wide grosses, a billion of that from *The Blue Cyclone* alone. He's charming and debonair and has an easy way with people. He can have his pick of any woman on the planet but he picked Lola. They met at a fundraiser five weeks ago and have seen each other when-ever their schedules allow, which has been two dates so far with a third pending. Though it's not yet bedroom serious, they talk regu-larly and plan to meet up when he's back in town tomorrow. Lola hesitated about telling Corey, but the fact is it's only a matter of time before it hits the media and, well, she didn't want him to find out that way.

Corey nods slowly. 'Right, well, I'm really glad for you.' He forces another grin but she doesn't have the heart to return it.

In stark contrast to the drive to the beach, which had been fun and full of promise, the trip back is awful and silent and pretty damn depressing.

Scott bloody Ford! Good God. It's impossible to compete with a guy like that. Even with Corey's limited understanding of who was 'hot or not' in the entertainment universe, he knew Scott Ford was a big deal. Whatever fame Corey had accidentally stumbled upon through helping save the hijacked shuttle or during his trip around America, they were but minor footnotes compared to that bloke's career. And, ironically, Corey thought *The Blue Cyclone* movie totally rocked.

Lola turns to him. 'You okay?'

'Yep, no wuckers.'

'What does that mean?'

'It's short for "no wucking forries", which is the reverse of —'

'Oh. Yeah, got it.'

Corey guides the BMW along the road. That's the third time she's tried to start a conversation and it's the longest response he's given. He can tell she wants to talk but he doesn't know what else there is to say. The more he thinks about what happened the more embarrassed he feels. Did he completely misread the signs? Obviously. It doesn't matter, though. This is the end of it.

She tries once more. 'Look, I feel like I should explain —'

'There's no need.'

'But I really want —'

'It's okay, Lola, really.'

He pulls up beside her McMansion, doesn't kill the engine, keeps his eyes forward. 'In spite of everything, I appreciate you telling me, instead of just not returning my calls, or, you know, letting me see it in a magazine or something.'

She takes a breath, meets his eyes. 'I'm sorry.'

He shrugs. 'It is what it is. Nothing to be sorry about.'

'Well, I am. And I meant what I said. I'd like to be friends.'

He looks at her. 'When has that ever happened in a situation like this?'

She studies him for an uncomfortable moment, then shakes her head. 'Never.' She opens the door, steps out of the vehicle, walks towards the very big house and out of his life.

He watches her go, wills her to stop, turn around, run back to the car, tell him that it's all been a terrible misunderstanding.

That does not happen.

He slots the car into gear and pulls away from the kerb.

'Well, *that* blew chunks.' Corey rubs his face as he pulls the BMW onto Santa Monica Boulevard. He can't remember the last time he felt this bad. Yes, he'd often been lonely back in the Northern Territory, but this is different, and, in many ways, worse, because he'd caught a glimpse of what life could be like with someone extraordinary – and then it was gone, like smoke on the wind. It feels like he's lost something precious that will be impossible to replace.

And, to ice the worst cake *ever*, he asked her who her boyfriend was, thinking he might be able to learn something from the answer, like what kind of guy you had to be to date a woman like her. Well, he learned something all right: *never ask questions like that*! The answer is a guy who is so far out of Corey's league that they aren't even playing the same game.

On the bright side, at least he didn't have to explain Spike to Lola. Funny how the things you worry about are never the things that bite you on the arse.

Spike barks.

'Well, I apologise if my lack of success with the opposite sex reflects poorly on you.'

Another bark.

'Taking my shirt off would *not* have made any difference.'

Corey drives on. The memory of the night in '97 when the quake hit and he lost his mum floods back. It's funny, that memory only resurfaces when he feels bad – and then makes him feel worse, which truly sucks. He finds the best way to deal with it is not to. Just bury it as deep as possible and ignore it. Eventually it will go away on its own. Of course, that means it will come back again later, but he'd cross that bridge when it reared up unexpectedly.

He did try to deal with it once. He was in his late teens and his need for answers became so strong that for a while he began reading about fault lines and earthquakes in his spare time, not just the ones in Australia but wherever they occurred across the planet. For a brief moment he'd even considered heading to Sydney University to study seismology and research earthquakes, but the call to fly was too strong and he didn't think he could sit in a classroom for years on end, no matter how interesting the subject.

Corey pulls up at a red light. It's an intersection. As he said to Lola earlier he's not great at understanding subtext, but he can't help but think he's reached a crossroads in his life too.

Spike barks.

It's actually a good question and takes his mind off the horrendous feeling-sorry-for-himself-fest he's been indulging in for the last couple of minutes. What do they do now? He's in no hurry to return to Central Australia. He loves his home but he wants to experience a world outside the desert. So where to next? He can stay in Los Angeles, try to find some work. He likes the vibrancy of the city, that there's always something going on, but the Florida Keys are also tempting.

He'd visited them at the beginning of the tour around America, travelled the two-hundred-kilometre-long Overseas Highway, the one they blew up in *True Lies,* one of his favourite movies, and even though he'd only spent a week there, the place captured his heart more than any other spot during the journey. He's pretty sure that's because of the ocean: every time he looked at the Florida Strait it was a different shade of blue. There's just something about the sea that, after living a desert life for so long, makes his heart sing. When the movie deal is finalised he'll have the dough to move down there and, as Cape Canaveral is close, it'll be easy to catch up with Judd and Rhonda when they're in Florida.

The dog barks.

Corey glances at the animal and grins. 'Yep, I'm thinking Florida, too.'

4

Alvy Blash is almost certain this is the day he will change the world.

Almost.

The next five minutes will tell him for sure.

He moves to the metre-wide fan positioned in front of the curvy, high-waisted Hyundai iX35 and flicks the power switch. The fan spins up and the large room, with cement walls, floor and ceiling, reverberates with the deep, flat chop of rotating blades. The torrent of air slams into the front of the car with such force it rattles the windscreen wipers.

Alvy points at Jacob, who sits behind the Hyundai's steering wheel. Jacob pushes the start button on the dash and the engine cranks to life. He slides out of the vehicle and exits the room through the only door, situated directly beside a long, thin horizontal window that's double-glazed with shatterproof glass and built into the wall at eye level.

In front of the vehicle the woolly-haired Alvy holds a small, metal spray can in his left hand and turns to Bunsen, who stands behind the shatterproof glass. Bunsen nods then Alvy takes a deep breath and presses the button on top of the can. Once. It emits a fine puff of clear mist that is whisked by the airstream straight into the Hyundai's front grille.

That clear mist is why they are here. Alvy almost called it *Hedorah*, after the fictional Japanese smog monster, but went with the Swarm instead because it better describes what it actually is: a very large group of very tiny particles working in perfect unison to complete a very sophisticated task. Granted, calling it the Swarm isn't as exciting as naming it after one of Godzilla's nemeses, but it feels right for an invention at the forefront of molecular nanotechnology.

Bunsen triggers a digital Seiko stopwatch as Alvy exits the room, closes the metal door behind him and moves to the window where they all study the Hyundai, its engine ticking over at a thousand revolutions per minute.

Alvy's heart races. He's never felt this nervous. He's been fiddling with the Swarm's formula for the last week, working on the molecular assembler, tinkering with the messenger RNA and tweaking the sequences of amino acids that construct the protein molecules. He'd really wanted to spend another day on it – he always wants to spend 'another day' on everything he works on – but gave in to Bunsen's demand that they perform a live test to see where they stood.

'Come-on-come-on-come-on,' Alvy says it through an exhaled breath and glances at the stopwatch. The numbers blink and change, ten, eleven, twelve seconds. He's spent the last thirty-four months, every day and night since Bunsen recruited him, creating and finetuning the Swarm, and now he's about to find out if all of that time, effort and money were worthwhile.

He's suddenly overwhelmed by a sense of dread. Did he miss a step? Is the self-replication sequence correct? He thinks so, but you never know until you run a real-world test. He's actually glad Bunsen pushed him to do this. If it were up to him he would have put it off, then put it off again. It helps to have someone cracking the whip, not that the twenty-nine-year-old needs much motivation. He has embraced Bunsen's worldview wholeheartedly, has not only drunk the Kool-Aid but come back for more until the jug was empty, then mixed up his own batch.

Alvy always worked on his own in the past, which meant he was a bit of a lonely guy, his excess weight, facial hair and actual hair, and his preoccupation with *Grand Theft Auto*, not doing him any favours socially (that is, with the ladies). He guessed that's why Bunsen sought him out: his skill set and solitary lifestyle – there was nothing at home to distract him from the job at hand. Of course, he's not working alone here, he's part of the team and he enjoys the dynamic immensely. It reminds him of when he was young and his brother and father were alive. He's sure they'd be proud of what he's doing, would realise that the Swarm will one day change the world for the better.

He studies the stopwatch in Bunsen's hand. Nineteen seconds, twenty, twenty-one. He glances at Jacob and they exchange a nervous smile. Jacob's been invaluable in the lab, eager to help and quick to learn. The shared experience has brought them close. Alvy likes having a friend, even if he is actually a work colleague. If the Swarm is a success a good part of the credit will go to Jacob. Bunsen, on the other hand, hasn't been around that much and didn't even pretend to understand the science of what Alvy was doing. He made up for that by not only building and paying for a state-of-the-art lab but providing all the equipment Alvy needed to complete the task. And it had cost a fortune – well over nineteen million dollars so far. Alvy once asked Bunsen where all the money came from. 'Reruns,' Bunsen said, but never elaborated.

Alvy looks at the stopwatch again. Twenty-eight seconds, twenty-nine.

Christ, the tension is unbearable.

It's like waiting for the world's most important kettle to boil. His eyes move back to the Hyundai. 'Come-on-come-on-come-on.'

He doesn't bother saying it under his breath this time. He hopes it will happen but fears it won't. Hope and fear. Don't those two words just sum up life? You hope for the best but fear the worst.

The Hyundai's exhaust turns a light purple colour. *Yes!* It's something Alvy expected, a key design feature of the Swarm that had taken him three months to perfect. It's thrilling to see.

Bunsen turns to him with a smile. 'Excellent.'

Actually, it's more than excellent. It's *fuckin' fantastic*. Alvy returns the smile and glances at the stopwatch. Forty-four seconds. He looks back at the exhaust. The purple exhaust is darker now, and growing darker by the second.

The exhaust turns black.

It happens, just like that. It's extraordinary, shocks Alvy even though he's expecting it, has been working towards it for the better part of three years. It's terrible and beautiful and sickening and inspiring all in the same moment. All the tension he's been feeling is instantly released.

Bunsen turns to Alvy with a wide grin. 'Congratulations. You just changed the world.'

Alvy has done exactly what was asked of him and he's done it *two months* faster than he said he would. The guy is even smarter than Bunsen realised.

Bunsen puts an arm around him, pulls him close. 'You did it. You did it!' Not wanting Jacob to feel left out, Bunsen hooks an arm around the assistant and pulls him into the huddle too. 'You guys – you made something out of *nothing*. Something important. Something vital.'

Bunsen takes in their shining faces. They look so happy. He wants to remember this moment forever, the moment the mission became a reality, before the machinery cranks to life and everything changes, before he must be cruel to be kind and set Kilroy in motion, to do the things Kilroy does so well.

Alvy looks at Bunsen. 'What now?'

'Make a batch. Three thousand litres of the Swarm, three litres of the counteragent.'

'Jeez. Okay. That's – a lot.'

'I want to impress them.'

'Of course.'

'How long will it take?'

'If we start now? Fourteen, fifteen hours.'

'All right then. I'll make some calls, set up the demonstration for tomorrow afternoon.'

'Excellent.'

'Call me as soon as it's done.'

'Will do.' Alvy nods and Bunsen moves off, then stops and turns back to him.

'I'm proud of you.' A little positive reinforcement always goes a long way with Alvy.

Alvy grins. 'Thanks, man.'

Bunsen nods and keeps walking.

5

Houston Oilers cap on. *Check.*

Fifty-eight millimetre American Optical mirror-lensed aviator sunglasses on. *Check.*

Beats by Dr Dre Pro headphones on. *Check.*

Collar of navy blue Penguin polo shirt up. *Check.*

Judd Bell is first down the boarding ramp towards the United Boeing 787, the aircraft that will take him to Los Angeles on this fine day. He doesn't want to get caught in line with the other passengers so he moves fast and stays ahead of the pack, his cap, oversized sunnies, enormous headphones and raised collar doing their best to make him incognito.

So far so good.

He steps into the plane and hands the flight attendant his boarding pass. He managed to reserve the seat he wanted. Not that it was difficult. Row 56, seat A is, arguably, the worst seat on the aircraft and in no demand at all. 'Row 56, seat A. Right to the back.' Judd takes the boarding pass from the nice lady before she has a chance to look at his face and walks on.

He moves quickly down the aisle. Ah, good old 56A. What would he do without it? It's the only way he can fly domestic any more. It's the last row on the left at the rear of the plane, against the window. It's far back enough so none of the passengers will have to pass him to get to their seats, and it's far enough from the rear toilets so none of the passengers will have to queue nearby when they visit the bathroom. Sure, he'd prefer the larger seats in business class but he's found, from experience, that if he sits at the front of the aircraft he's much too visible.

Judd takes his seat, pulls his cap down as low as it will go, then settles back and stares out the window. The seat beside him is empty, and as the plane is only half full it should stay that way.

It's been almost a year so hopefully the attention has waned a little anyway. It's the reason he doesn't get out that much any more. Sure, he leaves his house and drives to work at Johnson Space Center every day, but everyone he comes in contact with knows him, and if they don't they tend to be shy about approaching *Judd Bell*, saviour of shuttle *Atlantis* and the great state of Virginia. Interestingly, when he's outside the work environment, the opposite is true. He's mobbed, because he's *Judd Bell*, saviour of shuttle *Atlantis* and the great state of Virginia. Over the last year he hasn't been to a restaurant once. It was just easier to stay in than be mobbed and have to deal with –

'Excuse me, mister, are you Judd Dell?'

Two minutes! The tap on the shoulder comes exactly two minutes after he sits down. Judd turns from the window and sees a little girl, maybe seven years old, standing in the aisle opposite him, an expectant expression on her face.

'No, I'm not.'

The little girl is crestfallen. *Crestfallen!* Man, he hates that expression. It breaks his heart. He can't do it. He can't lie to a child. He raises his sunglasses and whispers: 'But I might be Judd *Bell*.'

Her face lights up. 'That's what I meant!'

'Just don't tell anyone.'

'Okay! Well, my name is Holly and I just need to tell you that you saved my grandma who lives in Richmond, Virginia, and she's really nice so thanks for that and also you're very nice, too.'

'Thank you, sweetheart, but it wasn't just me, lots of people helped out that day —'

The little girl turns and runs up the aisle, shouts at the top of her voice: 'Momma, it is him, it's Judd Dell! It's Judd Dell!'

Judd sighs, watches her go. 'I thought we weren't going to tell anyone.'

As one, the passengers turn and search – and find 'Judd Dell' in row 56, seat A. He forces a smile and they clap. The clapping then changes and becomes applause, then changes again and becomes – *good Lord* – cheering. They're *cheering*. That's a first. All Judd wants is for it to stop. He half rises out of his seat and tries to tamp it down. Unfortunately that just means the few people who aren't already cheering because they don't know what the hell is going on see him for the first time and join in.

Two hours into the flight the last of the wellwishers have returned to their seats. Twenty-seven different people visited him during that time, some from Virginia but most with friends and family there, and all of them credit Judd with saving either their lives or the lives of loved ones. Also amongst the wellwishers were some supporters of NASA who wanted Judd to know they thought the space program was in safe hands with him, and then there were a few people who just wanted an autograph and a momentary brush with fame.

When he's finally able to sit back, he feels terrible. *Terrible*. The whole reason he booked row 56, seat A and wore the old cap and the silly headphones and the ridiculous sunglasses and turned up his collar like he was Rob Lowe in 1985 is not because he doesn't want to be mobbed by wellwishers. He doesn't mind that at all. He likes chatting with people and signing autographs and spruiking NASA, it's an important part of the job. No, what he doesn't like is the feeling that he's fooling people. What's the saying? *You can't fool all of the people all of the time?* Well, it seems you can, and he's been doing a pretty good job of it for almost a year.

Judd pulls out his iPad and lays it on the tiny tray table. He has two hours before they land at LAX and there's plenty to do. He needs to read the *Atlantis* 4 screenplay so he doesn't sound like a complete moron when he talks to the studio execs and director about it. Then, time permitting, he should take a power nap, which is the same as a regular nap except with a cooler name.

He does neither of those things.

Instead he swipes open the iPad and watches a video he downloaded from YouTube six months ago, a video he has watched many, many times – a wobbly, hand-held, shot-on-an-iPhone-in-portrait-mode affair that lasts forty-six seconds.

He leans back in his seat and starts the video. It begins innocently enough, a young woman films two of her friends outside the Imax Theatre in Houston before an early evening show. The setting sun throws a warm, orange hue across the groups of people who mill about in the background and wait to enter. One of those groups is Judd, his partner Rhonda, his Aussie mate Corey and his blue heeler, Spike. It's a couple of months after the *Atlantis* hijacking.

All is fine and dandy as the crowd displays the usual expectant buzz before a show – then a man shouts: 'Everybody get down!' The man is Judd. The crowd scatters as the camera phone whip pans to a tall blond guy holding a sawn-off shotgun. *Bang.* He fires the weapon and the camera phone films the sidewalk for a moment as the camerawoman takes shelter behind a nearby truck, then turns and aims the camera phone at a white car. On one side Rhonda, Corey and Judd are crouched as they take cover, on the other the gunman approaches the vehicle. *Bang*. He fires again, blows out the windshield. The tinkle of glass on bitumen is heard.

The camera phone wobbles and Judd pauses the video. Past the stunned and panicked faces of Rhonda and Corey he can see himself in profile and remember exactly what he was doing at that moment. Astronaut Judd Bell, hailed as the great American hero, who not only helped save the hijacked space shuttle *Atlantis* but prevented the detonation of a nuclear dirty bomb in Virginia, was trying – and failing – to come up with a plan to save his friends and himself.

Judd un-pauses the video. The man with the shotgun is the towering German Dirk Popanken, who the world thought was dead. He is not, and as the lone surviving member of the crew that hijacked *Atlantis* and attempted to detonate that dirty bomb, strides around the white car to where Judd is crouched to enact his revenge. Fortunately, because of the angle, Judd is unsighted by the camera phone at this point. Otherwise the whole world would have seen him cowering, without a plan of action.

The gunman raises his weapon and aims it directly at Judd's unseen face. And that, you would think, is that: Judd's life cut short with the pull of a trigger. Except something else happens to fill the last twelve seconds of the video, something that changes his fate.

Judd's friend, ex-astronaut, launch director and fellow member of the *Atlantis* 4, Severson Burke arrives. Usually it's extremely difficult to stop a motivated gunman without serious firepower, but Severson manages to do it – with a Toyota Prius.

The vehicle, almost silent because it runs on electricity most of the time, strikes the oblivious gunman in the back of the legs at forty-five kilometres an hour. The weapon is knocked from his hands and he is launched ten metres across the sidewalk, straight into the glass doors of the Imax Theatre, bounces off and slumps to the sidewalk, broken and unconscious. Considering the speed of the action the camerawoman manages to capture it surprisingly well.

The camera phone then whips back to the Prius as Severson exits the vehicle to a round of applause. Judd had invited Severson to the movie but, as usual, he was running late. Severson humbly accepts the crowd's applause, turns to Judd, who has found his feet, and says with a wry grin: 'Sorry I'm late. Parking was a bitch.'

Sorry I'm late. Parking was a bitch. It became the catchcry of summer. The clip had over one hundred and seventy million views on YouTube and, it seemed, just as many memes. Judd loved those seven little words because, and thank God for this, it drew attention away from pretty much everything else in the video, most importantly Judd's inaction.

That didn't stop Judd's embarrassment, though. The fact is, when he needed to rise to the occasion he hid behind a Buick. And even though he's the only one who knows the truth he still feels the failure acutely. That's why he doesn't want to be congratulated by well-wishers, and why the constant hero talk sticks in his craw. It's like he's pretending to be something he isn't. And succeeding in the Orion simulator didn't make up for it because, as difficult as that was, it was still just a very expensive video game and no one's life was at stake.

So why the hell does he watch the video so often? Because he wants to remember that he needs to be better if there's ever a next time, and nothing motivates him more than being embarrassed, and this video is the most embarrassing thing he's ever been a part of. It's walking-naked-down-a-city-street-in-the-middle-of-peak-hour embarrassing. It's so embarrassing he's not mentioned it to anyone and never plans to.

Judd reclines his seat and picks up the iPad. He better get cracking with this screenplay. As soon as he lands he'll be busy. There's an interview with Corey at CNN, then lunch with the studio head and his posse at Spago, then they head over to the official press announcement at the Twentieth Century Fox lot, where he'll link up with Rhonda and Severson, who are due in later this afternoon.

He glances at his PloProf to check the time. They should be taking off any moment now.

6

The Southwest Boeing 737-400 sits on the tarmac of the General Mitchell International Airport in overcast Wisconsin, engines turning.

Rhonda Jacolby climbs the stairs to the front door. She always wonders what it would be like to pilot a commercial jet. This 737 is roughly the same size as a shuttle, but she knows that's where the similarities end. They have nothing in common except wings and a tail.

Rhonda has spent the last two days in Wisconsin, vetting a prospective contractor who reached the final round to build the Orion's solid rocket launch system. As the astronaut member of the selection committee her job is to interview the company's management, meet the workforce, inspect the facilities then write a report. She's glad it's over. The last forty-eight hours have been arduous, to say the least, for the blonde thirty-eight-year-old with the ski-jump nose. She's looking forward to getting to LA, attending the movie's announcement then spending a couple of days decompressing at the Beverly Wilshire with Judd. She wants to clear her head before getting back to JSC and tackling that Orion simulator. She hasn't mastered the damn thing yet and it's starting to piss her off. She knows, as does everyone else involved with preparations for the Mars missions, that she is the frontrunner for FOM, but if she doesn't get a handle on the sim soon that opportunity will slip away.

For the life of her, she doesn't understand why she can't crack it. In the past she has excelled at this type of training. The shuttle simulator took her one day to figure out. *One day!* So why is she dropping the ball on this? It's like she's so used to flying the shuttle that she can't adapt to Orion. Granted, the two are nothing alike, but still, she should be able to do it, she's a member of the *Atlantis* 4, for Chrissake. Whatever it is, whatever is missing, she needs to find it – and fast.

As she reaches the top of the stairs the man in front of her stops abruptly and she bumps into him. 'What are you doing?'

'What? Oh, sorry. Nothing.'

'Get a move on, will you?'

Rhonda watches the man enter the aircraft and rolls her eyes. The reason the last two days have been so arduous is because *that* man, good old Severson Burke, who is also a member of the selection committee, accompanied her on this trip. Good Lord he's a tool. Yes, he can be charming in a Downey Jr-ish sort of way, but mainly he's a selfish son of a bitch who thinks of no one but himself. He's also the reason they're the last to board the aircraft. He took so long in the bathroom they almost missed the final boarding call.

Severson would happily miss the flight and drive to Los Angeles if he could. Unfortunately that'd mean he'd also miss the movie's announcement and he can't have that, no matter how much he hates flying, or being in an aircraft, or being near machines designed to lift him off the ground. In fact, they don't even have to be machines. As far as he's concerned ladders are not be trusted. Christ, sitting on a bar stool can cause his collar to feel tight and a prickly sweat to break out across the back of his neck, which is exactly what's happening now. Yep, his fear of heights (and flying and aircraft) is as intense as when it first afflicted him during his one and only shuttle flight four years ago. He can't believe it. He's forty-six and afraid of heights. *Forty-six!*

How embarrassing.

He grits his teeth and wills himself into the 737's cabin. The tiny, single-aisle jet usually seats about one hundred and fifty, but there's fewer than half that number on board today's flight. There's an audible gasp from the passengers as they recognise two members of the *Atlantis* 4, then a rousing round of applause. Severson laps it up, Rhonda not so much, then the starstruck flight attendant directs them to their seats halfway along the cabin.

Rhonda takes the window seat and settles in. The jet starts to taxi almost immediately. After a moment Severson leans over and whispers to her, slightly annoyed: 'I thought we were flying business.'

'There is no business. The whole plane is coach.'

'Oh. Right. These seats are very narrow.'

She looks at him with an expression of mock horror. 'Oh no, Severson's seat isn't big enough! Somebody call the cops! How awful! And just when you need to rest – it must have been so exhausting lying around the hotel pool drinking margaritas for the last two days.'

He turns to her, eyes narrowed. 'And what, *exactly*, do you mean by that?'

She taps an imaginary microphone. 'Hello? Is this thing on? What I mean is that you are a lazy prick who did sweet fuck-all while we were in Wisconsin – which meant I had to do *everything*.'

'I went in to the head office.'

'*Once*. And ponced about for ten minutes, signed a couple of autographs, then left to see a *movie* with one of the receptionists.'

'There was a Woody Allen retrospective on and she'd never seen *Annie Hall*.'

Rhonda fastens him with a laser stare and shakes her head. 'Wow, it's like they took all the things that are annoying and put them in one person.' She turns, pulls on her headphones and looks out the window.

Severson doesn't attempt to engage her. She's giving him the silent treatment which, if everything goes well, will last until they reach LA. Gee, she really does need to loosen up, though, she's so damn serious all the time. And she doesn't seem to realise these committees are for show. The decision on who wins the contract will happen at a much higher pay scale than theirs, so the trip is just a chance to junket it up and party-hearty for a few days.

The 737 swings onto the runway as the turbofans run up. They bite the air and jolt the Boeing down the runway. Severson pulls on his eye mask and clamps on his noise-cancelling headphones. He found that if he eliminated as much stimuli as possible it could almost make a plane trip bearable. *Almost*. That's why he took so long in the bathroom before this flight. He'd misplaced his last Valium and had to empty out his carry-on to find the little bastard, which had somehow lodged itself in the headphone port of his iPad.

Unfortunately the pill doesn't seem to be working yet.

The 737 gathers speed as it rushes down the runway. His collar feels even tighter than before; the hot prickly sweat on his neck back with a vengeance. As an added bonus, his stomach feels über-queasy. He takes a deep breath, grasps the side of his seat and squeezes. *Ah, that's better*. It's soft and comforting and, now he thinks about it, much *too* soft –

He pushes up his eye mask and glances down. He's squeezing Rhonda's thigh. She fixes him with a dark stare.

Severson instantly removes his hand as the 737's nose tilts up and the jet rips into the iron-grey sky.

7

Crouched on a helipad in the middle of the five-hectare compound, the Tyrannosaur is hidden on all sides by a series of grey-rendered, two-storey buildings. When Bunsen built this place three years ago his priority, apart from making it earthquake-proof, was to locate it in a section of Santa Monica near the airport with no restrictions on helicopter use. He didn't want neighbours complaining about the Tyrannosaur. After all, it's the loudest helicopter to ever fly.

Bunsen and Enrico work at the centre of the Air-Crane. A large V-shaped tank rests in a cradle as they bolt it to the underside of the helicopter's spindly airframe. The tank is specifically designed so the chopper can haul and drop large quantities of water on fires. It won't be used to drop water today.

Kilroy Jones, the aging, ponytailed head of security, cuts across the helipad towards them, a frown on his crinkle-cut face. Bunsen looks up as he approaches. 'What's that expression? Everything okay?'

'Everything's fine.' His Tennessee drawl is thick as molasses.

'Then why do you look so annoyed?'

'I'm not – I just need a word.'

'Go on.'

'Privately.'

Bunsen studies him for a moment then turns to Enrico. 'Give me a sec.' Enrico keeps working as Bunsen points Kilroy towards the open garage, which faces the heliport. Once they're inside Bunsen raises his eyebrows, his cue for Kilroy to speak.

'I think you need to release the video *before* we begin Phase Two. People need to know.'

Bunsen studies the old man with the long grey ponytail and sun-wrecked skin, a man he has known since he was four years old and loves more than the father who hired him. Kilroy's the man who made sure Bunsen was fed and rested and clothed and on time for school, taught him baseball and football, played catch with him when he couldn't sleep and talked to him about anything and everything for hours on end. 'You know why that can't happen.'

Kilroy exhales, frustrated. 'It's our city.'

'This isn't about one city. This is about – everything.'

Kilroy looks down, studies the ground.

'And you know this because *you* were the one who taught it to me. About what's right. For the future. Not *our* future, *mankind's* future.'

'I understand that, but – people will die.'

'We all die in the end.'

'Don't be glib.'

'It's true, and I prefer that to the alternative. Don't you?'

'But you could warn them. Release the video. Let them leave.'

'There needs to be collateral damage. You have to get your head around that. People must understand the threat is real. It's the point of the exercise.'

Kilroy stares at him for a long moment, then nods reluctantly. 'But afterwards, then you'll release it and let them know?'

'I promise. And if I forget I'm sure you'll remind me.' Bunsen smiles and wants Kilroy to as well. When he doesn't, Bunsen puts a hand on the old man's shoulder. 'Let me remind you of a few things you taught me over the years. I think they're important to remember, today of all days.'

Kilroy nods for him to go on. Bunsen can see he wants to be convinced.

'Over a quarter of yearly greenhouse gases are directly related to the acquisition, processing, distribution and burning of fossil fuel for transportation.'

Kilroy nods, more to himself than Bunsen.

'And the burning of coal for base-load power accounts for over twenty per cent of yearly greenhouse gas, a number that is constantly rising as China brings two power stations on line every week.'

Again Kilroy nods.

'And finally, the kicker – the one nobody seems to take notice of – the sunlight that strikes this planet in one *hour* contains more power than the world uses in one *year*.'

Kilroy nods once more.

Silence between them.

Bunsen breaks it. 'You know I can't do this without you, right?'

Kilroy nods.

'I need to know you're with me one hundred per cent, that you've got my back.'

'I do, of course.'

'Okay then.' Bunsen smiles, glances at his Patek. 'Are you ready to begin?'

'Yes.'

'Then do it.'

Kilroy turns and moves across the helipad to the right. 'I'll let you know when it's done.' Bunsen nods and watches him leave through the helipad's only access point, a large metal door.

8

'How's it going?'

Alvy looks up from his microscope as Kilroy enters the laboratory. Alvy's surprised Bunsen isn't personally checking how production of the Swarm is progressing, but keeps it to himself. He gestures to the line of black plastic Rhino drums on the far side of the lab. 'We've made thirty batches of one hundred litres each and are testing each individually. The first twenty are good.' Alvy turns to Jacob. 'You have slides for the last ten?'

'Indeed I do.' Jacob brings them over on a metal tray and places them beside Alvy. Each slide sits in a sealed petri dish. Jacob jabs a thumb towards the door. 'Gonna hit the john.'

'I'll alert the media.'

Jacob shoots Alvy a wry grin then makes an exit. As the heavy metal door hisses closed behind him, Alvy raises his head to remind him to lock it. Too late, he's already gone. For nearly three years Jacob has forgotten to lock the door behind him. It's the only thing Alvy finds annoying about his assistant.

The scientist turns back to his microscope, inspects the remaining slides, then looks up at Kilroy with a smile. 'They're all good. We're ready to roll.'

Kilroy nods. 'And the counteragent?'

'All done.' Alvy points at three canisters, each the size of a large thermos, milled from solid aluminium, which sit on a table to the right.

'Excellent.' Kilroy might be saying something positive but it's not registering on his face. Alvy had taken to calling him *Killjoy* when he wasn't around.

'It is. It really is.' Alvy believes the Department of Defense will be so impressed by the Swarm's raw potential when they see it in action that it will fundamentally alter their approach to warfare and, as a happy bi-product, save countless lives. It is, far and away, the most important thing Alvy's ever worked on, a game-changer that will, he believes, make the world a safer place. 'So what time is the test scheduled for?'

Kilroy's expression remains neutral. 'There isn't going to be a test.'

'It's been cancelled?' Alvy's clearly disappointed.

'It was never going to happen.'

'It – what? What are you talking about?'

'The Swarm wasn't created for military use.'

Alvy's just confused. 'I don't – what does that mean?'

'Exactly what I said.'

'Then what's it for?'

'Urban deployment.'

Alvy thinks it's a joke, a bad one but a joke nonetheless. He grins – then takes in Kilroy's blank expression and realises it isn't. 'You can't be serious.'

'I'm dead serious.'

Alvy stands instinctively, his face grim. 'No, no, no!' His voice rises an octave as he says it. 'You can *never* do that. *Ever*!'

'And yet we can and we will – today, in fact, and as you're the only person who can synthesise the counteragent you can't be around when it happens.'

'"Can't be around?" What the hell are you talking about?'

Alvy understands exactly what he's talking about as light glints off the silenced Glock 9mm pistol Kilroy draws from inside his jacket.

'Oh, shit —'

The weapon swings towards Alvy as he drives a hand forward and bats the metal tray off the table in front of him.

Bam. The pistol fires and Alvy feels a sharp pain high on his left shoulder.

Clank. The spinning tray smashes into the bridge of Kilroy's nose. He cries out and both hands fly to his face.

This is a positive development for Alvy as the pistol now points at the ceiling. Belying his husky appearance the scientist is surprisingly nimble and springs forward, swings a foot and connects with the side of Kilroy's left knee.

Kilroy grunts and crumples to the ground. As he falls, Alvy grabs the Glock in his hand. The big surprise is that the pistol twists out of Kilroy's grasp with minimal effort. Alvy was expecting some resistance but the pistol's grip is slick with blood, courtesy of the metal tray, which has, he can now see, not only stunned Kilroy but also left a deep gash across his nose.

Alvy sprints ten metres to the lab's door, the bullet wound on his shoulder stinging like crazy. He reaches for the doorhandle. Thank God Jacob was the last person to use the door. He always forgets to lock it. Alvy wrenches on the handle –

The door is locked tight.

No! Is Jacob in on this? Is he on the other side, waiting to see if the execution has been a success, ready to act if it hasn't? There's only one way to find out. Alvy punches the five-digit code into the keypad, raises the pistol and pulls the door open.

There's no one there. The walkway is empty. Maybe Jacob isn't in on it after all –

Thud. A bullet rips into the wall in front of Alvy. He turns. Behind him a groggy Kilroy aims a smaller pistol at him and fires again.

Alvy pivots clear and runs backwards along the walkway, pistol raised and aimed at the door he just exited. Kilroy pokes his head out from behind it and Alvy fires, too low to be anything but a warning shot. Alvy's never consciously hurt anyone in his life so the idea of actually *shooting* Kilroy doesn't cross his mind, in spite of everything that just happened. Kilroy pulls back into the room and disappears from view.

Alvy's back thumps into the door that leads outside. He turns, taps five numbers into the keypad and it unlocks. Gun raised, he yanks the door open and steps into dazzling sunlight –

Bam. A gunshot rings out. Alvy feels hot pain in his hip as he swings the pistol around, fires in the direction he thinks the bullet came from.

It is silent.

Alvy blinks through the sunlight, looks down, sees he's been shot in his left thigh. Stunned, he turns and sees Jacob, slumped on the ground in front of him, a pistol in his hand, a bullet wound to the chest. Dead.

'No.' Alvy feels sick to his stomach. He just shot and killed a man he thought was a good friend – a man he has eaten lunch with *every day* for almost three years. Unfortunately, he's also a man who just tried to end Alvy's life with the bullet now lodged in his hip. Just thinking about it is doing the scientist's head in. Everything Alvy thought was true is a lie.

'Gotta move.' That's what he must do if he wants to live. He needs to get away from here as fast as possible, before Kilroy reappears. He takes a step – and instantly feels lightheaded, wants to lie down.

'No!' He pulls in a deep breath, grits his teeth, looks right, to the car park. His old blue Toyota Corolla is fifty metres away. He moves towards it as fast as he can, which isn't very fast as a bolt of pain shoots down his left leg with every step. He ignores it, keeps going.

Kilroy likes Alvy, couldn't help but be impressed by his outsized intellect, knew that Bunsen's plan was not possible without it. Unfortunately for Alvy, that outsized intellect is also the reason he must now be put down.

Grey ponytail swishing behind him, blood on his face from his still-throbbing nose, Kilroy reaches the end of the walkway, works the keypad and shoulders the door open, weapon raised, finger tight around the trigger of the .38 he kept strapped to his calf in case of emergency.

There's no sign of Alvy but Jacob is down. Jacob wasn't the brightest bulb in the chandelier but he's still surprised Alvy managed to get the better of him. Kilroy scans the area, hears an engine running in the car park, focuses on the exhaust that puffs from the tail pipe of Alvy's old blue Corolla.

Clearly the scientist planned to make a decidedly unstylish getaway in the sun-faded rust bucket. Kilroy's best guess, and he tended to guess right, is that he, or Jacob, had hit Alvy with at least one bullet and the guy had collapsed in the driver's seat before he could clunk the transmission into reverse.

Of course, it's only a guess so Kilroy approaches the car cautiously, pistol raised. He has privacy. The compound is boarded on all sides by a dense, tightly packed line of two-metre-tall shrubs in front of a high chain-link fence. Bunsen had them installed to protect the compound from unwanted guests and prying eyes when it was built.

Kilroy creeps forward, just five metres away from the Corolla. He glances down, scans the asphalt below his feet. A drip of red blood glistens in the sun. Then another. Alvy *is* hit. The next step is simple. Line him up and pull the trigger. Kilroy crouches low and moves on. Two metres from the Corolla he peers in through the left rear window. The tint is so dark and blistered he can't make out a goddamn thing inside. Finger tight on the pistol's trigger, he glides onward, reaches the open passenger window.

There's no one inside.

Alvy's plan has worked beautifully, leading Kilroy right to where he wants him. Now he must finish the job. Camouflaged within the tree line that rings the compound, he stands just five metres from Kilroy. Through the foliage Alvy aims the weapon at Kilroy's chest and squeezes the trigger.

He can't do it.

Jesus H! *He can't pull the trigger!* This bastard is trying to kill him and Alvy's hesitating. *Hesitating*! He's about to hesitate himself into an early grave. He must make the most of this moment because he knows Kilroy will keep coming after him.

Alvy pulls the trigger. The gunshot rings out – and Kilroy slumps to the ground beside the passenger door. Alvy moves fast, pulls open the driver's door, slides inside, doesn't look at Kilroy, just wants to get out of there as fast as possible.

Alvy doesn't feel any better sitting down. He actually feels worse. His arm and leg scream in pain and his head goes light. 'Wake up!' He shouts it, widens his eyes, wills himself to stay conscious. He thumps the Corolla into reverse and hits the accelerator. The car jerks backwards and he points it towards the main gate. He clunks the transmission into drive, floors it and presses the button on his gate remote.

Thud, thud, thud. Bullets thunk into the Corolla. Alvy instinctively ducks but has no idea where the fire is coming from so doesn't know if it will do any good.

Smash. The back window explodes, showers the interior with glass. Alvy looks in the rear-view mirror. Kilroy sits up from his position on the ground, shirt open to reveal the bulletproof vest he wears. He turns and aims his pistol at the Corolla again.

Thud, thud, thud. Three more bullets pepper the car's boot as it speeds through the gate. Alvy steers onto the empty street and accelerates away, tyres screeching as they scramble for grip.

'Christ almighty.' He takes a breath, tries to process what just happened. It's inconceivable and yet here he is, on the run with two gunshot wounds. He needs medical attention but first he must tell a cop, or someone in authority, about the Swarm and what is planned for today.

He wonders if anyone will believe him.

9

Bunsen paces the heliport, iPhone in hand. He doesn't feel good about ending Alvy's life, but there was no choice. Alvy is one of maybe three people on the planet who understands this nanotechnology well enough to create the Swarm, and is the only man who can disable it.

Bunsen's iPhone rings.

He sees it's Kilroy calling and knows it can't be good news. If everything had gone to plan he would have received a short text from the old man such as: 'it's done' or 'it's over' or something equally pithy. But Bunsen just heard gunshots from the opposite side of the compound and now the phone is ringing. He fears the worst.

He answers with a short 'Yes?' then listens. The update from his 2IC takes less than thirty seconds and is worse than Bunsen could have imagined. Jacob is dead and Alvy has escaped. It's a screw-up of epic proportions.

Bunsen keeps it simple. 'We continue Phase Two as planned. Find him. Deal with it. If he talks to anyone, deal with them too. Call me when it's done. Be quick.' He waits for a 'yes' then hangs up. This is not the time for recriminations or Monday morning quarterbacking, and it's not like there's anything else that can be done. Bunsen can't replace either Jacob or Kilroy. His crew is small for a good reason – it's extremely difficult to find people who are dedicated to such a cause, have the correct skill set and are trustworthy.

This is the first time Bunsen can remember Kilroy screwing up. The old man has been completely reliable over the years, not only for Bunsen but before that, as his father's general 'fixer', doing everything that needed to be done to keep his myriad productions running smoothly. Kilroy persuaded whoever needed to be persuaded, made sure the actors and directors were on time and in good health (that is, not high), and quietly and efficiently cleaned up any mess they made along the way. Though Bunsen's father wrote and produced light and fluffy sitcoms for a living, it took a surprising amount of strong-arming, bribery, wire-tapping and, yes, even the occasional 'accidental' death, to keep the shows on track and profitable. It never occurred to Bunsen that Kilroy would have trouble dealing with *Alvy*. Granted, he is getting older but, still, he's only sixty-four and he's been dealing with these kinds of issues since his twenties.

He can't dwell on it. Whatever the reason for Kilroy's slip-up it doesn't change what Bunsen does next. He gestures for Enrico to follow him and they enter the main building through the locked heavy steel door, move along the well-lit walkway and enter the laboratory. Bunsen directs his pilot to use the large trolley to move the black rhino drums containing the Swarm to the helipad while he deals with Jacob's body.

Bunsen drags the poor bastard inside the building and deposits him in the coolroom amongst the chemicals and lab supplies. Once the mission is completed he will dispose of the body appropriately. It strikes Bunsen as he closes the door behind him that Jacob is the mission's first collateral damage.

Bunsen moves back into the lab and on the central table finds the three aluminium canisters that contain the counteragent. Each flip-lid contains a small numeric keypad with an LED screen built into it. He slides them into his backpack then heads to the helipad.

He arrives as Enrico pushes a long hose from a four-horsepower electric pump into one of the drums of Swarm he brought up from the lab, then attaches another hose to the chopper's empty water tank. He switches on the pump and it whirs to life, transferring the contents of the drum into the tank. He turns to Bunsen. 'How much do we want on board?'

'One thousand litres.'

Enrico nods.

Bunsen knows that will be more than enough for today's mission, though it will use only a fraction of the water tank's ten-thousand-litre capacity. It will also leave them with two thousand litres of the Swarm to use later.

Bunsen moves to the front of the chopper and unscrews the Tyrannosaur's heavy fuel tank cap. The Air-Crane is currently full to the brim with 5114 litres of av-gas in its tank. He reaches into his backpack, pulls out one of the large aluminium canisters and thumbs 612 (his birthdate) into the keypad. The flip-lid unlocks with a burst of compressed air and he pours the contents of the canister into the fuel tank. He screws the fuel cap back on and turns to Enrico. 'How much longer?'

'Fifteen minutes.'

Bunsen nods, then draws in a deep breath. He needs to prepare himself for what comes next. He pulls earbuds from his pocket, slips them in place, hits play on his iPhone's screen – and lets the recorded screams of those tortured plants fill his world.

10

Judd strides down the passenger bridge from the 787 and steps into the LAX terminal. He glances at his watch then scans the crowd of people nearby.

'Sssuuup, Mandy?'

Judd turns. It's the Australian, with a crooked grin that'd make a Chimpanzee envious.

'See what I did there? Made it sound like I'm a local.'

'Excuse me, have you seen Corey Purchase? I believe I'm meant to meet him here.'

They embrace. Somehow shaking hands just doesn't seem like enough. They hold it for a moment, then part.

'How are you, man?'

'Mate, never better. How's it hanging?'

'Low, but with a curve to the left.'

'That's right, I saw the pictures on the Tweeters.'

'Ha. And it's "Twitter". Where's the puppy?'

'In the car with Bowen. They're circling. We should haul arse.' Corey points the way and they move off. 'We'll hit CNN first and do the interview, then drop by Spago for a feed, then head over to Fox for the announcement. They want to film it then release it to the networks for the news tonight.'

'Sounds like a plan.' Judd studies the Australian for a moment.

There's something about him that doesn't seem quite right. 'So, how are you?'

'Travelling beautifully, like I said.'

Judd's not buying. 'So what's going on?'

'Actually, I'm remembering how much of a pain in the arse you can be.' Corey tries to grin it out but Judd is undeterred.

'Fess up, Blades.' Blades is Corey's nickname, after Blades of Corey, the heli-services company he ran in Central Australia. Mandy is Corey's nickname for Judd, because he dances like Barry Manilow, who had a big hit back in the day with a ballad called, unsurprisingly, 'Mandy'.

Corey takes a breath. 'Well, there was this girl. I liked her. Thought she liked me. I didn't know she had a boyfriend. It was embarrassing. Boo-hoo. The end.'

Judd's about to say something 'there's-plenty-of-fish-in-the-sea' glib, then sees Corey's actually cut up about it and changes tack. 'Sorry to hear that. Who is this lady?'

'She works at Bowen's agency. She's great – funny and interesting and clever and . . . she gets me.'

Just not enough. Judd doesn't say it. He stays positive. 'Well, if you feel that strongly, you've got to fight for her, pursue her – without being a stalker about it, of course.'

Corey's face brightens. Judd knows this is new ground for the Aussie. He hasn't had a lot of positive experience with the opposite sex so he's looking for any kind of guidance. 'Really? Do you think that could work?'

He continues to stay positive. 'I have no idea, but it's worth a try. Who's the boyfriend?'

'Scott Ford.'

'Excuse me?'

'His name is Scott Ford —'

'*The Blue Cyclone* Scott Ford? The actor? In the tights, with the body?'

Corey nods.

Judd turns serious. 'I may have led you astray with the advice I just gave you.'

'But you said if I feel strongly, I should fight for her —'

'That was before I found out she's dating the biggest movie star in the world. You kinda buried the lead on that.'

Corey studies his feet, no longer trying to hide how miserable he feels.

'Sorry. But that's kind of hard to top.'

'Yeah, I know. I'm just a bloody chopper pilot from the Alice.'

Judd places a mollifying hand on his shoulder. 'And it's her loss. And, you know, plenty of fish in the sea and all that.'

Corey takes this in with a half-hearted nod and they continue walking. Judd sees the usual spring is gone from his step. 'Why didn't you want to tell me?'

'I didn't want you to feel sorry for me.'

'Oh, come on, I wouldn't do that. Last year I told you everything about, you know, my troubles with Rhonda.'

'Exactly.'

'And you felt sorry for me?'

'Of course.'

'Oh.' Now Judd is despondent – and it's Corey's turn to place a mollifying hand on his shoulder.

They pass through the terminal's sliding doors and step outside. The dry heat slaps Judd across the face. LA: one season, all year around.

Corey searches the roadway.

'What are we looking for?'

'A blue Bimmer, seven series – there it is.' Corey points at the navy BMW as it approaches, Spike in the front passenger seat. It pulls up beside them and they slide into the back seat. Judd pats the ugly white dog on the head and takes in Bowen, who sits behind the wheel.

The agent is on the phone, a Bluetooth gadget jammed in his right ear. He turns, holds up a single 'one minute' finger and continues to talk on the phone: 'Why? 'Cause my guy's the one you need on this. Sure, his last movie was a hundred different clichés celebrating a reunion and yes, it was too long – I wanted to tap it on the shoulder and ask, "Hey, shouldn't you have ended fifteen minutes ago?", but it made six hundred and fifty million international.'

Bowen pulls out from the kerb, turns and looks back at Judd, mimes a 'nice to meet you' that ends with a wink, then continues talking on the phone: 'And that's the point – it was awful and it opened everywhere because my guy is a star. He was a star thirty years ago when he started out, he's a star right now and he'll be a star the day the sun explodes and you can't say that about anyone else. Think of him as insurance against that Russian first-timer you hired to direct.' He listens for another moment, then, 'It means this: you can't polish a turd, but you can roll it in glitter – and my guy's the glitter. I want your answer ASAP, as in www-dot-you-got-fifteen-minutes-dot-org.'

Bowen hangs up and looks back at Judd and Corey with a grin. 'Well, lookee here, I got me a car full of bona fide heroes! Oh my Lord. I'll instagram it as soon as we get out.' He focuses on Judd. 'I must open with a heartfelt thank you. For what you did for our country. It's greatly appreciated. It's an honour to be on your team. It's the highlight of my career.'

Bowen keeps talking and Judd takes him in. With the exuberant overstatements, hollow platitudes and folksy inflection, the

COMBUSTION   71

agent is just as Judd expected. In his late forties, Bowen is short but good-looking in that I-was-once-a-child-star way, which he was. Judd remembers him from *First Son*, a hit sitcom that ran for seven years on CBS during the eighties. He played James, a smart-mouthed, liberal-minded teen who had an almost Svengali-like control over Barry, his dimwitted, ultra-conservative father – who just happened to be the President of the United States.

From what Corey's told him, Bowen never considered himself anything more than a low-rent Michael J. Fox and despaired at the thought of being unemployed like all the other young actors he knew, except Michael J. Fox. So, when *First Son* was cancelled he started his own talent agency to represent those actors and give himself some career security. He was only twenty-four, but using everything he'd learned from his time on the sitcom, B&A quickly became a premier boutique agency in Beverly Hills.

As Bowen drives he brings Judd up to speed on *The Atlantis 4* movie, or *Atlantis 4* as it is now called, because apparently 'it's a much stronger title without the "The".' He then tells him how Fox is looking to commit to a sequel before the first movie is even released and want to talk money soon.

Money. It's never held much interest to Judd – if you want to be rich you sure as hell didn't become an astronaut – but he is excited that a successful movie, or series of movies, might help the program win over the non-believers who think the NASA budget is an extravagance and the Mars mission frivolous. He's happy to be involved in anything that will rekindle America's love affair with the space program.

Corey turns to Judd. 'Mate, nearly forgot, the studio needs us to choose a song for the bit when my character swoops in and saves your arse at the end. We can have "Can't Fight This Feeling" by REO Speedwagon or "Baby Come Back" by Player.'

'Can we have something from this century?'

'It's meant to be nostalgic and ironic.'

'I remember the "fight this feeling" one but how does the "baby goes back" one go again?'

'Oh! I know!' Corey puts up his hand, excited.

'You don't have to raise your hand, just sing it.'

Corey puts his hand down and sings it: 'Baby come back! Da da da da da da da and then something, something something something something – baby come back!' He stops with a grimace. 'That sounded horrible.'

'I have even *less* idea now.'

'Sorry. Anyway, download them and have a listen. We need to make a decision before Monday.'

Judd nods and looks out the window as the dirty grey freeway whips past. He turns and takes in the skyline, notices sunlight reflects off the black glass windows of the distant CNN building, their destination this afternoon. Behind it, in the distance, his eye is drawn to a dark helicopter that cuts across the horizon. It's one of the big ones they use for firefighting. What are they called again? That's right – it's an Air-Crane.

11

Kilroy guns the Prius.

The bridge of his nose stings like a bastard, the right side of his chest throbs from where the bullet hit the vest, but neither hurt as much as his pride. Alvy Blash, the geekiest of scientists, a tubby, pigeon-toed hairball, brought him down with a metal tray, stole his gun, shot him with it and then *escaped*.

It's so humiliating he can't bear to think about it. He should have taken more care, shouldn't have assumed Alvy would be an easy target. He could tell Bunsen was über-pissed about it, even though he barely said a word on the phone. And why wouldn't he be angry? This is exactly the kind of distraction they don't need today, of all days. Kilroy glances at his Tag Heuer. The Tyrannosaur will be airborne by now. He'll need to be quick to get this mess cleaned up before Phase Two begins.

Kilroy can see Alvy's faded blue Corolla ten cars ahead as it navigates light traffic on Cosmo Street in Hollywood. He has no idea where it's heading, just knows he must deal with it now.

He can't underestimate that chubby scientist again.

Alvy needs to lose Kilroy.

He scans the road before him. Where's a cop when you need one? He hasn't seen a police station or a police cruiser since he made his getaway.

He glances in the rear-view mirror, takes in Kilroy's Prius, a good ten cars behind. He needs to warn the authorities about the Swarm, then get himself to a hospital, but he can't do either with the pony-tailed son-of-a-bitch on his six. He's managed to escape Kilroy once today but he doesn't like his chances of a repeat performance. He's sure if he stops the car he'll be dead before he gets out – though he might not have to worry about Kilroy killing him if he doesn't get some medical attention ASAP. His head feels even lighter than before as blood pools on his seat from the wound on his thigh. He keeps pressure on it as best he can but it doesn't stop the bleeding.

A police cruiser. Driving on the opposite side of the road. Two officers inside. That's it. That's what he needs. He makes a decision.

Alvy yanks the Corolla's steering wheel, sends the vehicle careering into the opposite lane and braces for impact.

Crunch. It's much heavier than he expected. The police cruiser ploughs into the front of the Toyota and destroys its grille and bonnet, sends a shudder through the chassis that cracks the windscreen and triggers the driver's airbag. It whacks Alvy in the face and he feels even groggier than before.

He couldn't be happier.

The two police officers slide out of the cruiser, dazed but with guns drawn. One shouts at him: 'Get your hands where I can see them! Now!'

Alvy is more than happy to comply, though the act of raising his hands makes him *extremely* lightheaded. One of the cops opens his door, drags him from the vehicle and pushes him to the bitumen.

'Jesus!' The cop sees the blood, calls to his partner: 'We need an ambulance, now!'

'On it.' The partner calls it in as Alvy looks back and tries to locate Kilroy's Prius. He can't see it, but then he can't see anything because the world goes dark.

Kilroy watches the arrest unfold as he drives past. In spite of everything, he can't help but be impressed by Alvy's resourcefulness. Drive into a cop car and they'll have no choice but to call an ambulance when they see your injuries. Clever boy.

Kilroy pulls over and studies the scene in his side-view mirror. It's clear Alvy is unconscious; he won't be telling anyone anything in the short term, but how long will that last?

Kilroy's first thought is to walk over there and start shooting, take out Alvy, the cops and anyone with the bad luck to be rubbernecking. Then a second police cruiser and an ambulance pull up beside the crash site. There goes that idea. With four cops in attendance he is outgunned. He glances at his watch. Phase Two will begin in a matter of minutes. He needs to take care of this pronto.

12

The Tyrannosaur slices through the beige smog cloud that hangs above Los Angeles.

In the chopper's cockpit Bunsen listens to those screaming plants on his headset as he glances at the Air-Crane's altimeter. They're at three thousand feet. He unplugs the headset from his iPhone, plugs into the aircraft's console then turns to Enrico beside him. 'How long until we're in position?'

'Two minutes.'

Two minutes until the world has the motivation it needs.

It's incomprehensible to Bunsen that of the almost seven billion people on the face of the earth, not one has yet created an efficient mechanism to harness the sun's power and unshackle the globe from its unsustainable reliance on fossil fuels. There is, he feels, an overwhelming lack of motivation for mankind to make the necessary change to clean energy.

Well, today Bunsen will create that motivation – and it will not be gentle. He knows a carrot won't work. He needs a stick – a *big* stick – and with the Swarm he wields the biggest stick since the dawn of the atomic age. Like the first nuclear weapons created during the Manhattan Project, the Swarm's power will profoundly alter the way people think about the world.

Enrico turns to him. 'We're in position.'

'You know the route?'

'Absolutely.'

'Then let's do it.' Bunsen reaches for the small, red switch attached to the side of the chopper's control panel, touches it, can feel his heartbeat through the tip of his finger. He takes a breath, tries to settle the butterflies that swirl in his chest, doesn't succeed. Three years of his life and the better part of twenty million dollars have led him to this moment. He can't quite believe it all begins now.

He flicks the switch.

Directly behind him he hears a faint whir as a spigot opens and a fine mist of the Swarm is released from a two-metre-long crop-dusting spray rail fastened to the bottom of the water tank. Bunsen looks back and watches the vapour fill the sky, then fall towards the Santa Monica Freeway, the ugly ribbon of cement and bitumen gridlocked with traffic below.

13

Ding.

The elevator door opens onto the top floor of the CNN building. Corey steps out, Spike beside him, Bowen directly behind and Judd bringing up the rear. They enter a wide foyer, empty except for a pair of sleek, black leather sofas.

Bowen speaks into his iPhone: 'Yes, it was very funny. Really. I drank milk while I was reading it so I could have it run out of my nose every time I laughed – hold on a sec.' He turns to Judd and Corey and points down the hallway to the distant reception area. 'Hang here. I'll find out when you're on.' He moves off, resumes his conversation: 'Really? *He's* doing the next draft? The autocorrect on my *iPhone* writes better dialogue than him.'

Judd and Corey turn to the large window that offers a panoramic view of Los Angeles. Judd takes it in. He lived here, briefly, as a boy. His father was in the army and the family moved all around the country. Judd doesn't remember much about their stay in LA, it was only for eight months or so, but he does remember one thing: this city is the reason he became an astronaut.

Most people think astronauts choose their career for the rush of being strapped to a vehicle travelling faster than a bullet. Not Judd. He became an astronaut because, as a thirteen-year-old, he had an epiphany. It happened on one of the rare Saturdays his father wasn't working and they could spend the day together. It was a strange day, a day of two halves. In the morning they visited Disneyland for the first time, a pristine, magical place, the 'happiest place on Earth' as the motto trumpeted. Judd was the perfect age, not too old to be jaded, but big enough to go on all the rides, Space Mountain being his favourite.

Near the end of their stay an older man in his sixties stepped off the Big Thunder Mountain roller-coaster and fell over, dizzy after the ride. A swarm of people ran to his aid, including Judd's father. Medical attention was quickly forthcoming and the man was stretchered away, Judd's father staying with him until he was loaded into the ambulance. The old guy was fine at the end and the episode just added another element of excitement to an already exhilarating day.

That afternoon Judd accompanied his father to visit an old army buddy of his on San Pedro Street, in Central City East, a place, Judd realised years later, also known as Skid Row, the most economically depressed area of the city at the time. Simply, it was the polar opposite of Disneyland. If it had a motto, 'the unhappiest place on Earth' would have been spot on.

As Judd and his father walked along the desolate street, searching for his father's friend's apartment, a man who had 'fallen on hard times', they approached a young guy lying unconscious on the footpath. Judd remembers two things. The first was that, unlike Disneyland, no one stopped to help, including his father. Instead they stepped over the young guy and walked on. The second thing Judd remembers is how tightly his father gripped his hand as they did it.

As they walked away his father turned to him and said: 'One day you'll understand.'

Even at thirteen Judd knew he didn't want to. Why didn't anyone, including his father, a good man, a good *soldier*, not stop to help the young guy? Years later, Judd realised the young guy was probably drunk or on drugs, but still, how did the world get to the place where it was okay to ignore it? Or accept it? Why was the world like that? Why didn't it work the way it should?

Judd was a clever boy and once he was aware of this schism he saw examples everywhere. Inequality between the haves and have-nots, between the sexes, between the races. He saw how the environment was being destroyed through stupidity and greed and how religious superstition created division and ran roughshod over scientific fact.

So how did a young boy fix this world, make it work the way it should? He quickly realised he couldn't, but as a man he could find *another* world, a red planet where the human race could start over with a new set of rules, where the environment was respected, where religion was a personal choice with no role in government or science, where equality and fairness, no matter who you were, was guaranteed because everyone would be Martian. It would be a place where no one would ever step over you.

Something in the urban sprawl below catches Judd's eye. 'What's that?'

Corey turns to him. 'Hmmm?'

Judd points. 'That. What's that – down there?'

Corey follows the direction of his finger and takes it in. 'Oh.' He looks closer, surprised. 'I don't – I don't know.'

A giant orange fireball silently rolls skyward from the Santa Monica Freeway five kilometres away, the sound too distant to register. In quick succession three more explosions blast into the sky.

'Christ.' Judd can't see what's causing the explosions, but he remembers reading about a multi-car pile-up on Germany's autobahn years ago. It killed ten people, caused dozens of fires and destroyed fifty cars. Was something similar happening here? Another two explosions punctuate the skyline, one with the flaming shell of vehicle within it. 'What the hell's going on?'

Matty Bowen's voice echoes as he approaches along the hallway and talks into his phone: 'No, it's so bad my DVR refuses to record it. I'm not saying his style of writing is old-fashioned, but I just saw it out shopping for a single-level house because its kids have left home and it doesn't want to climb the stairs any more. Yeah, we'll talk later.'

He hangs up and Corey turns to him. 'Matty?'

'Guys, you're on in fifteen —'

'Look.'

Bowen turns and looks where the Australian points.

Another giant orange fireball rips skyward from the freeway. The agent takes it in, unperturbed. 'They must be shooting the new *Transformers* down there —'

The dog barks.

Judd and Corey turn to Spike as he raises a paw and points at the Hollywood Freeway on the other side of the city.

It bursts into flames. At the point where the freeway crosses Vine Street, a series of explosions launch giant fireballs into the sky. Unlike the distant Santa Monica Freeway this one is less than half a kilometre away so they can see and hear everything clearly.

'Migod.' Even though Judd looks directly at it he can't quite process what is happening. He blinks, to make sure his eyes aren't playing tricks, then refocuses. Cars and trucks and motorcycles explode – but not because they're part of an accident. No, they just – blow up, like they've been filled with explosives then detonated. He glances at Corey. 'What's happening?'

The Australian shakes his head as he stares at the flames, dumbfounded. 'Never seen anything like it. Looks like a bloody terrorist attack. Could it be a film shoot?'

Judd doesn't know the answer. It doesn't feel like a film shoot, but why would terrorists attack a *freeway*? Granted, if you were going to do it LA was the place, but if you wanted to do some serious scar-the-country's-psyche damage in this city surely you'd take out the Santa Monica Pier or the Universal Studio Tour – or Disneyland.

Spike barks.

Corey turns to him. 'I reckon the safest place is right here, mate—'

Boom. The explosion on the street directly below them flashes white and the building shakes, the noise like thunder. The window-pane directly in front of them cracks from side to side.

'Jeez-us.' Judd recoils, then looks down at a roiling ball of flame which kisses the side of the building as it races past, turns the world orange for a split second.

Bowen's voice trembles. 'What was that?'

Judd studies the road directly below and takes in the twisted remains of a burning vehicle. He's pretty sure it used to be some kind of van. His eyes move, find a shiny silver Caltex tanker truck that trundles to a stop just near the wreck.

The first question that pops into his mind is whether or not the gleaming tanker is full of fuel. The *second* question is what kind of damage it would do if it exploded while full of fuel –

Ka-boom! The tanker explodes and Judd has his answers. The first is '*absolutely*' and the second is '*much more than you could imagine*'. The initial flash is brighter than the sun, burns a ghost image into his retinas.

'Get down!' His words are cut off as the brutal shockwave punches in every window. The three men duck for cover. Judd shields his head with his arms but feels the sting of glass on his face. Corey drops to his knees and covers Spike as he is showered with debris. Bowen ducks and crouches, hands over his face as what appears to be the truck's engine block crashes through the roof, bounces once and slams into the wall between the twin elevators.

A deep groan cuts across the soundscape. Corey glances at Judd. 'What the hell was that?'

The building twists beneath them – then lurches to the right.

Bowen looks extremely unhappy. 'Guess they're not shooting *Transformers* after all.'

Corey finds his feet. 'We need to get out of here.'

The building leans to the left and they fight to keep their balance, stumble towards the elevators – and realise the engine block has destroyed the button pad.

'Fire stairs!' Judd jabs a finger in the direction of the green EXIT sign twenty metres away. As one they turn for it –

Shwump! Metal shears and cement shatters as the left side of the building falls away like a giant, terrible curtain, revealing a sheer drop and the sprawling city beyond. They all sprint for the fire stairs but now they're running *up* an incline as the floor beneath them tips and slides towards the open side of the building.

Spike leads, Judd behind him and Bowen behind him, and Corey at the rear. The floor beneath the Australian collapses.

'Corey!' Judd pivots to grab him but he's too far away. He falls –

Wham. Bowen catches Corey's hand. 'I got you!'

Terrified, Corey dangles over the gaping chasm, sixty metres above the ground. 'But who's got *you*?'

The shattered floor beneath Bowen collapses and drops –

Slam. Judd catches his hand. 'I do.'

Corey and Bowen dangle over the abyss and their weight wrenches on Judd's shoulder. It feels like it's about to pop its socket. '*Jesus Christ,* you guys are heavy—'

The floor beneath Judd tips and he slides towards the chasm too. 'Oh, damn . . . '

14

Crunch.

'Ahhh!' Something clamps around Judd's right shoe, stops him from sliding over the edge. He looks back.

Spike.

'Good dog!'

The canine bites down on Judd's foot. Surprisingly it doesn't hurt that much because the shoe leather is thick. Spike pulls back with everything he's got but still the weight of the two men drag him and Judd towards the edge.

Shoulder screaming, Judd's eyes find a metal rod, part of the cement floor's reinforcement, which dangles a metre from the Australian. 'Can you grab that?'

Corey reaches for it, can't quite get to it.

'You can do it!' Bowen's voice is a terrified croak.

Corey strains for the rod again, touches it – grabs it. 'Yes!'

It comes free in his hand.

'No!' They say it in unison, their disappointment profound.

Judd slides towards the edge, can hear Spike's paws rip at the carpet as he scrambles for traction.

Corey looks up at the shattered concrete above him. 'Got an idea.'

Judd reaches the edge. 'If you're going to do something, do it fast!'

Corey reaches up with the metre-long rod and jams it between two bent pieces of pipe visible within the broken concrete. 'Here goes.'

He lets go of Bowen, grabs the rod with both hands – and swings free. The pipes bend, but hold his weight. 'Yes!'

Instantly the pressure on Judd's shoulder is halved and he drags Bowen up. The agent snatches at the shattered floor with his free hand, grabs a handful of carpet and pulls himself to safety.

Judd's eyes flick back to Corey. He holds the rod tight, but the pipes crack and buckle under the weight. He falls –

Judd's right hand shoots out, seizes the metal rod. But now Corey's weight drags him over the edge again. 'Oh, man —'

Bowen grasps Judd's belt, heaves him backwards, yanks Corey upwards too. The Australian grabs at the floor, clambers up and they collapse to the ground, pull in big air.

Judd turns to Bowen. 'Thanks.'

Bowen nods as he catches his breath. 'Just part . . . of the comprehensive service . . . we offer at Bowen & Associates.'

They can't help but smile. Corey shoots Judd a thumbs up. 'Mate, owe you one.'

'I had some help.' Judd reaches back, pats Spike on the head. 'Good dog. If I had a biscuit it'd be all yours.'

The building shudders again. Judd looks to the others. 'We gotta move.' They don't need to be told twice. They find their feet and rush for the fire stairs. Judd gets there first, drags the fire door open.

They file inside and move down the stairs three at a time. Other office workers are in there too, but no one speaks. They all have just one focus: *get out now*.

Creak. The sound echoes around them. The building sways to the right. The lights above flicker. Still no one speaks. They just increase their pace.

It feels like an eternity before they reach the ground floor. Corey shoulders open the fire door and they burst outside – then stop dead.

The city looks like a war zone.

15

Heavy smoke drifts between the buildings, the smell of gasoline thick in the air. Explosions echo, some distant, others close. On the road before them every car, truck and motorbike is either on fire or a smoking wreck. There are bodies everywhere.

Judd moves to an elderly woman who lies on the sidewalk. As soon as he kneels beside her he sees the left side of her face is missing. 'Oh, Christ.' On the ground beside her is a burning piston from a car's engine.

Judd glances back at the CNN building. It reminds him of the one that was bombed in Oklahoma in the 1990s. One third of it has collapsed and the rest leans at a profound angle. They were lucky to get out alive.

His attention moves to a car that turns onto the road. Since he exited the building it's the only vehicle he's seen that's not on fire. It's an LAPD cruiser which drives fast and swerves between the burning wrecks. There's a young cop behind the wheel. He looks terrified.

Judd points to the rear of the cruiser. Its exhaust is a light purple colour. 'What's that?'

Corey sees it too, shakes his head. 'Don't know, but it doesn't look right.'

Judd waves at the young cop to pull over but he accelerates past, the cruiser's V8 engine thundering. The exhaust turns a darker purple.

Bowen sees it too. 'What's going on there?'

As he says it the engine note changes from a deep throb to that of a cement mixer filled with gravel. It's a terrible sound, like the engine is eating itself –

Boom! The cruiser detonates.

The explosion is so bright it's like a star going supernova. The blast wave picks up Judd and slams him against the side of the CNN building, the sting of shrapnel hot on his face. His ears ring like a five-alarm fire as he opens his eyes and sees nothing but swirling smoke and dust. He blinks, tries to find his bearings, staggers to his feet. 'Corey?'

There's no answer.

The dog barks but he sounds a mile away.

'Mate? You there?' It's Corey, his voice groggy.

'You okay?'

'She'll be right. Where's Matt?'

'Don't know.'

'Matty!'

There's no response. The dog barks again, closer this time. Judd follows the sound through the wall of smoke and dust – then sees Bowen lying on the sidewalk, Corey kneeling beside him. The agent has a shard of metal embedded in his throat and blood pours from the wound. Corey tries his best to staunch it with his hands.

It doesn't work. Bowen stares up with wide, stunned eyes, his breathing fast and rough. He opens his mouth to speak but no sound emerges. 'We're going to get you some help, mate. Just gotta stop this bleeding.'

Judd pulls off his jacket, a heavy cotton Carhartt, and presses a sleeve against the wound. Corey pulls Bowen's iPhone from his breast pocket and dials 000.

Judd watches. 'What are you doing?'

'Calling emergency.'

'ooo is in *Australia*! *911* in America!'

'Oh, bugger! That's right.' Corey hangs up, dials 911.

It's busy. He tries again as he looks back at Bowen. 'It'll be okay, mate.'

The jacket's cotton sleeve is already soaked with blood. Judd replaces it with the other sleeve. 'You just have to hold on.'

Bowen smiles weakly – then stops breathing.

'Matt!' Corey checks his pulse. There isn't one. 'Come on, mate. Come on.' Corey pumps his chest, checks again. Nothing. He pumps his chest again, keeps at it.

Judd puts a hand on his shoulder. 'Corey.'

The Australian stops and his chin drops to his chest, stricken. A moment passes. 'I didn't know him very long but he was always really nice to me —'

Craaack. The sound shakes the street. Corey looks around, confused. It wasn't an explosion. It sounded different, sharper somehow. 'What was that?'

Judd's eyes flick to the CNN building that looms above. It teeters, then lurches towards them. 'We've gotta move!' He scrambles up, drags Corey to his feet.

The Aussie points at Bowen's body. 'We can't just leave him —'

'*Now*!'

Corey looks up at the building and suddenly understands the gravity of the situation. 'Oh Christ! Spike! We're going!'

They turn and run.

The building falls.

16

The sound is a thundering, biblical roar, like the world is coming to a conclusion.

Judd runs as fast as he can, the only escape route straight ahead as there are buildings to the left and right. Corey is three metres ahead, Spike in front of him and pulling away.

The roar behind Judd grows louder. He glances back as the building's wall of black windows smash into the street like a tidal wave breaking on a beach. The torrent of concrete and steel and glass rolls over Bowen's body and surges onward. If they'd tried to move him they would not have survived.

The rubble keeps coming, seems to *gather* speed. Judd turns forward, tries to lift his pace. He doesn't think he can outrun it, doesn't think *Usain Bolt* could outrun it.

He can't see Corey or Spike. *Where the hell are they?* The roar is deafening now. He looks back again, wishes he hadn't. The rubble is *right* at his heels. He can't outrun it –

A hand yanks him left, into the recessed entrance of a car park as the river of debris thunders past like a runaway train, the noise echoing off the buildings. It goes on and on – then stops abruptly.

Judd turns, sees Corey, then Spike between them. The astronaut exhales, relieved beyond all measure. 'Thanks, man.'

Corey grins his crooked grin. 'We're even.'

•

A solid cloud of grey dust hangs over the road as Judd and Corey emerge from the car park entrance. Judd holds his hand over his mouth and nose, remembers how dust from the Twin Towers made so many sick after 9/11. Corey follows suit.

They turn back to where the CNN building once stood and see a thick column of the same grey dust rise in its place. Judd looks up at the sky. The usual smog that hovers above the city is darker now, fed by columns of black smoke. It dulls the sun, casts an eerie orange pall across the city.

People emerge from surrounding buildings, scared, stunned and confused. Something strikes Judd as odd. Usually, if this happened in the middle of a major city, ambulances and fire trucks and police cruisers would quickly converge on the scene with engines roaring and sirens blaring. But there are no emergency vehicles to be seen and no sirens to be heard. The only sounds are the regular thud of explosions, some distant, some close, which are, he is sure, vehicles detonating. Something terrible is happening in this city, something that makes the collapse of a large office building almost inconsequential.

Corey turns to him. 'Why is this happening?'

Judd thinks it through. 'It's the engines, isn't it? Before that police cruiser exploded it sounded – strange, and its exhaust was purple, right?'

'Yeah. As it accelerated it got darker, turned black right before it blew up.'

'That must have something to do with it —'

A flash of yellow to the right. Judd turns, notices a school bus fifty metres away. He looks closer. There are children on board. Lots of them. It turns down Sunset Boulevard. Judd shifts position, focuses on its exhaust.

It's a light purple colour.

'No.'

'What? What's "No"?'

'We've got to stop that bus.'

'Bus? What bus?' Confused, Corey turns, follows Judd's eye line, catches sight of the school bus – and sees its purple exhaust. 'Oh, *that* bus.'

Judd takes off after it and Corey follows, Spike just behind. They circumnavigate the debris field and sprint towards Vine Street.

It is horrifying.

The street is littered with the twisted, flaming hulks of vehicles which loom through the smoke haze. Worse, there are burned bodies everywhere, many still alight. The bus swerves past a series of blazing wrecks, then slows as it reaches a bottleneck where two abandoned cars almost block the road. The bus noses into the gap between them.

Judd runs towards it. Blistering heat radiates off the burning cars, forces him to duck his head and shield his face. He keeps moving, focuses on the bus's exhaust, which he can't quite see through the haze. Corey and Spike are right behind him.

The dog barks.

Corey looks at him. 'I don't care if you're tired, there's no time to have a rest!'

Judd glances back. 'Is that exhaust black?'

Corey peers at the bus. 'Can't really see it properly.'

'No, not the bus, *that*!'

Thirty metres away Corey sees an old Mercedes pull out of a parking station. Its exhaust is dark purple, *very* dark purple. 'Almost.'

Judd veers towards the car, shouts at the top of his lungs: 'Turn it off! Turn off the car!' The young blond guy behind the wheel takes in the destruction on the street, stunned, then sees a shouting man run towards him, clunks the car into reverse and backs up.

'No, no! Don't do *that*!'

The Merc's engine note shifts to a sound that resembles gravel in a cement mixer and its exhaust turns black.

'Turn! It! Off!'

Boom. The explosion is even bigger than the police cruiser. The parking station protects the street from the full brunt of the blast but the gush of hot air slaps Judd and Corey to the ground.

A moment passes. Dazed, they pull themselves up. Judd looks at Corey unhappily. 'He didn't turn it off.'

The Australian turns, sees his dog lying on the road. 'Spike!' He scrambles over to the animal, kneels beside him, heart in throat. The dog's eyes are closed. 'Mate, you okay?'

There's no response.

'Oh God.' Terrified, Corey puts a hand on Spike's chest, feels for a heartbeat, looks for an injury. The heartbeat is there – and there's no sign of an injury. Corey leans closer, confused. 'You all right?'

The dog's eyes blink open and he lets out a sharp bark.

'You're having a *rest*?'

Another bark.

'I don't care if you told me you were tired. Get up!'

Judd focuses on the bus as it scrapes between the two burning cars. 'We have to go.' He takes off after it. He's a little unsteady at first but quickly finds his balance. Corey and Spike follow.

They close in on the vehicle. Judd can see its exhaust is darker. Three kids, two girls and a boy, no older than ten, look out the back window. Too scared to cry, they stare out in horror at the destruction on the street – and the two strange men with a dog who follows them.

The bus turns sharply onto another street and heads east. This road is not as congested as the last, only a few burning vehicles which don't block the way. The bus picks up speed.

So do Judd and Corey. Judd's chest is tight from inhaling smoke but he ignores it, keeps moving.

The bus rides up onto the sidewalk, knocks over two garbage bins and takes a sharp turn to the left.

The boys follow it, cross a parking lot, reach another street. It's untouched by explosions, save the burning motorcycle flopped over in a driveway next to the remains of an unlucky dude in a helmet.

They glimpse a flash of yellow in the distance, run on, duck down an alleyway, overgrown with brush, pass a row of single-storey houses, then emerge onto a narrow street.

Directly below is the Hollywood Freeway. Its eight lanes are peppered with burning vehicles but it's not impassable. Cars, trucks and motorcycles zip past, swerve around anything that's stationary.

'They're all purple.'

Judd looks closer. Corey's right. Every vehicle's exhaust is a shade of purple. He turns, takes in an overpass that crosses the eight lanes, scans the freeway. He can't see the bus –

Corey points. 'There!'

It heads down an on-ramp towards the freeway, takes to the grass verge to avoid a burning van, then drives directly towards them. Judd can see its exhaust is dark purple.

'Come on!' He moves fast, reaches an embankment, looks over the railing at the freeway below. There's a steep, fifty-foot slope of dirt and gravel that runs down to the shoulder of the road-way. Corey arrives beside him. 'So what are we going to do – oh Jesuschweppes!'

Judd vaults the guardrail, plummets to the embankment five

metres below and roll-thumps to the bottom. He finds his feet beside the freeway and swings around to stop the approaching bus.

Honk! A Mack truck fills his world and careers straight towards him as pitch-black exhaust blasts from its stack. It's barely thirty metres away when the sound of its thundering engine mutates into that horrible noise Judd now knows too well –

Boom. The truck's cab vaporises in a vivid fireball and its tanker jack-knifes, flips over – and rolls directly towards him.

'Oh faark!' He turns and sprints, the giant flaming rolling pin right behind him and closing fast. To the right a burning vehicle blocks his path so he veers left, towards the metre-high cement divider that separates the left and right lanes of traffic. He vaults it and lands in the middle of the next lane –

Honk. A Corvette roars towards him from the opposite direction. Judd pivots left and it brushes past with an inch to spare – then ploughs into the rolling tanker as it crashes over the cement divider –

Boom. The explosion is huge. The shockwave throws Judd to the bitumen. His eyes flutter open and he staggers to his feet, shields his face from the wall of fire that dissects the road, and searches for the school bus.

It punches through the flames just thirty metres away. Judd sprints towards it. Its engine sound changes and his eyes flick to the exhaust. It's pitch black. He yells at the top of his lungs: '*Stop the bus!*'

Ka-boom. It explodes and the fireball is enormous. The blast catapults Judd back over the cement divider and into a pylon. He crumples to the ground, his ears ringing, his face numb.

He failed, and all he can think about are those three children, staring out the back window, too scared to cry.

A distant voice floats to him: '—andy—'

Andy? Who's Andy?

'Mandy!'

Oh! Mandy. That's right, it's my nickname.

Judd's eyes blink open as Corey kneels in front of him. 'You okay?'

Judd takes a deep breath, nods dully.

'Mate, when you hit that pylon I thought it was curtains. It looked *really* painful.'

'I didn't get to the bus in time —'

'No, you didn't.' Corey jabs a thumb to the left. Judd follows it to the unharmed group of schoolchildren and their elderly bus driver, who climb an emergency stairwell beneath the overpass. 'But I did.'

A profound sense of relief sweeps over Judd. 'Well done, son.'

Corey grins his crooked grin. 'I only told them to get off. You did the hard bit.'

That's true, and Judd couldn't be happier the children are safe, but still, he can't help thinking that, once again, at the critical moment, he didn't rise to the occasion, he didn't save them, he wasn't the man the world thought him to be.

A siren blares and an engine strains. Judd and Corey turn to the sound, see an ambulance speed along the freeway's far lane. It's the first emergency vehicle they've seen since the explosions began. Their eyes flick to its exhaust.

It's pitch black.

Corey shoots Judd a concerned look. 'That's never good —'

Boom. The explosion flips the ambulance onto its side and it skids along the freeway for fifty metres. Golden sparks spray as fast steel meets stationary bitumen, then it clips the cement retaining wall, flips over it and disappears into the brush on the other side.

17

Alvy Blash comes to with a gasp.

He lies on the ceiling of the ambulance, the vehicle upside down and tilted at a steep angle. He can see thick brush out the shattered front windscreen. From the panicked comments of the paramedics as they raced him to hospital, he knows the Swarm is to blame for his current predicament. Bunsen sure didn't waste any time with his 'urban deployment'.

Alvy feels woozy, not from the accident so much as his twin gunshot wounds, which the paramedics tried to patch as best as they could. Alvy turns, looks at the medic who was in the back with him. Blood trickles from his ears and nose, evidence of a traumatic head injury. The guy is dead, no doubt about it. Alvy shifts his eyes and takes in the driver. The poor schmuck's been impaled by the branch that shattered the windscreen.

Alvy is horrified. This is *his* fault. He created the Swarm. Even if he never intended it to be used this way it is still his responsibility to put right. He must tell the authorities what is going on and give them a sample of the counteragent. He's the only one who can do it. But first he must get out of this ambulance before Kilroy finds him. The old man is nothing if not thorough and will not stop until he knows Alvy is dead.

Alvy turns towards the rear doors and the ambulance shudders, slides down the incline, then stops. Alvy looks out the shattered front windscreen. What's left of the vehicle's nose pokes through the brush that blocked his view a moment ago.

Directly in front of the vehicle is a bracingly steep twenty-metre incline to a wall, then a sheer drop to a car park that is, at best guess, ten metres below that, a fall that would either be fatal or never-walk-again-bad if he were to make it in this upside-down ambulance.

He turns to the rear doors again and the ambulance slides towards the drop once more – then stops.

A noise in the distance. Someone crunches through the brush towards the ambulance.

Kilroy.

Damn it.

The sound grows louder, draws closer quickly, then stops. Alvy waits, heart in mouth, for a volley of bullets to strafe the vehicle, or for it to be simply kicked down the incline and over the edge.

'Anyone in there?'

That's not Kilroy's voice. It doesn't have the ponytailed bastard's flat southern twang.

'Yes – yeah! I'm okay, but the paramedics are dead.'

'Need some help, mate?'

That's a second voice. He's pretty sure the accent is Australian.

'Yes! Every time I move, it slides down —'

The ambulance slides down the incline.

'Grab it!'

Alvy hears bushes thrash, then thumps on the side of the vehicle – then the ambulance stops.

'I didn't even move that time!'

'Christ!' The American voice is strained.

'Jeez Louise!' The Australian voice is little more than a grunt.

'Okay, mate, get out.'

'Are you sure?'

'She'll be right.'

'I don't know what that means!'

'It means get moving 'cause we can't hold this bloody thing all day!'

'Oh. Okay!' Alvy starts towards the rear hatch and the ambulance slides again.

The Australian voice rings out. 'Crikey! You got it?'

The American answers. 'Yeah, but the ground – it's collapsing under my feet! I can't get a foothold.'

A dog barks.

'Unless you just grew a pair of hands, no, you can't help! Now get out of the bloody way!'

What's a dog doing there? Alvy pushes the thought from his mind and continues towards the rear doors. It's slow going. His head swims and the gunshot wounds throb but he ignores it all because he can feel the ambulance pick up speed.

He pushes the rear doors open and sees two men trying their best to slow the ambulance as it skis down the incline. Alvy is momentarily stunned to realise they look just like the astronaut and chopper pilot from the *Atlantis 4*.

The Australian barks at him: 'You waiting on an invitation, mate?!'

And the American doubles down: 'Get out now!'

Alvy leaps out – and the men let go of the ambulance. Sprawled on the ground, the scientist watches the vehicle slide noiselessly down the incline, reach the bottom, flip over the edge and crash into the parking lot below. He lets out a deep sigh of relief – then everything fades to black.

•

Corey and Judd carry the unconscious bloke to the freeway's cement retaining wall, not far from where the ambulance flipped into the brush, and lay him down. Corey studies his blanched face. 'He doesn't look so hot.'

Judd feels his pulse. 'He's alive but he needs a doc.'

The man's eyes flutter open and he takes in Judd and Corey. 'It *is* you.' He grins weakly.

Corey knows that smile, has seen it many times before. The guy is a fan of the *Atlantis 4* and, in spite of everything that's happened to him, is excited to be in their presence.

'You saved me – that is so cool. You're my biggest fan – I mean I'm your biggest – you know what I mean.' He forces another smile then realises he doesn't have the energy for that. 'Oh boy, I'm not feeling so great.'

'I'm gonna call for help.' Corey instinctively pulls out Bowen's iPhone and dials 911, then immediately realises that it's a useless gesture. Even if he managed to have an ambulance sent here, wouldn't it just explode on the way? It's a moot point anyway as the line is engaged. 'It's busy.'

The man nods resignedly, his voice a low rasp. 'I deserve it – it's – this is all my fault.'

Judd checks the dressing on his wounds. 'What's your fault?'

'This.' He raises a finger skyward. 'What's happening to the city.'

Judd glances at Corey, then turns to the man. 'You're saying – what are you saying, exactly?'

'I designed it – the Swarm – it's my fault.'

Corey studies him like he's a crazy person. 'The Swarm? What's the Swarm?'

'A nanotech virus. Enters a combustion engine through the air

intake, infects the gasoline, turns the exhaust purple, then – boom.'
His eyes turn to the sky. 'It's airborne, adheres to particulates in smoke
and exhaust, uses carbon monoxide for fuel as it self-replicates. Lives
in the smog – has a half-life of fifteen years.'

Corey finds this very hard to believe. 'It *lives* in the smog? Are
you – is this a joke?'

The man shakes his head, sees the scepticism on his face.
'I wish. It was designed for military use as a first-strike weapon – to
disable the enemy's war machines before the fighting began. It was
never meant for urban deployment. I tried to stop them, but —' He
shifts painfully, his voice barely a whisper. '— that didn't work out
so well.'

Judd leans close. 'Who did this to you?'

'Ponytailed mofo – from Louisiana.' The man's breathing is
laboured now, his face drained of colour. 'They wanted me dead –
so I couldn't stop it —'

Judd leans closer. 'How *do* you stop it?'

'The counteragent.' The man's eyes move between Judd and
Corey. 'It's like an antidote – the only thing that will work. The *only*
thing. It needs to be synthesised, replicated, added to the gasoline
supply – you must take it to the authorities.' The man drags in a
ragged breath. 'The only samples are at – 1138 – South Carmelina –
Apartment 7 – the freezer – the code is 274.'

Judd's confused. 'The code? What code?'

The man's head slumps to the side, his pupils pinned.

'Oh.' Corey feels his neck for a pulse, then shakes his head,
surprised. 'He's gone. Poor bastard.' They study him for a grave
moment, then Corey gently closes his eyes. 'Jeez, what a story.'

'You don't believe it?' The tone of Judd's question says he's not
sure himself.

'An airborne virus? That infects gasoline? And lives in the smog? No.'

'It explains what's going on.'

'Or that he made up a story.'

'Why would he do that?'

'It's *Los Angeles*. The town was *built* by people who make up stories.'

'I guess.'

'I mean, really – and the stuff about the ponytailed mofo from Louisiana? Sounds like a bad movie, mate.'

Spike barks.

'What?' Corey turns to Spike, who peers over the retaining wall. Corey looks over it too and suddenly he's very unhappy. 'Remember when I said it sounded like a bad movie?'

'It was five seconds ago.'

'Well, I think this is the part where the scary music starts playing.'

'What?' Judd follows Corey's line of sight to a ponytailed man who strides across the freeway towards them from a parked silver Toyota Prius. He's thirty metres away and closes fast.

Judd watches him closely. 'Is that —?'

'Looks like a ponytail to me.'

'The ponytailed mofo from Louisiana.'

Corey nods at the dead man with a hopeful expression. 'Maybe he's just coming over to check on his buddy here —'

From inside his jacket the ponytailed man draws a Glock 9mm pistol.

'— though that seems unlikely.'

Ponytail aims the pistol and fires.

'Down!' They both duck behind the retaining wall.

Thud, thud, thud. Bullets slam into the cement.

Spike barks.

Corey nods. 'Yes, he *is* a mofo.' He turns to Judd. 'We gotta get the flock outta here.'

Judd nods and surveys the immediate area. There are only two options. The freeway in front or the undergrowth behind. He turns to Corey. 'You thinking what I'm thinking?'

The Australian nods, and they move fast, stay low.

Weapon raised, finger tight on the trigger, Kilroy peers over the cement retaining wall. Alvy's body lies on the ground but the two good Samaritans who pulled him from the ambulance are gone.

Kilroy raises his eyes, scans the steep incline. He can't see them because the vegetation is so thick and he can't hear them over the distant explosions, but he knows they're in there. He silently glides into the brush. They have a lead on him but don't appear to be armed so he doesn't think they'll be difficult to deal with. What does concern him is the fact he missed them in the first place. Yes, he's well over sixty and yes, he's lost a step this last year, but still, he's never missed *twice* in one day. He's never considered retiring, but, well, maybe this is a sign. He'll think on it when this is over and done with.

After Alvy crashed into the police cruiser, Kilroy followed the ambulance he was transferred into for a good fifteen minutes, then lost it as Phase Two kicked in and the roads became gridlocked. He picked the ambulance up again as he crossed the freeway's overpass, then saw it explode and flip over the retaining wall. He was on his way to make sure Alvy was dead when the two men turned up and saved his tubby arse.

Looking at them from a distance he could swear they were two of the guys from the *Atlantis 4*. If he's correct, Kilroy would like nothing better than to sit down, have a beer with them and discuss their feats of derring-do. Instead he will have to kill them because they were in the wrong place at the wrong time. He must presume Alvy told them everything. He may be wrong, of course, they may know nothing, but he needs to be sure there are no comebacks. That's the reason he's on Bunsen's payroll after all, to fix problems like this, though usually the problems are not of his own making.

For many years Kilroy performed the same job for Bunsen's father. He was enlisted by the old man to, amongst other things, watch over and, if need be, rein in, his idealistic son. Kilroy had indeed watched over the boy, had been his only functional parent once the mother left, but had never reined him in because, well, he approved of everything the boy did. Until today. Today they'd had a difference of opinion, but Kilroy had let himself be persuaded by the boy's arguments. It wasn't that difficult to do because he trusted Bunsen implicitly.

Pistol up, Kilroy glides through the undergrowth. It's difficult terrain, the ground is surprisingly steep and he can't hear much over the explosions that bang and pop in the distance. He reaches the bottom of the incline and peeks over the steep drop to a sprawling car park below. It looks like it belongs to some kind of church, which burns furiously, watched by a handful of parishioners. He can't help but wonder where their god is now. There is one fire truck in attendance, but that is also alight. Directly below he can make out Alvy's ambulance, upside down and still smouldering. There's no sign of the men or the dog, though he doubts they're down there anyway. There are no stairs and to jump would be a death wish.

Where'd they go? He turns back to the brush and listens, tries to hear something, anything, over the explosions.

•

Judd slides through the last of the vegetation, Corey right behind him, Spike bringing up the rear. They vault the cement retaining wall and land on the shoulder of the freeway. They're about fifty metres down the road from where they entered the undergrowth.

Corey turns to Judd and whispers: 'It worked!'

Judd looks at Corey, presses his index finger to his lips and speaks in a very low voice: 'When you whisper it's louder than when you speak normally. Keep it down.'

Corey nods apologetically, mouths: 'Sorry.' He knows the last thing they need is for the ponytailed guy to know they're out of the brush.

Judd turns, searches for options, takes in the overpass above, then looks to the opposite side of the freeway and the emergency stairwell near the far pylon, the one the schoolkids used earlier. It seems a long, long way away, at least twenty seconds at full speed, but it's the only place that offers them an escape or, at the very least, cover. Judd points to it. There's no argument from the Australian. Those stairs are the only game in town. They go, sprint for it.

Judd takes in the freeway as they run. It looks worse than it did even a couple of minutes ago: packed with burning vehicles for as far as he can see, countless pillars of dark smoke swirling skywards. In the slanting afternoon light he notices the smoke has a purple tinge. What did that guy say? *It lives in the smog.*

Judd hears the brush thrash behind them.

Ponytail.

Christ.

Judd glances back at the undergrowth. He sounds close. It won't be long before he's out. They need to be at the stairs before that happens. Judd glances at the Aussie. 'Must run faster —'

Boom. The loudest explosion yet spanks the air. It sounds like the end of the world. Judd and Corey flinch involuntarily but keep running, unsure what just happened. Judd scans the freeway, searches for the source of the sound.

'Look up.' Corey sounds both frightened and amazed.

Judd looks up – then wishes he hadn't.

It's not good news.

A kilometre away a large airliner – he can't see if it's an Airbus or a Boeing – lists sharply to one side and veers directly towards the freeway – and them – a burning stump where its left engine used to be. A blanket of burning debris, pieces of that lost engine, tumble to earth behind it.

They keep running but Judd's not sure what good it will do. That large airliner is going to belly-flop onto the freeway right in front of them and destroy everything in its path for kilometres – and it's going to happen in about fifteen seconds.

He glances back as the brush thrashes and Ponytail emerges, pistol in hand. He clocks Judd and in one smooth movement raises the weapon and aims at the astronaut. Judd's eyes meet his – and then he does the only thing he can think of.

He points at the doomed airliner.

It *is* Judd Bell.

Kilroy squeezes the trigger, can't quite believe he's about to kill one of the *Atlantis* 4 –

What's he doing? He's pointing at something. Kilroy's first thought is that it's a ruse, the oldest, simplest ruse in the book actually, pointing at something 'over there' that doesn't exist, the guy hoping Kilroy will look at it so he can escape. Kilroy won't fall for that – yet there's something about the expression on the guy's face that tells him it's no trick, that Kilroy should, in fact, turn and look. He decides to do just that, as soon as he shoots him.

Kilroy's finger tightens on the trigger –

It's not the man that makes Kilroy turn and look, it's the noise. He does it involuntarily because the sound is so loud and terrible. Kilroy's surprised to find it comes from the turbofan of a large airliner, which drops towards the freeway he is standing beside. By Kilroy's rough calculation its left wing will land on him within the next ten seconds.

'Shit.' He pivots and launches himself back into the brush, to put as much space between him and that wing as possible. So it was a ruse, and it worked perfectly. Props to Judd Bell. Not only is he a national hero, he was clever enough to save his own life by sparing Kilroy's.

It's a shame he must die.

Judd can't believe pointing at the jet worked, though he's not sure he can classify it as a success as it may have only extended their lives by a couple of seconds. Instead of being shot by Ponytail they're about to be crushed by a very large airliner.

They sprint towards the stairwell but it doesn't seem to be getting any closer. Christ, it feels like they're running on the spot. Judd glances up at the jet and is shocked by how close it is. The only positive thing is that he can now see it's a Fed Ex Boeing 777 cargo jet so there are no passengers on board, just an unlucky flight crew who are surely wondering why one of their engines just exploded and why the remaining engine sounds like it's devouring itself from within.

Corey sprints hard, but knows they're not going to make it to the stairs in time. They're about to die and he has just one regret: that he won't see Lola again, even as 'friends'. In spite of everything that happened last night he hopes she's okay.

Corey glances up one last time.

The jet fills his world.

18

The 777's right engine detonates, ejects flaming chunks of metal in every direction, including straight up, into the wing. There's a pregnant pause – then the av-gas inside the wing's fuel tank explodes and the aircraft vaporises in a vivid starburst.

For a fleeting moment a second sun hangs in the sky above Los Angeles. Then it dissipates and Judd and Corey slow to a jog as they realise the jet no longer exists in any meaningful way.

A burning section of the tail is the only part that isn't vaporised and it cartwheels into the brush where good old Ponytail took cover. A moment later the brush bursts into flames.

Judd wonders if he survived, hopes he didn't, but doesn't want to take a chance if he did. 'Come on, gotta keep moving.' Corey nods and they resume running. They reach the stairs then climb to the overpass.

First order of business for Judd is to call Rhonda. He's sure she's airborne, but just maybe she isn't, so it's worth trying to warn her about what's happening here. He pulls out his iPhone, dials – and it goes straight to voicemail. He leaves a message for her to call him urgently, then turns to Corey: 'The guy said 1138 South Carmelina, right?'

Corey glances at him. 'What? Which guy?'

'The dead guy.'

A blank expression from the Australian.

'From the ambulance?'

'Oh. Yeah. 1138.' Corey takes a moment, then regards Judd suspiciously. 'Why?'

'It's just – I know South Carmelina. It's right off Santa Monica Boulevard. I was thinking we should go there.'

'Why in all the world would we do that?'

'To find the counteragent.'

'What counteragent?'

'The one the guy was talking about.'

'Which guy?'

'The dead guy! From the ambulance.'

'Oh, right. The "counteragent" to "stop the explosions". That's "hidden in his freezer".' Corey makes air quotes as he speaks. 'You actually believe all that?'

'Well, not when you say it with air quotes.'

'So tell me, is it behind the cookie dough ice-cream or the rum and raisin?'

'He was right about the ponytailed guy.'

'That guy could have been anyone. His girlfriend's ex, an angry bookie, a bloody debt collector.'

'Then why did he try and kill us?'

'I don't know! Because he's a dickhead? Because we know he topped that guy? Because Americans are always shooting people they've never met?'

'No. He did it because he thinks the dead guy told us about the counteragent. We have to get over to South Carmelina and check it out.'

Corey's eyes narrow, unconvinced. 'Mate, it's not our job.'

'But I think —'

'Not. Our. Job.'

They continue up the stairwell in silence. Judd knows Corey's right to be sceptical, but there was something about what the dead guy said, or maybe it was the *way* he said it, that makes Judd think he was telling the truth, as crazy as it sounds. 'So what do you want to do?'

Corey glances at him. 'What I want to do is – well, I'd like, I guess I – I want to make sure Lola's okay.'

'The girl who's going out with the movie star?'

Corey nods.

'She blew you off, buddy.'

Corey stares at him unhappily.

'What's that face? She did. Let the Blue Tornado make sure she's okay.'

'Blue *Cyclone*.'

'Who cares? Really. I don't mean to be harsh but come on. She's got a boyfriend.'

They reach the top of the stairs and step onto the footpath. Judd turns to the Australian. 'So what's it going to be? Cookie dough or rum and raisin?'

Corey studies him for a long moment, then smiles resignedly. 'I've always been partial to cookie dough.'

Judd's happy. 'Okay.'

'Which way?'

Judd points to the right and they set off across the overpass.

Spike barks.

Corey nods at the dog. 'He's hoping for lemon sorbet.'

Kilroy ploughed into the scrub like a rampaging elephant as the Fed-Ex jet approached, then dived to the ground when he heard the explosion. He can now smell smoke and hear the crackle of burning undergrowth so he pulls himself up and moves fast, works his way up the incline through the brush then pushes himself out onto the freeway.

His eyes flick to the spot where he last saw the two men. Of course there's no sign of them – no, there they are! Running along the overpass above, just their shoulders and heads visible.

'Shit!' He swings his pistol up, aims.

They pass behind a burning truck and disappear into the haze.

'Damn it!' Kilroy moves fast, makes a beeline for his Prius. He needs to deal with this *Atlantis* 4 problem ASAP.

Judd and Corey jog along the freeway. Spike leads the way.

Corey pulls Bowen's iPhone from his back pocket, swipes it to life, scrolls through the address book and finds Lola's number. His finger hovers above the call button –

No. Judd's right. She made her choice. He slides the phone into his back pocket and runs on.

19

Lola has it all organised.

Half an hour ago she closed the sale of a raunchy e-book, originally a raunchy piece of *Hunger Games* fan fiction, to Paramount Studios for three million against six. It was an exhausting, week-long auction so, as a treat, she's decided to give herself the afternoon off. She has a date with Scott Ford tonight, only their third, so she's going to have a manicure, pedicure and facial, her first in over a year, at that Korean place on Doheny she keeps hearing about, then head home, take a long bath and a short nap. As her Grandmama used to say, she doesn't want 'to hold back on the pretty'.

Scott said their date is going to be a 'big surprise' so she can only wonder what that means, though he's well known for making extensive use of his Lear jet. Perhaps they'll head to Vegas for the night. Or Acapulco. Lola doesn't care where they go, she's just looking forward to seeing him – and finding out if she actually likes the guy.

She isn't entirely sure. They've spent a lot of time on the phone, but not much time face to face, so tonight's a chance to confirm she's made the right decision. The reason she wants to be certain is that she's been thinking about Corey. A lot. She really enjoyed his company last night – right up until the moment she dropped the bomb and told him she had a boyfriend. In fact, she's been thinking about him so much she's worried she might have made the wrong call.

Oh, man. *Did* she make the wrong call? And if she did, is there any way on God's green earth she could walk it back? Could Corey ever forgive her for the embarrassment she caused him last night? She's not sure *she* could –

Stop it. She needs to stop thinking about it. She's seeing Scott and he's great. Sure, the Australian is tall and charming and funny, but she completely blew it with him so, end of story. *Fugetaboutit*. She pushes it from her mind and her thoughts turn to why she's so *über-successful* in her career but an *abject failure* in her personal life. She's twenty-nine and yet to have a regular, happy relationship that lasts for more than six months. What's up with that?

And what is up with this traffic? It's moving at a snail's pace. She glances at the diamond-encrusted platinum Rolex Day-Date on her wrist, a watch Scott sent over after their second date. It's a little too blingy for her taste, but it's the thought that counts so she's been wearing it. She's running late for her appointment at the nail joint –

Boom. A bright flash lights up the street and her world shudders. A wall of fire rises before her as the car in front explodes.

'What the hell–?'

A truck two lanes to the left detonates like it's been hit by a missile. Flaming shards of metal rain down on her Lexus. She looks down Doheny Drive, sees another explosion in the distance, then another, then something catches her attention: the exhaust of every car she can see is purple. Some are light purple, some are dark purple and some are almost black.

Her driver's door is wrenched open by a wild-eyed young man. He's tall, white and well dressed, looks like a lawyer, definitely a white-collar professional. 'Get out!' He jabs a small penknife towards her. Make that white-collar *criminal*. She doesn't argue, just nods and grabs her handbag from the passenger seat –

'Now!' White Collar yanks her from the vehicle and she crashes to the bitumen, grazes an elbow. The man climbs into her Lexus, slams the door shut and accelerates away.

'Fucker!' She catches sight of the tailpipe as it departs. The exhaust is a dark purple colour, then turns black –

Boom. The car detonates in a vivid fireball. 'Oh!' Lola recoils, shields her face from the heat blast. The Lexus grinds to a halt and the driver's door swings open. White Collar lurches out of the vehicle, his body completely alight. He staggers across the road for a couple of metres, keels over and slumps to the ground.

Lola's stunned, horrified and relieved in equal measure – being carjacked never felt so lucky. She takes a moment to process what just happened and realises she can't. The colour of the exhaust was purple, then it became darker, then it turned black – and then the car exploded? Is that right? Could that be right?

Another explosion rocks the road nearby. She instinctively ducks and shields her face, realises the air reverberates with the constant bang and crack of explosions, both distant and close. What the hell is happening?

She drags in a deep breath, rises off the roadway and makes it to the footpath. She must let people know what's happening, how the exhaust turns black and then the car explodes. She pulls her iPhone from her bag and studies the screen. It has service. She swipes it open, accesses her address book and remembers the woman she met a while back, who works for CNN as a news editor. She has her number. She'll call her. That's the right place to start. She flicks her way through the names, searches for the woman. What was it? Cindy, Candy – Stacey! Stacey something. Kagan! Stacey Kagan. Lola finds the number and dials. The call goes directly to voicemail. Lola speaks as clearly as possible, explains what's going on.

Boom. Another explosion shakes the street to her left. She needs to get away from here now. She runs. Burning cars clog the road as shell-shocked people mill around like zombies. Lola shouts at a group as she passes by: 'If the exhaust turns black the car explodes! Tell everyone!' They just look back at her dully.

She runs on, then realises she doesn't know where she's running to. She needs to get off the street, out of harm's way, but her house is miles from here. Her grandfather's place isn't, it's only twenty minutes away on foot, give or take. She inherited it a few months back. It's empty, awaiting a renovation before it's rented or sold. She could head there –

Boom. Another explosion shakes the air as she approaches an intersection. The smoking wrecks of three cars block the road. A telephone pole is on fire. Two bodies lie on the bitumen, burning. Smoke drifts across the road. It looks like a carefully staged scene from a Michael Bay extravaganza. It's not. It's real, and it's the most terrible thing she has ever seen. She sprints past the horror and makes up her mind. She's going to her grandfather's place. Right now.

Doheny is gridlocked with cars, many on fire. How did this happen *so fast*? She must get word out about the exhaust. She wishes she'd embraced social media more wholeheartedly than the MySpace profile she'd never once updated. If she were on Twitter she could tell the world instantly.

Scott Ford. He has *thirty-three million* followers on Twitter. If he can tweet about the exhaust changing colour it could make a huge difference. She dials his number.

Boom! An explosion right behind her. She's hit hard in the back, slapped to the ground, the wind knocked out of her. Her ears ring as she gulps air, tries to catch her breath, looks back through the smoke, sees she was struck by a car seat – with a young guy still strapped to it. *That's not good.* She takes a moment to recover her composure, stands shakily and checks the guy. He's dead.

Smash. That's not an explosion. She turns. A young white man sprints towards her from a shattered shop window cradling what looks like a Nespresso coffee machine. A shopkeeper, an older Asian gentleman with a severe buzz cut, swings out of the store's front door and aims a pistol at him – as he runs right past her.

'Oh shit!' Lola ducks low. The shopkeeper fires and Nespresso man is hit in the back of the leg and drops the machine, which shatters on the ground beside her. Nespresso man keeps moving, limp-runs away as the shopkeeper brandishes the weapon and screams after him in Korean.

This is insane. Lola stands, keeps her head low, passes the shop-keeper and runs on. She remembers watching the 1992 LA riots on television when she was a kid and never forgot the crazy mob mentality that spiralled out of control and killed, if she remembered correctly, fifty people. Whatever's happening in the city right now has the potential to be worse than that. She can feel it.

She realises even her grandfather's house is too far away. She needs to get off the street *now*. She scans the area, searches for a place to take refuge, if only temporarily, that isn't a store or a house with a gun-toting owner on the lookout for looters.

A tall white and blue building appears through the smoke that blankets the street, maybe three hundred metres away. It has – she counts – six floors. Is it an office building? Whatever it is she's sure she'll be safer inside it than out here. She can wait for things to cool down a little, make some calls, get Scott to tweet about the black exhaust.

Boom. Another explosion shocks the air. She feels the sting of debris on her cheek. *Man, that was close!* She sprints towards the building, cuts through the haze, fear turning in her chest. If she can just get to it in one piece she'll be right. *She'll be right.* Corey said it last night when she blew him off. She wonders if he's all right now. She wants to call him, make sure he's okay, but, really, would he even pick up? He didn't even want to be friends. Then she remembers he doesn't have a mobile phone.

The building looms out of the haze and suddenly she's in front of it. She scans the flagstone wall for a way in but can see no obvious doors or windows –

There! What's that? She sees a vehicle has hit the building, dented a metal roller door and created a gaping hole. There's no one inside the car and both doors are open, surely the first time a Mercedes Gullwing has been abandoned with keys in the ignition.

She has a way in, except she'll need to roll the Merc out of the hole to gain access. She leans in, thumps the gearbox into neutral, releases the handbrake until it clears the hole where the dented roller door has pulled away from its tracks, leaves herself a half-metre gap, then pulls on the handbrake again. She ducks low, works her way through the hole and enters the building.

She instantly feels safer; the explosions outside now remote. She looks around, realises it isn't an office building, it's a self-storage facility. There doesn't seem to be anyone around. She knew these kinds of places didn't need many people to operate but she'd have thought there'd be at least one person there, just to keep an eye on the joint?

Boom. The explosion is vast, comes from her left and blows in part of the flagstone wall. She's knocked to the floor.

Crunch.

'Ahhh!' Something very heavy lands on her left leg. The pain is horrible and instantly she feels dizzy. She can't see anything

through the haze of smoke and dust and she can't move either –
she's pinned to the ground. The dizziness gets the better of her and
she decides she just might have a little nap. As she closes her eyes
she wonders if she'll ever open them again.

20

The Baldwin Hills Overlook offers a three-hundred-and-sixty-degree view of Los Angeles. Actually it's not quite three hundred and sixty degrees, more like three hundred and twenty, but you can pretty much see everything that's going on in the city.

Bunsen stands atop the overlook and takes in the destruction he has wrought. Phase Two has been a total success. The Swarm has performed exactly as intended, though watching it work its terrible magic has been difficult. The human toll – just an abstract idea previously – is very real to him now. Even so, he has no regrets.

The plan was, simply, to make people switch off their combustion engines. That's why the Swarm was designed to turn a vehicle's exhaust purple as soon as the engine was infected, then black before it exploded. It was a *warning*, so people understood that if they *didn't* turn off their engines they would die. Of course, for the warning to be effective, some people needed to die early in the process.

Kilroy didn't agree with this. Even though he is a stone-cold killer with years of experience in the ways and means of death, he baulks at hurting anyone he believes is innocent. That's why he wanted Bunsen to release the video this morning. Kilroy had created a two-minute Flash animation that explained the virus, what the purple and black colour of the exhaust meant, told people to turn off their combustion engines before there was any chance they could explode and urged them to leave Los Angeles ASAP.

Kilroy wanted to post it online and send it to all the news outlets before the Swarm was released but Bunsen overruled him, explaining that the threat needed to be real and obvious or it would have no power. Bunsen did, however, promise to release it before Phase Three, and he expects Kilroy to remind him of that as soon as he returns from dealing with Alvy.

Bunsen takes in the burning city and draws a deep breath, steels himself for what comes next.

Phase Three.

He moves towards the Tyrannosaur, which is parked nearby. The irony is that everything he has done today is to free mankind from its reliance on fossil fuels by forcing it to develop clean energy alternatives, and yet his primary mode of transportation is an Erickson Air-Crane, the thirstiest, dirtiest, most inefficient and polluting helicopter to ever grace the skies. Oh well. After today it will never fly again.

He climbs into the cockpit beside Enrico, buckles up and pulls on the headset. In a flash the giant chopper lifts into the sky and Bunsen takes in the hundreds of smoke spires that dot Los Angeles and snake towards the heavens.

Phase Two has laid this city low.

Phase Three will change this planet forever.

21

Judd, Corey and Spike run hard, keep to the edge of the freeway in case they need to use the cement retaining wall as cover.

The destruction is overwhelming, the sound of distant explosions constant. The lanes are littered with abandoned or burning vehicles, but few people. Traffic is almost non-existent: the odd car or bike races past with a purple exhaust, but that's it. It seems most people have had the good sense to get off the road.

They skirt a line of smoking wrecks and Judd glances behind him, can't see any sign of Ponytail or his silver Prius. Maybe the old guy didn't survive the plane crash, or maybe he just cut his losses and went home. Here's hoping.

Judd pulls in a deep breath and looks across at Corey, who, in spite of all the running they've done, doesn't seem to have cracked a sweat. Judd tries not to breathe too deeply as he speaks: 'You know, when I was a kid I thought LA would be great if it wasn't for all the cars. Now I'm not so sure.'

'You lived here?'

'Not for long. We spent a year here in the eighties. My dad was in the army so we moved around a bit, up and down the west coast mainly.'

'I moved with my dad too.'

'Really? Where did you guys live?'

'Started out in Adelaide, in South Australia. Biggest move was to Broome, over in the west. Then up to Darwin for a while. Ended up in the Alice eventually.'

'Why'd you move so much?'

'He was a heli-musterer so he had to go where the work was.'

'How'd you find it? Gotta say I didn't love it myself. As soon as I'd settle somewhere, make some friends, we'd be up and going again. Pissed me off for years.'

Corey takes it in with a nod. 'Yeah. We were never in one place for very long.'

They run on in silence. Corey doesn't tell Judd the reason his father was always looking for work was because he was a shocking drunk. Once he was hired it was only a matter of time before he'd be found inebriated on the job (not a good look for somebody who flies helicopters for a living) and would be let go. The poor bastard just never got over the death of his wife, something Corey completely understood. Once he lost his pilot's licence it only took a year before he drank himself into the grave. He was fifty-two.

Corey never speaks about it, his mother's death or his father's truncated life afterwards. Of all the people he's ever known, Judd is the one person he's come closest to telling – just a moment ago, as they ran along this freeway. The Yank knows everything else about Corey's life, knows he can communicate with the bloody *dog* for heaven's sake, so why doesn't he just tell him about his parents? He thinks about it and realises he knows the answer: he wants at least one part of his life to be unaffected by it.

Spike barks.

Corey glances at Judd. 'He wants to know how much further. The question had a lot more uppity attitude than I can convey.'

'A while. Never done it on foot before —' Judd stops running. Corey and Spike pull up too.

'What?'

Judd points. 'And might not have to.' Across the road is an SUV, a large, black Cadillac Escalade, jammed between a cement dividing wall and a truck. On the SUV's roof are strapped two mountain bikes. 'We use those we'll be there in twenty minutes.' Judd sets off for the SUV. Corey and Spike follow.

They approach the vehicle and Judd sees it. 'Oh, come on!' The engine runs and the exhaust is light purple. Inside, a guy is slumped over the steering wheel, quite clearly dead.

Corey turns to leave. 'Oh well, we tried. Let's get out of here before it blows.'

'No. We switch off the engine.' Judd moves to the rear passenger doorhandle, the only one he has access to, and pulls on it. Locked.

'Like I said, we tried.' Corey turns to leave.

'Wait.' Judd's hands face each other and turn, like he's working an invisible Rubik's cube.

Spike barks.

Corey nods. 'Yeah, I see it.'

'See what?'

'You're doing that Rubik's cube thing with your hands again.'

'It helps me think – we can break the window!' Judd steps forward and hits the rear windscreen with his fist.

Whack. It bounces off, painfully. He wrings his hand. 'Well, that's not going to work.' He searches the road, finds a piece of the SUV's bumper bar, picks it up, feels its weight, swings it at the rear window.

Whack. It bounces off. He tries again. No joy. 'Come on!'

Corey stares at the exhaust, concerned. 'Mate, it's getting darker.'

'I can do this!' Judd swings the bumper at the window again. It bounces off, barely leaves a mark. 'If we can get them it'll save us hours and we won't be wandering around like sitting ducks on the road —'

Corey's not convinced. 'Just step away from the vehicle.'

Judd drops the bumper and clambers onto the Escalade's roof.

'That is the opposite of stepping away!'

Judd goes to work on the clamps that hold the bikes' rear wheels to the roof racks.

Corey's eyes move to the tail pipe. 'The exhaust is really dark.'

Judd's having trouble undoing the first clamp. 'Tell me when I need to get down.'

'*Now*! Now is that time. *Right now*.' Corey's eyes are locked on the puffing exhaust. It's dark purple.

Judd's frustrated. The clamp will not come off. 'I just can't – this thing – it won't come loose.'

Corey looks at what he's doing. 'Don't *pull* it, *push* it.'

'That's not going to work —' *Click*. The clamp unfastens. 'Oh, good tip.' Judd moves to the second rear wheel. Click. He then turns to the front wheels.

Corey stares at the exhaust. 'Must go faster!' He backs away from the vehicle. 'It's turning black!'

Click. Click. Judd unfastens both front tyres then flings one bike off the roof. It bounces on its tyres and Corey grabs it as Judd jumps down with the second bike and runs hard –

Boom. The Escalade detonates.

The blast hits them like a hammer, the heatwave extraordinary. Corey can hear the hair singe on the back of his head as the wall of flame reaches out for them – then dissipates. They both stay upright, but only because they have the bikes as support. Judd turns to Corey with a smile. 'See? No problem.'

Corey's furious. 'What the hell are you *doing*?'

'What?'

'Do you have a bloody death wish?'

'I got the bikes, didn't I?'

'Yeah, and nearly – rolled them, to our deaths.'

Judd looks at him. 'That doesn't make sense.'

'It sounded better when I was thinking it —'

Judd hears a noise over the crackle and pop of the burning SUV. It's a high-pitched whir. It is distant but grows louder. Judd turns and scans the freeway, then sees it through the flames. A car swerves through the wrecks and races towards them. It whirs because it's a hybrid. A Prius.

A silver Prius hybrid.

'Ponytail.'

Corey's not happy to see it. 'Oh, come on!'

The car will arrive in twenty seconds.

Spike barks.

'Yes, he *really* is a mofo.'

Judd glances at the mountain bike he holds. 'See? Aren't you happy I got these things now?' He pushes the bike, skips once, throws his leg over the seat, finds the pedals and rides away. 'Follow me.'

Corey push-runs his bike behind him.

Judd glances back. 'What are you doing? Get on.'

'I can't.'

'What's wrong? Is it broken?'

'I don't think so.'

'Then what?'

'I can't.'

'That's not an answer —'

'Ride a bike! I can't ride a bike.'

Judd is dumbfounded. 'You're thirty years old. Didn't you learn when you were a kid?'

'You don't ride a bike if you have your own *helicopter*!'

'Why didn't you say something?'

'I was hoping you'd teach me.'

The Prius whirs.

They turn.

It's just ten seconds away.

Judd looks back at Corey. 'First lesson! Throw your leg over the seat, sit down and put your feet on the pedals.'

Corey doesn't need to be told twice. He pushes off, throws his leg over the seat, sits and finds the pedals with his feet – then topples over. 'Christ!'

Spike barks.

'I'd like to see you do it.' Corey pushes off again – and stays upright this time. 'Yes!' Cocky, he looks over at Judd, then realises the astronaut is riding beside him and holding his bike's seat to keep him upright. 'Oh.'

'Second lesson! When you pedal, push down hard to stay balanced.' Corey does it and they pick up speed. Judd turns them towards the wreck of a semitrailer twenty metres away. If they can reach it, it might offer them some cover. *If.* Spike gallops ahead.

Tyres screech. Judd looks back, sees the Prius swerve around the burning SUV and head straight towards them.

Kilroy watches the two men on bikes. Interestingly, one doesn't seem to know how to ride and is held steady by the other – not something you see very often. They furiously pedal towards a wrecked semi-trailer because, Kilroy guesses, they think it will offer them some cover.

It won't. He mashes the pedal and the Prius surges forward. With the car running on battery power its acceleration is swift, much better than with the petrol engine.

The wreck is close, but is it close enough? Corey hears the thrum of the hybrid engine behind him. He glances back.

The car is three metres away! *Jeez!* Fear twists in his chest. Who'd have thought a *Prius* could be so menacing?

Judd yanks him right, pulls him behind the wreck as the Prius whips past. Its bumper grazes Corey's back tyre and the bike wobbles violently, but he pushes hard on the pedals and keeps balance.

'The gap in the wall!' Judd nods at the right side of the freeway. There's a narrow service gap in the cement retaining wall three lanes away, wide enough for a bike but too small for a car.

Corey ups his pace. 'Okay. I got this.'

'You sure?'

'Bloody oath.'

'I have no idea what that means.'

'It means you can let go now.'

Judd lets go and aims for the gap, the Australian follows and Spike bounds ahead of them both.

The Prius's tyres screech on the bitumen, but Corey has no idea where the car is. He's too focused on getting to that gap –

Wham. 'Jeez!' Corey looks back. The Prius's nose has slammed into his rear wheel. The bike shudders, wobbles violently, but he hangs on and keeps it upright.

The gap in the wall is close. The dog bounds through it, then Judd follows. They disappear from view.

Wham. The Prius hits Corey's rear wheel again, but this time it propels the bike forward and he spears through the gap to safety.

Or not.

'Sweet Jesus!'

The ground drops away like it's the Grand Canyon and suddenly Corey's airborne, ten metres above a steep, grassy hill, his bike's gears clicking as it freewheels through space.

He has time to turn and watch the Prius slam into the cement retaining wall. Then he looks forward to see where he's headed. The hill is thirty metres long and ends abruptly at a steep drop-off to another road three metres below.

Spike slides down the hill and reaches the drop off. Hard as he tries he can't stop himself from sliding over the edge, so he jumps and lands nimbly on the road below. Next, Judd lands his bike just before the drop-off, then, like one of those Red Bull stunt rider guys, jumps again and lands safely on the road too.

As Corey's bike arcs through the air he realises he's not travelling fast enough to land *beyond* the drop-off and not slow enough to land *before* it. That big nudge from the Prius has increased his pace just enough so the bike comes down right *on top* of the drop-off, after which it will flip or snap or do God knows what.

He pulls back on the handlebars and tries to alter the bike's trajectory.

It doesn't work.

He then pedals hard, thinks that might increase his speed.

It just looks silly.

Now what?

He lets go of the bike and watches it fly away as he falls to earth.

The bike lands right on the drop-off and violently flips onto the road as expected. A split second later Corey slams into the hill, back first.

Crunch. His head thumps the ground and rattles his teeth. *Jeez-it-hurts!* He slides towards the edge, snatches at the ground to stop himself going over –

Slam. He catches hold of a clump of grass and jerks to a halt, right at the edge. He takes a deep breath. His head vibrates like a tuning fork and his back aches from the impact but he's in one piece. Groggy, he looks over the edge at Judd and Spike on the road below. 'I really didn't enjoy that —'

'Move!' Judd frantically points back up the hill.

'Huh?' Corey turns to see the slab of cement retaining wall the Prius hit slide down the slope – directly towards him. 'Oh, man!' He pulls himself up, but he's slow. His back screams and his head feels light and he slumps back down to the grass.

Spike barks.

'I'm trying!'

The cement slab picks up speed. It's the size of a single bed and must weigh a tonne.

Judd watches it. 'Get up, man!'

'I said I'm trying!' Corey wobbles to his feet and the slab's *right there.* He jumps awkwardly and it thunders under him, flips off the edge and shatters on the road below.

Corey crumples to the grass. 'Jesuschweppes.'

'Come on. We gotta go!' Judd's voice is low but firm, his eyes pinned to the Prius at the top of the hill.

Corey raises his head, concerned. 'Is Ponytail coming?'

'Not yet, but I don't want to be here when he does.'

'Can you see him?'

'No, that's why I want to get going! Hurry up.'

Corey slides over the edge and drops down to the road as Judd quickly picks up his bike. It's scratched and dinged and the seat is skew-whiff but otherwise appears functional. He straightens the seat and presents it to the Australian. 'She'll be all right.'

'It's "she'll be right" —'

'Just get on the friggin' bike.'

Corey does it. 'I'm really getting the hang of this —' The bike instantly keels over and Judd catches him. Corey takes a moment to compose himself. 'Maybe I should walk.'

Judd's eyes flick back to the Prius. 'We don't have that much time. Come on.' The astronaut grabs his own bike and they ride away. Corey wobbles violently.

Spike follows, lets out a sharp bark.

'I'll put training wheels on *you* if you don't zip it.' Corey picks up speed then finds his balance.

They ride on.

Judd looks back at the Prius one more time, sees no sign of Ponytail, then pulls the iPhone from his rear pocket, swipes it open and dials Rhonda. He's hoping word of what's happened in Los Angeles has reached her flight and it's been diverted to another city, which hopefully isn't experiencing the same problems. Her phone rings and rings – then goes through to voicemail.

'Damn it.' He hangs up, prays she's okay.

22

The Southwest Boeing 737 rips across the deep blue empyrean at forty-one thousand feet.

Rhonda Jacolby sips a bottle of water and reads the *Atlantis 4* screenplay on her iPad. She laughs then shakes her head, incredulous: 'Fuckin' Hollywood.' She turns to Severson to discuss the outrageous liberties the screenwriter has taken with their story, but, with his headphones and eye mask on and his mouth half open, he's clearly asleep. She turns and looks out the window –

'What the hell?' She leans forward and focuses on the turbofan attached to the aircraft's wing. The exhaust has a light purple tint to it. She works the touchscreen of the entertainment unit built into the headrest of the seat in front of her then swipes through the various menus until she pulls up four windows that show different views of the aircraft's exterior, including the engines. Yes, a light purple exhaust billows from *both* engines.

She elbows Severson. 'Wake up.'

He turns away, uhappy at being disrupted. 'Sleeping.'

She elbows him again. 'Now, Buttercup.'

'Be nice. I saved your life six months ago.'

Rhonda grits her teeth. The fact that it was *Severson*, of all people, who saved her and Judd and Corey outside the Imax Theatre is a source of deep annoyance to her. She sends in another elbow. 'You need to see this.'

Severson pushes up his eye mask, annoyed. 'Omigod, *Nagatha Christie, what?*'

She points at the touchscreen. 'What's going on here?'

He blinks rapidly and takes a moment to focus on it. 'What? Oh. Is that – why is that – is that purple?'

'Ever seen anything like it?'

He shakes his head, unnerved. 'Never.'

Rhonda turns and sees the aircraft's captain, grey-haired, mid-fifties with a slight paunch, exit the cockpit and move down the aisle with a concerned expression. The passengers quietly watch as he stops midway down the fuselage, five rows ahead of Rhonda and Severson, leans across the empty seats and looks out at the engine. He studies it for a long moment and his expression morphs from concerned to troubled.

Severson watches him. 'That doesn't look good.'

A strange noise cuts across the soundscape, reverberates like gravel inside a cement mixer. Rhonda looks out at the turbofan again. 'And that doesn't *sound* good —'

Bang!

All the air abruptly leaves the aircraft.

Rhonda is yanked against her safety belt by the cabin's explosive decompression. Dust swirls through the air, momentarily blinds her as the airframe convulses and yellow oxygen masks drop from the ceiling. She blinks the grit from her eyes and takes a moment to find her bearings.

Five rows in front of her there is now a gaping, two-metre long gash in the starboard side of the fuselage. The captain is gone, and so is the row of seats he was leaning across. The gash is like a giant vacuum and sucks everything into it. Stunned, she looks out the window and sees the starboard turbofan is gone, a smoking nub all that remains. It has exploded.

The 737 noses down abruptly and Rhonda realises the shrill noise she can hear is not just the rush of air leaving the cockpit but the screams of passengers. She looks up the aisle to the cockpit. The vibrations are severe and the door swings open and shut so she can't see very clearly – and then she can. One of the aircraft's cabin crew, a flight attendant, is kissing the copilot. *What the hell?*

Rhonda looks closer. No, the flight attendant isn't kissing the copilot, she's giving him mouth-to-mouth resuscitation. *Oh damn.* The flight attendant turns and sprints from the cockpit as the co-pilot slumps in his seat, a large gash across his head.

The flight attendant runs down the aisle, fights to keep her balance, reaches a point three rows before the gash in the fuselage and shouts at the top of her lungs. Rhonda can just hear it over the screaming passengers and the roaring air: 'Can anybody fly a plane?'

Rhonda unbuckles her belt, levers herself over Severson and lands in the aisle –

Hey! The 737 noses down again and Rhonda grabs hold of the nearest seat back to stay on her feet. She moves forward, but the torrent of air is overpowering and drags her towards the gash in the fuselage. She keeps a tight hold of the seat back beside her, then grabs the next, then the next, edges past the gash – and reaches the flight attendant. 'I'm Rhonda Jacolby. I'm a pilot.'

The expression on the flight attendant's face is one of abject relief. 'Come with me, please.' They turn and head for the cockpit as a smattering of applause rises from the passengers.

•

Severson's worst nightmare, of dying in an aircraft accident, is about to come true. His second-worst nightmare, of someone else getting all the kudos, is *also* about to come true. The combination is a particularly unpleasant double whammy. If they die they die, but if they survive he'll be the one who sat around and did nothing while Rhonda Jacolby saved the day. He can't have that. He has to at least *look* like he's involved.

He unbuckles his belt, pulls himself out of the seat and moves down the aisle towards the cockpit, grabs hold of seat backs as he goes. He watched Rhonda do exactly the same thing only a moment ago so it can't be that hard –

Whoa! The jet lurches to the right and he loses his grip. The buffeting rush of air drags him towards the gash. He grabs a seat back with his right hand, stops himself from being sucked out, the rip in the fuselage just a metre behind him. The blast of air is overpowering. His hand slips. He won't be able to hold it for long. He glances back, sees nothing but blue sky and clouds through the jagged tear. His hand slips again. He's about to die because he couldn't stand the idea of someone else getting all the credit. His hand slides off the chair and he's dragged out of the aircraft –

Slwump. Rhonda grabs his hand, yanks him away from the gash and pulls him down the aisle to safety. He takes a breath, his pale face a portrait of relief and terror. 'Thank you.'

She looks him straight in the eye. 'I saved your life so we're even. Never speak of what happened at Imax again.'

He nods, surprised. 'I didn't know it bothered you so much —'

'Shhh! What do you think "never speak of" means? Now come on, we're going to land this aeroplane now.' She turns and moves up the aisle. Severson takes another breath and follows her into the cockpit.

●

Rhonda slides into the captain's seat, takes the controls in hand and slowly but surely levels out the jet. Beside her Severson lifts the unconscious copilot out of his seat and parks him in the jump seat in the galley behind the cockpit.

Rhonda scans the instrument panel. The jet is currently at 38 765 feet and descending, but not that quickly. Its speed is seven hundred and twenty kilometres an hour and slowing, but gradually. 'Okay. It's under control. We're gliding.'

Severson tentatively approaches the copilot's seat but doesn't sit.

She glances at him. 'What are you doing?'

'Just – girding my loins.'

'Gird 'em on your own time. Sit down.'

He does it. 'So what happened?'

'We've lost one engine and the other has been shut down. I'm guessing they did it after the first one exploded.'

'Christ, so we have no power?' Severson looks even paler than he did a moment ago.

She turns to him, her voice low and flint hard: 'Listen, if you want to sit up at the big kids' table you stay positive and do as I say. Otherwise, go take your seat with the rest of the passengers and I'll get one of the flight attendants to help out. Is that clear?'

Severson nods. 'Crystal.'

'Good. Get air traffic control on the horn. They need to know what happened and that we have to land ASAP.'

'What are you going to do?'

'Read.'

He looks at her like she's mad. 'Read? Read what?'

She pulls an iPad from a rack beside the pilot's seat and holds it up. 'The flight manual. I have to learn how to fly this thing – without engines.'

23

Kilroy's eyes flutter open. His head aches and his vision is blurry and the left side of his face is numb from where the airbag hit.

Christ, he is *screwing this up*. Maybe he *should* retire before he really hurts himself. He has enough money to do it in style, both Bunsen and his father always paid him well.

He pushes the thought from his mind. He's not going to retire. What the hell would he do all day? *Play golf?* Tomorrow the world will be a very different place and Bunsen will need him around. And it was just one accident, after all. It could have happened to anyone. He was so focused on the guy riding the bike that he misjudged the braking distance and hit the cement retaining wall, a part of which then, it seems, took a trip down the hill in front of him.

The front of the Prius is crumpled but the damage doesn't look terminal from the driver's seat. He cranks the electric engine and it starts first time. Relieved, he engages reverse and the vehicle shudders as it backs up. He slots it into drive and the Prius pulls away with a slight crab to the left and a deep scraping sound that sets his teeth on edge. It's not perfect, but it works. Now he just needs to find those guys.

He sees them on the road below, three specks on North Cahuenga Boulevard. They're maybe a kilometre away, riding the bikes, the dog beside them. Good. He needs to finish this job so he can meet up with Bunsen.

Third time had better be the charm.

24

A colossal fireball splits the sky.

Bunsen takes in the explosion from the Tyrannosaur. A reservoir tank buried beneath a gas station, owned by BP, has detonated, causing the surrounding ground to subside. He smiles. The company can consider it payback for the Deepwater Horizon spill in the Gulf of Mexico that spewed *five million barrels* of crude oil into the ocean back in 2010.

Bunsen may feel regret regarding the human damage of his actions today, but he will never regret the destruction of petroleum industry infrastructure. Considering the overwhelming devastation that business has inflicted on the planet over the last century it only seems fair they get a little of their own back. Or more than a little.

The Tyrannosaur drops towards his Santa Monica compound and lands with a blast of dust on the helipad. This changeover had been well rehearsed, but always with four people. They are two men down today. Bunsen will have to push through with Enrico and do it as quickly as possible. It's not ideal but he has no choice.

They climb out of the cockpit. Enrico instantly wheels the cradle under the water tank that contained the Swarm, then goes to work removing the bolts which hold it to the central section of the chopper's airframe.

To the right Bunsen unlocks the garage's roller door and pushes it up.

It sits on a trolley in the middle of the garage.

It is both terrible and beautiful.

Alvy did a sterling job designing and, along with Enrico, building the Item, as they named it after spending a week trying to think of a suitably understated name. Three metres long by two metres wide, it is the centrepiece of Phase Three.

He locates the electric water pump Enrico used earlier, still with its hoses attached, and removes the lid on top of a hundred-litre rhino drum that contains the Swarm. He pushes in a hose then unscrews what looks like a radiator cap on top of the Item and pushes in the other hose. He then fires up the pump. It whirs to life and the Swarm sloshes along the hoses from drum to Item. Once this drum is empty Bunsen will need to repeat the process four more times.

He glances at his Patek. He still hasn't heard from Kilroy. He hopes the old codger is okay. It'd hurt Kilroy's pride to call for help, but he'd do it if he really needed it. Bunsen adores the man, but he can, at times, be the bane of his life. The trouble stems from the fact that although Kilroy is an employee, he is also family, which can make the relationship difficult. Bunsen can never fire him, or discipline him, or even hold him to account. He just has to trust the old bastard will do a good job, which he usually does, and hope for the best. And if Bunsen ever wants to do something that he knows Kilroy won't agree with, then he has to lie about it, or accept that he's going to hear the old fella bitch and moan about it.

The water pump whirs steadily as Bunsen checks the first rhino drum. It's only half empty. This will take a while. He heads out of the garage to help Enrico remove the water tank.

25

Lola Jacklin's eyes flutter open.

It takes a moment before she remembers she's not waking up at home in bed but in a building full of storage lockers on Doheny Drive.

She takes a deep breath. She can move both arms and her right leg, but her left thigh is trapped under a heavy metal beam and hurts like hell. She must get it off quickly or risk suffering crush syndrome, which she knows all about from an episode of *Grey's Anatomy* one of her clients wrote. She remembers that it occurs when a ruptured muscle dumps an excess of chemicals, usually potassium and phosphate, into the bloodstream, which can then cause cardiac arrest. The longer the muscle is crushed, the more intense the release of chemicals.

She takes a deep breath, grabs the beam with both hands – it's about a foot square – and pushes upwards.

Good God! She manages to raise it half an inch and take some pressure off her thigh, but that's it. It's just too heavy. She can't even wriggle free. She holds it up, her yoga-toned arms take the strain admirably for a good ten seconds, then they start to shake uncontrollably and she has to let it down. Reintroducing the beam to her thigh hurts like an absolute *mofo*.

'Hello? Need some help over here!'

There is no response.

'Can anybody hear me?'

It would seem they cannot.

'Damn it.' She takes a breath, tries to process what's happened. She knows when you live in LA you must always expect some kind of disaster to befall you at some point. It's a dangerous place. For example, wildfires are common, so you must take precautions. Earthquakes are not so much common as a daily occurrence so, again, you must take precautions, and if you're clever like Lola, you study the fault lines, even the ones that are lesser known, and make sure you don't buy a house on one. But this? Exploding vehicles all over town? Well, she can't imagine how you could ever prepare for that.

With difficulty she drags the iPhone from her back pocket, swipes it open with her thumb and is surprised to find it has a pretty strong signal in spite of everything that's happened. She dials 911.

It's busy.

'Of course it is!' She dials another number. Bowen. 'Come-on-Matty-come-on-Matty.' It goes to voicemail. 'Christ.' She leaves a detailed message which describes her predicament. She then hangs up and dials another number. It rings – and is answered.

'Hello?'

'Scott!'

'Hello, sweetness.' That's what Scott Ford calls her. *Sweetness*. 'Everything okay?'

She keeps it upbeat. 'Well, yeah, actually I'm trapped. I have a – I think it's a metal beam – lying across my thigh and I can't seem to move it.' She says it like it's some minor inconvenience she often has to deal with.

In fact she says it in such a breezy manner that Scott thinks it's a joke. 'Are you serious?'

'Oh, yeah, absolutely.'

'Oh, man. That's terrible. Jeezus.' He sounds concerned. 'Can anyone help you?'

'Well, no, the place seems to be empty. When the explosions started I took shelter in a building thinking it'd be safer inside. So I was wrong about that. Anyway, there was a huge blast, part of the building caved in and, well, here I am.'

'That's terrible. I hear it's pretty bad out there.'

'It is. Anyway, I know it's a big favour, but can you come and help me?'

'Where are you?'

'Doheny, near Pico. It's a big storage building painted white and blue. I'm on the ground floor.'

'Oh, yeah, we shot *Galaxy Chef* around there.'

Lola remembers that last year Scott starred in a film about a time-travelling, universe-hopping, short-order cook who's searching for a long-lost recipe book but ends up saving the planet from annihilation in an intergalactic bake-off. It managed to capture the zeitgeist by fusing the audience's long-standing love of science fiction with its newfound interest in cooking competitions. It did 250 million domestic and 400 foreign and wasn't even in 3D.

'I'll be there ASAP. Might take a while. I can't drive, obviously.'

'No, and if you see a car, or any kind of vehicle, with exhaust that's purple, or turning black, get away from it fast because it's about to explode.'

'Yeah, they've been saying that on the TV.'

'You should tweet it if you can.'

'Oh, yeah, good idea. Okay. Hang in there.'

'I will. If I manage to get free I'll call you.'

'Okay, sweetness.'

He hangs up and she looks at the phone for a moment. That seemed kind of – formal, but then his usual laid-back, half-mast, gravelly-voiced flirty talk wouldn't have been appropriate considering the situation. What's important is that he said he'd come. She remembers reading somewhere, probably in one of her clients' screenplays, that you get a true sense of someone's character in a crisis situation. Well, so far so good. Scott had volunteered to help her immediately.

Lola's leg is really throbbing now so she decides to lift the beam again to alleviate the pressure. She grabs hold of it, takes the strain and pushes it upwards. *Man!* It seems even heavier than before, takes all her effort to raise it half an inch, and she can only hold it for five seconds this time. She rests it back on her thigh and it hurts like a bastard, makes her eyes water.

She smells something. Pungent, sharp. She lifts her head, scans her surroundings.

Smoke.

A light haze hangs in the air. It must have blown in from outside –

A flame jumps to the right. The smoke didn't blow in. Fifteen metres away a clump of insulation burns, must have been set alight by the explosion. The flames are not big, not yet anyway, but they're big enough.

'Perfect!' She needs to get out of here.

Very soon.

26

The sun drops through the purple-grey smog towards the horizon and casts a dull, eerie glow across the city.

Corey finally has the hang of this riding thing, almost finds the rhythmic tick of the gears relaxing as he follows Judd down Santa Monica Boulevard; Spike is close behind.

The Australian glances behind him to make sure the ponytailed mofo isn't following in the Prius. He isn't, but if he was he'd have a tough time navigating Santa Monica Boulevard this afternoon. Not only is it gridlocked by the smoking hulks and flaming wreckage of every kind of vehicle imaginable, but scores of people wander through the destruction in a daze.

Corey's never seen anything like it. 'How much further, mate?'

'It's close. This way.' Judd takes a right turn, navigates a side-walk, passes a burnt-out van and crosses onto a quiet street. A line of towering eucalyptus trees casts a large shadow across a row of neat apartment blocks. 'What was the number again?'

'1138. Apartment seven.'

'Here.' They pull up under a eucalyptus and Judd nods at the white, three-storey apartment block opposite. 'That's it.' He thinks about it. 'Number seven should be . . . on the first floor, second from the end.'

'How do you know this?'

'We lived around the corner, just off Wilshire. I used to ride my bike down this street.'

'Right.' Corey takes in the building. It has a security door at the front. At the rear is a narrow alleyway that runs the length of the block and services the ground-floor parking area. Overhanging the alleyway is a line of eight balconies, at the very end of which sits a large dumpster. The alleyway faces the blank wall of the next block so it's relatively private.

The Aussie grins his crooked grin. 'Think I have a way in.'

They hide the bikes behind a row of large-leaf plants in the building's front garden then move down the driveway to the dumpster. It's both heavy and unwieldy, but they muscle it to a position under the seventh balcony, then climb on top, grab the railing and pull themselves up. On the balcony sit two sad, rusty metal chairs and a rickety wooden table.

Corey looks over the railing and speaks in a low voice to Spike on the alleyway below: 'I need you to be a *watch* dog, for a while, okay? Keep a look out and if you see anything, don't be shy.'

Spike barks up at him.

'Yes, if there's lemon sorbet I'll get it for you.'

Corey turns to Judd as he pulls on the handle of the balcony's sliding glass door. It's locked. 'How are we going to —'

Smash. Judd swings one of the chairs into the glass and it shatters.

'What are you *doing*?'

'What? It's not like the guy's going to mind.'

'I'm trying to keep everything low-key and quiet, whispering to the dog, and you're smashing windows? What's got into you?'

'Nothing.' Judd leans through, unlocks the door and slides it open. 'I just want to get on with it.'

They step inside. It's dark. The place has the dank smell of unwashed laundry. Burger King wrappers and drink containers cover the cheap, nasty furniture. It's a classic bachelor pad, lacks both charm and even a nod to basic hygiene.

'Looks like he's already been robbed today.' Judd heads straight for the small, rusty refrigerator in the corner of the kitchen. He grabs the freezer doorhandle and yanks it open. 'Rum and raisin or cookie dough?'

Neither. It's empty. Judd's surprised and disappointed. 'There isn't even any ice-cream.'

'Mate, I never thought that bloke was fair dinkum.'

'Fair what?'

'*Dinkum*. It means he was full of crap.'

Judd pushes his hand into the icebox and feels around, hopes the counteragent is hidden in there, that Alvy was under the misguided notion that a few ice cubes would add a layer of impregnable security.

Corey looks around the kitchen. 'I don't know why you're so surprised —'

Judd draws out two metal canisters and shows them to Corey with a wide grin. 'I guess he was fair dinky after all.'

Corey studies the canisters in shock. 'Dink*um*. Fair dink*um*.'

They examine the canisters. They are each slightly larger than a can of Red Bull, but much heavier, milled from solid aluminium. Their flip-lid contains a small numeric keypad with an LED screen built into it. Judd reads the handwritten sticker attached to the bottom of both canisters. '*One drop per litre.* I'll keep one, you keep the other. Just in case.' He passes it over.

Corey takes it. 'What was the passcode again?'

'274.'

He punches 274 into the keypad. With a heavy click and a swoosh of compressed air the lid unlocks. Corey flips it up and looks at the residue on the cap. It's a bright red viscous liquid. 'What should we do with them?'

'Get them to the authorities.'

'And who's that?'

Judd thinks it out. 'The – ahhh, the police – no, Centre for Disease Control? No – the FBI? Yeah, the FBI. The Federal Building's not that far from here, if I remember. I had to go there during my last press tour. We should get moving.'

Corey's sceptical. 'Mate, we're not even sure it works. It could be red cordial for all we know.'

'We'll test it when we get there —'

Spike barks in the distance.

Judd turns to Corey. 'What?'

Corey's expression is grim. 'Ponytail.'

Kilroy followed the two guys until he hit the gridlocked carnage on Santa Monica Boulevard, then lost them. He then surmised – he preferred that word to guessed – they were heading to Alvy's apartment and took a back street route to get here. The dog in the alleyway, which seems to have run off now, and the dumpster in position below the balcony and the smashed glass door seem to indicate they are inside. But why?

The counteragent.

It's the only thing that makes sense. Alvy must have kept some offsite, in case of an emergency, or as insurance, then told these guys about it before he died. He must have been pretty damn convincing to prompt two complete strangers to come down here and get it.

He checks that his Glock 9mm's magazine is full then looks out from his parked Prius and takes in both the front and rear exits of the building. No one will be able to leave that building without him seeing them.

Flat to the floor, Judd and Corey crawl towards the balcony window and look left. They scan the far end of the alleyway and South Carmelina beyond it – and can't see any sign of Ponytail or his Prius.

Judd's confused. 'Where is it?'

'He said he's sitting in the car but I don't – wait, there it is. Reflected in the car opposite.'

Judd looks closer, sees the outline of the Prius reflected in the white paint of a van parked on the opposite side of the road. 'Yep. Got it. I'm pretty sure he can see both the front and rear exits from there.'

'Jesuschweppes.'

'You know it's Jesus *wept*, right? As in, "boo-hoo, I'm having a tear", not *Schweppes* as in, "Thank you, Stephan, I'll have another gin and tonic".'

'Are you sure?'

'One hundred per cent.'

Corey's not at all convinced. 'Anyway, you have any ideas?'

'I should never have come back to LA? There's one.' They crawl away from the balcony window and find their feet. Immediately Judd's hands go Rubik. 'There's got to be a way out of here.' He needs a plan. Unfortunately he can't think of a damn thing. 'Christ.'

Corey turns to him. 'I got an idea.'

Judd squints. 'Hmmm?'

'What's that sound?'

'Well, you know, sometimes —'

'What?'

'— your ideas aren't always, you know —'

'No, I don't know.'

'Fantastic.'

'Excuse me? That's not true. At all.'

'Hmmm.'

'Would you stop making that sound. It's a good plan.'

'What is it?'

'Well, now you've made me self-conscious. But it is good.'

'You keep saying that but I haven't heard anything yet.'

'I can tell you it's better than standing around twisting your hands in the air hoping for the best.' Corey mimics Judd's hands when they go Rubik, then heads for the front door. 'Come on. I'll tell you on the way.'

'On the way where?'

'To where we're going to carry out the plan!'

Judd takes a moment, then follows Corey out.

On the open walkway outside the apartment the Australian looks around, finds a stairwell that leads to the ground floor and moves down it. He glances back at Judd. 'What's going on with you?'

'What?'

'You don't have any ideas, then you criticise me when I do?'

'Sorry, my bad.'

'Should bloody hope so.'

Corey has every right to be annoyed. There *is* something going on with him. Yes, Judd wants to prove that he's deserving of the world's adulation, but he can't do that if he can't come up with a goddamn plan and that pisses him off, especially if Corey has one. That's part of the reason why Judd desperately wants the counteragent to be genuine. If he can bring it to the world's attention and somehow stop what's going on, he might feel like less of a fraud. He doesn't want to tell Corey this for a number of reasons: the first being that it's embarrassing, which is also the second and third reasons. It always amazes him what he'll do *not* to be embarrassed.

They reach the ground floor. Corey moves fast, searches, finds a door, opens it. It's the communal laundry. He moves on, opens another door – and grins when he sees what's inside. He gestures for Judd to look in. 'That's my plan.'

Kilroy keeps one eye on the apartment and one on his iPhone as he swipes his way through the main news sites. There's breaking news about the explosions in LA, but no sign of the video he created, not even on YouTube. Strange. Bunsen said he'd post it once Phase Three began. Of course, he is undermanned, which is partially Kilroy's fault, but still it should be up by now. The old man quickly taps out a text message to Bunsen, tells him Alvy has been been dealt with but there is one other issue to resolve before they can meet, then reminds him to post the video. He'd do it himself, but the file is on Bunsen's MacBook Air and needs to be posted with the relevant software filters so the IP address is untraceable.

He places the iPhone on the passenger seat beside him and turns back to the apartment. 'Come on.' This is taking too long. His impulse is to rush in there, gun blazing, and deal with the problem head on, with deadly force. He doesn't. They could slip away if he isn't pinpoint accurate. No, softly, softly is the best approach. He just needs to wait for them to emerge then take them out, unawares.

Clunk. The roller door to the parking area shudders and slowly rises. He turns to it, pistol on his lap, and waits, ready for whatever the afternoon may bring.

Clank. The roller door shudders to a stop to reveal a white, two-door Buick LeSabre, a big old heavy tank from the early eighties.

The Buick's engine revs and its rear tyres light up at it lunges out of the garage and swerves towards the Prius.

'What the hell?' Kilroy realises he is not, in fact, ready for whatever the afternoon may bring – especially when it's two tons of hurtling Detroit iron. He presses the Prius's start button, slams the vehicle into reverse and hits the accelerator. The car lurches backwards, but it's not fast enough –

Crunch. The Buick spears into the front quarter of the vehicle and knocks it a metre sideways, pops a front tyre. The side airbag triggers and slams into Kilroy's head and shoulder. Dazed, he looks into the other car and locks eyes with the driver.

It's the Australian guy from the *Atlantis* 4, the one with the sheep dog. Kilroy saw him on Jon Stewart once. The guy slides out of the car and sprints towards the garage.

Kilroy grabs the Glock from his lap, pushes open the door, steps out and aims the pistol at him: 'If you're going to kill me you better make sure I'm dead.'

Corey sprints towards the garage and the safety of a wide cement pylon, where Judd takes cover. He steals a look back and sees Ponytail swing a pistol towards him.

Damn. Corey realises he's not going to make it to the pylon in time. Maybe Judd was right. Maybe his ideas aren't that fantastic after all. That car should have exploded by now. Why in hell hasn't it exploded? His eyes flick to the Buick's exhaust.

It's pitch black –

Ka-boom. The vehicle detonates – and rocks the world. The car rises a metre off the ground as the blast wave hits Corey and drives him into the floor of the parking garage's entry.

Ears ringing, the Australian forces his eyes open and sees Ponytail lying on the driveway ten metres away, his left shoulder on *fire*. He *must* be dead. Surely he couldn't have survived that blast –

Ponytail twitches. His right hand rises – and tamps out the flames on his shoulder, then reaches for the pistol that lies on the ground in front of him.

'Oh, come on!' Corey drags himself to his feet, but he's groggy and isn't moving as fast as he should.

Ponytail picks up the weapon and aims it at the Australian, pulls the trigger –

Bam. Judd yanks Corey behind the pylon as the bullet pings off the cement and ricochets into the parking garage.

Corey turns to the astronaut. 'Thanks, mate.'

'This way.' Judd pulls him into the parking garage.

Kilroy finds his feet and swings around the pylon, pistol raised, finger tight on the trigger –

No one there. They can't have gone far. He keeps the pistol raised and enters the parking garage, scans the dimly lit space. It's large, takes up the whole ground floor of the apartment block. It must have forty car spaces though half are empty.

Judd and Corey crouch by the passenger door of an old Ford Mustang. Corey rubs his temples, tries to wake himself up.

Footsteps echo across the garage, then stop.

Corey whispers: 'He's here.'

Judd whispers too: 'Shhh. Voice down.' He looks around. 'We need to find a weapon.'

Corey scans the garage. There isn't much to choose from. An old tyre leans against the wall nearby, but there are no tools that could be used as weapons. On the adjacent wall there's a tall, thin metal locker. He points at it. 'Might be something in there.'

'Should have a look.'

Judd stays low to the ground and sets off towards it, creeps past the front of the Mustang. Corey follows. Judd sees him and stops. 'You're coming with me?'

'Sorry. I thought we were doing it together.'

'No, I'm doing it.'

'Okay. So we're going to split up?'

'We're not splitting up, it's fifteen metres away. I'll be back in thirty seconds.'

'Oh. Right. But if we do get separated, where should we meet?'

'I don't know.'

'Well, think.' He says it a little bit too loud.

'Shhh. Voice down.'

Corey racks his brain. 'I know! We'll meet where we hid the bikes.'

'Okay. Whatever.' Judd moves off.

'One more thing.'

Judd turns back to him, frustrated. 'What? I could have been there and back by now.'

'We should come up with an emergency word, in case, you know, one of us gets in trouble. I was thinking "tomato".'

'Tomato? No. Just shout my name.'

'Oh. Okay. So you'll shout out your name too?'

'No, I'll shout out your name.'

'Right.' Corey's confused. 'So we both shout my name?'

'No. I shout *your* name and you shout *my* name.'

'Got it.' Corey thinks about it. 'Wouldn't it be easier to use "tomato"?'

'I'm leaving now.' Judd turns to go.

'Alrighty.'

'Shhh. Voice down.' Judd moves off.

Corey whispers after him. 'See you at the bikes.'

Judd stops. 'No! I'm coming back *here*. We're not meeting at the bikes. We're meeting *here*.'

'I thought we were meeting at the bikes.'

'Only if we get *separated*. Otherwise, we meet here. And if you get in trouble you call my name. If I get in trouble I'll call your name.'

'So we're not going to use "tomato"?'

'At no point is *anyone* going to use the word "tomato"—'

'Shhh. Voice down.'

Judd drills Corey with a withering look then turns and moves off.

Kilroy stands in the middle of the garage and is sure he can hear whispering. He just can't work out where it's coming from. With all the hard surfaces in this place the sound bounces around like a pinball. He scans the dim surroundings, tries not to think about how much his shoulder hurts. He doesn't even want to look at the burn. He'll ignore it until these guys have been dealt with.

He hears a short, sharp scratch. To the left, like a leather sole on a cement floor. He turns towards an old Mustang in the opposite corner of the garage.

•

Corey winces.

Bugger! His left boot just scuffed the bloody floor. He raises his head and peeks through the Mustang's cabin to make sure Ponytail didn't hear it.

He heard it! And now he strides towards the vehicle. The fact his shoulder was recently *on fire* doesn't seem to have slowed him down at all.

Their eyes meet.

Oh, damn it!

Ponytail breaks into a run, raises his pistol and fires.

Thud, thud, thud. Bullets strafe the Mustang's bodywork as Corey ducks behind the front passenger door. He stays low, tries to think of a way out of this.

The Australian! Kilroy saw him – but was he inside or outside the Mustang? Weapon raised, Kilroy approaches the vehicle and looks inside.

There's no one in there.

He moves to the front of the car.

Nothing.

Where the hell is he?

A faint sound behind him. He pivots, swings the pistol to the boot of the car, finger tight on the trigger.

Not there.

Under the car. He must be under the car.

Ponytail drops flat to the ground, thrusts the pistol under the vehicle.

He's not there either.

Where is the bastard?

•

Corey holds his breath as he crouches behind the Mustang's front wheel on the passenger side, balanced on one foot. He looks over at the exit. If he ran for it he'd be out in the open for too long. Ponytail would see him straight away.

Bugger.

Kilroy pulls himself up and circumnavigates the Mustang's boot, swings the gun down the passenger side of the vehicle.

No one there.

He turns.

'Where is he?'

Lying under the car a metre away from you.

Corey watches Ponytail's feet stride across the floor, then he loses sight of them in the darkness. Corey backs up, pulls himself out from under the vehicle, crouches beside the passenger door and peeks through the Mustang's cabin again. He can't see Ponytail anywhere, and he can't see any sign of Judd either. He takes a breath and stays low.

Now what? Does he wait for Judd to return? He said he was only going to take thirty seconds. Does this mean they're now separated?

He smells something unpleasant. What is that? Sharply toxic and instantly headache-inducing.

Corey turns.

Ponytail towers above him. The odour is his cheap and nasty cologne. It's the first time the Australian's seen the guy up close. Damn, he's positively *ancient*.

Ponytail points his pistol at Corey's face. 'Give me the counteragent.' His accent is thick Louisiana.

'Counteragent? What's a counteragent?' Playing dumb is not Corey's strong suit.

Ponytail steps forward, the pistol's muzzle an inch from the Australian's forehead. '*Where is it?*'

'I only have one thing to say.'

'And what's that?'

'Tomato!'

'What the hell are you –?'

'To-ma-to!'

Wiif-Clunk! Ponytail's head jerks sharply to the left as something clips him across the back of his skull. He sways unsteadily for a moment, then keels over and slumps to the cement like a large sack of extremely old potatoes. He's out cold.

'The locker only had one thing in it.' Judd steps forward and holds up a floor mop with a heavy wooden handle. 'You okay?'

'Took your sweet time coming back. Where were you?'

'I thought we were meeting at the bikes.'

Corey's confused, then sees Judd's grin and realises he's taking the piss. 'Thanks, mate.'

'Anytime.'

Judd and Corey study the crumpled, unconscious ponytailed man on the floor of the garage. Judd picks up his pistol and checks the magazine. There are four bullets inside.

Corey watches the astronaut closely. 'We're not going to . . . kill him, are we?'

Judd shakes his head and pushes the weapon into his belt at the back of his pants. 'Just because he's a dickhead doesn't mean we have to be.'

Corey nods in agreement. 'And he's so old he could die of natural causes really soon anyway, so what's the point?' A moment passes, then he looks at Judd. 'What *are* we going to do with him?'

Judd and Corey drag Ponytail to the dark corner of the parking garage behind the old Mustang. They prop him up so he sits against the wall then search him. Judd finds nothing, but Corey discovers a small walkie-talkie in his jacket. He checks to see if it's functional. It is so he pockets it.

Judd looks at the old fella. 'We need to tie him up.'

Corey thinks about it for a moment. 'I got an idea.'

The Australian rolls over the bald tyre he saw earlier, picks it up and drops it over Ponytail's head. Judd steps up and they both push it over his shoulders, then jam it down his torso until his arms are trapped tight.

Corey takes in their handy work. 'Beautiful.'

Judd turns to him. 'Let's deliver those canisters.'

They move fast.

Spike pants at the entrance of the parking garage as Judd and Corey exit. He barks.

'Sorry, mate, no lemon sorbet.' Corey pats him on the head as he turns to Judd. 'So, where are we going?'

The astronaut works his iPhone and reads the screen. 'We head for the Federal Building. It's on Wilshire. That's where the FBI office is. Shouldn't take too long on the bikes.'

They move past the wrecked cars. The Buick burns loudly, almost completely gutted. The Prius is only half alight.

'Hold on a sec.' Judd shields himself from the heat as he approaches the vehicle and looks inside. He uses his sleeve to pull on the doorhandle, which is hot to the touch, then reaches in to the passenger seat and flips something onto the street. It's on fire so he lightly tamps out the flames with his shoe.

Spike sniffs it and barks.

Corey studies it. 'Don't know what it is, mate.'

'I do.' Judd crouches beside the smoking item for a moment, then flips it over. 'It's Ponytail's iPhone.'

Kilroy comes to with a start.

He looks around the empty parking garage and realises his predicament. He's trapped in an old tyre, he can't see his pistol anywhere and the back of his head throbs worse than his burned shoulder. Overall his day has not gone to plan. The only upside is the fact those two guys didn't kill him. It's a pleasant, if not particularly shocking, surprise. They're not the kind of guys who kill people, especially when they're unconscious, though they will regret not killing Kilroy.

Kilroy knows he must get moving. Unfortunately he no longer has a car so Bunsen will need to pick him up. The boy won't be happy about that, and will be even less impressed when Kilroy explains how he ended up in this situation. But before any of that can happen he needs to get out of this damn tyre.

He tries to wriggle out of it. No joy. They really jammed it on tight. He tries to stand, to walk out of here, maybe find a stranger to help pull the thing off, but without the use of his arms he can't even get up. So he grits his teeth, pushes himself onto his side and rolls across the floor towards the old Mustang.

He's sure it's a 1967, though it could be a '68. It doesn't actually matter because what's important is that it has the chrome front bumper which wraps around the side of the car and ends in a point. Facing the ceiling, he works himself close to the vehicle and rams the sidewall of the tyre against the pointed end of the bumper. He then pushes his right leg under the car, braces it against the exhaust system and pushes hard. The bumper presses into the tyre's sidewall and slowly edges it down his body. After what feels like a minute but is probably only twenty seconds, he stops, exhausted and sweating like a pig, and checks his progress. The tyre has moved about an inch and a half down his body.

An inch and a half! This is going to take an age. No use whining about it. He braces himself and pushes again.

Judd and Corey briskly circumnavigate the apartment building and arrive at the spot where they hid the bikes behind the large-leaf plants.

Judd studies the burned phone then presses its home button. The screen blinks to life but it's melted and cracked and only about twenty per cent of it is readable. He swipes a finger across the blackened glass and the phone unlocks. 'It works.' He's happy.

Corey turns to him. 'What are you looking for?'

Judd stares at the screen. 'A clue to who this bastard is and what he's up to.'

27

Judd and Corey ride along Wilshire Boulevard. Fast. Spike lopes along just behind.

To the Australian there seem to be fewer people on this road than Santa Monica Boulevard, and fewer burning and abandoned vehicles too. Even so, he stays focused, keeps his hands firmly on the handlebars and his eyes locked on the road. In spite of everything that's happened today, he's happy to have picked up the riding thing so quickly.

He glances over at Judd and realises he shouldn't get too cocky. Judd's hands aren't on the handlebars and his eyes aren't on the road. Instead, he swipes his way through Ponytail's iPhone, occasionally glancing up to check if anything is ahead. When he does need to alter direction he casually leans to one side or the other.

'Can you read this?' Judd lifts his head from the screen, veers across the bitumen towards Corey and holds out the phone.

The Australian takes it. He makes sure the road ahead is clear, then studies the small portion of the screen in the lower right-hand corner that isn't burned. 'Phase – Phase Three? What's Phase Three?'

Spike barks.

'Yes, I realise it comes after "phase two", but what is it?'

Judd shakes his head. 'No idea. Look at the next bit.'

'Five p.m. MHS.'

'Are you sure it says MHS?'

'MHS. Yep. What's MHS?'

'Don't know, but it's familiar. They must have something planned there.' He glances at his Ploprof. 'In just over an hour.'

'Is there some way you can send this document to your own phone? So you can see it more clearly?'

'No, it's in the calendar section. There doesn't seem to be anything else on there that's of much use.'

Corey passes the phone back. 'Show it to the feds when we meet 'em.'

'Yep.' Judd turns and points. 'And that's where we're going.' Behind a line of skyscrapers they catch a glimpse of the tall, boxy Federal Building, which could only have been designed and built in the 1960s. It houses everything from the Passport Office to the Office of the FBI. For anything related to the United States Federal Government, it's a one-stop shop in LA.

Corey turns to Judd. 'So what are we going to say to them? The Feds.'

'The truth. We have two canisters of a counteragent to the virus that's causing the explosions.'

'Will they believe us?'

'We're half the *Atlantis* 4. They'll believe us.'

'Mate, we don't even know if the stuff works —'

They pass another skyscraper and see the Federal Building fully for the first time.

The left side of the building is alight, the flaming chassis of an exploded bus on the road in front of it the ignition point of the blaze. A small group of people mill about outside and watch the flames.

There are, of course, no fire trucks in attendance.

The left side of the building collapses and slides onto the road below, scattering the group of people. There's a pause – then a series of five explosions rock the structure. Windows blow out and the centre of the building collapses in on itself like a failed soufflé. There's another pause – then a giant flame shoots out from the roof. It lights up the sky with a fireball that burns a vivid blue.

Corey and Judd recoil as the heatwave rolls over them. Even from a hundred and fifty metres away it's like putting your head inside a pizza oven. They freewheel along Wilshire and watch the destruction unfold for a moment, then Judd turns to Corey. 'So that didn't turn out the way I hoped.'

'Where to now?'

'Good question.' Judd consults his iPhone, works the screen for a couple of seconds, points down a side street. 'This way.'

They make a hard right turn and ride fast.

'There.'

'Is this where they shot *Beverly Hills Cop*?'

'Yep.' Judd and Corey cycle towards the Beverly Hills Police Station. Yes, the same one used in the Eddie Murphy movies, and countless TV shows. It's surely the best-looking police station on the planet, with its handsome tower, Art Deco details and spotless appearance. It looks like it was built to be a palace, not a cop shop.

Judd takes it in. 'And you know what I like most about this place? It's not on fire.'

Corey grins. 'How'd you know to come here?'

'When I was a kid it had just opened when my mum – someone stole the tape deck, yes, *tape deck*, out of her car. We had to come to this station to file a report. Spent a couple of hours here. A cop showed me around. It was very cool.'

They cycle closer. There aren't many people around. Judd was expecting the place to be packed with citizens in need of assistance but no, it's all but empty. Odd. 'Where is everyone?'

'Must be inside.'

They cut through the car park where half the police cruisers, almost ten by Judd's count, are burned out, then ride up to the main entrance, dismount and push the bikes through the sliding doors, which open into a giant foyer.

Inside it is both gloomy and empty. There are no lights on and nobody around. They glance at each other.

Corey looks around. 'Is it closed? Do police stations close in America? Is that wise with all the guns?'

They park their bikes by the door and Corey turns to Spike, forks his middle and index finger into a V, points them at his eyes, then the dog's eyes, then the bikes. 'Stay here. Anybody tries to take them, you know what to do.'

The dog barks.

'No, I don't think the police will need to take your statement.'

Corey and Judd turn and walk across to the reception desk.

There's nobody sitting behind it.

Judd looks around. 'What the hell is going on here?'

There's a faint noise from the other side of the desk. They peer over. A young, dark-haired woman is huddled beneath it.

Judd's instantly concerned. 'You okay?'

She looks up at him and shakes her head, petrified.

'What are you doing down there? Where is everyone?'

'Are they still here?' Her voice trembles.

Corey leans forward. 'Is who still where?'

'The men, with the machines. Are they still there?'

Judd looks around, even checks right behind him. 'Men? I can't see any men. Or machines.'

Corey pipes up. 'There's *us*. We're men, but we don't have any machines – unless you count our bikes, which aren't really "machines". Well, I guess you could make an argument that they *are* machines but – anyway. Sorry. So, what kind of machines are you talking about?'

The young woman rolls out from under the desk, finds her feet, sprints across the foyer and out the main doors. They watch her go.

Corey is confused. 'Is she coming back?'

Judd shakes his head. 'I don't think so.'

They scan the list of offices on a large plaque bolted to the wall beside the reception desk. Judd points at the word *Detectives*. 'Third floor.'

'Seems like a good place to start.'

They turn towards the bank of elevators and see no one is manning the security screening gate that visitors pass through before they can enter the elevators on the other side. They glance at each other and it hits home how peculiar this situation actually is.

Corey looks around. 'Really, what's going on here?'

Judd shakes his head. 'Don't know, don't care. We just need to find a cop, pass on the counteragent and tell them about the MHS thing.' He glances at his watch. 'Whatever's happening there is happening in fifty minutes.'

They reach the bank of elevators and Corey presses the up arrow.

'MHS.' Judd mumbles it to himself. He knows those initials. What do they mean?

Corey turns his head. 'Hear that?'

'What?' Judd listens, then notices a very distant buzzing sound.

Ding.

The doors to the elevator in front of them slide open and they step inside. The large elevator is wood panelled, has a mirror on each wall and a button panel on both sides of the doors. A jaunty muzak version of 'The Girl from Ipanema' plays from a speaker above. The boys don't really notice any of those details, though. What strikes them is the pungent smell. Corey knows what it is straight away. 'Gasoline.'

Judd looks down. There's a small pool of liquid on the dark marble floor. He crouches, touches it, smells it. 'Yep. Why would that be here?'

Corey shrugs. 'Jeez Louise, it's strong. Want to take the next one?'

'Nah. It's only three floors.'

Corey nods and hits the button for the third floor. The doors slide together and the elevator rises. As it does the buzzing sound recedes into the distance.

Ding.

The doors slide open.

The third floor is empty.

They step out, look around. There's no one there. Judd's baffled. 'That's just – strange, don't you think?'

Corey nods. 'It's actually weird, mate. I reckon we should head down to the lockup.'

'The what?'

'You know, where they put the crims when they're brought in. That plaque thingy downstairs said it was on the lower ground floor. There's got to be someone down there who can tell us what's going on.'

'Let's do it.'

They step back inside the elevator and Judd presses the LG button. The doors slide shut and the elevator descends. 'The Girl from Ipanema' continues to play.

The buzzing sound returns, and becomes louder. Judd can hear it clearly now. 'What is that?'

'Sounds like a leaf blower or something.' Corey glances at the liquid on the ground. 'Why would there be gasoline in the elevator?'

Judd thinks about it. 'What did that woman say? About the men?'

'That they had machines.' Corey stares straight ahead, lost in thought. 'And machines run on gasoline.'

'And what's been happening to machines that run on gasoline today?'

They look at each other.

Ding.

The doors slide open.

The throbbing buzz-scream of a chainsaw echoes across the large room.

Fifteen metres away a man dressed in black and wearing a white hockey mask rises from behind a booking counter, swings his arm high and hurls a chainsaw across the room.

Engine screeching, it spirals through the air, then drops like a brick, slams into the ground, bounce-rolls across the cement floor and slams into a barricade of three office desks, behind which three uniformed cops take cover.

Judd's eyes flick to the chainsaw's exhaust. It's dark purple, then turns black, its engine note rough, like rocks in a blender. 'Take cover!' Judd and Corey roll behind the elevator's button panels –

Ka-boom! The chainsaw detonates like a Claymore landmine – but worse. It sends a blast of white-hot shrapnel in every direction, the soundwave deafening.

Smash, thud, crash. The shrapnel slams into the elevator, shatters the mirror on the rear wall. The office desk barricade is obliterated, the police officers behind it slump to the blackened floor.

Corey glances at Judd. 'Guess we know what the buzzing sound is now.'

Judd scans the lockup, stunned. It's strewn with bodies – every one a police officer. At least twelve that he can count. They've stumbled into the middle of a siege. He jams his thumb onto the door-close button. Nothing happens. 'Won't shut.'

Corey tries the button on his side. 'Not happening! The explosion stuffed it.'

Still crouched behind the counter, Hockey Mask shouts at a man fifteen metres behind him. 'How long till it's open?'

This guy has no shirt on his heavily tattooed back but wears large safety goggles over his eyes. 'Thirty seconds!' He trains a flaming welding torch on the lock of a holding cell door, egged on by three prisoners inside. On a small cart beside him are the cylinders of oxygen and acetylene that feed the torch.

One of the uniform cops, stunned by the explosion but still alive, drags himself across the ground towards a 9mm pistol.

Hockey Mask dives his hand into the open, oversized duffle bag beside him, drags out another chainsaw, yanks the ripcord to start it and hurls it across the room. It spirals through the air, engine screaming, and lands a metre in front of the police officer. He reaches out, grabs it to throw it back –

Ka-boom! It detonates and blows the poor bastard to pieces.

Smash, thud, crash. Judd and Corey take cover as another wave of shrapnel slams into the elevator.

Judd winces. 'Oh, man. Really wish I hadn't seen that.'

Hockey Mask and Safety Goggles turn to see Judd and Corey in the elevator. And Judd and Corey see them.

'Damn it!' Corey jams his thumb into the door-close button again and keeps it there. 'Come on!'

Nothing happens.

'Continuing to push it isn't going to make it work!'

'You got a better idea, I'm all ears.'

Safety Goggles draws a pistol and swings it towards the elevator. The prisoners in the holding cell cheer him on.

'Jesus!' Corey turns to Judd. 'Use the gun.'

'The what?'

He points at Judd's back. 'The gun! Use the bloody gun!'

'Oh Christ, that's right!' Judd had forgotten all about Ponytail's pistol. He drags it from his belt, aims it out the elevator's doors and fires once.

The bullet slams into the oxy-welder's acetylene cylinder.

Boom. It detonates. The explosion isn't as big as either of the chainsaws but it's big enough, smacks Safety Goggles flat to the ground, knocks him out cold. The deflated prisoners in the holding cell let out a disappointed groan.

Hockey Mask takes in what just happened, then disappears behind the booking counter again. It's silent for a long moment – then a buzz-scream cuts across the room.

Judd and Corey watch Hockey Mask rise from behind the booking counter and hurl a chainsaw towards them.

Time slows.

Corey turns to Judd. 'We gotta close the doors!' He grabs the door on his side and pushes it shut as Judd does the same on his side. They slide towards each other – slowly.

The shrieking machine spirals directly towards them.

It's larger than the others.

Judd and Corey frantically push the doors closed.

But it's taking too long.

The roaring chainsaw is halfway there.

And the doors are only halfway shut.

Judd's hands slip on the polished metal as he pushes for all his worth. 'Must go faster!'

The chainsaw is right there.

The doors slam shut.

Thump. The chainsaw lands on the ground inside the elevator. Its engine thunders as its exhaust turns a deep purple.

Time speeds up.

Judd and Corey frantically pull the doors open.

They won't budge.

Corey pivots to the chainsaw, kneels, finds the ON/OFF switch, flicks it.

It doesn't work. The engine still runs. 'The switch has been disabled.'

They stare at the machine for a terrible moment.

'I'll pour out the gas.'

Judd shakes his head. 'Won't work. It's in the fuel lines. You'd have to flush the whole system.'

They look at each other.

'The counteragent!' They say it at exactly the same time. Judd grabs the canister from his jacket as Corey twists off the chainsaw's fuel cap.

Judd stares at the keypad built into the lid of the counteragent's aluminium canister. 'What was the code again?' He can't remember the number the dying guy told him. '724?'

Corey can't remember it either. '742?'

'No, 274!' Judd punches in the numbers. With a heavy click and a swoosh of compressed air the canister's lid unlocks. Judd flips it open.

'Quick!' Corey holds up the screaming chainsaw.

Judd tilts the canister towards the fuel tank's filler neck. 'How much?'

'Just pour it in!'

Judd sloshes half a cup of the counteragent into the tank. Corey places the chainsaw in the far corner of the elevator and they stand back, side by side, eyes locked on the exhaust. It turns black and the engine note sounds like rocks in a blender.

Corey takes a breath. 'I'm starting to think coming down here was a bad idea.'

Judd almost smiles.

The exhaust is pitch black.

The engine runs rough.

Then it doesn't – and the exhaust clears.

They exhale, long and deep, more relieved than words can express. Corey rubs his face. 'Far out. Well, the upside is that we now know the counteragent works, so that's nice.'

Judd presses the ground floor button. No joy. The elevator does not move. 'Now we just have to find a way out of here.'

Corey looks up at the wood-panelled ceiling, then down at the running chainsaw, then up at the ceiling again. 'Got an idea.'

The roaring chainsaw blade slices into the ceiling's wood panelling, cuts out a large square piece that drops to the floor.

Corey rests a foot on the railing that rings the elevator and propels himself up through the hole. Once on the elevator's roof he reaches down, grabs Judd's hand and helps him up. He carries the still-running chainsaw with him.

Corey looks at it. 'Really?'

Judd shrugs. 'I got a feeling it's gonna come in handy.' As he says it the chainsaw runs out of gas and cuts out.

The Australian moves to the right wall, where a series of small metal rungs have been cemented into the shaft and act as a service ladder. 'Excellent.' He quickly climbs the rungs towards the ground floor elevator doors. 'Never been in a lift shaft before. We call them "lifts" in Oz, by the way.'

Judd is just behind him. 'I've been in one.'

'Really? When was that?'

'Just before *Atlantis* was hijacked – would've loved a ladder built into the wall that night.' Remembering shuttle *Atlantis* immediately makes Judd think about its commander, his partner, Rhonda. 'Man, I hope Rho's okay.'

'When's she due to land?'

Judd glances at his Ploprof. 'In just over an hour.'

'Word will be out about what's happening here, mate. I'm sure they've already landed a couple of states away and she's sitting in the airport lounge, sipping a crappy latte, pissed off that she has to listen to Severson bang on about some nonsense.'

Judd nods hopefully, wishes it were true, knows in his heart she would have called him if it was.

They reach the ground-floor elevator doors. Corey grabs one and forces it open. He pokes his head out, checks there are no chainsaw-wielding mofos about, and slides out. He reaches back and helps Judd up.

As soon as he's on his feet Judd pulls out his iPhone and dials Rhonda. It goes to voicemail. He hangs up, tries not to worry about her, fails miserably.

Paws click on the marble floor as Spike bounds towards them and lets out a sharp bark.

Corey pats him on the head. 'Let me just say this: I want to leave this place and never return.'

They head straight for the bikes, which are right where they left them. Judd rests the chainsaw across his handlebars and they run-roll them onto the street, hop on and start to pedal, the dog right behind.

Corey turns to Judd. 'We need to find another cop shop, tell them what happened here.'

Judd nods but his mind is elsewhere. 'I gotta work out the MHS thing.' He glances at his watch. 'Man, forty minutes. *MHS*. It's – I know what it is – it's right there – I just can't put my finger on it.'

'If only there were a service that could instantly answer annoyingly difficult questions like this.' Corey looks at Judd, then nods at the phone in his hand. 'I believe some call it "Google".' He throws in a pair of ironic air quotes on "Google".

Judd glances at the phone and stops pedalling. 'Worth a try.' He swipes open his phone, thinks about it. 'I should search, what – MHS Los Angeles.'

'Good place to start.' Corey decides to help him search for it and stops too. He reaches into his back pocket, draws out Bowen's iPhone and looks at the screen.

Lola called – and left a message. The mute button was switched on so he didn't know it rang. Even though the call isn't for him he feels a buzz in his chest. The intensity of his excitement surprises him. He's desperate to hear her voice and to know she's okay. He's not surprised she called Matty. Not only did she work for the guy but they were great mates.

Jeez, he'll have to tell her what happened to him.

Spike barks.

'What? I'm fine. Nothing.'

Judd looks up from his phone. 'Why is your face flushed?'

'No, it isn't. What?' Corey tries to play dumb and again fails miserably.

'You look like a beetroot. Who called?'

'Umm, well . . . Lola. She left a message.'

Judd stares at him blankly for a moment. 'The one whose boyfriend is Steve Ford?'

'Scott Ford, and thanks for the reminder.'

'You're going to call her back?'

'I'm not, I mean I just . . . ' He trails off.

'As long as you're clear about it.'

Corey's head drops to his chest. 'I don't know what to do.'

'Nothing is what you do. She has a boyfriend. She blew you off.' Judd looks back at his iPhone. 'Why are you even thinking about it?'

'Because when I'm with her it feels – right, like I don't have to do it all on my own. I've never felt that way before. I think I should tell her and see where the chips fall.'

'But you know where they fall. They fall on "I have a boyfriend who is the biggest movie star in the world so thanks for dropping by and don't let the door hit you in the arse on the way out".'

Corey takes this in unhappily.

'I don't mean to sound like a dickhead again, but, really, you don't want to get hurt, or, you know —' He says it in a low voice. '—embarrassed again, do you?'

Corey listens, but his finger still hovers over the iPhone's screen. Does he play the message or not?

Judd watches him. 'Let it go, Blades.' He looks back at his own iPhone's screen then takes in a sharp breath. 'Of course.'

'What?'

'I know what MHS means.'

'And?'

'It's short for Moreno High School. I played baseball there when I was a kid. T-ball actually. That's where I know it from.'

'Why would they – what would be happening at a high school?'

'That's what I'm going to find out —' He glances at his watch. '—in thirty-eight minutes.'

'You're going there?'

'Of course.'

'Shouldn't we tell the cops? About, you know – what happened here?' He nods at the Beverly Hills Police Station in the distance.

'You can. I have to do this.'

'You sure that's a good idea?'

'Absolutely not. It could work out really badly, or I could be going to the wrong place, but if something *is* going down I don't wanna be standing around twiddling my thumbs at some police station.'

'You're doing it again.'

'Doing what?'

'Acting like you're the only one on the planet who can fix anything, like it's your personal responsibility. You've been doing it all day.'

'I just need to do what's right.'

'We all need to do that, mate. What's going on with you? And you need to be fair dinkum with me.'

'I still don't really understand what that means.'

'It means different things at different times, but right now it means tell me the truth.'

Judd stares ahead. 'It's embarrassing.'

'Spill it.'

'Right.' It's difficult to say. 'I just – since – the incident at Imax, I've felt – like a fraud.'

It's not what Corey was expecting to hear. 'What?'

'The *heroic* Judd Bell of the fabled *Atlantis* 4, unable to deal with a single terrorist, couldn't even come up with a *plan*, *cowering* behind a car with a shotgun pointed at his face.'

'That's why you've been running around like a chook with its head cut off, trying to save everyone?'

Judd nods. 'Pretty much, though "chook with its head cut off" seems a tad harsh. I guess, I don't know, I'm – I'm trying to make up for it, be the man the world thinks I am.'

'I didn't have a plan either, mate. Neither did Rhonda. We were all dead if Severson didn't turn up, so don't beat yourself up about it.'

Judd takes it in with a nod, but Corey can tell he doesn't quite believe it. The Australian looks at the iPhone in his hand again. Curiosity gets the better of him and he plays Lola's message.

It's not good. Her voice is reed thin, like she's in pain. She's trapped in a building on Doheny, her leg caught under something heavy. He can't quite work out what it is because the sound is distant and echoey, but she's asking Bowen for help.

Concerned, Corey instantly returns the call. It goes straight to voicemail. 'Bugger.'

Judd turns to him, notices his strained expression. 'Everything okay?'

Corey shakes his head. 'Lola needs help. She's trapped in a building.'

'What? Christ.'

'I need to go there.'

'Where?'

'Doh– Don– Don Henley?'

'*Doheny* Drive. Know how to get there?'

'Just follow the map app.' Corey works the iPhone screen, swiftly finds the location.

'Be careful. LA's a shark pit, if you hadn't noticed.'

'I just spent fifteen minutes dodging exploding chainsaws. I noticed.'

Judd gestures to the chainsaw that lies across his handlebars. 'Do you want to take this? In case.'

'Had more than enough of those for one day.'

'What about the pistol?'

Corey shakes his head. 'Better if you have it, I think. In case.'

Judd nods. 'Okay. Just – let me give you my number.' Corey passes over the iPhone and Judd taps his digits into the address book, then passes it back. 'Be careful.'

'Yes, Mother. *Second* time you said that. I'll be fine.'

They exchange a nod, but it's difficult to say goodbye. To lighten the moment Corey gestures to the bulge in his pants. 'Is that a canister of counteragent in my pocket or am I just happy to be leaving?'

Judd thinks about it, then grimaces. 'That was just weird.'

'It was, wasn't it? It was meant to be funny but ended up being gross.'

Judd grins. 'I'll see you.'

Corey returns it. 'Not if I see you first.' He thinks about it. 'And what does that mean, anyway? Why does it matter if I see you first if we're both seeing each other at the same time?' He pedals off, wobbles violently, finds his balance, increases his pace and rides away. 'Come on, dog.' Spike gallops after him.

Judd watches them go, then rides off in the opposite direction, consults the map on his phone for the fastest route to his destination, then builds speed quickly.

He doesn't feel great about letting Corey ride off on his own. He worries about him like he would a kid brother, feels responsible. After all, he's the one who brought him to this country in the first place.

Judd takes in the road, astounded by the amount of destruction. He doesn't know what he'll find when he reaches the school, but hopes he's up for the challenge. He can feel the weight of the pistol in his jacket pocket. He's glad he has the weapon with him.

Corey pedals the bike so hard Spike has trouble keeping up.

The dog barks.

'Well, you'll just have to lift, won't you? We're in a rush. There's no time for a rest stop.'

Another bark.

'I miss having the chopper, too.' He doesn't add that he's not sure if he'd be able to fly it even if he had one.

Another bark.

'No, I've never seen a "shark pit".'

Another bark.

'I guess it's like a snake pit but worse, because it has sharks.'

Another bark.

'I don't know. It must be full of water otherwise the sharks would be dead and that wouldn't be scary, it'd be sad.'

The Australian takes in the road before him, littered with smoking wrecks and displaced people. The number of buildings and houses on fire is the biggest surprise. He keeps an eye out for any vehicle with a dark exhaust, though it looks like every car has already exploded, is on fire or has been abandoned.

The dog barks once again.

Corey glances at the map app on the iPhone. 'Not far.' He stops pedalling and freewheels past a line of wrecks that litter Doheny, the bike's gears ticking furiously, and scans the road before him. 'Where is it?'

He sees it in the distance, the towering white building with the large blue stripe Lola mentioned in her voice message. It's not that far away –

Boom. The explosion is enormous, blows him off the bike and knocks him clean across the sidewalk. He hits a building ten metres away, then slumps to the ground. It feels like he's been bitch-slapped by Goliath.

His head throbs and his ears ring. He opens his eyes. His vision is blurred. Smoke cloaks the road. He can just make out the burning wreckage of the car that exploded on the opposite side of the street. He pulls himself up unsteadily, the bike crumpled against a shop-front, both wheels buckled, the iPhone smashed on the sidewalk in front of him. He can feel something licking his ankle. He turns to look at it, but his eyelids get very heavy very quickly and he needs to have a little lie down. He rests his head on the warm pavement and can't help but think Judd was right: he really needs to be careful. Maybe if the astronaut had told him a *third* time he would have paid better attention.

Spike bounds over to Corey. His master is unconscious.

The dog barks.

There's no response.

Spike turns, sees the cuff of Corey's left jeans leg is on fire. He barks again.

Corey does not wake up.

Spike trots over to the left cuff, assumes the position and releases a short squirt of urine. The flames are instantly extinguished – but Corey does not wake.

The dog lies down beside him.

28

Finally.

It took Bunsen five one-hundred-litre rhino drums to do it, but the Item is now filled with the Swarm.

He removes the electric water pump's hose, screws on the radiator cap, then uses an oxy-welder to seal it tight. He eases the trolley loaded with the Item out onto the helipad. It's both heavy and unwieldy, but he eventually parks it beside the Tyrannosaur, where Enrico continues to remove the water tank from the airframe. Bunsen then pulls out a swathe of black-green netting from the trolley's bottom shelf, which will be used to camouflage the Item's true shape and nature.

He returns to the garage and rolls out a second trolley. The contents of this one are not as visually arresting as the Item, but just as important to the mission. Bunsen deposits two long bags, one black, the other light grey, into the chopper's rear cabin, then joins Enrico in removing the tank. Once it's detached they will fasten the Item to the Tyrannosaur's airframe.

He glances at his Patek. The only thing he's concerned about at this point is the same thing that has concerned him all day: *Kilroy*. After sending a text about making sure Bunsen posted the video online, the old guy has gone AWOL again, hasn't responded to any texts or picked up his phone.

The old man is really cutting it fine. He should be here by now.

29

'Come on, Scott! Where are you?'

Lola turns and looks at the fire. The flames are much higher now. The insulation is well alight and produces a thick blanket of acrid smoke that hangs in the air and smells like cancer.

She coughs, pushes on the beam that lies across her thigh, can't even lift the damn thing off her leg now. She has no energy and feels nauseous, the charming effects of crush syndrome kicking in as it dumps those deadly chemicals into her system.

She hasn't heard anything from Scott since she spoke to him last. That must have been thirty-five, forty minutes ago. She guesses that's how long it would take for him to get here on foot, which means he should be here any minute. She'd tried 911 a couple more times but couldn't get through.

The flames flare and the smoke billows. Lola realises she's not going to burn to death, or die from the crush injury, she's going to be asphyxiated. She pushes her face low to the ground, the air a little fresher down there, and takes in shallow breaths.

'*Come on*, Scott.' Her head throbs and her lungs are tight and her eyes sting. Jesus Christ, she came in here to take shelter, not to die –

A sound, to the far right.

She turns to it.

Twenty metres away a towering figure is silhouetted through the smoke haze.

She'd know that outline anywhere.

Scott Ford.

The Blue Cyclone.

Yes! He came! Just in the nick of time. The guy is a hero, on screen *and* off. He has something in his hands. A long cylinder – a fire extinguisher! He rushes towards the flames, releases a blast of fire retardant, instantly douses them. He pivots, cuts through the smoke towards her, drops the extinguisher, grabs the beam across her thigh and in one fluid motion lifts it off and tosses it to the side.

Lola's relief is overwhelming. She looks up as he drops through the haze to kneel beside her.

'G'day.'

'*Corey?*'

The Australian looks like he's been to hell and back, his face covered in cuts and soot, blood and grime, his hair singed, clothes ripped, torn and burned. Then he grins his crooked grin. 'Sorry I didn't get here sooner.'

Lola takes him in, stunned, thrilled and confused all at once. It's the strangest feeling.

He sees it. 'You look surprised.'

'I was expecting —' Someone else. She doesn't finish the sentence, changes the subject instead. 'What happened to you?'

'I'm pretty sure it was a Chevy Impala. Or maybe a Buick Riviera. Either way, the explosion was a humdinger. Took a few minutes to wake up. Still feel a bit groggy, actually. How are you?'

'Better now. Thank you.' She nods at the fire extinguisher. 'Where'd you find that?'

'It was on the wall beside the roller door.'

'How'd you know I was here?'

'I, it was – I heard your message. On Bowen's phone.'

'Oh, right. Where is he?'

Corey realises he should have devised a lie so he could delay telling her about Bowen until a more suitable time and place. But then he's terrible at lying, and when he thinks about it there will never be a suitable time and place for news like this. So he tries to find the right words. 'We were at CNN and – and there was an explosion.'

'Oh, God.' Her hand covers her mouth. 'Is he okay?'

Corey blinks, then shakes his head.

'No.' She buries her head in her hands, grief-stricken.

'It was – it happened fast. He didn't suffer. We tried to help, but there was nothing —'

'He's my best friend.' Her tears flow.

Corey rests a hand on her shoulder. 'I'm so sorry.'

Spike moves to Lola, nuzzles against her leg. She rubs his head absently.

A moment passes.

'I didn't want to tell you like this. I just didn't know how else to do it.'

'It's okay.' She wipes her eyes. 'I'm glad you did.'

A harsh squawk bursts from Corey's pants.

Lola looks at him. 'What was that?'

'Sorry.' He dives a hand into his trouser pocket and pulls out Ponytail's walkie-talkie. A distant voice echoes from its speaker: '*Where are you? I haven't heard from you in over an hour. We're on the way to Moreno High now. Do you need assistance?*'

Corey takes it in gravely, thinks aloud. 'Moreno High. Damn. He was right. They really are going there.'

Lola looks at Corey, then the walkie-talkie, then Corey again. 'Who's going where? Who is that?'

'The people responsible for the explosions.'

'Say what?' She looks at him like he's mad.

Corey sees it. 'I know it sounds crazy, but Judd's on the way there and I need to tell him they're coming.'

She's confused. 'To Moreno High School?'

'Yes, but my phone's screwed. Do you have Judd's number?'

'Um, no. We dealt with him through a NASA liaison. And I don't have that number either.' She still doesn't really understand what's going on. 'Why do you need to tell him they're coming?'

Corey's expression is grim. 'Because I'm pretty sure they will try to kill him.'

'What?' She half laughs as she says it because it sounds so strange. 'What are you talking about? Why would they do that?'

'Because they have something else planned and he wants to stop it.'

'What do they have planned?'

He opens his hands wide, palms up. 'No idea.' He nods at her phone. 'Can I borrow that for a sec?' She passes it over and he launches the map app, works the screen.

She watches him. 'What are you doing?

'I need to go there.'

'Moreno High?'

'Yes. Can I . . . run there?'

'Not unless you're training for a marathon. It's on the other side of town.'

Corey stops working the iPhone's screen and exhales. 'Man, I wish I had my chopper.'

'You couldn't fly it anyway. Everything with a combustion engine explodes.'

'Not everything.' From his pocket he draws the aluminium canister containing the counteragent. 'Not if I use this.'

'And that is – what?'

'A counteragent to the virus that's making the engines explode.'

She studies him for a long moment.

'I wouldn't believe me either.'

'No, I . . . actually do.'

'Then why are you looking at me like I'm insane?'

'I'm not. I'm having a thought – which I'm turning into an idea.'

'And it is?'

'Hero car.'

His brow furrows. 'You've lost me. What does that mean?'

'It means I think I know a quick way to Moreno High.' She stands, gingerly puts weight on her injured leg and winces.

'How's it feeling?'

'*Fuck!* is how it's feeling, excuse my French.' She puts a little more weight on it. 'I need to run it off. Come on, follow me.'

They move quickly, navigate the dent in the roller door and step out onto the sidewalk. The sky is slate grey with a purple hue, much darker than it was before Lola took cover in the building. Fat tendrils of purple-grey smoke hang above the bitumen like serpents in the still afternoon air. The road is littered with the burning shells of vehicles, including the charred remains of the semitrailer that exploded and caused Lola to be trapped in the first place.

'This way.' She points them left and they jog down a quiet side street that has not seen much action. Even with a painful leg, Lola is quick. Corey follows, a little confused. 'So we're going to the school?'

'Yes. It won't take long. I want you to tell me everything, but I need to make a call first.'

'Sure. Okay.' Corey gets the hint and drops behind her a polite distance, Spike in tow.

She dials the phone and puts it to her ear. The call is answered.

'Hello?'

'Scott?'

'This is he.'

She can barely hear his voice over a high-pitched flapping noise. It's a familiar sound, but she can't quite place it. 'Hey, it's Lola.'

'How are you, sweetness? I was just about to call.'

'Are you close?'

'Well, we haven't made a lot of headway —'

'Are the roads gridlocked?'

'Yeah, it's pretty bad, the gridlock.'

The flapping returns and momentarily drowns out his voice. What *is* that sound?

'I can't hear you. Where are you? Are you okay?'

'We're – yeah – we're fine.'

'I got out.'

'That's great to hear.'

The flapping returns, and just like that she knows what the sound is. 'Are you on a *boat*?'

'Actually it's a yacht.' The noise is a sail flapping in the breeze. 'I was told it's the safest place to be at the moment. No engines. Just wind power.'

There is a long silence.

Lola breaks it. 'So, let me recap. I was trapped under a beam in a building and you said you'd come and help me, but instead you went sailing. Is that right?'

'Oh, don't be that way, sweetness. It was just a management call.'

'You manage yourself.'

'I didn't say it was an *easy* call, but I knew you'd be okay. You're resourceful. That's what I like about you.'

She keeps jogging and takes a breath. Her first impulse is to launch the full *Bitchkrieg*, verbally destroy him, ridicule his acting as a pants-down humiliation, tell him the town regards him as the Derek Zoolander of action movies and wonders if he'll ever perfect a second facial expression, explain that no one except him thinks *Avatar* would have been better if the humans had defeated 'those blue hippies', clarify that he only has a career because God hates Mel Gibson and remind him that with every moment he grows older and less worthy of the public's attention.

But what, exactly, would be the point of that? Sure, she'd feel like a hero for fifteen seconds, but she works in a business where criminals and bullies roam free and the careers of good women die like dogs in the street, or at least fade into anonymity, if they don't work every angle to keep their head above water. As Scott is currently the biggest gorilla in every room of this town, she should hold on to this golden chit and cash it in the future, not blow it on some meaningless tirade now. So she decides to cool her jets and play the long game. She feigns bad reception: 'I —an't hear yo— Sco—' and ends the call.

She looks up, takes in a gigantic billboard of Scott Ford as *The Blue Cyclone,* which looms above the roadway. It must be ten metres long and three metres tall and highlights his ripped and buffed physique under blue tights.

It's on fire.

She watches the billboard burn and has an epiphany. She's an idiot. That guy was never right for her. How could she have not seen it? Well, she knows how: she was swayed by all the wrong things. The guy is good-looking, he's an action star, he's successful and has plenty of industry cache. She had wilfully disregarded the fact he was vain and shallow and didn't have her best interests at heart. She knows there's only one thing she can do about that. From now on she must date *men* instead of *boys*. The problem is she's not very good at working out which is which because age has nothing to do with identifying them.

There was one guy she knew who was a man, the guy she'd worked with for the last decade. She turns to Corey behind her. 'Sorry about that. Can you tell me what happened to Matty? Please?'

'Of course.' The Australian catches up to her, Spike right beside him, and lays it out in broad brushstrokes. She appreciates that he doesn't weigh her down with the awful specifics, but she needs enough detail to get it straight in her mind, so she interjects from time to time and asks for clarification.

When he finishes she doesn't say anything for a good while. They run on in silence, both breathing hard now, the distant bang and pop of explosions filling the space between them. She wipes at her wet cheeks, realises it's going to take a long time to come to terms with what happened. She takes a breath and pushes the pain way down, so she doesn't have to think about it now. She needs to concentrate on getting through this day in one piece, and helping the man who just helped her. She turns to Corey. 'Thank you. You're being – great.'

'No wuckers.'

'After last night I didn't think you'd talk to me again.'

'Well, you said you wanted to be mates, so, you know, *this* is mates.'

'Guess it is.' And it *is* mates. She can see the spark has left his blue eyes, the one that was there every time they'd met in the past. She now realises how much she misses it. It's gone and has been replaced with a polite, reserved distance.

Corey scans the destruction on the roadway. 'Gotta say I'm looking forward to getting out of this town.'

'Where are you going?'

'We're going to head down to the Florida Keys.'

'For a holiday?'

'No. I'm thinking about moving down there. Maybe start a business.'

'Right. Well, great. It is beautiful.' This news actually throws Lola more than what just happened with Scott, which had been disappointing, but predictable. This is – well, an unhappy surprise. But then what did she expect? Last night she'd dropped the Aussie like a hot potato and now he's moving on.

Corey feels surprisingly good. He's happy he was able to help Lola out of her predicament but the fact is she chose another guy over him, who, he is almost certain, she was just on the phone to. Judd was right. He has to let it go and move on and that's exactly what he is doing.

They turn a corner and stop dead. Before them a gigantic sound stage – it must be forty metres high – burns fiercely and pumps black smoke into the sky. Again, there are no fire engines or fire fighters in sight.

Corey takes it in. 'What is this place?'

Lola looks around, stunned. 'What's left of Twentieth Century Fox.'

Corey sees the company's logo and immediately recognises it from a bunch of his favourite movies – *Star Wars*, *Aliens*, *Independence Day*. He remembers hearing something about the guy who owned the joint. He can't remember his name but he used to be an Aussie but decided to become a Yank. He must have had a really good reason because Corey couldn't imagine why anyone would want to do that.

Lola points the way forward. 'Down here.'

They run on, pass through the main gate. There are no guards around and the boom has been smashed by a speeding vehicle, which, it would seem, then exploded and burned the guardhouse to the ground. The place is all but deserted. Two vehicles lie smouldering on the road that cuts through the studio, another three buildings are well alight from vehicles that have exploded nearby, and a smattering of people mill around, dazed and confused. No one tries to stop them, no one even tries to speak to them.

'Is it much further?'

Lola leads them onwards. 'Almost there. So, tell me, how did you end up with this counteragent?'

'Well, right after the CNN building collapsed we saw a school bus . . .'

30

Kilroy drags himself clear of the godforsaken tyre. It took much longer than he expected. Pushing the damn thing over his elbows proved to be the hardest part.

He reaches into his jacket pocket for his phone. Not there. 'Shit!' He left it in the car. He searches for his walkie-talkie. He knew there was a possibility the mobile phone system might crash after the Swarm was released so he'd prepared a back-up plan. All members of the crew were given a small, hand-held Midland walkie-talkie, chosen for its thirty-kilometre range.

It's gone. What the hell happened to it?

The *Atlantis* 4 boys, no doubt.

'Pricks.'

Hopefully his iPhone is still in the car, in one piece.

He pulls himself up, moves through the parking garage stiffly, his back aching, and exits to see what is left of both cars. Not much. They are burned up, almost unrecognisable. His iPhone is clearly toast. Now he's going to have to find a payphone to call Bunsen. A *working* payphone? In *LA*! Even on a good day, when the city isn't in chaos, that's an all but impossible task.

He sets a course for Santa Monica Boulevard. It's not that far away and seems like a good place to start looking.

31

Lola punches through the thick layer of smoke which blankets the Twentieth Century Fox backlot and sprints past a large sound stage. Corey and Spike are right behind her.

Corey just told Lola everything that happened today, from the dying guy in the ambulance to the old ponytailed mofo in the Prius to the chainsaws in the police station. Only by saying it out loud did he realise how much he'd been through, and how bonkers it was. It's not what he expected when he woke up this morning.

'How much longer?' He really wants to be on his way to Moreno High School as quickly as possible, hopes this detour isn't a wild goose chase.

'Almost there. This way.' Lola ducks down a narrow walkway that cuts between two towering buildings. She seems to know exactly where she's going and what she's doing, which alleviates his concern a little.

They reach the end of the walkway and run towards another long building, about half the size of the sound stages. Lola leads them to the main door and works the handle. It's locked. She knocks. No answer. 'We need to get in here —'

Corey hits the door just above the handle with the heel of his boot and the door flies open. Lola is impressed. 'Well, okay then.'

They enter the pitch-black room. Lola reaches out, feels along the wall for a light switch, touches something that resembles a button and presses it. Instead of lights blinking on, a large roller door at the far end of the room clanks, then rolls towards the roof. Blazing light spills inside and illuminates the machine in the centre of the room.

Corey stares at it, astonished. 'You've gotta be kidding me.'

Spike barks.

Corey has to stop himself from answering the dog and confirming that they aren't seeing things. The Australian knows he needs to get moving, needs to help Judd, but he's frozen in place.

It's *his* Loach.

Or at least a perfect replica of his Huey OH-06 helicopter, nicknamed 'Loach' after its designation LOH (Light Observation Helicopter) during its service with the US Army in Vietnam.

Corey turns to Lola, opens his mouth to say something, but nothing emerges. He is gobsmacked.

Lola speaks instead. 'It's the hero car from the *Atlantis 4* movie – except, it's not a car, obviously.'

'But – how?'

'Remember the guy you spoke to on the phone a while back? The one with all the questions? We emailed him those photos you had in your wallet? Well, he's in charge of art design on the *Atlantis 4* movie. Anyway, we represent him, so I took a personal interest in the project, wanted to make sure they got it right.'

'Well, they got it right.'

The chopper is perfect. It's doorless, painted yellow, with 'Blades of Corey' emblazoned on the side, and has all the rust and scorch marks just where he left them. He steps forward, studies the fuselage, realises the rust marks are not rust at all, but skilfully applied and coloured plaster. It even has automobile side-view mirrors bolted to each side of the fuselage. It's uncanny, the attention to detail astounding – and he knows this chopper well. Corey had used it every day of his life for a decade in Central Australia, until it was shot down over the Pacific Ocean by the German hijacker, Dirk Popankin, last year.

He can feel moisture at the corner of his eyes. Jeez. He didn't realise how much he missed the damn thing. 'Can it fly?'

'That's why we're here. They started camera tests with it last week.'

Corey peers into the cabin. It's exactly the same as he remembers, the beaten-up cassette deck under the instrument panel, the old tapes strewn across the floor, everything from Player to REO Speedwagon to Def Leppard, the large loudspeaker attached under the fuselage, the winch with the blue, high-tension rope positioned between the front seats above a rough-cut hole in the floor, an assortment of hooks lying in a perfect copy of his lucky bucket. There's even the brass telescope in the leather pouch beside the pilot's seat. Everything's the same – except for the two parachutes under the rear bench.

'Parachutes? We didn't use parachutes.' Corey had parachuted out of planes a few times in the past, but didn't enjoy the sensation of freefalling. He'd certainly never jumped out of a chopper.

'In the latest draft of the screenplay, when the chopper is destroyed and you jump out, you're wearing a parachute. The studio thought it was more believable. I was going to tell you.'

Corey's eyes narrow. 'But we did it without parachutes in *real life* —' He catches himself. 'Forget it, we need to get going.'

He takes in the small helipad beyond the open roller door then slides into the pilot seat and wakes the little chopper's instrument panel. Gauges spring to life and lights blink on and his eyes find the fuel gauge. The tank is full, which means they have 242 litres of avgas on board. At one drop of counteragent for every litre of av-gas he can only hope there's enough in the metal canister. He climbs out of the cabin, unscrews the Loach's fuel tank cap, taps the code into the canister's keypad, unlocks the lid, then tips the contents into the tank. He saves a portion, a tenth maybe, which he thinks – hopes – will be enough for it to be analysed, and synthesised, if necessary. He realises how lucky it was that they used the counteragent from Judd's canister for the chainsaw back at the police station.

Lola watches. 'Is there anything I can do?'

'Stand well clear.' He points to the far side of the room, near the open roller door. She moves there quickly, Spike in tow, and turns to watch.

Corey cranks the Loach's engine to life. A light clicking emanates from the turbine, then it catches and spools up. He turns and studies the stream of exhaust from the chopper, ready to kill the power if need be. 'Please-no-purple-please-no-purple.'

There's no sign of purple in the exhaust.

Lola calls out: 'So far so good!'

Corey nods. 'Yep, it looks okay.'

Then the exhaust turns a light shade of purple.

'No!' Corey and Lola say it at the same time.

It gets dark fast.

'Jeezus.' Corey kills the power and studies the canister in his hand. 'I need to use all of it.'

Lola approaches. 'Why didn't you before?'

'Wanted to save some, in case it needs to be synthesised later.' He unscrews the fuel tank cap again and pours in every last drop, hopes to God Judd isn't doing the same thing somewhere right now, then cranks the turbine once more. It spools up.

They watch the exhaust.

It's purple immediately.

Corey's head drops, the disappointment crushing. He reaches to shut down the turbine.

Spike barks.

Corey looks up at the exhaust again. The purple hue fades – then disappears completely. He exhales, his relief enormous. 'Okay, let's go. Everyone in.' He nods at Spike. 'The back.' The dog jumps in.

Lola looks confused. She takes in the twenty metres between the chopper and the roller door. 'Don't we need to push it out?'

'She'll be right. Hop in and belt up and put on the headset.' She does it, then he does the same himself.

Jeez. He almost forgot. This is the first time he's flown in almost a year. He takes a breath. Okay. His hands work a series of switches and the rotor blades turn. He feels right at home. All good so far. He was worried that being shot down will come back and bite him on the arse, but he's fine. Absolutely fine! Fine *and* dandy, in fact! His feet touch the tail rotor pedals as his hands find the cyclic stick and collective lever –

He freezes – and flashes back to that moment over the Pacific when his Loach was blown out of the sky.

Damn-it-damn-it-damn-it-damn-it-damn-it-damn-it!

It's come back to bite him on the arse.

Lola's voice fills his headset. 'Are you okay?'

He nods, breathes out. 'Yep, I'm good.' But he isn't good. At all. He feels sweaty and panicked. *Panicked!* Not once in his life has he felt panicked while flying a chopper, even when he was *nine years old* and on his first solo. And it's happening in front of Lola! How bloody embarrassing! What the hell is he going to do?

Spike pushes himself between the front seats and rests a paw on his master's arm.

Corey looks at him.

The dog barks – and Corey listens as he lays it out. Corey's done this a million times before. Being shot down was not his fault. Judd needs his help right now so man up and get on with it.

Corey takes a breath and nods. 'Yep.'

It's like a switch has been flicked. His self-doubt instantly recedes. He takes the controls in hand and throttles up. Ever so gently the chopper lifts three inches off the ground then tilts forward and skims the ground towards the open roller door –

And blasts outside.

Corey threads the Loach through the tangle of buildings on the Fox lot then pulls it into a steep climb.

Lola's impressed. She's never seen him fly before. His deft touch with the chopper is quite something. She turns and watches the ground fall away and for the first time sees the scope of destruction across the city. It's horrifying. Everywhere she looks a pyre of smoke reaches for the heavens.

'Where are we going?'

She completes a quick scan of their surroundings, gets her bearings, then points left. 'That way.'

Corey works the controls and tilts the little chopper into a steep turn.

Next stop Moreno High School.

32

Twelve minutes.

That's how long it takes Kilroy to find a working payphone on Santa Monica Boulevard. He's surprised it happens so fast.

The bigger surprise is the sheer number of walking wounded on the street. They are everywhere, thousands of dazed and injured people. It makes him sick to his stomach. He understands what Bunsen is trying to accomplish with the Swarm, but this is wrong, worse than 'collateral damage'. *Much worse.* These people should have been warned – and *must* be warned before Phase Three begins in earnest.

Thump, thump, thump. Kilroy looks up from his spot beside the payphone and scans the dark sky. That sound can only mean one thing –

With a hurricane blast of rotor wash, the Tyrannosaur swoops low, then drops quickly and settles onto the only clear spot on the road, fifty metres away. Kilroy runs towards it.

An old guy slumped against a nearby shopfront, his face blackened with soot and one trouser legs burned away, shouts at him in a hysterical voice: 'No! Don't go near it! It'll explode!'

Kilroy ignores the advice, picks his way through the wrecked cars, ducks under the thundering rotors and pulls open the chopper's rear cabin door. He steps in, buckles up and pulls on his headset, all without meeting Bunsen's eyes.

The chopper rises off the roadway.

Kilroy can't see Bunsen's face from the rear cabin, but as soon as he pulls on the headset he can hear his voice. 'Nice of you to join us.'

Kilroy knows he's angry. He only uses sarcasm when he's really pissed off and this unscheduled detour has done just that.

'What the hell happened?'

'Judd Bell.'

'What?' Bunsen is stunned. 'You mean – *the astronaut*?'

'Yes. He's with the Australian, the other one from the *Atlantis* 4, you know, with the dog.'

'Can't remember his name but he was funny on Jon Stewart. Are you sure about this?'

'I saw them up close after the Prius was destroyed.'

'How did that happen?'

Kilroy takes a breath and runs through the whole sorry tale, doesn't try to dress up the truth or leave anything out because he knows Bunsen will see straight through it.

'*Did* they get the counteragent?'

'They had a conversation with Alvy before he died and then they were at his apartment so I'm guessing yes.'

Bunsen winces. 'Jesus. It was your job to *contain* this.'

'Tell me what you want me to do.'

Bunsen thinks long and hard. 'We continue as planned, then we hunt them down.'

No one speaks for a moment, then Kilroy breaks the silence: 'Have you posted the video yet?'

'No.'

'It should be the priority, Zac.' If Bunsen didn't yet understand how important this issue was to Kilroy he would now: Bunsen may have only used sarcasm when he was pissed off with Kilroy, but

Kilroy only used Bunsen's first name when he was pissed off with Bunsen. 'People need a chance to leave the city before Phase Three begins —'

'We'll do it as soon as the prep work is complete. There's no point warning anybody about anything until we know all the elements are in place and functioning. Thanks to this little detour we're now behind schedule.'

Kilroy concedes the point begrudgingly. 'Understood.' He turns and looks out the rear window, watches the smoke haze whip past. He will hold Bunsen to his word.

33

Judd pedals the bike hard.

He glances at his Ploprof. He's late. If the information in Ponytail's iPhone is accurate, whatever's happening at MHS began fifteen minutes ago. He hopes he hasn't missed it.

He pulls out his iPhone and dials Rhonda once again. No joy. It goes straight to voicemail. Listening to her voice on the message makes him feel better for a moment. Man, he really hopes she's okay. He hangs up and pockets the phone –

A bald guy bursts from behind a van and charges Judd, his expression hostile. Legs pumping, Bald Guy closes fast, extends his hands to grab the astronaut –

Judd pulls his pistol and points it directly between Bald Guy's eyes. 'Fuck off!' Bald Guy throws up his hands and stops running, watches the bike speed away, clearly pissed off at the missed opportunity.

Judd ups his pace, pushes the pistol back into his belt line. 'Christ.' *That's* how valuable bikes are now. They're the only viable transport in town. *Bicycles rule LA*. In a city built for automobiles, the car capital of the world no less, who'd have imagined that would ever happen?

He sees a Caltex service station to the right. It is, unsurprisingly, not only deserted, but filled with the smoking hulks of burned-out vehicles. Judd mounts the kerb, rides into the station and pulls up beside the only gas pump that hasn't been destroyed by an explosion or melted by fire. The chainsaw still lies across the handle bars. He quickly fills its gas tank then rides on.

He takes a quick left then sees it in the distance: Moreno High School. It is dominated by a single piece of architecture that towers fifty metres above everything else. The soaring edifice, like a boxy, unsophisticated rocket ship, or a very thin ziggurat, is clad in soundproof panels painted with swirling flowers to conceal its true identity. The paint job isn't fooling anyone. Everyone knows it's an oil derrick.

Yes, an *oil derrick*. Only in LA would an oil-drilling island be built *inside* a school. Judd remembers he was covered in a fine spray of 'black gold' during the games he played there. He didn't recall the details, but the school pretty much had every facility it needed because of those oil wells. The company that operated the drilling island paid a generous stipend for every barrel of oil they produced a year – and they produced a lot, around five hundred a day.

Thump, thump, thump. Judd glances up as a helicopter thunders overhead. For a moment he thinks it must be LAPD, then he gets a better look and realises it's one of those giant, water-bombing Air-Cranes. Didn't he see one earlier today? His next thought is that it must be on loan to the fire brigade –

Wait a second! How is that thing even flying? Why hasn't it exploded?

The answer is in his jacket pocket. He unconsciously touches the canister of counteragent. That chopper must be using it. How else is it flying? He watches it slow, bank to the right, then descend – directly towards the school.

Judd increases his pace and sets a course for the oil derrick.

•

The oil derrick towers above Judd, fifty metres to his right.

He turns into a narrow alleyway that runs adjacent to the oil drilling island. An eight-foot chain-link gate blocks his path. He dismounts the bike, throws it over, then, chainsaw in hand, scales the fence. He drops to the other side and moves along the alleyway, the drilling island's cinderblock wall to the left, open ground to the right.

He can hear the Air-Crane's turbines howl though he can't see the chopper. It's so loud he knows it must be close, guesses it's parked on the baseball diamond that sits behind the oil drilling island.

Ka-boom! An explosion shakes the air. Judd looks right. A fireball rolls into the sky directly above the drilling island. A moment later, a shower of white-hot metal shards rains down. He takes cover against the wall as they clink and thud onto the road. 'What the hell is that?'

He props the bike against the cinderblock wall, steps onto its seat, levers himself up and looks over. He can't see much except a tangle of pipes and reservoir tanks. He pulls himself over, drops into the drilling island and draws the 9mm pistol from his jacket, does it almost nonchalantly. A year ago he'd never held a gun in his hand but now he's well practised with a weapon. He doesn't know if that's a good or a bad thing but it certainly feels like a necessary thing because he's making this up as he goes along. He doesn't have a plan because he doesn't know what to plan for.

His eyes flick from the pistol in his right hand to the chainsaw in his left – he's sure it will come in handy for something, but what, exactly, he does not know. He moves deeper into the facility, navigates those pipes and tanks, searches for what he does not know. The sound of the Air-Crane is even louder in here, the shriek of its turbines magnified as it bounces and echoes off the hard surfaces.

He rounds a three-metre-tall reservoir tank and sees a man in the distance. He studies the remains of a destroyed wellhead. On the ground in front of him a stream of oil flows out of a five-inch-wide pipe. He turns, kneels and from a long grey bag pulls out what looks like an aluminium baseball bat, but is in fact a three-foot-long, three-inch-wide cylinder with a two-inch-wide propeller at one end. He works his iPhone's screen and the propeller spins up. He then slides the cylinder down the pipe and it disappears.

The man consults his iPhone for a moment, grins, then zips up the long bag, slings it over this shoulder and turns to leave –

Judd stands in front of him, points the pistol at his chest. 'What are you doing?'

The man stops. He is, Judd realises, movie-star handsome. He is also surprised but not unhappy to see the astronaut. 'Well, well, *Judd Bell* from the *Atlantis* 4. I heard you'd been gumming up the works today.'

Judd steps forward, aims the pistol at his chest. 'I said, what are you doing?'

'You'll know very soon.'

Click. A pistol is cocked. Judd glances left, sees Ponytail aim a 9mm pistol directly at his temple. 'Drop it.'

Judd takes a moment – then reluctantly complies.

Handsome Guy steps forward and studies Judd, surprised. 'Wow, you're *terrible* at this.'

Bunsen takes in the astronaut with a keen interest. 'I was expecting you to be taller.'

Judd glares at him. 'Why did you do it?'

'Do what?'

'Release the Swarm.'

'So Alvy told you what it's called?'

'Is he the guy –?'

'Husky fella. Frizzy hair. Multiple bullet wounds. You met him in the ambulance.'

Judd nods. 'Yeah.'

'The short answer is that I did it for motivation. To jump start the use of renewable energy so mankind no longer chokes this planet to death with greenhouse gas. That's also the long answer.'

It's not what Judd expected to hear. 'That's crazy.'

'I don't know about *that*. It's better than your idea. I saw you on TV a while back, I think it was *Nightline*. What did you say?' Bunsen tries to remember. 'Something about colonising Mars because, once Earth is uninhabitable, we'll need to go somewhere else and start again.' He looks at Judd. 'That's right, isn't it?'

Judd just stares at him.

'I'll take your blank gaze as a yes. So we agree on the problem. We just differ on the solution. I think mine's better than yours, though. At least I want to save the planet. You just want to abandon it. And *that*, to me, is crazy.'

'What you did today is not a solution.'

'Actually, it is, and it's a pretty good one, even if I do say so myself.' Bunsen moves toward Judd, pushes a hand into his jacket pocket and pulls out the canister of counteragent. 'There it is.' He shows it to Kilroy with a smile. 'Wasn't so hard to find after all. Now all we have to do is locate the Australian.' Bunsen turns to Judd. 'Any idea where he might be?'

Judd ignores the question, nods at the destroyed wellhead beside them. 'What are you doing here?'

'Remember a couple of minutes ago, right after we met, when you asked exactly the same question, and I said "you'll know very soon"?'

Judd nods.

'I lied.' Bunsen nods at Kilroy, who steps forward, aims his pistol at the back of Judd's head and pulls the trigger –

Boom! The explosion is huge.

And no one expects it except Judd.

Handsome and Ponytail flinch as the blast wave hits and shrapnel rains down. Before they can regain their composure, Judd is in motion. He swings a knee, nails Ponytail in the gut and knocks him on his arse, then pivots, sweeps Handsome Guy's legs and snatches the canister from his hands as he falls. 'Wow, you're *terrible* at this.'

Judd doesn't have the time to bend and grab his pistol so he kicks it like a football. It flies ten metres and lands beside a reservoir tank. He sprints after it.

Ponytail recovers and swings his weapon towards the astronaut but he ducks behind the tank –

Ping. The bullet ricochets as Judd takes cover, glad he bought the chainsaw with him, happy no one heard it over the rasp of the chopper's turbine before it exploded. He picks up the pistol.

Ping, ping, ping. Three more bullets strafe the tank. Judd pulls in a rough breath and moves fast, ducks low, weaves through the maze of pipes until he reaches a heavy door built into a cinderblock wall. He twists the handle. Locked. *Of course!* He sizes up the wall. It's about three metres high. He steps onto the door's handle, grabs the top of the wall, levers himself up, clambers over, drops to the other side – and lands at the edge of a beautifully manicured baseball diamond, the one he'd played on as a boy.

The matte-black Air-Crane looms before him like some kind of enormous, mutant grasshopper. It's parked fifty metres away in the outfield. A man sits in the cockpit, but what draws Judd's eye is the gigantic appendage that hangs from the centre of the chopper's airframe. 'Appendage' is the only way he can think to describe it. It's an oval shape and is covered in what looks like dark green camouflage netting.

What the hell is it?

He's sure it's important but he needs to get a closer look at it.

Judd sprints across the baseball diamond towards it, his feet kicking up red dirt as he goes. The guy in the Air-Crane's cockpit sees him almost immediately and disappears from view. What's he doing? Either hiding or arming himself. The astroanut's finger tightens around the pistol's trigger and prepares for a fire fight.

He approaches the appendage quickly. From twenty-five metres away he can make out what's beneath the camouflage netting.

Christalmighty.

He realises 'appendage' is not the right word. *Bomb* is. And he could also add 'giant friggin' to that because it is the single largest weapon Judd has ever seen. It looks like three huge bombs – are they *bunker busters*? – have been welded together with metal pipes.

Judd runs on. If he can take out the Air-Crane with a bullet to one of its turbines then maybe he can end this thing now. He raises the pistol and aims –

Thud. The pain in his left thigh is horrendous. He falls and his elbow slams into the ground, jars the pistol from his hand. It bounces across the dirt in front of him. He looks back.

Gun raised, Bunsen steps through the door in the cinderblock wall then strides across the diamond towards him.

Judd turns to his pistol. It's five metres away and out of reach.

He is screwed.

34

The song reverberates across the baseball diamond and momentarily drowns out the Air-Crane's engines.

It's a tune both old and familiar, summer ear candy from a more innocent age. White soul vocal harmonies float above the melodic tinkle of electric piano as an electric guitar gently shreds in the background. 'Baby come back . . . '

'*That's* how it goes.' Judd looks up to identify the source of Player's 1977 number-one power ballad and sees a yellow shape punch out of the grey smog, fifty metres above, two hundred metres away.

It's like something from a dream.

'How is that possible?' He must be hallucinating from the bullet wound. He blinks, then focuses again. It's no dream. It's a bright yellow, doorless Huey Loach, exactly like the one Corey flew in the Northern Territory. The song blasts from the speaker beneath its fuselage.

'Blades!' He lets out a delighted laugh. Two unrelated thoughts swirl through Judd's mind. Where on earth did Corey get that chopper, and that song will be *perfect* for the *Atlantis 4* movie.

The Loach swoops towards him. Fast.

Eyes locked on Judd, Corey kills the music. His mate is injured and lying in the middle of a dusty baseball diamond as some guy advances on him with a pistol in hand.

'Drop the hook!'

Beside him Lola works the winch. The hook and rope plummet towards the ground. 'It's away. Will he know what to do?'

Jaw set and face grim, Corey's eyes move from Judd to the gunman heading towards him. 'I bloody hope so.'

Judd watches the hook hit the ground and drag along the dust. It's a hundred metres away and moves fast.

Gobsmacked, Bunsen sees the yellow chopper close in, then follows the rope to the hook that dangles below it. It takes a moment before he realises what's happening.

He turns back to Judd Bell and raises the pistol. That prick cannot leave with the counteragent.

Lola sees it and points. 'I guess you were right about them wanting to kill him.'

'Change of plans. Hold on!' Corey tips the Loach into a steep dive – directly towards the gunman.

Bunsen squeezes the trigger.

Whomp. A blast of dirt from the baseball diamond slams into him, knocks him sideways. He stumbles, just manages to stay on his feet.

The little yellow chopper thunders overhead, then banks hard left and swoops towards the astronaut. Bunsen recovers his footing, aims at Judd again – and can't see him through the dust cloud. He fires anyway.

Judd doesn't hear the bullet zip overhead because the sound of the Loach's turbine is so loud. And he can't see the hook because it's lost in the dust cloud. He can see the rope, though.

Thump, thump, thump. The Loach skims over him with a metre to spare – then the dust cloud rolls in and he loses sight of the rope too. He guesses where it is and grabs at it.

He misses.

'Do we have him?' Corey drags the little chopper into a tight turn, its turbine wailing.

Lola hangs out the side of the cabin and stares down at the blanket of dust. 'I can't see anything! There's too much dust!'

Judd reaches into the dust again –

Wham. His left hand catches the hook and it yanks him along the ground, his shoulder screaming blue murder. He reaches down with his right hand, snags the pistol and jams it into his belt. His hand is slick with blood from the wound on his leg and slips on the hook.

Corey's heart is in his mouth. 'Do we have him?'

Lola strains to see. 'I can't – he's there! He's holding the hook!'

Corey exhales in relief. 'Okay, hold on.'

He powers up.

The Loach rises quickly. 'Whoa!' Judd's yanked skyward and his left hand slips off the hook –

Wham. His right hand grabs it.

From the rear cabin of the Tyrannosaur, Bunsen pulls out the long black bag, unzips it, extracts the two sections of an SA-7 Grail man-portable, shoulder-fired, low-altitude surface-to-air missile (SAM) and snaps the warhead into the firing canister. With a high explosive, one-and-a-half-kilo warhead and passive infrared homing guidance system, the Russian-designed rocket has more than enough firepower for this job.

This SAM and four others just like it were stolen from Gaddafi's personal weapons depot in Libya after he was overthrown and Bunsen bought all five, at a million bucks apiece. Yes, they were expensive, but they were just the insurance policy he needed after the RPG's range proved ineffective when he stole the bunker busters. He knew the SAMs would come in handy, though the fact he's firing one at a world-famous astronaut as he dangles at the end of a rope beneath a canary yellow Huey Loach, is quite a surprise.

He hefts the weapon to his shoulder and aims at the rising chopper.

'What is that?' Lola peers down at the man on the baseball diamond. 'There's a guy down there with a – is that – he has a rocket launcher!'

Corey scans the surrounding area, takes in a cluster of skyscrapers to the far left and nods to himself.

Lola looks at him. 'Why are you nodding?'

'Because I have a plan.'

'Did you hear me when I said the thing about the rocket launcher?'

'*That*'s why I have a plan.'

Lola's eyes flick back to the baseball diamond. 'The guy he's, he's – oh – he fired it!'

Horrified, she watches the missile zip low across the baseball field, trailing thick white exhaust behind it. Then it changes direction abruptly and shoots upwards, directly towards the Loach. 'It's coming straight at us!' Her voice cracks in terror.

Corey glances in the side-view mirror and sees the missile approach. 'Fasten your seatbelt and hold on.'

She does up her belt then looks around the cabin. 'You keep saying "hold on" except there's nowhere to hold on to except the doorframe —'

Corey wrenches the controls and the Loach tips into a steep dive.

'Ohsweetbabyjesus!' Lola grabs the doorframe and grits her teeth.

'Faark!' Judd holds the hook tight as the rope swings him back, then jolts him forward. It's like he's riding a flying fox from hell.

He sees the missile hiss towards him. Man, it's quick. It's like he's watching it in fast forward. He points the pistol at it and fires.

Bam. It has no effect whatsoever. He jams the gun into his belt and seizes the hook with both hands as the rope swings him back, then jolts him forward again.

The roadway rushes up to greet him.

'Oh, damn.'

Corey yanks on the controls, pulls the chopper up just twenty metres above the road.

Which means Judd is only *five* metres above the ground at the end of the rope. He hurtles towards a burning fire truck that's directly in front of him. 'What the hell? Pull up! Pull up!'

Corey can't hear or see him. His eyes are locked on the rear-view mirror and the missile that follows. It's close, just thirty metres away.

Spike's head is pushed out the rear of the pilot's door and he looks down. He barks.

'*What?*' Corey looks forward and sees the fire truck below. 'Judd!' He pulls the chopper up and tips it hard left.

'Yaah!' Judd is jerked right and swings out like he's at the end of a pendulum. He pulls his legs up so they don't spank the burning fire truck, can feel the heat as they pass through its flames.

'Is he okay?'

Spike looks down and barks.

Corey lets out a relieved breath. 'Good.'

The Loach shoots along a narrow street, fifty metres above the ground, skyscrapers towering on either side.

The Aussie glances in the side-view mirror. The missile is still there, fifty metres away and closing. Fast.

Spike barks.

'I see it!'

Oh, damn. Corey realises he's been talking to Spike. He glances at Lola to see her reaction, but he's sure she didn't hear anything. She's hunched over, her eyes are jammed shut and her face is drained of colour, one hand clamped to the doorframe and the other gripping her seat.

'You okay?'

'I'd like to go home now.'

'It's going to be fine.'

'I don't know if I can do this.'

'You're already doing it. Now come on, eyes open! I need you to navigate. I don't know these streets.'

In the short time she's known him, Lola's never heard Corey speak like that. His tone is gentle but tough and compels her to snap out of it. She takes a breath, opens her eyes and nods stoically. He shoots her a reassuring wink. It's incredibly corny and completely genuine and makes her feel better.

'Find me a tall building.'

'How tall?'

'Biggest you got.'

She nods, thinks about it for a moment. 'Take the next left.'

On the street below, an intersection quickly approaches.

'This one or the next–?'

'This one!'

He yanks on the controls and the chopper tilts hard right, makes the turn down a narrow road.

'Ohmijeez!' Judd swings out – holds on for dear life as a building brushes past his feet just a metre away. He's almost horizontal to the ground, hangs there for what seems like an eternity – then swings back down.

He looks up the rope, realises the higher up he is the better his chance of not being thrown off, or hitting one of these buildings. He puts his right hand above his left and hauls himself upward.

Corey stares at the missile in the side-view mirror. It's not as close as it was.

'Where now?'

'Third street on the right.'

The missile closes in and he loses sight of it. 'Need a visual on that rocket. It's in my blind spot.'

Spike and Lola both look back. Spike barks as Lola says: 'Twenty metres away.' Corey hears the information in stereo.

The Loach thunders past the first street.

'It's getting closer!' Lola's voice rises as she says it.

Corey tries to increase power but the chopper is already at its maximum speed. 'If this bloody thing was any slower it'd be going backwards.'

'*Really* close now!'

'Does it have to be the third street?'

'The third!'

Corey looks in the side-view mirror again. The missile hoves into view, fills the mirror.

'You sure?'

'Absolutely!'

They pass the second street.

The missile surges closer.

The third street approaches fast.

Judd heaves on the rope, drags himself up, then again, gets his feet on the hook. He feels as secure as he can considering the situation. He looks back.

The missile is so close he can see the rivets on its casing. It's just five metres away now. They won't outrun it. It's only a matter of time before it –

The Loach jinks hard right, turns down another street. The missile turns too but not as fast. Suddenly it's twenty metres behind again.

'Whoa!' Judd grips the rope white-knuckle hard as he swings out again, even wider than before, more than horizontal this time – hangs there like he's in suspended animation –

Clang!

The chopper shudders.

Corey is horrified. 'What was *that*? Is he okay?'

Lola and Spike look down.

Judd swings back down. He's fine but the hook below his feet is gone. It struck the side of a building and has been severed from the rope.

Spike barks as Lola speaks: 'He's all right! He lost the hook but he's all right.'

Corey exhales, relieved. 'Okay, where to now?'

Lola turns and points out the windscreen. 'You wanted a tall building.'

Corey follows her finger and takes in the towering blue glass edifice before him. It must be three hundred metres high. He grins his crooked grin. 'That'll do.'

He glances in the side-view mirror. The missile is right behind. He pulls on the controls and the Loach points up at a forty-five degree angle, thunders towards the heavens like a bat out of hell.

He wills the little chopper onwards. 'Come on, baby, you can do it.'

What the hell is that Australian *doing*?

Judd holds tight but without the hook to stand on, gravity goes to work. He watches himself slide down the rope in the mirror windows of the building in front of him. He's surprised he doesn't look as terrified as he feels – then he sees the white missile close in and he does.

The g-force jams Lola back into her seat. 'Oh jeez.'

Corey glances at her. 'Don't worry, there's a plan.'

She's petrified – and yet she's never felt so alive. It's the first time she's seen Corey fly and it's like watching a maestro conduct an orchestra. She's seeing it but she's not quite believing it. She glances in the side-view mirror. The missile is close. 'Must go faster!'

'Almost there.'

The Loach goes up and up –

This building seems to go on forever –

The missile is *right* there –

'This might get a little bumpy.'

Judd grips the rope tight but that just seems to make it slide through his hands faster. There's a foot left – then half a foot – then the severed end slips through his fingers –

He falls.

35

Crunch.

Judd slams into the skyscraper's roof and lands on the bed of white pebbles that insulates the surface.

He skids to a stop. It should hurt, the fall was over three metres, but the pain is cancelled by pure relief. He watches the Loach thunder overhead.

'How is he?'

Lola looks down, clocks Judd, then turns to Corey, amazed. 'He's okay!'

The Australian drops the Loach onto the pebble surface with a skid-bump then turns and watches the missile sweep overhead and rocket towards the heavens. 'Okay, time you ran out of fuel, mate.'

Lola studies Corey, her face flushed. 'That was amazing. I mean – you're so good at flying this thing.'

Corey nods politely but he's not really listening, he's focused on the missile as it rips into the sky. He whispers to himself: 'It's gotta be low on fuel.'

'The way you threw it around. I had no idea you could do that sort of stuff in a helicopter.'

Again Corey nods politely, but he's still not really listening.

His eyes are locked on the missile as it accelerates away. 'Come on, run out of fuel, you bastard.'

'And the plan, with the serpentine through the tall buildings, that was very clever —'

He holds up a finger and she stops talking. 'What?'

He points towards the distant missile, unsure. 'Is it turning?'

She watches it. 'Um, well, I think – '

The missile gently curves to the left – then keeps turning.

'Yes.' Lola frowns. 'We don't want that, do we?'

'No, we don't.'

The radius of the missile's turn tightens, then tightens again.

Corey can't believe it. 'No, no, no, don't do that!'

It heads straight back towards the Loach.

'Oh, come *on*!'

'That's not good.'

'No, it's not. Get out.'

Lola turns to Corey. 'I'm coming with you.'

Corey looks at her. 'No, you're not. Out.'

'But I want to.'

'Two minutes ago you were asking to go home.'

'I changed my mind.'

'It's too dangerous. Out! I need to draw it away from the building.'

She unhappily unbuckles her belt and slides onto the skyscraper roof.

'Stick close to Judd.' Corey's eyes flick to Spike. 'You too. Out.'

The dog hops out as Corey looks back to the missile. Its hissing rocket motor coughs and splutters – and cuts out.

It has finally run out of fuel.

And that's *really* bad.

'Oh, damn.' Now the engineless warhead tumbles directly towards the roof of the building and there's no way Corey can draw it away.

Fifteen seconds until impact.

Corey shouts: 'Everybody in!'

Lola turns to him, confused. 'But you just said —'

'I know what I said! In! Now!' She does it. Spike jumps in behind her.

'Mandy!' Corey leans out and waves Judd towards the chopper. 'In!'

Judd limp-runs to the Loach as he watches the warhead silently plunge towards the roof. He swings into the backseat. 'Go!'

Five seconds until impact.

The Loach's rotor blades thunder and it springs into the sky.

The warhead slams into the roof.

Ka-boom. The explosion is massive.

Time slows.

'Jesus H!' Through the Loach's open door Lola looks back and sees the top of the building blow apart. An orange fireball fills her world, reaches out for the chopper like a giant claw. It's the most beautiful and terrifying thing she has ever seen.

Then the blast wave hits and it's no longer beautiful.

Time speeds up.

The rush of hot air spanks the Loach onto its side.

Every alarm in the cabin shrieks.

'That's me!' Corey tries to drag the Loach upright.

It doesn't work.

The helicopter falls like a dropped shoe.

Corey glances right, sees Lola's terrified face, then back at Judd, who holds the dog. He turns, looks out his open door at the ground as it rushes up to meet him.

In five seconds everything important to him will die.

36

The Loach falls.

Corey wrenches the controls.

The Loach rights itself, but it's slow.

One hundred metres from the ground.

He gives it full power.

It makes no difference.

Fifty metres.

The turbine screams as the rotors bite at the air.

Twenty metres.

The rotors kick up a wave of dust.

Five metres.

Corey, Judd and Lola all brace for impact.

The Loach stops dead.

One metre off the roadway.

They look at each other, relieved and euphoric. Judd leans forward with a smile. 'Doesn't get much closer than that —'

Crack. A deep rumble from above. They peer up through the spinning rotors and are no longer relieved or euphoric. The top three floors slide off the building – and drop towards them like a cement waterfall.

Lola turns to Corey. 'We gotta go.'

He nods but there's nowhere *to* go. There are skyscrapers on either side and they won't outrun the debris if they fly forward or back.

He drags the chopper hard left, aims it at the building's ground floor entrance. It's a narrow archway.

Judd sees it and braces himself. 'You sure that's wide enough?'

'Not really!'

'I don't think we're going to make it!'

'Neither do I!'

The Loach flies through the entrance –

Zzzrt! The tips of the rotor blades touch the sides – and the Loach enters the cavernous foyer intact.

Corey grins his crooked grin. 'No wuckers.'

Lola furiously waves at a dumbfounded group of office workers who stand and stare as the chopper thumps towards them. 'Out of the way, ladies!' They scurry clear.

Smash. Corey swings the Loach around as the stream of cement and glass slams into the road outside. It gets heavier and louder – then stops abruptly.

Judd claps Corey on the shoulder. 'Good call.'

A deep thump and a high-pitched whine reverberate within the foyer.

Judd listens. 'The Air-Crane.'

They wait.

It gets louder.

Lola points to the entrance. 'There.' The shadow of the giant chopper drifts across the rubble outside. She swallows hard. 'It's searching for us.'

Corey nods. 'I won't be able to outrun a missile in here.'

The Air-Crane's shadow eases to a stop.

They hold their breath.

•

From the cockpit of the hovering Tyrannosaur, Bunsen surveys the giant mounds of rubble and wreckage on the road below. He's seen no sign of the yellow Loach since the missile hit the building.

Enrico turns to him. 'What's the call? Do we keep looking?'

Bunsen studies the rubble for a long moment – then shakes his head. 'No. It's under there. Let's put this to bed.'

Enrico nods and pushes the Tyrannosaur onwards. It gains altitude quickly.

Seeing the yellow chopper airborne answered one question for Bunsen. They had used the counteragent, which raised two more questions: did they have more than one canister and had they given it to the authorities? Bunsen will need to investigate this when Phase Three is complete, though he assumes that what remained of the counteragent is buried under that rubble with Judd Bell and the chopper.

Judd, Corey and Lola watch the Tyrannosaur's shadow slide across the rubble and disappear. They breathe out as one, their relief golden.

Judd leans forward. 'We need to follow it.'

'Say what?' Corey turns to him, stunned. 'Why?'

'They're going to detonate a bomb.'

Corey's both confused and unhappy. 'There's a *bomb*?'

Judd nods. 'A big one, it's hanging under the Air-Crane's fuse-lage – you didn't see it?'

'I was too busy saving your arse, mate.'

'And I really appreciate that. Thank you.'

'Any time. Do you know where they're taking —' Corey sighs. '— this bomb?'

Judd shakes his head. 'That's why we need to follow it.'

'Before we can do that we need to find a way out of here.' Lola points to the archway where they entered the foyer. It is now blocked with debris and there is no other spot large enough for the chopper to exit.

Corey scans the foyer and his eyes land on something to the far left. He glances at Judd. 'You still have Ponytail's pistol?'

Judd draws it from his belt line. 'May I ask why you need it?'

'Got an idea.' Corey holds out a hand. Judd passes it over.

Corey pivots the Loach to the left. Office workers mill about everywhere, gawk at the thundering chopper that hovers in the middle of their foyer. The crowd blocks the way and there's no room to go over them because of the long, oval-shaped light fixtures that hang from the ceiling.

'Spike! Plough the road.'

The dog barks once, leaps out the pilot's side door and lands on the marble floor two metres below. His paws scrabble for traction then he finds grip and bounds into the crowd, barking, growling and nipping at ankles. Startled, people hop and jump out of the way – and the crowd parts like the Red Sea.

Corey works the controls and the Loach's nose tips down as it thumps along the freshly cleared path – towards a giant window. It approaches fast.

Lola sees it coming, winces. 'Oh, good Lord.'

And so does Judd. 'Christ.'

Corey points the pistol out the pilot's door. 'I know today's been pretty full on —'

Bam, bam, bam. Click. Three bullets thud into the window. The glass hangs in place for an impossibly long moment, then collapses in a cascade of sparkling fragments. The Loach soars through the window's frame and into the courtyard outside.

'— but there's no reason we can't have some fun.' Corey grins and passes the pistol back to Judd. 'Sorry, it's out of ammo.'

Corey dips the chopper low and Spike bounds towards the open passenger door, leaps high and lands beside Lola. 'Oh!' Surprised but delighted, she pats the dog. 'You're a good boy.'

'Back seat.' Spike jumps into the back as Corey pulls on the controls and the Loach ascends.

Judd grabs the brass telescope from the leather pouch on the side of the pilot's seat and extends it. It's weighty and a full thirty-eight inches long. 'This is much nicer than the one you had in Australia.' He pans it across the cityscape, searches for the Air-Crane. 'Where the hell are you?'

Lola glances at Corey. He smiles at her politely. Again. She realises she wants more than that from him. She knows it's a strange thing to be thinking about right now, with everything that's going on, but there you go – the heart wants what the heart wants. The irony is she's been searching for a *man* rather than a *boy*, but didn't realise this one had been staring her in the face the whole time.

Gee, she really screwed this up.

So how does she fix it? If she comes right out and says she made a mistake, that she likes him and Scott is toast, will she come across like some flighty schoolgirl who can't make up her mind, or worse, changes it on a whim? Of course she will, and that's not the kind of person you take seriously, or trust with your heart.

Gee, she *really* screwed this up.

'I see it!' Eye pressed to the brass telescope, Judd focuses on the Air-Crane in the distance. 'To the far right, three o'clock, about – five clicks away.'

Corey scans the area, takes in a black dot slicing through the purple-grey smoke haze. 'Righto. Got it.'

'Can you catch it?'

'This thing isn't exactly a speed demon but I can try. I'll stay low. Don't want them to see us and fire any more of those missiles.'

Corey drops the Loach low, barely fifty metres off the ground, guns the turbine and sets a course for the Air-Crane. They fly on for a moment, then he realises something. 'Sorry! Where are my manners. Lola, Judd, Judd, Lola.'

They exchange nods and hellos and shake hands, then Corey turns to Judd. 'So, what were those guys doing at the high school?'

The astronaut shakes his head. 'Not sure exactly, but it had something to do with the oil well.'

37

The Southwest 737 glides silently across the wild blue yonder.

Severson turns to Rhonda. 'We should see LA any minute now.'

'Thanks.' Rhonda scans the Boeing's controls. This plane glides so much better than a shuttle. The spacecraft's glide ratio is 1:1, which means for every one foot the shuttle flies forward it also drops one foot. The 737 is currently providing her with a glide ratio of 12:1, twelve feet forward to every one foot down. To lighten the jet's weight and extend that glide range further, she read the relevant section in the flight manual on the pilot's iPad and worked out how to dump fuel from its wing tanks. She ditched three quarters of the av-gas twenty minutes ago.

The jet is currently at 28,000 feet so they have a hundred kilometres of range. Since Los Angeles is only seventy kilometres away they will reach their destination with altitude to spare. The autopilot is set to direct them to the airport, and then to the runway, where Rhonda will land the unpowered jet just as she has landed the unpowered shuttle two times for real and over five hundred times in the simulator.

Rhonda feels like she has everything under control. She managed to deal with the cabin's depressurisation, work out how to maintain an optimum glide speed, dump the excess fuel, restart the remaining engine if need be, even use reverse thrust for landing. There's only one problem. They can't raise anyone on the radio, air traffic control included. Severson's been trying ever since they took charge of the aircraft, but they've heard nothing but static. She hopes the turbofan's explosion didn't affect the airliner's communication systems. They're going to need priority to land and she'd really like the tower at LAX to know the situation before they arrive at the airport unannounced.

The 737 drops through a cloud bank and they see Los Angeles for the first time.

Rhonda catches her breath. 'What the hell?'

Even from seventy kilometres out, the city looks like a war zone, *worse* than a war zone. Thousands of fires dot the horizon as smoke pyres feed a strange purple-tinged smog cloud that hovers above the city like a giant alien spacecraft.

Severson's voice is a stunned whisper. 'Guess that's why we can't raise anyone on the radio.'

Rhonda's first thought is for Judd. Fear rises in her chest. He's been there for *hours*. Is he okay? *Christalmighty*. She hasn't told him she loves him in almost a year. She thought it showed weakness, probably because that's what her father always said –

Stop it. Focus on the job at hand. 'Try the emergency frequency again.'

Severson changes the radio channel, tunes in the emergency frequency. Through their headsets they hear the distant echo of a woman's voice:

'— affecting the greater Los Angeles area. The public are strongly advised to stay indoors. Do not operate combustion engines. If there is a combustion engine in operation it must be shut off immediately. If the exhaust from the combustion engine is purple in colour vacate the area immediately. All airports are closed and the airspace above the city is a no-fly zone until further notice.

All aircraft are to proceed to their alternate airports. This message is part of the Federal Emergency Management Agency Alert System and will be updated half-hourly. There is an unspecified threat —'

Severson turns to Rhonda. 'Well, fuck-a-doodle-do.'

She nods in agreement. 'We saw the purple exhaust. That's why the starboard turbofan exploded. The pilots shut down the port engine before it blew.'

Rhonda no longer feels like she has everything under control. The FEMA message told her the one thing she didn't want to hear: that all airports are closed due, she could only guess, to problems similar to the one this jet experienced. As for proceeding to their alternative airport, which the pilot's iPad told her was San Diego, well, they wouldn't make it a quarter of the way there without engine power. It was LA or bust, no-fly zone or not.

She takes a deep breath, can feel her heart rate increase. This is how she feels in the Orion simulator when the techs throw the kitchen sink at her. This is when she needs to think on her feet to solve the problem, when time is critical and she can't go by the book. Trouble is she loves the book, she's done everything by the book her whole life and it has always worked out well for her. But now she must throw the book away and – literally – wing it. For a moment she wonders if she can pass the responsibility to Severson, let him land this jet, but as soon as she thinks it she realises it's crazy. Even if he'd agree, he's not half the pilot she is.

Severson turns to her. 'We need to think outside the box.'

She nods. 'It's not my – strong suit.' Admitting even that, especially to the person she respects *least* at NASA, a person who would happily trade personal information to benefit his own career, is one of the hardest things she's ever done.

'There are seventy people on this plane that need it to be.'

'I don't know if I can.' Her voice is small.

'You can. Improvise.'

'I'm landing a jet, not doing stand-up. There's no room for improv.'

'But there is. A little. And your job is to find it.' He smiles. 'I've been seat-of-the-pantsing-it-and-making-it-up-as-I-go-alonging-it my whole life. You just need to – loosen up a little. I can help.'

She looks at him, breathes out to steady her nerves, then nods. 'Okay. So we rule out both LAX and Santa Monica airports. That means we need to find something very flat, long and straight –'

'And close. Let's have a look.' He picks up the pilot's iPad, swipes it open and consults the map of Southern California.

She takes another breath and steels herself. The irony is, as lazy and hopeless as Severson was during their trip to Wisconsin, he just might be the best person to be stuck in this plane with.

Or then again maybe not.

She will find out one way or the other very soon.

38

The little yellow chopper thunders across the rooftops.

'Okay, take us up. Let's see where it is.' Corey's voice rattles in Judd's headset as he works the controls. The Loach quickly gains altitude and rises above the smoke haze that cloaks the city.

Judd sweeps the brass telescope across the horizon and finds the Air-Crane in the distance. 'Got it. One o'clock. We're catching it, but it's still a good three clicks away.'

Corey keeps the chopper just above the haze as Judd pulls the telescope from his eye. 'Okay, two questions. Where in hell did you get this thing and can it go any faster?'

'I'm thrashing it, mate. It's the hero car from the *Atlantis 4* movie – except it's not a car, obviously. We got it from Twentieth Century Fox.'

Judd takes this in with a nod. 'Thank you, *Rupert*.'

Corey's confused. '*Rupert*? It was *Lola's* idea to use it.'

Judd leans between the front seats and nods to Lola. 'Good one.' He then turns to Corey. 'Rupert Murdoch owns Twentieth Century Fox.'

'Oh, that's right. He used to be an Aussie.' Corey glances back at Judd. 'I had to use every drop of the counteragent to get this thing in the air. Tell me you still have yours.'

Judd gestures to the bulge in his pants: 'Is that a canister full of counteragent in my pocket or am I just happy —' He realises Lola is sitting right there and stops abruptly, embarrassed. 'Oh, sorry – that was completely inappropriate.' He clears his throat, turns to Corey. 'Yes, I still have it.'

Lola finds a small container under the passenger seat and passes it to Judd. 'Is that a medi-kit in my hand or are you just bleeding from a bullet wound?'

'Thank you.' Judd examines the bullet wound on his thigh. It is bleeding, but not too badly. 'It's a flesh wound with delusions of grandeur.' He opens the medi-kit, pulls out a wide bandage and wraps it tightly around his leg.

Corey looks back at him. 'Need a doc?'

'Nah, this'll do it.'

'So what's the deal with this bomb?'

'It's huge, at least three metres long with three warheads. It's like the Godzilla of explosive devices. I've never seen anything like it.'

'And who are these people? Why are they doing this?'

'I met the main guy, this handsome prick, said something about trying to motivate people to use renewable energy . . . ' Judd trails off as he focuses the telescope again. 'The chopper's descending. Take us down.'

The Loach follows the Air-Crane down through the smoke haze. They watch the giant chopper land in the middle of a small, tree-lined park, opposite a large building with a tall beige tower.

Judd scans the area. 'Is there anything important round here? A reason to detonate a bomb?'

Lola shakes her head. 'Not really. It's just West Pico. Nothing out of the ordinary.'

Judd turns to Corey. 'We need to land close by – but not too close. They can't know we're here.'

Corey nods and plays the Loach's controls.

•

Bunsen pushes open the Tyrannosaur's cockpit and turns to Enrico. 'Be ready to leave in five.' The pilot nods and Bunsen slides out.

From the rear cabin Kilroy passes him the long grey bag. Bunsen takes it with a nod and moves off. As he goes he glances over at the Item. The trio of BLU-116 bunker busters have been combined to create an explosive device with more destructive power than any non-nuclear weapon in the history of the world, or at least since people have been dropping bombs on each other. To Bunsen, the Item is even more useful than a nuclear weapon because it doesn't spread radiation – just the Swarm.

Corey searches for a spot to put down. 'There.'

In a swirl of dust and ash the Loach settles on a quiet street, about a hundred and fifty metres away from the park. They quickly step out of the cabin. Corey forks his fingers into a V, points them at his eyes, then the dog's, then the chopper. Spike gets the message, barks once and takes up a guard position in front of the Loach.

'This way.' Judd points them towards it and they run hard, though the bullet wound definitely slows Judd down a little.

'Is that one of them?' Corey indicates a figure who walks briskly out of the park.

Judd pulls out the brass telescope and focuses it. It's difficult to see through the haze – and then it isn't. 'Yep, that's the guy in charge. Mister Handsome.' Judd follows him with the telescope until he disappears into the beige building with the tower. 'What is that?'

Lola doesn't know. 'Could be a synagogue. This is a Jewish area.'

Corey glances at Judd. 'Should we follow him?'

'No, we have to prioritise.' Judd looks over at the giant chopper. Corey watches him study the Air-Crane. 'Are you thinking what

I think you're thinking?'

Judd pulls the telescope from his eye. 'We take the chopper and ditch the weapon in the ocean.'

'Yep.'

Lola is stunned. 'So – you just decided that?'

They both nod.

'You aren't serious? Are you?'

Judd glances at her. 'We have to get that thing as far from the city as possible.'

'But what if they —' She lowers her voice to a whisper. '— you know, detonate it —' Her voice returns to normal. '— while you're, you know, *nearby*?'

Neither of them have an answer for her.

'So that's an acceptable risk?'

Judd shrugs. 'You haven't seen that thing close up. It's *enormous*. We have to get it out of here.' He turns to Corey. 'You can fly that chopper, right?'

'Sure.'

'You've flown one before?'

'Nuh, but I'm a quick learner.'

Judd doesn't doubt it.

Lola studies these the two crazy people for a moment, then: 'So, what can I do?'

'Nothing.' Corey probably says it too quickly.

She gestures towards the building with the beige tower. 'What about that guy, Handsome-man-or-whatever-he's-called? Why don't I follow him, check out what he's up to?'

Corey shakes his head. 'It's not worth putting you in harm's way.'

'Hello, have we met? I'm *already* in harm's way. I've *been* in harm's way all day. And if he comes out before you've stolen his chopper you're going to need a heads up 'cause I'm sure he'll be pretty pissed.'

'It's too dangerous. You should head back to the Loach.'

She stares at the Australian. 'You know I'm not asking permission, right?'

Corey turns to her. 'This isn't a movie, Lola. If he catches you spying on him he will try to kill you.'

He sees that gives her a moment's pause – then he sees her push the fear away and steel herself. 'I know, but I'm going to help anyway.'

Corey exhales, realises this is not an argument he can win. 'Just keep your distance, okay? *Stay out of sight*. Don't let him know you're there under *any* circumstances.'

She nods.

They run on, approach a burned-out van and crouch behind it, the Air-Crane now thirty metres away. Corey addresses the two others: 'You guys need to swap numbers.' They pass over their phones, tap in their respective numbers, then pass them back.

Corey turns to Lola. 'If something goes wrong just head for the Loach, okay? Whatever you do, don't engage these people. *Please*. Do. Not. Engage.'

'I'll be fine. *You* be careful. I'll call *when* he comes out.'

He studies her for a moment, then takes the telescope from Judd's hand, collapses it, and passes it to her. 'In case you need to hit something with a heavy piece of brass.'

She takes it with a grateful smile. 'Why, you shouldn't have.'

They move off. Judd and Corey towards the park, Lola towards the building with the beige tower. Corey watches her go and realises he's more concerned for her safety than his own.

Corey and Judd stay low and move fast, take cover behind

a large tree at the edge of the park, just twenty metres from the chopper. The park is not that big, maybe fifty metres square, and is cloaked in a drifting haze.

They can see both the cockpit and rear cabin from where they are. Judd looks closer: 'Two men. One in the cockpit, one in the rear who looks suspiciously like a Mister P. Tail, Esquire. So how are we going to do this?'

Corey turns to him. 'I got an idea.'

Lola searches for a way into the building but there is no obvious spot from the road. She moves down a narrow side alley and finds an entrance. The lock has been shot through and the door is ajar. She steps inside.

As soon as she enters she knows what it is and it's not a synagogue. It's the hidden world of Los Angeles she'd heard about but never seen before, a sprawling oil-drilling island of forty wells, cleverly disguised within a soundproof building. She knew these structures were located all over town, hidden from the world as they exploited LA's vast oil reserves, the second largest in the continental USA.

Lola surveys the football field-sized platform five metres below her. It's filled with wellheads and pipes and reservoir tanks. The building doesn't have any windows so it's gloomy, lit only by the glow of the odd yellow light bulb. Forty metres away she sees the handsome guy walk quickly through the machinery then stop in front of a two-metre-high structure that looks like a Christmas tree constructed from metal pipes.

Handsome crouches and unzips the long bag he carries. He pulls out a four-inch-wide, metre-long strap and wraps it around the base of the metal Christmas tree. He then takes cover behind a reservoir

tank ten metres away, draws out a small black box the size of a cigarette pack and thumbs the button on top.

Boom. The strap detonates the metal Christmas tree and sends
burning hot shrapnel in every direction, including Lola's. She takes
cover, then realises everything is now coated in a fine mist of oil, including her good self. She wipes it from her eyelids and studies the man.

What the hell is he up to?

The Air-Crane looms through the smoke haze, the rasp of its twin
turbines shrill and unpleasant. From the rear Judd and Corey
quickly move towards its tail rotor.

'You realise this whole thing would have been a lot easier if you
hadn't used up all the bullets.'

'Sure, and we'd still be flying around inside that building.'

They reach the tail rotor, bend low and crawl under the chopper. Ponytail can't see them because his view out the back cabin is
blocked by the weapon which hangs low and wide under the airframe.

It's the first time Corey's seen the bomb up close and he's amazed
– and horrified. 'It's bloody enormous.'

They crawl on until they are under the cabin. Judd nods to the
right. 'Okay, I'm going this way.'

Corey holds up a hand for him to wait. 'Look, I can fly this out
on my own. There's no need for both of us to do it.'

'I'm coming with you.'

'There's no point, mate. Really. Just make sure Lola and Spike
are all right.'

Judd takes a moment before he realises Corey is right. 'Only if
you promise me something.'

'What?'

'As soon as you get the chance to fly it out, take it. Don't hesitate, just go. If you think I need help or, whatever – ignore it. I'll be fine. Just get it done. You might only get one chance.'

Corey is reluctant to agree.

Judd sees it. 'Promise.'

Corey stares at him, then nods. 'Okay.'

'Okay.'

Corey tries to lighten the moment. 'So, what's the emergency word? I'm still leaning towards "tomato".'

Judd smiles. 'Just call out my name if you're in trouble, but *don't worry about me*. Concentrate on getting this monstrosity out of here.'

'All right. Good luck.'

'You too.'

They move off in separate directions.

Pistol in hand, Enrico waits in the cabin. He scans the park but can't see much through the drifting haze. He will lift off if there is any threat that could endanger the aircraft but so far there's nothing to be concerned about –

Knock, knock. Enrico looks out the pilot's side window – and sees Judd Bell. *Judd Bell!* He's right there. Beside him! The astronaut smiles and waves.

Enrico is stunned. Judd Bell's meant to be buried under a large mound of rubble on the other side of town, but here he is, *right outside* his cockpit window –

He's gone.

Where'd he go? Does this count as a threat that could endanger the aircraft? Yes, because he might sabotage the chopper.

Enrico wonders if he should take off. No, because he might have already sabotaged the chopper. Better to eliminate the threat then check that everything is okay. He speaks into his headset. 'Kilroy, Judd Bell is outside.'

The old man's stunned voice rattles back at him. '*What?*'

'I'm going to deal with it.'

Enrico pulls off his headset, pushes the door open and slides out.

Judd lies under the cockpit and watches the pilot step out. As soon as his feet touch the ground the astronaut springs forward, tackles him hard and drives him into the grass. The pistol is jarred from the pilot's grip and Judd scrambles after it. This is going to be *easy* –

The pilot throws out an arm, hits Judd's ankle hard. He trips and falls and slams to the ground, the pistol just out of reach. *Oof!* The pilot lands on Judd's back, loops an arm around his neck and squeezes hard, cuts off his air. This isn't going to be easy after all.

The astronaut pulls an elbow back and thrusts it into the pilot's ribs. The guy cries out like a mummy's boy and loosens his grip just enough for Judd to twist free, clamp his arms around the guy's torso and pull him to the ground. Now neither of them can move so no one has the advantage. It's like a Greco-Roman wrestling match between two guys who don't know anything about Greco-Roman wrestling.

Corey is crouched under the left side of the cabin. He watches Judd Greco-Roman with the pilot. He's not winning, but then he's not losing either so that's okay. Judd is the bait today. It's not the most sophisticated plan ever devised, but it's the best they can do without access to weapons. The Australian just has to wait for Ponytail to climb out of the rear cabin to help the pilot, after which Corey will surprise him, just as Judd surprised the pilot. The only wrinkle in the plan is that Ponytail is yet to take the bait.

Corey smells something unpleasant. What is that? Sharply toxic and instantly headache-inducing –

Oh, crap!

Ponytail's cologne.

Corey turns. Ponytail is crouched right behind him, pistol raised and index finger tight on the trigger. The Australian throws out a hand and hits the weapon –

Bam. It fires and the bullet thuds into the grass beside them. The old guy must have climbed out through the cockpit. He aims the pistol again but Corey drives a hand up, knocks the weapon from his grip and unleashes a sharp jab.

Thud. The old man cops it on the nose and slumps backwards. Corey scrambles from under the chopper and searches for the pistol, can't see it anywhere, the smoke haze not helping visibility. He has to make a decision. Spend valuable seconds searching for a gun he may never find or finish the job he came here to do?

Finish the job.

He pivots towards the Air-Crane's cockpit and sees that Judd still wrestles the pilot. The astronaut locks eyes with Corey and shouts: 'Go! Now!' At least that's what Corey *thinks* he says, it's hard to tell over the wail of the chopper's turbines.

Against his every instinct the Australian does as he's told and doesn't help his mate. He pulls open the pilot's door, vaults into the cockpit – and is immediately dragged out by Ponytail, his nose bloodied but his spirit unbowed. The old codger hasn't found the pistol either.

Corey kicks out a foot and hits him in the thigh, not hard, but hard enough to knock him off balance. Ponytail trips backwards, falls awkwardly, whacks his head on the grass – and doesn't get up.

Corey clambers back into the cockpit, slams the pilot's door shut and takes in the controls. It doesn't look that complicated. He flicks a series of switches, his feet find the pedals, he takes the cyclic and collective controls in hand – and powers up.

Thump, thump, thump. The turbines howl as the rotors turn, slow then fast. The Tyrannosaur lifts off in a blast of dust and smoke.

A metre off the ground Corey looks down at Judd as he Greco-Romans the pilot, who now has a clear advantage. Corey knows he promised to get on with the job and not worry about Judd, but can he really leave him like this?

Judd looks up at Corey and mouths: 'Go now!' Well, that answers that question – wait! Did he say 'Go now!' or did he say 'Tomato!'? No, it's neither of those. He said, 'Behind you!'

'Behind you?' Why would he say 'Behind you'? What's behind me? Confused, Corey turns.

Ponytail! He wrenches the passenger door open and dives inside the cockpit. Bloody hell. Isn't he lying on the ground unconscious? The old bastard slams into Corey and drives him against the pilot's door. It flies open and they tumble out –

Slam. Corey hits the grass hard and Ponytail lands right beside him. The Australian elbows him across the jaw and Ponytail cries out in pain. Corey looks up as the now pilotless Air-Crane ceases to fly and its huge front wheel drops directly towards his chest –

Jeezus! Corey rolls left as the tyre slams onto the grass beside him. The chopper bounces twice – then turns and rolls straight towards him. He scrambles clear, finds his feet, realises he's right beside the open cockpit door again and climbs inside –

Crunch. Ponytail crash-tackles him to the grass.

39

Bunsen takes in the destruction. The wellhead is gone, leaving a five-inch-wide pipe from which a low-pressure stream of crude oil flows. He kneels beside the hole, unzips his bag, and draws out a long, thin aluminium cylinder, same as the one he used at Moreno High School. He works the iPhone's screen and the cylinder's propeller spins to life. He then slides the cylinder down the pipe and it disappears.

He studies the numbers which update on the phone's screen: forty, one hundred and twenty, three hundred and seventy. Seconds pass until the number reaches fifteen hundred and stops. One point five kilometres. It's at depth and all systems are nominal.

He heads for the exit. He's happy and there's a spring in his step. Phase Three is almost complete.

Lola watches the handsome guy move towards the exit. What the hell did he just send down that well? Didn't Judd say he did something similar at Moreno High? She moves off quickly and quietly, follows him through the jungle of pipes and tanks as she dials Judd's number.

It rings, but nobody picks up.
Come on!

•

Judd feels his phone buzz in his pocket but his hands are full and he can't answer it. The pilot, he now realises, may not be trained in the art of hand-to-hand combat but he's one strong son of a bitch. He's currently on top of Judd and has him pinned to the ground.

Whik, whik, whik. The spinning tail rotor cuts through the smoke haze and swings straight towards them as the Air-Crane continues to turn. Judd sees it coming and realises the bottom edge of the blade is in line with the pilot's head. Excellent. All Judd has to do is hold him in this position and the guy is toast.

The pilot sees the rotor, instantly collapses an elbow, rolls right and flips Judd over so now he's on top. Now the bottom edge of the blade is in line with *Judd's* head. Not so excellent.

Whik, whik, whik. The thundering rotor is three metres away. Judd tries to roll clear but the pilot has the arm strength of a silverback gorilla and holds him tight. *Christ!* Judd shifts his knee, pushes it down into the guy's cahones and presses as hard as he can.

Whik, whik, whik. The rotor is right there. Judd presses harder. The pilot flinches –

Whik, whik, whik. Judd rolls clear as the rotor sweeps overhead. The astronaut scrambles to his feet, searches for his opponent –

Crunch. The pilot tackles Judd from behind and drives him into the ground.

Bunsen exits the building – and takes in the scene in the park. He's no longer happy and has most definitely lost the spring in his step. 'What the fuck is going on?'

The Tyrannosaur spins around in circles. To the right Enrico fights – is that *Judd Bell*? And to the left, Kilroy fights – the Australian whose name he can't remember.

Apoplectic, Bunsen draws his pistol and sprints towards the park. Judd Bell dies first.

Ponytail has Corey in a headlock and try as he might he can't get free –

Something soft and grey brushes against the Australian's face, then again. What the hell is that?

It's Ponytail's *ponytail*.

Errr, gross – but also, potentially useful. Corey reaches up, grabs at it, misses, tries again, gets a handful of it and yanks hard.

Ponytail's head jerks to the right and Corey wrenches himself free, twists the hair around his fist, pulls it hard and slams Ponytail's head into the Air-Crane's cockpit door.

Ponytail bounces off and drives an elbow into Corey's gut. Winded, the Australian backpedals – then sees the pistol lying on the grass five metres away. Ponytail sees it too and they both sprint, dive, slide across the grass for it –

Ponytail gets there first, grabs the weapon with his right hand and swings it towards Corey's face. The Australian shoves Ponytail's arm up –

Bam. The pistol fires into the sky –

Whik, whik, whik. The tail rotor swings around and the bottom edge clips the gun and all five of Ponytail's fingers.

They're instantly vaporised. Ponytail screams blue murder and slumps to the ground, tries to stem the flow of blood from the nub that is now his right hand. Covered in a fine mist of the red stuff, Corey rolls left and finds his feet –

Whik, whik, whik. The tail rotor is right in front of him! He stops dead as it swings past, centimetres from his face, then runs for the Air-Crane's cockpit. He's going to fly this thing out right now.

•

Why don't they answer?

Phone jammed to her ear, Lola clears the doorway and sees the handsome guy run on to the park, a pistol in hand.

Damn it.

What did Corey say? 'Whatever you do, don't engage these people. Please. Do. Not. Engage.'

He was very clear. He said it twice. He even said 'please'.

What does she do?

She can't just stand here and watch this guy shoot them. She breaks into a run, picks up speed instantly, sprints directly towards the handsome guy. She's fast, but most importantly, she's faster than him, all those years spent on track at UCLA finally proving useful in the real world. She catches him quickly, armed with nothing but her iPhone, a brass telescope and the element of surprise.

She hopes it's enough.

Slam. She tackles him hard, drives him into the grass. *Wow.* She feels like a damn superhero! Now what? She wants his gun. She springs to her feet, scrambles forward, bends to grab it. This is working out brilliantly –

Wham. Handsome swings around and kicks her in the breadbasket.

Damn, that hurts!

All the air leaves her body. She stumbles backwards, arms windmilling, and crashes to the ground.

She doesn't feel like a superhero any more.

'What is that bloody woman *doing*?'

Astonished, Corey stares out at Lola from the pilot seat of the Air-Crane, which continues to rotate because he can't find the wheel brake. He told her *twice*. Do. Not. Engage. But what did she do? She engaged, and is now laid out flat on the far side of the park. Pistol in hand, Handsome pulls himself to his feet and turns to her.

Jeezus. This is *exactly* what he feared would happen. He can't fly the Air-Crane out now, can't leave her like this. He pushes the door open, jumps out of the cockpit and runs –

Whik, whik, whik. The tail rotor swings towards him.

'Oh, come *on*!' He sprints hard, outruns it, sets a course for the handsome guy, who's a good thirty metres away. The only thing Corey has going for him is that the bloke won't hear him coming over the Air-Crane's turbines. The Australian has no idea what he'll do when he gets there, he just knows he must get there.

Slam. Judd Bell nails Enrico with an uppercut.

Groggy, the pilot slumps to the ground. He takes a moment to shake it off, looks up – and can see no sign of the astronaut. Where'd he go? Enrico *can* see Kilroy, though, and he doesn't look well. What happened to his hand?

Whik, whik, whik. The tail rotor thunders towards Enrico again. He needs to get that chopper under control and help Kilroy. He pulls himself up.

Bunsen studies the young woman who tackled him. Who the hell is she and why did she do that? It doesn't actually matter. She dies now. He raises the pistol.

Lola feels the weight of her phone in her hand. It's an older iPhone 4S so it's quite a bit heavier than the new version, so that's good. Even so, it's not much of a weapon, but then she doesn't have time to pull the brass telescope out of her jacket pocket so it's the only show in town. *Man.* She can't believe she bought an *iPhone* to a gun fight. She draws her arm back and hurls it at the handsome guy.

Bunsen watches the white shape rocket towards him.

What is that –?

Whack. It hits him flush on the cheek and stings like hell.

'Hey!' He touches the point of impact. Whatever it was has split the skin and really hurts. He glances at the ground, sees the woman threw an iPhone, looks back at her, re-aims and squeezes the trigger.

She won't need a phone where she's going –

Whump. Corey hits Handsome Guy like a train.

The Australian drives him into the grass and the guy doesn't fire the shot. He scrambles to his feet and swings the pistol towards Corey. Before he can pull the trigger the Australian springs forward, twists the weapon from his grip and kicks him in the gut.

Handsome staggers backwards, trips and lands on the ground with an almost comical exhalation of breath.

Corey steps forward and points the pistol at him. 'Not so tough without your gun, are you?'

The man looks up at him and grins.

'You got nothing to smile about, mate. You are done.'

'What *is* your name?'

'You can call me "the Australian who just kicked your arse". It doesn't really trip off the tongue but I think it captures my general vibe.'

The man's grin widens. 'You're going to die today, like all the others. You just don't know it yet.'

'You're kinda mouthy for a guy without a gun.'

'That's because I'm a guy with a detonator to a really big bomb.' Bunsen holds up a cigarette-pack sized box, his finger touching the green button on top. 'I guess I have something to smile about after all. Now tell me, do you think you can shoot me before I press this button?'

Corey hesitates.

'Drop the gun or we'll find out.'

Corey reluctantly does it.

Thump, thump, thump. The Tyrannosaur skims across the park directly towards Bunsen, Enrico in the pilot's seat. The rotor wash kicks up a blizzard of smoke and leaves that blasts into Bunsen and almost knocks the Australian off his feet.

A rope ladder drops from the rear cabin door and swings low. Kilroy steadies it as Bunsen grabs hold. He quickly climbs it to the cabin as the giant chopper lifts into the purple sky.

Corey recovers his balance, picks up the pistol and aims it at the Air-Crane. He's pretty sure that if he hits one of the rotors the chopper will auto-rotate to the ground and the landing will be soft enough not to detonate the weapon. Unfortunately 'pretty sure' isn't really good enough. So he releases the trigger and lowers the weapon – and immediately has second thoughts. Will history be kind to him? Would it be better for this neighbourhood to be destroyed rather than whatever location the weapon is being transported to now? Is it on the way to a crowded Disneyland? Or the Santa Monica Pier? Or Universal CityWalk? He can't help but think it was better that Flight 93 crashed into a field in Shanksville, Pennsylvania, rather than its intended target on 9/11. Did he just send that bomb to the equivalent of the White House?

What *did* that prick have planned for it? Corey knows there's only one way to find out. He must follow it. He turns for the Loach then catches sight of something under the rising Air-Crane and stops dead. 'You've gotta be kidding me.'

Judd lies on top of the giant weapon under the chopper's airframe, his face a picture of steely determination. He waves at Corey.

Dumbstruck, Corey waves back. Suddenly he's very glad he didn't shoot down the Air-Crane. Lola approaches, her retrieved iPhone in hand. 'What on earth are you waving at?'

Corey just points at the climbing chopper. She looks up and sees Judd. Stunned, she instinctively waves too. 'Is he insane?'

Corey turns and runs for the Loach. 'We gotta follow them.'

Lola's right beside him, astonished. 'Why would he do that?'

'To prove a point.'

'What point?'

'That he's the hero everyone thinks he is.'

'But he *is* a hero.'

'He doesn't believe it.' Corey takes a moment. 'I just realised I probably shouldn't have told you that. Please keep it to yourself.'

'Of course. And thanks for helping me out with that guy back there.'

Corey doesn't respond. They run on, their footfalls and breathing the only sound. After a moment she turns to him. 'What?'

'Nothing.'

'When someone says "nothing" it's always "something".'

'You ignored everything I said.'

'See? Always something.'

'Do not engage those people. I said it *twice*. I even said *please*. It was just dumb luck that I got to that guy before he shot you.'

'*That guy* was marching across the park to shoot *you*. And Judd. I wasn't going to let that happen so I tackled him.'

'Don't help me, please. I can look after myself. I don't want you to die trying to help me unnecessarily.'

'I wasn't "trying to help you" I was *actually* helping you and it looked pretty *necessary* to me. You should thank me.'

He shoots her an incredulous look. 'You don't get thanked for doing crazy-dangerous stuff. There's no thanking for that. Just please, don't do it again.'

'But *you* do it all the time. Flying the chopper through those sky-scrapers was the most crazy-dangerous thing I've ever seen in my life.'

'I didn't *choose* to do it. I was *forced* to.'

'And so was I. That guy was going to kill you. That's why you should thank me.'

'And we're back to where we started.'

They run on in silence, their footfalls and breathing, which is heavier than it was a moment ago, the only sound.

He glances at her. 'You're good at arguing your side.'

'That's why I've got such a big house.'

He can't help but smile at that. 'I just – I don't want you to get hurt.'

'And I don't want me to get hurt either.' She looks at him. 'I'll be careful.'

He regards her for a moment and realises that's the closest they'll get to an agreement. 'Okay. And thanks, for tackling that guy.'

She nods. 'Anytime. And thank you for doing the same.'

He sees the Loach appear out of the gloom. A young guy lies on the ground in front of it, terrified. That's because Spike stands on his chest and growls at him with bared teeth, his snout inches from the poor sucker's nose.

Corey takes in the tableau. 'You picked the wrong dog, mate.'

The guy's voice trembles. 'I was just looking at the chopper, I didn't mean anything by it, honest.'

Lola climbs into the passenger seat. 'I think we all know anyone who says "honest" at the end of a sentence usually isn't.'

'You gotta get this crazy mutt off me.'

Corey slides into the pilot's seat. 'You'll need to be much nicer than that.'

'Get this . . . lovely animal off me?'

Corey fires up the Loach's turbine. 'And what's the magic word?'

'Please?'

The rotors start to turn. 'Not in the form of a question.'

'Please.'

'There you go. Spike, get behind.'

The dog hops off the guy, who immediately scrambles away. Spike chases him for a moment, then doubles back and leaps into the cockpit and lands beside Lola. She rubs his head. 'Oh, you're a good boy.' He nuzzles against her. Corey takes this in as he works the controls and the Loach springs off the roadway.

They both pull on their headsets and survey the horizon. The haze is thick and Corey can see no sign of the Air-Crane. 'Where is it?'

Lola drags the telescope out of her jacket pocket, scans the smoke. 'There!' She points to the far left and up. 'It's high.'

Corey looks high and sees a distant black dot. 'Right. Thank you.' He sets a course for it and shakes his head. 'What the hell was he thinking?'

Lola holds up her phone. 'Why don't we find out?'

Corey points to a cable that protrudes from the communications panel. 'If you plug it in we should both be able to hear him.'

40

It seemed like a good idea at the time.

In reality it's possibly the worst idea Judd's ever had. *Ever*. He's so desperate to prove he's not a fraud that he's going to dig himself an early grave. And by 'early' he means a little later today.

At least it's not as loud up here as he expected. From his position directly under the airframe and above the weapon he is protected from the worst of the wind and noise. The only real negatives are the vibrations that have made his hands numb from holding the weapon and the fact *he's about to die*.

What the hell was he thinking?

He watches the ground sweep past for a moment, then turns and looks into the rear cabin. He can see only the legs and torsos of Handsome Guy and Ponytail in the Air-Crane's rear cabin. The old man seems to be injured in some way. Handsome is holding what appears to be a missile launcher across his knees. Judd's certain he's surveying the horizon to make sure they're not being followed, which, Judd is also sure, is exactly what Corey and Lola are doing right now.

Judd turns and studies the weapon he's lying on. The sides are cloaked in camouflage netting but from the top he can see the whole thing clearly. The three weapons inside the football-shaped lattice are surely US Army bunker busters from their length, width and markings.

Somehow he has to disarm them. That's the reason he climbed up here after all. Being so close to the weapon he can see it is completely handmade, which gives him hope, for an exposed wire or a loose detonator or some other manufacturing defect that will present him with a way to disable it.

He goes in search of it.

Corey drops the Loach low, maybe fifty metres off the ground, skims the smoke haze. Beside him Lola studies her phone. The call to Judd still isn't going through. She hits redial, then peers through the brass telescope and focuses on the Air-Crane as it cuts across the darkening horizon above them. 'It's closer, but we're still two clicks away.'

'Okey-doke.'

She looks at the Australian. He got a little annoyed with her before, but she takes it as a good sign. If he didn't care he wouldn't get upset, would he? She's always thought the opposite of love isn't hate so much as indifference. Then she realises she really shouldn't read too much into anything he said. She blew him off and embarrassed him last night so he was probably just venting frustration.

The call fails again. She hits redial.

Judd shakes his head. Amazing. He's searched this thing and found no manufacturing flaws *at all*. The weapon may be handmade but the craftsmanship is first rate. He can tell by the quality of the welding used on the metal tubes that connect and surround the three central bombs and make up the latticework. He can't even find any exposed wires for the electronics systems. And that means just one thing: catching a ride on the back of this thing has been a monumental waste of time –

He hears sloshing. *Liquid* sloshing. Is it coming from the av-gas in the Air-Crane's fuel tanks directly above him? No. It's definitely coming from the weapon, specifically those metal tubes. He sees what looks like a welded radiator cap at the centre of the weapon. He feels around the base and touches liquid. It's clear, but has an almost grainy texture when he rubs it between his fingers. He smells it. Sweet, but with a synthetic edge. Definitely not oil or gasoline or any kind of accelerant he's aware of.

It's the Swarm. He's sure of it.

This bomb is full of the Swarm.

That cannot, under any circumstances, be a good thing.

There's a buzz in his pocket. Judd pulls out his phone and answers it with a shout, the microphone's noise-cancelling feature working overtime. 'Hello?'

Judd's voice is distant and muffled, but Corey can hear him well enough. 'What the hell are you *doing*, mate?'

'Trying to disarm this friggin' thing.'

'Did you?'

'No – but I'm pretty sure it's full of the Swarm. There'd have to be four or five hundred litres inside it at a guess. Enough to infect something really big.'

Corey listens. 'Like what?'

'Somewhere with a lot of oil. A reservoir maybe? A refinery?'

Lola hears this as she scans the horizon with the telescope, focuses on the Air-Crane, then something beyond it. She studies it for a long moment then yanks the telescope from her eye. 'I think I know where they're taking it.'

Judd's voice echoes down the line. 'Where?'

'La Brea. You're flying straight towards it.'

'Christ, that makes sense.'

Corey has no idea what they're talking about. 'What's a La Brea?'

Lola turns to him. 'The La Brea Tar Pits. There's like a – cluster of oil lakes around the Miracle Mile on Wilshire Boulevard. One of the lakes is huge – like, millions-of-gallons huge. The Air-Crane's heading straight for it.'

'You're telling me there's a giant lake of oil *in the middle of LA*?'

She nods. 'The oil seeps up through the 6th Street Fault from the Salt Lake Oil Field. It's a major tourist attraction. There's a museum with all the fossils they've found over the years, schoolkids go there on excursions, it's a whole thing.'

Corey thinks about this. 'So, they detonate the bomb there and ignite and infect the oil. What for?'

Judd's voice is distant but certain: 'To pump all that infected smoke into the atmosphere and send the virus global.'

They all process this for a moment, then Lola breaks the silence: 'That's just evil.'

Corey's eyes move to the Air-Crane. It's a long way above them, but they're almost parallel with it now. 'So, Mandy, what's the plan for getting off that thing?'

'I was hoping they'd land and I'd just sneak away. Or maybe they'd fly over open water and I could jump.'

'You just didn't think this through *at all*, did you?'

'Yeah, definitely turned into a bit of a chook-with-its-head-cut-off situation, if I'm honest.'

'They don't know you're there, do they?'

'No, but when they release the bomb and see me plummet to my death I'm pretty sure they will.'

'There's nothing to hold on to when they drop it?'

'Not really.'

'Okay. I've got an idea.'

'Before you say anything you gotta know they have a loaded missile launcher in the rear cabin.'

'I'm sure they do.'

'Good old Mister Handsome has it lying across his knees, just waiting for you to drop by.'

'Okay, good to know. Now, tell me, are you still wearing your jacket?'

The Tyrannosaur churns across the burning skyline.

In the rear cabin the rocket launcher lies across Bunsen's knees, but he's not spending a lot of time searching for airborne threats. His primary concern is Kilroy as he wraps a fresh bandage around the old guy's now fingerless hand.

The rudimentary medi-kit in the Tyrannosaur isn't sophisticated enough to treat this wound. Normally Bunsen would take him straight to the private hospital in Santa Monica he'd used previously, but that will have to wait until they have completed Phase Three. Bunsen gives the old man three tabs of codeine so at least he'll feel okay until then.

'Have you released the video yet?' Kilroy's voice is low and thin.

'Soon. Don't worry about it. Just rest.'

Kilroy takes a deep breath, leans back and closes his eyes.

Bunsen remembers when Kilroy was the one tending his wounds, inevitably from a schoolyard scuffle brought about by Bunsen espousing some left-of-centre ideal, unpopular and unappreciated by the greater student body at the conservative prep school he attended in Brentwood. With his mother long gone and his father focused on his career, this old man was there for Bunsen when the pressure of that school became too much. Sometimes they'd play hooky together, go explore the city in Kilroy's black Lincoln, or eat chilli fries on Venice Beach, or watch one of his collection of action movies on VHS. Whatever they did, this man was *always* there for him. So Bunsen would be here for him now.

Judd looks out at the smoke cloud below, searches for the little yellow Loach.

'Where is it?'

Thump, thump, thump. It stabs out of the layer of smoke, low and to the left, almost directly behind the Air-Crane, the better to stay out of sight, and thunders towards the giant chopper.

Lola ties the severed end of the rope onto the largest hook in the bucket, drops it through the hole in the chopper's floor for the winch, then turns to the Australian: 'How long do you want it?'

Corey's eyes are glued to the giant chopper as he adjusts the controls. 'Twenty metres, please.'

Lola fires up the winch and watches the hook drop away. She estimates twenty metres as best she can, then kills the winch, the rope and hook now trailing behind the Loach.

In the Air-Crane's rear cabin Kilroy's eyes are half open as he stares out the window. 'You really need to release the video ASAP.'

Bunsen turns to him with a nod. 'I don't want you to worry about that now —'

'What the *hell*?' Kilroy's eyes spring wide open and with his good hand he points out the rear window.

Bunsen turns and looks – and gets the shock of his life. Five metres away, Judd Bell hangs off the side of the Tyrannosaur.

•

Judd has one foot on the bomb and one on the wheeled landing leg directly beside it. He holds on for dear life in the one-hundred-knot breeze as he studies Handsome and Ponytail frantically searching the cabin for something. He's certain they're looking for a weapon to blow him off the side of this aircraft.

Judd turns and looks back at the Loach. 'Come on, Aussie!'

Turbine screaming and rotors thundering, Corey corrects the Loach's angle of attack. 'Okay, you need to hold on because this might be a little . . . ' He doesn't finish the sentence.

Lola grips the side of her seat in preparation. 'Be a little *what*?'

Corey really concentrates as he finetunes the chopper's controls again. 'Tricky. I really need to be . . . quite accurate . . . to get this right.'

'What can I do?'

'Tell me if you see any missiles.'

She swallows hard. 'Okay.'

Corey stares at the Air-Crane as he make one last adjustment to the controls. 'Alrighty, here we go.'

Judd watches Handsome and Ponytail scour the Air-Crane's rear cabin for – oh, yep, *there it is* – they've found what they're looking for. A 9mm pistol. Handsome cocks the weapon, unbuckles his seatbelt and leans across to open the door.

Judd's eyes flick back to the little yellow chopper as it surges towards the giant chopper. Two hundred metres becomes one hundred becomes fifty becomes fifteen –

The Loach is right there, fills the sky, then tips into an impossibly sharp turn. The trailing rope is yanked into the turn too, and like a cracked whip, flicks out towards the Air-Crane, the heavy hook leading the way. It swings straight towards Judd –

Clang. It snags the Air-Crane's landing gear upright, directly in front of the astronaut. The airframe shudders.

Twang. The rope yanks tight between the two choppers. Judd is stunned. When the Australian told him the plan, he never expected it to work but here they are. Judd turns back to the rear cabin as Handsome, pistol in hand, pushes the door open, then stops.

Christ!

What should he do?

Bunsen is in two minds. Shoot Judd Bell with this gun or blow that chopper out of the sky with the SAM? By the time he has the missile aimed the chopper could be gone. But if he hits the chopper then all his problems are solved, including the Australian.

What should he do?

One thing he knows he shouldn't do is waste any more time making a decision.

Judd can see Handsome can't decide what to do next. He's not sure if he should shoot the astronaut or blow up the chopper.

Perfect.

He who hesitates is lost.

Time to go. Judd yanks his heavy-duty cotton Carhartt jacket from around his waist, flaps it over the rope, grabs the arms of the jacket in each hand, winds his fists tightly around them and pushes off –

Ohmigod! It's the Flying Fox From Hell – *Part Deux.* The Loach is a little below the Air-Crane so gravity is Judd's ally and he slides towards it *super* fast. Halfway across he glances back at good ole' Handsome and sees muzzle flash. So he went with the pistol instead of the missile in the end. The pistol is not directed at Judd, though; he shoots at the rope that's attached to the hook that's attached to the Air-Crane –

Boom. The rope collapses behind him as a bullet hits the mark.

'Damn—' Judd falls, drops, plummets, still holds the jacket in his left hand –

Clang. He hits the Loach's skid and grabs at it with his right hand, catches hold, dangles over the abyss. His hand slips –

Wham. Lola grabs the jacket in his left hand. She might be slight, but she's strong as steel. She pulls on the jacket and yanks him up and into the Loach.

'Hold on!' Corey tips the Loach hard right.

'Whoa, momma!' Judd clambers into the back seat as the chopper drops into a horrendously steep spiral dive, down and down and down. It plunges into the smoke layer.

And suddenly it's upright again. Nobody says a word as they just catch their breath.

A moment passes.

Corey glances back at Judd, gestures for him to put on his headset, which the astronaut does. 'Yep?'

'*Never* do that again!'

'Deal.' Judd claps both of them on the shoulder. 'Thanks, guys.'

In the Tyrannosaur high above, Bunsen scans the blanket of smoke below, SAM missile in hand as he attempts to locate the yellow Loach. He cannot. He went with the pistol instead of the missile and now believes it was an error.

Enrico's voice echoes in his ears. 'Now what?'

'We continue as planned.'

'What about the Item? Should we check it?'

'Unless he had an oxy-welder back there there's nothing he could have done to it. What's our ETA?'

'Six minutes.'

'Good. Let's ice this cake and go home.'

41

The Loach cuts through the haze as the setting sun turns the world an eerie orange-purple.

Lola pats the dog beside her then turns to Judd. 'So, it sounds like they did the same thing at the West Pico and Moreno High School. Injected something into the oil wells.'

Judd nods. 'But what? And why?'

'Could they be explosives?'

Judd's unsure. 'Maybe, but you'd think that bomb would be enough.'

Corey has a thought. 'Are those wells linked in some way? I mean, are they pumping oil from the same field or something?'

Lola shakes her head. 'Don't think so. They're too far apart.' She thinks about it and talks to herself in a low voice, though Judd and Corey can still hear her through their headsets. 'Moreno High and West Pico and La Brea. What do they have in common?' She absently looks at Spike's back and the splotches of blue that spot his white coat. She points at one. 'Moreno High.' Then another. 'West Pico.' Then a third. 'La Brea.' She draws a line to link the three then studies it – then stops dead. 'Oh, fuck!'

Judd leans forward. 'That doesn't sound good.'

She pulls out her iPhone and works the screen, launches the web browser, taps letters into the search engine.

Corey watches. 'Everything okay –?'

'Hold on! I gotta check something.' She stares at the screen, waits for the browser page to refresh. It takes an age. 'Come on!'

It refreshes.

She studies the screen – then pulls in a deep breath.

Corey glances at her. 'What?'

She looks at him. 'They're on a fault line. Moreno High, West Pico and La Brea. They're *all* on a fault line.'

'Which one?'

'Puente Hills. I think they did inject explosives and they're going to detonate them – and rupture it.'

The blood drains from Corey's face. 'So they can start an earth-quake.'

Lola nods as Judd leans forward again. '*What?*'

Corey turns to him. 'The Puente Hills fault runs right under downtown LA. When it goes it'll be huge. Some people think it'll be twice as big as the North Ridge quake.'

Lola nods. 'It's true.'

Judd looks at Corey, surprised. 'How do you know this?'

'I spent some time studying quakes and fault lines.'

'Really? Why?'

Corey hesitates – then forces himself to say it: 'My – my mother died in a quake in '97.'

The mood shifts in the cockpit. Lola turns to him. 'I'm so sorry to hear that.'

Judd puts a hand on his shoulder, concerned for his friend. 'Why didn't you say anything before?'

'I just – it was a long time ago.' Corey stares into the distance, lost in the pain of the memory. *Jeez*. Fifteen years later and it's still terrible. 'I wasn't able to save her – so I . . . ' He breathes in, shakes it off, pushes it away. 'Anyway, afterwards I was trying to understand what happened so I read. California is the earthquake capital of the world after all, so I read all about it. It was the only thing that made sense of it.'

Lola places a hand on his and looks at him. Corey can't meet her gaze, just wants the moment to pass. He changes the subject. 'Anyway, why would they do something like this?'

Judd thinks it through as he speaks: 'They know the city will be so busy dealing with the aftermath of a big quake that no one's going to worry about putting out a single oil fire in the middle of parkland that's not a threat to anyone.'

Lola takes this in. 'But why does that matter?'

Judd does his best to work it out. 'They must need the fire at La Brea to burn for a certain amount of time, so enough infected smoke is pumped into the atmosphere to send the virus global.'

Corey looks at the astronaut. 'You really think that's it?'

Judd shrugs. 'I don't know. I'm guessing, but it makes sense, doesn't it? Whatever it is, we have to stop them detonating that bomb.'

Corey nods. 'You got a plan?'

'I'm working on it.'

'Good, 'cause I got nothing.' The Australian immediately slows the Loach, searches the roadway beneath them, sees a clear spot and drops the chopper towards it.

Lola watches. 'What are you doing?'

'You're not coming with us.'

'Excuse me?' She's instantly furious.

'They have a huge bomb that might set off a huge earthquake. I don't want you anywhere near the blast radius or the epicentre. It's too dangerous. I can't take that risk.'

'That's not your decision.'

'It is when I'm the one flying the chopper.'

'You wouldn't even know about this chopper if it wasn't for me!'

'True, and I'm grateful – but that doesn't change anything.'

The Loach settles on the roadway, which is empty except for coils of drifting smoke. Lola glares at Corey for a moment, then steps out of the chopper. Corey looks back at Spike. 'You too, dog face.'

Spike growls.

'I don't care if you're hungry. Out.' Then Corey leans close and whispers: 'Keep an eye on her.' The dog barks and hops out.

Corey beckons Lola to his side of the cockpit. She has to shout over the whine and thump of the chopper: '*What?*' She is royally pissed.

Corey shouts too: 'Stay in this area and take cover. We'll be back to pick you up soon.' He nods at Spike. 'If anything happens – look after him, please.'

She draws in a surprised breath, taken aback by the request. 'Oh. Yes, of course.' She steps closer and the anger drains from her face. 'Be careful.'

Corey grins his crooked grin. 'She'll be right. Now stand back.'

Lola steps away and shields her eyes as the Loach spools up and lifts skyward.

Lola pivots, scans her surroundings then looks at Spike. 'Well, *this* sucks.'

They've been dropped in the middle of nowhere. It looks like some kind of semi-industrial wasteland and is dominated by the pungent smell of burned gasoline. Lola doesn't know where she is and as the place seems to be deserted, she can't ask anyone. The fact that the streets are empty must mean people now understand that *inside* is the safest place to be. Trouble is, if the Puente Hills earthquake theory is correct, *outside*, well away from buildings and structures, will definitely be the best option.

So what does she do now? Wait for the monster explosion? Or the massive earthquake?

Neither.

'Screw it.' She runs, beckons Spike to follow. 'Come on, boy.' They jog along the road, past a vacant lot, turn a corner, and then she knows exactly where she is. 'Right.' She finds her bearings then runs on, sees a lone figure on the sidewalk in the distance.

It's a little girl. She sits on a pink dragster bicycle and watches a solitary car burn on the opposite side of the street. Lola stops beside her, smiles warmly. 'Hey there.'

The little girl looks her up and down warily. She's no more than nine years old but she has the knowing eyes of a wise soul. ''Sup?'

'I'd like to talk some business with you.'

The little girl leans back on the dragster's seat and takes in the well-dressed lady. 'I'm listening.'

The little girl studies the diamond-encrusted platinum Rolex Day-Date that hangs loosely on her tiny wrist, then turns and sprints towards a modest, single-storey house. 'Hey, momma, look what *I* got!'

Lola rides the pink dragster like she stole it, rainbow-coloured handlebar ribbons fluttering in the breeze. It's almost too small for her but she doesn't care, running will take too long and she's happy to be rid of that garish watch. She turns and looks down at Spike, who bounds along beside her. 'You're a good boy!'

The dog lets out a sharp bark and they race onwards.

42

'Take it up.'

Corey eases the Loach above the smoke haze and Judd pushes the brass telescope to his eye, scans the sky, picks up the black Air-Crane. 'There! About a kilometre and a half away. Heading straight for the tar pits. Take it down.'

'Right.' Corey drops the Loach into the smoke layer, where it is almost completely cloaked.

Judd turns to the Australian. 'So, I get what you see in her.'

'Lola? Sure, but you were right.'

'Yeah.'

Corey glances at him. 'That didn't sound very convincing.'

'Well, maybe you should – rethink your approach.'

'*Rethink my approach*? *My* approach is *your* approach! I got it from *you*!'

'I may have been – premature with my advice.'

'Premature?'

'A better word might be – inaccurate.'

'Good God, what *are* you saying? And stop pausing in the middle of your sentences.'

'I'm saying she may be worth fighting for after all.'

'*I* said that to you before! And you're all "oh-no-she's-got-a-boyfriend-who's-a-movie-star" and "you-know-how-it-ends".'

'That was before I met her. Look, I don't know what the hell I'm talking about when it comes to relationships so don't listen to me.'

'I have to.'

'Why?'

'Otherwise the only advice I'm getting is from a cattle dog, which is actually *better* than yours now that I think about it, *not* that that would be hard.'

'I'm just saying you should fight for her. Even if it ends badly or, you know, gets embarrassing again.'

'But you just said I shouldn't listen to you!'

'*Exactly*. So let's just deal with these pricks.' He nods at the Air-Crane. 'And then I'm sure everything will become apparent.'

'What the hell does *that* mean?'

'I have no idea. I told you I'm terrible at this stuff.'

Corey exhales and his eyes find the Air-Crane. 'Okay. So what's the plan?'

'I'm working on it.'

'We're getting close so don't be shy with the details.'

Judd nods and his eyes narrow as he thinks.

43

'We need to find a place to land now!' Rhonda's voice is thin as she pulls the Southwest 737 into a steep turn. 'Otherwise we have to ditch.'

Severson nods. He knows ditching in the ocean is the very last option. So many things can go wrong even when a plane is intact, but ditching with a two-metre gash in the fuselage means the plane will sink, and everyone will drown, in three minutes.

'Okay.' He surveys the ruined city of Los Angeles below, takes in the odd purple-coloured smoke that blankets the ground. The last half hour has been an education. As the jet slowed and lost altitude they searched through the haze for a spot to land. And searched. And searched. Any place they could see that was flat, long and straight was blocked or clogged with vehicles, most of them on fire. They even flew over LAX and saw the destruction there, the main runway littered with the wreckage of airliners. After telling Rhonda that he would help her improvise, Severson has so far delivered a big, fat duck egg. 'I can't see anything.'

'Then we are about to buy the farm.'

Severson does not want to buy *any* kind of farm. He hates farming. He wants to live forever so *meeting Swayze* before he's even fifty is not part of the plan. He takes a breath, tries to think of something, *anything*, to fix this.

LA. He doesn't know the city that well, hasn't been there for a couple of years. 'Who or what do I know in LA?'

Rhonda looks at him. 'That's it!'

'Of course!' Then he stops, confused. '*What's* it?'

Rhonda passes him her iPhone. 'Call Judd. If he's down there he could know something.'

Severson's not convinced. 'Will it even go through? We're still pretty high.'

She glances at the altimeter in front of her. 'Five thousand feet isn't high. Anyway, we won't know unless we try.'

She's right. He doesn't believe the call will go through but then how can it hurt to try? They're minutes away from ditching in the friggin' Pacific. He dials and nothing happens, he just hears static-laced dead air. He looks at Rhonda and shakes his head – then it rings. 'Oh, it's ringing —'

'Hello?'

'*Judd*?' Severson can't believe it. It's Judd! His voice is distant and echoey but it's him.

'Severson? God, it's good to hear you, man! You okay? Is Rhonda okay? Where are you?'

'Fine. We're both fine. Are you in LA? Are you okay?'

'Yes to both.'

'Fantastic.' He shoots Rhonda a thumbs up.

'Where's Rhonda?'

'She's busy flying the plane.'

'The what?'

'We're five thousand feet above you with no engine power and there's a large gash in the fuselage. The captain's dead, the copilot's unconscious and there are seventy passengers on board. The airports are all blocked and every goddamn road is jammed with burning cars. Even the *canals* are full of cars. We need a place to land ASAP.' Severson says it in one breath.

'Christ. What are you flying?'

'A Boeing 737.'

'Right. Okay.' Judd is horrified that Rhonda is aboard a crippled jet above LA – and relieved she's the one piloting it. If anyone can bring it down safely it's her. She's still alive and in one piece and in charge of her own fate.

Okay, mofo, time to think.

Judd knows that even though the 737 is a small commercial airliner, it's still a commercial *airliner*, so it needs plenty of space to land. He looks out the Loach's windscreen and can't see a spot that would be suitable. Then the haze clears momentarily and the La Brea Tar Pits loom in the distance. The museum, a low-slung, two-storey building, is borded to the left by a giant, kidney-shaped lake of black oil. In between the two runs a long, wide walkway that leads to an expansive, green park beyond. Apart from a stand of trees at the far end, the park is empty. 'La Brea. There's space there if you can't find anything else.'

Severson sounds sceptical. 'The tar pits? How do you know this?'

'I'm staring at it. There's a walkway that leads to a park beside the museum. You'll have to be super-accurate and bring it in slow to make it work. It's short.'

'Okay.'

'But – and I know this is going to sound strange – there's a guy with a bomb on the way there now.'

'There's a *what* now?'

'It's not *confirmed*, but I think he's heading there.'

'Is that a joke?'

'I wish. It's a *really* big bomb. We're on our way to stop it now.'

'We?'

'Corey and me. So, because of that, La Brea should be your *last* option.'

'Understood.'

'Can you put Rhonda on?'

'Of course.'

Judd hears a rustling sound, then Rhonda's voice: 'Hey, babe.'

Hearing her makes his heart hurt. Instantly he wants to get all lovey-dovey but he knows she doesn't respond to that kind of thing so he sticks with the tried and tested: humour. 'Well, I'm just loving this trip to LA. It's *so* relaxing.'

He's sure he can hear her smile on the other end of the line. 'Yeah, I'm really enjoying the flight too. Such great service.'

He laughs, then she surprises him. 'I love you, sweetheart, always know that.'

What?

'I lov—'

The line cuts out. 'Oh, come on!' Judd immediately calls her back but no joy, it goes straight to voicemail.

Man!

She told him she loved him *on the phone*, the *first time* she has *ever* done that, which makes him think she is either heavily medicated or her situation is much worse than he thought, and he's pretty sure it's the latter.

He should have said it *straight away*. As soon as he heard her voice.

Christalmighty

He hopes that isn't the last chance he gets to say it.

•

Severson redials Judd's number but the call goes straight to voice-mail. As he does it he realises, for the first time in his forty-five years, that he has no one to love in his life, no one to have a heartfelt conversation with in a moment of crisis. He decides that if he gets out of this alive he must remedy that.

But that's something for the future. Right now he knows that La Brea is not only their best option, but their *only* option. He makes an executive decision not to tell Rhonda about the 'guy with the bomb'. As far as he's concerned there's no reason to even bring it up until they actually get there. 'Okay, Judd said there's space to land at La Brea.'

Rhonda continues to wrestle the jet's controls, confused. 'What's a *Labrea*?'

'The tar pits. The La Brea Tar Pits. You know, with the tar.'

'Don't say it like I should know what it is. I need *directions*.'

Severson swipes open the pilot's iPad, works the screen, pinches and zooms his way across the map app. 'It's somewhere on – Wilshire Boulevard, I think. Near the Miracle Mile. Christ, I haven't been there since I was a kid – come on, where are you, you bastard?'

'Quickly.'

'I'm doing it – okay, I think – I got something.' He shows her the iPad's screen and points. 'We're *here*, we need to go *here*.'

Rhonda studies the map for a long moment.

'Can we make it?'

She looks anything but one hundred per cent confident. 'It's a way.'

Severson leans close. 'Hey, if you want to sit up here at the big kid's table you're going to have to stay positive.'

Rhonda stares at him for a moment – then cracks a grim smile. 'Okay, let's do it.' She works the controls and the jet tips into a steep turn.

Severson holds on tight.

Next stop La Brea.

44

The Tyrannosaur slows as it descends, now just fifty metres above the ground as it slashes towards the sprawling oil lake that dominates the La Brea Tar Pits complex. The giant chopper's shadow slides across a family of mammoths that stand next to the wide walkway beside the lake.

With the SAM again lying across his knees, Bunsen studies the three life-sized models, a long-time favourite of visitors to the tar pits, then speaks into his headset's microphone: 'Park it over the middle of the lake.'

'Will do.' Enrico directs the Tyrannosaur into position.

Bunsen turns to Kilroy. The old guy looks terrible now, his eyes shut, his face drained of colour. 'I'll get you to a doc really soon.'

Kilroy's voice is little more than a low croak. 'Have you released the video?'

Bunsen scans the horizon, searches for a threat. 'Not yet.'

'You said it would be done before Phase Three. *Before* we ignite the oil lake. Before the earthquake.'

'I know.'

Kilroy opens his eyes and looks at Bunsen. 'People must know before it happens. You must warn them.'

Bunsen looks at him and shakes his head. 'I'm sorry. That's not going to happen.'

'But – you promised me.'

'I'm sorry.'

Kilroy exhales noisily. Bunsen knows that sound well. It's the sound of disapproval. It hurt to hear it when he was a child and it has exactly the same effect on him now. He looks at Kilroy, expects to see that emotion on the old man's face, but it's not there. Instead of disapproval he finds disappointment, which, in many ways, is worse. 'You lied to me.'

Bunsen nods. 'I did.'

'Why?'

'Because I knew you wouldn't understand.'

'Understand what? I thought the purpose of the earthquake was to make sure the oil lake burned for two weeks so the virus went global.'

'It is but it's more than that. We need to make an example of this city. *Los Angeles* is the single most important place on the planet for the motor industry. We need to get rid of the old infrastructure and the old ideas and start again.'

Kilroy looks at him, horrified. 'You're talking about destroying a city, *our* city, killing thousands, maybe *hundreds* of thousands of innocent people.'

Bunsen nods. 'It's the only way to be sure.'

'Didn't you learn anything from me?'

'Of course. That's why we're here.'

'No.' Kilroy shifts painfully in his seat, looks Bunsen in the eye. 'We don't want to *destroy* the world, we want to *save* it. We don't want to *hurt* innocent people, we want to make their lives *better*.'

'Yes, but to do that we have to change everything. It must be a revolution, otherwise we're just playing at the edges and everything stays the same.'

Kilroy stares at him for a long moment, speechless, then turns and looks out at the sun as it sets on the horizon.

Bunsen opens his mouth to speak, then realises there is nothing more to say.

The little yellow Loach stays low as powerlines zip past a metre below.

A gap in the haze opens up and Corey sees the giant tar pit for the first time. He's impressed. 'It's so big.'

'That's what she said.' Judd cracks a grin as he focuses on the Air-Crane hovering over the pit. 'So I guess we can confirm La Brea *is* the target.'

Corey pulls the Loach into a hover then turns to the astronaut. 'So, what's the call?'

Judd looks at him – and his hands go Rubik.

Corey can't believe it. 'You only do that when you don't have an idea! Don't tell me you don't have an idea!'

'No, I do it when I'm thinking.'

'Thinking was for *earlier*. This is happening *now*.'

Judd knows he's right. This is exactly what happened at the Imax Theatre, when he couldn't save himself or his friends. This is a moment when he needs to rise to the occasion and be the man everyone thinks he is – and yet he can't even come up with *one* goddamn idea. He realises saving *Atlantis* was just a fluke –

Wait.

Saving *Atlantis*.

Where was he when he realised he needed to save that shuttle? He was sitting in a Loach exactly like this, with the same Australian beside him. That's all he had then and that's all he has now – so he can do it again. He just needs to use what he's got and remember what he knows.

Use what you've got and remember what you know.

Ding!

It's like a light bulb going off. He turns to Corey. 'I have a plan I think might work.'

'Might?'

'It could also end badly, but let's stay positive.' Judd forces a grin.

Corey looks at him like he doesn't want to ask. 'What is it?'

'We let them know we're here.'

Corey takes a second, then understands what he means them to do. 'Jesus wept. Really?'

Judd nods. 'Fair dinkum.' Then he thinks about it. 'Did I use it right?'

Corey nods, and they share a smile, then: 'Righto, let's do this.'

'You sure?'

'Not at all. But we should give it a go anyway.'

The Australian grins his crooked grin then sends the Loach straight up. Fast. It punches through the blanket of smoke and bursts into clear air above. Corey slows the descent then pulls the little chopper into a hover. 'That should do it.'

From the Tyrannosaur's rear cabin Bunsen sees the Loach. Stunned, he barks into his headset's microphone: 'The yellow chopper is right behind us! Turn left. Now!'

'Will do.' Enrico pulls on the controls and the Tyrannosaur swings around.

'That's it!' The Tyrannosaur stops turning as Bunsen pushes the rear cabin door open, aims the SAM out at the Loach and pulls the trigger. 'This ends now.'

•

The missile blasts away from the rear of the Air-Crane and hisses directly towards the Loach.

Judd picks it up first. 'Missile!'

Then Corey sees it too. 'Got it!'

It's upon them very quickly.

'Hold on!' Corey guns the turbine and yanks the Loach into a steep right turn, ploughs into the smoke.

'Yahh!' Judd is flung to the side, grabs his seat and the door-frame with a tortured grimace.

Corey glances in his side-view mirror but can't see the rocket. He shouts into his headset: 'Tell me where it is!'

Judd cranes his neck to look back through the open doorway. He can't get into the right position so he unbuckles his seatbelt and tries again, sees the missile hissing behind them. 'It's – oh Christ, it's *right* behind us. And I mean *right* behind.'

'Good.'

'This'd be fun if I didn't think we were about to die.'

'Hold on!' Turbine screaming, rotors throbbing, Corey tightens the Loach's turn.

'Oh – man.' The g-forces go to work on Judd, squeeze him back into his seat. The last time he felt anything this severe was during a *shuttle launch*. It's difficult to breathe, even harder to talk.

Corey caresses the controls and tightens the turn again. 'Where is it?'

Judd cranes his neck against the g-force, again sees the missile hissing behind them. 'Same as usual – except *closer*.'

Rotors thumping, Corey tightens the Loach's turn a little more.

The chopper's tilted at such a steep angle that Judd can see nothing but the black oil lake rush past the pilot's open door. 'How – much – longer?'

'Almost – there.' Corey yanks the Loach out of the turn.

Hovering within the fog directly in front of them is the Air-Crane.

Corey smiles. 'And there it is.' The little chopper has pulled a giant arc. He eases the Loach up and over the giant black chopper with a foot to spare.

Ka-boom! The missile slams into the Air-Crane's tail rotor and vaporises the rear section of the chopper.

45

'We're going down!'

Enrico fights the Tyrannosaur's controls but there's nothing he can do to stop it. Without a tail rotor the giant helicopter twists into a wild spiral.

Whump, whump, whump. Bunsen holds on for dear life as the burning chopper whips around and around, faster and faster. He leans back into the cockpit, reaches across to the central panel and flicks a switch –

Clank. The Item is released from the Tyrannosaur's cradle and flies free, cartwheels across the sky –

Slam. It lands at the very edge of the tar pit, bounces high then smashes through the safety railing and lands on the grass by the side of the walkway.

Whump, whump, whump. The Tyrannosaur spins violently. Metal bends and tears as the rotor blades shatter in a blizzard of fibre-plastic. Bunsen glances into the cockpit. Enrico is dead, a shard of a shattered rotor blade embedded in his throat.

Whump, whump, whump. Bunsen turns to Kilroy, both terrified beyond measure. Their eyes meet.

Time slows.

A poignant moment passes between them, imbued with a bond of shared affection, for the years when they only had each other.

Time speeds up.

The left side of the cabin rips away and the old man is ejected from the spinning chopper. Bunsen screams after him, horrified: 'No –!'

Boom! The burning Tyrannosaur smashes into the tar pit, sends out a giant wave of oil.

Judd stares down at the flaming wreck of the Air-Crane as a wide patch of the oil ignites around it. He studies what remains of the chopper, can find no pity in his heart for the men aboard. The astronaut turns and takes in the bomb, which has come to rest on the grass by the side of the paved walkway. 'We have to get it out of here now.'

Corey turns to him. 'But he had a detonator. If he's dead or unconcious he can't trigger it.'

'It could be on a timer.'

Corey takes this in with a nod. 'Of course. You got a plan?'

Judd's eyes flick around the Loach's cabin, sees the rope wound around the winch nestled between the two front seats.

Use what you've got and remember what you know.

'Get me to that bomb and I'll tell you all about it.'

Handlebar ribbons fluttering, Lola rides the pink dragster like it's Seabiscuit. She looks up, bleakly registers the plume of black smoke that arches into the sky above the tar pits. She ups her pace and turns to Spike, who runs beside her. 'Come on, boy.'

Judd finishes tying the frayed end of the rope onto a hook as Corey stares at him, appalled. 'It's not a fantastic plan, mate.'

'It's the only one going. Now, as soon as I have the hook you release the rope then get this thing in the air as fast and as high as possible. Then, if it detonates, we *both* don't bite the big one. Hopefully.'

Corey nods unhappily, drops the chopper onto the walkway beside the weapon. And takes it in. It appears to be even bigger now that it's not attached to the Air-Crane. And creepier, the black lattice metalwork gives it a particularly ominous aspect. The heavy impact has dug it into the grass beside the walkway, but it still appears to be in one piece. Corey turns to the astronaut. 'I'll wait for your signal.'

Judd shoots him a sharp nod. 'Okay, I'll see you.'

'Not if I see you first.'

They share a grim smile then Judd slides out of the cockpit, scrambles under the chopper, grabs the hook at the end of the rope and thumps on the underside of the fuselage with his fist.

The Aussie hears it and works the winch. It quickly unspools every inch of rope, almost forty metres. Hook in hand, Judd crawls from under the chopper and points skyward.

Corey powers up and the Loach rises quickly. He looks down, makes sure he isn't too high and there's enough play in the rope for Judd to work with, then pulls the little chopper into a hover.

As the astronaut approaches the weapon a cloud of black smoke drifts across the walkway from the burning Air-Crane and obscures Corey's view. The Loach is too high for its rotor wash to clear it. Corey holds position and waits for the signal, hopes to God that black lattice atrocity doesn't explode.

Hook in hand, Judd surveys the weapon for a spot to latch on. The problem is the smoke from the crashed Air-Crane. It smells like death, stings his eyes, irritates his throat and cuts visibility to a few metres. He tries his best to ignore it as he searches for a place –

Click.

The fact he can hear the sound of a pistol being cocked above the throb of the Loach's rotor blades means it must be very close. He turns.

It's Handsome Guy.

Christ. He's *still* alive? How did he survive that crash? He's covered in black sludge but doesn't seem to be injured. *At all.* He has a pistol in hand and aims it at Judd's face.

'Let go of the hook.'

Judd does it. It swings away, disappears into the smoke.

'Now give me the counteragent.'

Judd points at his jacket pocket. 'It's in here.'

Handsome steps closer. 'Slowly.'

Judd reaches inside his jacket with his right hand and very deliberately draws out the metal cylinder – then flicks it hard.

It extends. It's not the canister, but the brass telescope from the Loach.

Judd springs forward and clubs the pistol from Handsome's hand. It skitters across the walkway and disappears into the smoke haze.

Handsome charges the astronaut.

Judd swings the telescope.

And the battle is joined.

Clang. The heavy telescope slams into Handsome's torso. He staggers sideways, stunned. He recovers his balance but Judd steps forward and swings the instrument again.

Clank. It clips Handsome across the jaw. He turns with the blow, then swings back with a right fist, cracks Judd in the mouth. The astronaut jolts back and he stumbles to the ground, rolls to his feet and swings the telescope once more.

Clunk. Handsome throws out a forearm to block the stroke and the telescope snaps in two, never designed for hand-to-hand combat.

Judd drops it, then nails him with an uppercut to the chin. Handsome rocks backwards, then pivots and swings into a roundhouse kick, slams Judd in the solar plexus, knocks him off his feet.

Crunch. Handsome lands on top of the astronaut, jams a forearm across his throat. He might be shorter and lighter than Judd but he's stronger than he appears. Judd whacks him in the cheek with a left jab but Handsome holds the forearm in place and searches his clothes –

'Yes.' He wrenches the canister from the astronaut's jacket pocket, finds his feet, backs away, searches for the pistol within the smoke haze, scoops it up and aims it at Judd.

The astronaut freezes. Handsome steps towards him, nods at the bomb. 'Two good men gave their lives to make this a reality. And now you will too. Congratulations, Judd Bell, you're the first visitor to the new Ground Zero.'

He pulls the trigger.

Bam. The gunshot rings out.

Handsome staggers forward – then drops to his knees and slumps to the ground face first, a scarlet bullet wound in the middle of his back. The canister of counteragent falls from his hand, hits the ground with a clank and rolls to Judd's feet.

'What the hell?' Judd is both shocked and relieved. He looks from Handsome to a figure that looms through the haze towards him.

Ponytail.

The old man limps, appears to be badly injured, his body streaked with a mix of blood and oil. He holds a raised pistol.

'Oh, damn.' Judd is still shocked but he's no longer relieved. He pulls in a sharp breath and waits for the next gunshot. Ponytail limps towards him – then lowers the weapon, kneels beside Handsome and turns him over. Handsome weakly reaches for his jacket pocket but Ponytail gently pushes his hand away, reaches into the jacket pocket himself and pulls out a cigarette pack-sized black box that Judd thinks can only be the bomb's detonator.

Shit! He starts towards Ponytail – but the old guy turns and throws the box into the middle of the tar pit. It lands with a splash and disappears below the surface.

Judd exhales, feels like his life just flashed before his eyes. 'Thank you.' He doesn't know what else to say.

Ponytail doesn't look up at him. 'I didn't do it for you.'

Kilroy turns to Bunsen and cradles his head, overwhelmed with grief. 'I'm sorry.'

Bunsen stares up at him, confused. 'Why?' His eyes are glassy, his voice a low rasp.

'I had to stop you. The city is on its knees.'

'That was the *point*.'

'I spent the best days of my life exploring this town with you.'

Bunsen smiles at the memory. There's blood in his mouth.

'I just – I couldn't let it be destroyed. No matter what.'

The light fades from Bunsen's eyes. 'But it – will be —'

Kilroy is confused. Bunsen coughs blood, his voice little more than a croak. 'The bomb – it's on a timer – you must leave – now.'

Judd steps towards them. 'Did he say the bomb is on a timer?'

Ponytail doesn't answer, just stares down at Handsome.

'How long? How long is the timer?'

Neither of them responds.

'Answer me!' Judd crouches down – then realises they're not ignoring him, they're dead. Both of them. He sees a gaping wound under Ponytail's arm, the ground beneath him slick with blood.

'Fuck!' The astronaut stands, grabs the canister of counteragent, then searches the black smoke for the hook and rope which hang from the hovering Loach. He cannot see either, or the chopper. The haze is even thicker than before. 'Where is it?' he shouts into the fog, his frustration extreme.

He takes a breath, tries not to inhale too much smoke, fails – and coughs hard. People the world over think he is a hero. Well, this is where he gets to prove it. This is where the rubber meets the road. He has to get this right, *right now,* even if every fibre of his being tells him to leave this place and get away from this bomb as fast as possible.

He looks up, searches the sky, catches sight of the Loach's rotors as they strobe through the haze. From its position he guesstimates where the rope might be and moves in that direction, fast –

He glimpses the hook within the smoke, follows it, grabs at it – misses. It's so close. It swings in front of him again. He reaches out – snags it. He turns to the bomb.

Where the hell is it?

It was just here, but he can't see anything through this damn smoke –

There it is. It looms through the fog like an iceberg on *Titanic*'s maiden voyage. It's close, just two metres away. He tugs the rope towards it –

Twang. It pulls tight, won't reach.

It's ten centimetres short.

Ten centimetres!

Judd yanks on it again. 'Come on!'

Twang. It won't reach. The Loach has drifted and it's too far away. He pulls on it with all his might, leans into it, strains, uses every ounce of energy. 'Come on, you mutha!'

He drags the chopper across the sky –

Clank. The hook attaches to the bomb's latticework.

'Yes!' He pulls on the rope once, like he's plucking a gigantic guitar string.

Corey feels the vibration shake the little chopper. Then a second. Then a third. That's the signal. 'Time to go.'

He powers up.

Judd hears the chopper's turbine spool, can feel the rope tighten in his hand. It's actually happening. He'd smile if he didn't think it would somehow tempt fate and jinx everything.

Screw it.

He smiles. For just a moment –

A high-pitched whistling sound cuts the soundscape, instantly grows to an ear-splitting crescendo. It comes from his right. He turns to it.

A Boeing 737 punches through the purple haze and drops towards the walkway – right where Judd stands and the Loach hovers.

'Oh, damn.'

Rhonda.

He completely forgot about Rhonda – and her *jet*.

He guesses it's a kilometre away but who can tell through all this damn smoke? However far away it is, it will land on him in a matter of seconds.

He wishes he hadn't smiled.

46

Corey can't hear anything over the throb of the Loach's rotors, but he sees a flash of movement in the chopper's side-view mirror. He looks closer. 'What is that – oh, jeez!'

A 737 drops out of the sky straight towards the Loach, its wake turbulence swatting the smoke haze into a series of gigantic swirling vortices. It appears to be missing an engine.

This is not good. Descending will not work. The jet will just land on top of the Loach. He needs to go up. *Fast*. Corey gives the little yellow chopper full bananas. The turbine screams and the rotors throb – and the Loach does not rise an inch.

Judd watches the 737 approach. He knows it cannot change course or fly around because its engines aren't operational and there's nowhere else to land.

Corey must know the jet is coming because the Loach's turbine screams and its rotors roar – but nothing is happening. The bomb is so heavy and it's jammed into the grass so deeply that it will not move. No wonder they used an Air-Crane to ferry the damn thing around.

Judd wrenches the rope from side to side, lays a foot on the bomb and rocks it back and forth, tries to work it free.

It does not move.

•

Corey eyes the approaching jet as it grows large in his side-view mirror. Jeez, it's close. 'You-can-do-it-baby!' The bomb is either extremely heavy, or stuck, or both –

He feels the rope sway the chopper from left to right. Judd must be trying to work it free. Corey joins in, sharply jolts the chopper from side to side, hopes it might help pull it free.

Yes! Good one, Corey! Judd frantically yanks the rope side to side in time with the Loach as he rocks the weapon back and forth with his right foot –

Pop. It slides out of the dirt and rises. Judd holds the rope, keeps his foot on the weapon and takes the ride. He turns and checks the 737's position.

Christ!

It's shockingly close, less than a football field away and dropping straight towards him. He's rising directly *into the path of the jet.*

The little chopper climbs, but it's slow.

Too slow.

'Come-on-baby-baby-please!' Corey's eyes flick to the side-view mirror.

The airliner is right there!

The 737 sweeps past and Judd's eyes momentarily find the cockpit.

Time slows.

He looks inside and sees Rhonda at the controls, mouth frozen in a stunned 'O' shape as her eyes move from her boyfriend to what-the-hell-is-he-standing-on-it-sure-as-hell-looks-like-a-*weapon-of-mass-destruction*!

Beside her Severson has the same 'O' expression going on, but he's waving, which leads Judd to believe Rhonda's the one doing the flying – definitely the correct choice. He wonders if Severson told her about the bomb or if this is the first she's hearing about it.

Time speeds up.

The wing slices under the weapon with about half a metre to spare, but the tailfin is a different matter. The wake turbulence sends the bomb, and Judd, straight into it. It hits flush on and sets the giant weapon spinning wildly. Judd holds on to the rope for dear life as he whips around and around and around.

The 737's rear landing gear slaps the centre of the walkway then its front wheels touch down.

'Flaps up! Brakes on full!' Rhonda works the controls. She's really pissed. 'Why didn't you tell me there was a *bomb?*'

'Because I wanted you to stay focused on this!' He points at the end of the walkway. Through the haze they can see the grassy parkland and the stand of trees beyond. It's close.

Rhonda grits her teeth. 'Hold on!'

Severson grips the edge of the copilot's seat. 'I'm holding!'

The jet spears off the end of the walkway.

The wheels touch the grass and instantly dig into the moist surface.

Crack. They snap off and the jet belly flops onto the ground and skids. They no longer have control of the aircraft.

The fuselage convulses as Severson unhappily takes in the fast approaching trees. 'We're heading straight to the scene of the accident.'

Rhonda knows it. 'We need reverse thrust. I'm going to restart the engine.'

'*What?*'

'You wanted improvising, well, *this* is improvising!'

'It'll explode.'

'Which will also happen when we hit those trees.' She pushes the throttle lever for the starboard side jet full forward, hears the engine run up behind her, then triggers the thrust reversers.

With a jolt the aircraft instantly decelerates and Rhonda is hopeful. She lets the engine run and run, then she hears that terrible sound, like gravel inside a cement mixer, and pulls the throttle lever back to shut it down –

Too late.

The engine detonates.

Ka-boom. The explosion is massive. The jet violently twists and metal rips and the world turns over. For a moment Rhonda's vertical, then she's on the cockpit's roof with a terrified Severson right beside her –

The bad news is that the explosion rolled the jet and now it slides along the parkway *upside down*. The *really* bad news is that she hears metal tear again –

Riiip. Rhonda is flung sideways and suddenly grass rushes past her face. She looks up and sees the rear half of the jet's fuselage slide away to the left as the cockpit arcs to the right.

Her only consolation is that she told Judd she loved him.

The spinning bomb slows enough for Judd to see the 737, now in two pieces, slide across the parkland. 'No!' Horrified, he loses sight of it in the smoke haze.

He wishes he'd told Rhonda he loved her.

The little Loach surges towards the smog ceiling.

Corey's motivation is simple: get the weapon and its blast zone as far from the city – and Lola and Spike – as quickly as possible.

The best way to do that is by taking it straight up. Once he has enough height he will fly it to the coast and release it over the ocean. If it detonates before then, at least it'll be far enough above the population so no one will be affected – except for Judd and his good self, of course.

Lola furiously pedals the pink dragster along the sidewalk, Spike right beside her. Through the haze she catches sight of the yellow chopper as it climbs, then sees that someone is *surfing* what appears to be a giant bomb attached to a rope below it.

'What the hell are they doing?'

The dog barks, like he's answering her.

Then she knowns exactly what they're doing. *They're being heroes.* They're performing an incredibly dangerous, totally selfless act. She's read it in screenplays, watched it in movies, seen it on television shows, but she's never *witnessed* it in real life before. It's the strangest combination of breathtaking, inspiring and terrifying, and it strikes her with a feeling of cold dread and giddy euphoria at exactly the same moment.

If the bomb detonates now Judd knows he's toast, but if he can get to the chopper it might offer some protection. *Might* being the operative word. Either way it'll be better up there than down here *standing* on the damn thing.

He scales the rope towards the cockpit, wrenches himself upwards, hand over hand over hand. He doesn't look down. Not because he's afraid of heights, but because he doesn't want to look at that bomb.

Corey keeps the throttle at full power as the Loach ascends. In spite of everything that's going on he's loving flying again. He looks up, takes in the smog cloud that's lit orange by the end of day's sun. The Loach will reach it in a moment, then he'll head for the coast.

He glances down, sees Judd swiftly climb the rope towards the cockpit. He's close, only a few metres away. 'Come on!' He knows the astronaut can't hear him, but it feels better to be encouraging.

Lola watches the Loach disappear into the smog cloud – then it flashes a vivid purple and illuminates the city like God's sunlamp.

She recoils. 'What the hell – ?' It takes a moment before she processes what just happened.

The bomb detonated.

Ka-boom. The thunderclap echoes across the landscape to confirm it. Its ferocity is overwhelming.

'No!' Lola stares up at the glowing cloud, waits, hopes for the little chopper to emerge, unscathed and intact.

It does not.

The bright glow inside the cloud diminishes as the thunderclap fades.

They're dead.

Lola is stricken. She pulls to a stop and bends at the hips. It feels like she's been punched in the stomach so hard that she will never catch her breath.

Corey is dead.

Spike howls.

47

'This is not good!' Corey fights the controls as the Loach convulses.

'I noticed!' Judd hangs half in, half out the passenger door, reaches for the seat to grab hold and pull himself inside the cabin –

The chopper tilts to the left and he slides out. 'Tomato! Tomatooo–!'

Wham. Corey catches his hand, yanks him inside. 'Thanks!' Judd slides into his seat – then realises the soles of his shoes are on fire. 'Oh, shit!' He stamps them on the floor to put them out – and the floor collapses under him and he falls through the flaming hole –

Corey grabs his arm and pulls him back into his seat, then looks up at the spinning rotor blades. They are ablaze, a pulsating circle of flame against the purple smog cloud that surrounds them. 'We're losing lift!' The Australian wrenches the controls but the expression on his face tells Judd all he needs to know: the giant fireball from the explosion didn't destroy the chopper but set it alight and that's almost as bad.

Judd scans the cabin, searches for a solution.

Parachutes!

Two, pushed under the rear bench seat. He points at them. 'Are they movie props or are they real?'

Corey has no idea. 'Check 'em!'

Judd hauls one from under the seat. 'It's heavy!' That's a good sign. He slips his hand under the flap, feels the material. Yes! It's a parachute. He pushes it towards Corey. 'I think it's okay.'

Thud, thud, thud. The burning rotor blades disintegrate and flaming chunks of plastic fibre smack into the windscreen.

The Loach stops flying, hangs in the smog for an extended moment – then plummets to earth.

Judd grabs the second parachute from under the rear seat but it's lighter than the first. *Much* lighter. Is it a prop or is it real? He pushes his hand under the flap to check –

The Loach tilts hard left.

'Oh, Christ!' Judd is ejected from the cabin. He instinctively throws out a hand to grab the doorframe then sees it's on fire and thinks better of it. As he falls he sees the whole chopper is alight and realises he's better out than in.

He drops into the smog cloud, the parachute he's not sure is a parachute held tightly in his hand.

With a screech of bending metal the little chopper flips over completely and Corey is turfed out as well –

Bam. He's hit by the wall of air and the parachute is slapped from his grasp.

'No!' The word is lost on the wind as he pivots to grab it –

It's gone, lost in the smog. He didn't have a chance to put it on before he was ejected from the chopper so he thought he could do it while he was falling. He saw someone do it once and it didn't seem that hard – then he remembers that someone was *James Bond* and he saw it in a *movie* and he realises it's probably *very* hard.

There's only one thing for him to do now. Wait until he clears this smog cloud and hope Judd's nearby. Then, maybe, he can, *somehow*, latch on to him before his chute opens.

He's really glad he asked Lola to look after Spike.

•

Judd tumbles through the smog.

He's disoriented, doesn't know which way is up. To make matters worse his parachute is only half on and the air current drags it off –

He twists, jams his left arm through the pack's loop, grabs both sides of the waist buckle and slams them together. *Clack*. They lock tight. He's happy the pack's on his back but fears it's full of old copies of the *LA Times*, not just because he doesn't want to die, but because he wants to make sure the canister of counteragent isn't destroyed. If his chute doesn't open then he hopes the canister survives the landing and that Corey, or anyone, finds and uses it. The virus might not be going global but it's still in the smog above LA – and has a half-life of fifteen years.

Judd drops out of the cloud and takes in the city beneath him, bathed in a sunset glow that is an eerie combination of orange and purple. Directly below, the giant tar pit rises up to meet him. Stopping that bomb from igniting and infecting the oil lake feels like a real accomplishment – worthy of at least a little of that *Atlantis 4* adulation. He turns, looks to the park. He can't see any sign of Rhonda's plane through the smoke. He hopes to God she's all right. He's going to fly this parachute straight over there – if, in fact, it is a parachute.

Guess there's only one way to find out.

He reaches up and pulls the ripcord.

Bang. A big jolt. He looks up, sees a drogue release from the pack. It's the small chute designed to slow him down before the main chute opens. So it *is* a parachute. 'Thank-you-thank-you-thank-you!' He waits for the second, bigger jolt as the drogue pulls the main chute out of the pack.

It doesn't happen. The damn drogue doesn't catch air. It just
snaps and twists in the breeze. Judd wills it to inflate. 'Open, you
bastard!'

It does not.

Then he sees it.

Above and moving fast.

'Oh, come on!'

Whump, whump, whump. The Loach punches out of the smog
cloud and spins directly towards him, the burning nub of its rotor
blades leaving a thick black trail of smoke behind it.

If the main chute deploys now it will tangle on the chopper and
that'd be all she wrote.

Whump, whump, whump. The spinning Loach moves so fast
he can't avoid it. The left landing skid snags the fluttering drogue –

'Ohhhhchriiiist!' Judd is violently swung around and around
and around – like he's on an amusement park ride, except there's
nothing amusing about it at all.

Corey tumbles through the smog cloud. They were at over seven
thousand feet when they bailed and he's been falling for what feels
like an hour.

He drops through the base of the cloud and spies Judd below
and to the right. *Jeez.* His chute is tangled around the Loach's skid
and spins him around like he's hanging off the world's most dangerous Hills Hoist. Corey's horrified to see his friend in such trouble,
wishes he could help him, doesn't know how he can, realises any
hope of sharing his parachute is now gone.

Time slows.

The Australian turns his head and takes in downtown Los
Angeles. The distant skyscrapers stand tall. If a giant earthquake

had been planned today then it has been averted, or hadn't been big enough to affect those buildings. So, an excellent result – nobody should have to experience one of those things.

He looks down, sees the tar pits quickly approach. He doesn't want to die. He really doesn't, but the possibility that there's something beyond this physical world and he could see his mother again, speak to her one last time, tell her how much she was loved and missed, well, that makes the thought of what happens when he reaches those tar pits almost bearable.

The irony is that it took the threat of the quake for him to actually speak about the death of his mother, even if it was for a fleeting moment. He knew it would be terrible, and it was, but it wasn't as terrible as he thought it would be and now it feels like a weight has been lifted, if only a little. So he spent almost half his life, *fifteen years*, not dealing with something that took *fifteen* seconds to feel better about once he decided to open up. *Way to go, Corey, great time-management.* Of course, he knows it only happened because he was speaking with the two people he liked most in the world, the kind of friends he'd never had before.

That's the one thing that really pisses him off about this whole situation. Lola said she'd look after Spike and it now occurs to Corey that the bloody mutt will get to know her much better than he ever did.

Whack. Corey is hit across the back.

Time speeds up.

He turns and sees his parachute tumble end over end as it ricochets away from him. He's astonished, didn't think he'd see it again. He looks down. The tar pits come up fast, but there's still time before touchdown.

The pack is only three metres away and he needs to fly over to it. He's jumped out of planes twice before so he knows the basics of skydiving. Forward motion is generated by – he can't remember!

Extend the legs! That's right! If you straighten them against the airflow and keep your arms back it propels your body forward. He straightens his legs, jams his arms by his side, points himself at the pack – and flies backwards.

Lola looks up at the sky and watches it all unfold, open-mouthed.

The relief she felt at seeing two moving human figures drop through the smog cloud, having not been vaporised in the explosion, quickly disappeared as one of them opened his parachute only to have it snag on the remains of the burning chopper while the other frantically tries to grab something which, she can only presume, is a parachute.

A few moments ago she felt both dread and giddy euphoria. Now it's just dread.

Corey flies forward.

He has it down now, realises he needs to keep his arms right back if he doesn't want to go backwards. This time he veers to the left and is as far from the pack as when he started.

How does he steer?

Elbows!

Right elbow down, turn right, left elbow down, turn left.

'Come on!' He does it, pushes his arms and legs to the side of his body, drops his right elbow and curves towards the pack.

'Whoa!' Judd swings around and around, feels dizzy and sick.

He pushes his left hand across his chest, releases the drogue.

Twang. Its suspension lines fly free and instantly slap against the Loach's underside.

Whump, whump, whump. The chopper spins towards him. Judd tries to get out of its way so he can open his main chute in clear air –

Bang. The Loach slams into him.

Flat on his back, Judd is pinned to the bottom of the chopper's fuselage by air pressure and centrifugal force. Together, Loach and astronaut spiral to earth in a crazy aeronautic dance.

Time slows.

Judd watches that smoking, oozing expanse of La Brea approach. He's not scared – yet. If a pilot has time, he has hope. He needs to get away from this chopper and open the damn chute. With all his energy he attempts to overcome the forces at play and roll towards the edge of the fuselage.

He can't do it, can barely move. The air pressure is too great.

Time speeds up.

He has seconds until impact. If he can't move his whole body then maybe he can move part of it. With all his strength he pushes his right arm past the edge of the fuselage, jams it into the blasting stream of air –

'Goddamn!' His arm is wrenched back at the elbow, feels like it's going to snap off. He grits his teeth, ignores the pain, holds his arm within the airflow, tries to alter the aerodynamic balance just a little. Buffeted by the wind he pulls it forward. His shoulder screams in protest.

Absolutely nothing happens.

'Come on!' He jams his right foot sideways, pushes it into the airflow too. The chopper tips to the right slightly – and releases the air pressure. He pushes off the fuselage and flips away.

Freedom. He looks down. The tar pit is *right there*. He yanks on the ripcord. The chute zips out of his pack – *and doesn't open*. It just licks at the air behind him. After everything that's happened today his *goddamn chute won't open*.

The chopper drops past him towards the tar pit below.

Boom. It lands upside down and detonates in an immense fireball. Judd plummets directly towards the flames.

Wham. The chute explodes out of his pack and bites the air, yanks him to an almost dead stop as the giant orange flame rolls up to meet him. He wrenches the chute's suspension lines to fly right and avoid the fire but its rudimentary circular design means it's slow to respond.

The fireball engulfs him. All he sees is orange, all he feels is heat and all he smells is av-gas. He hopes the chute doesn't catch fire. Or his clothes.

Judd punches through the flames.

The good news is that his clothes didn't catch fire. The bad news is that his chute did. The canopy, the suspension lines, it *all* burns. Then the suspension lines melt and snap.

He falls.

Corey stretches for the parachute. The tips of his fingers scrape it but can find no purchase. He registers an enormous explosion that rolls into the sky from the tar pits, realises it's the Loach. He has seconds until he suffers the same fate as that chopper.

He lunges towards the pack – gets a hand on it, pulls it towards him, jams his right hand through a shoulder strap, loops it around his elbow then reaches for the ripcord –

He can't find it! He searches, grabs something, pulls it, hopes –

Wham. The chute explodes out of the pack, catches air, wrenches on his elbow. The pain is intense, but the chute is open.

Bam. He smacks into the tar, goes straight under.

It's like swimming through Vegemite, except this thick, black ooze doesn't taste any good. He should be happy because he's alive, but he isn't. The parachute is twisted around him and he can't get free. It's like he's been wrapped in a blanket and dropped in quick sand.

He needs air but can't breathe. He fights the chute but that just makes it worse. Jesus, he's going to drown in this tar pit, like every other prehistoric animal that's stumbled into it over the last fifty thousand years.

48

Corey's head is light, his lungs burn.

He needs air, but he doesn't even know which way is up.

He's dying.

A hand seizes the chute that's wrapped around him, wrenches him to the surface. He gasps air, blinks the tar from his eyes –

Lola.

He's stunned. 'Thank you.'

'No wuckers.' She grins, shoulder deep in the tar, helps him pull free of the chute, then takes his hand and leads him through the smoke haze towards the side of the tar pit. 'Walkway's over here.'

His arm is numb from when he opened the parachute but he doesn't even notice that at the moment. What registers is that the hand at the end of his numb arm is holding hers. It's the first time that's happened and he couldn't be happier about it. This happiness lasts for exactly *three seconds*, then he's concerned. 'Where's Judd? Did you see him?'

Lola shakes her head. 'I barely saw you through the smoke.'

He calls out. '*Judd!*'

There's no response.

The haze still blankets the tar pits and surrounding walkway but it's not as bad as it was before. They wade past the three large, life-sized mammoth models then reach the edge of the tar pit, climb the short embankment, scale the safety fence and drop down to the walkway.

Spike is right there, lets out a sharp bark. Corey kneels, pats him, is about to answer that yes, he *did* just destroy another perfectly good helicopter, but catches himself in front of Lola and instead says: 'Good boy.' He turns, looks round. There's no one on the walkway. The place is deserted.

His eyes land on the burning remains of the Loach lying in the tar pit thirty metres away. He moves towards it, shouts again: '*Judd!*'

No reply.

Panic rises in his chest. 'Where could he be?' He turns to Lola again. 'You didn't see a chute?'

She shakes her head, her expression grave. 'Only yours.'

'*Judd?*'

No answer.

'Jeez.' Corey bends at the waist, puts his hands on his knees, distraught. '*Judd Bell?!*' He says it again but there's no power in his voice this time.

'Just how many Judds do you think are out here?' Judd ploughs through the smoke, straight towards him. He moves fast, or as fast as he can at the moment. He's doing what looks like a painful limp-run and it's not pretty. He's streaked in tar though you can see his hair is singed, he has a vivid sunburn on his face and one of his shoulders doesn't seem to be working the way it should. 'Oh, and by the way, I saw you first.'

The Australian takes him in, couldn't be more relieved that he's in one piece. 'Mate, you look shocking.'

'I'd look a whole lot worse if I hadn't landed in the tar.' Judd smiles, thrilled to see the Aussie. 'I'm so glad you're not dead.' He doesn't stop, just limp-runs past.

'Where are you going?'

'To find Rhonda.'

The Australian falls in beside him, Lola and Spike right behind.

Corey looks across at the astronaut. 'Is that a canister of counteragent in your pocket?'

Judd pulls it out and inspects it. It's undamaged. 'Yep, and it's happy to see you.' He doesn't say it with any humour this time.

'She'll be okay, mate.'

Judd pockets the canister and nods tightly, hopes the Aussie is right, fears he's not.

They reach the end of the walkway and run into the park. The smoke is heavier and visibility is low. They pass a section of landing gear torn from the 737's undercarriage, then follow a deep gouge across the grass towards a large flickering light in the distance.

Heart in mouth, Judd increases his pace, pulls ahead of the others, ploughs through the fog. It burns his eyes and makes his chest tight but he doesn't care. He hears the pop and crackle of fire, then the tail section of the jet looms out of the haze, tilted to one side and alight.

He stops and scans the park. There are no passengers anywhere. He limp-runs on, sees the nose section of the 737, fifty metres to the right. It lies on its roof and the nose section burns. He sprints towards it. 'Rhonda.'

Boom. It explodes.

'No–!'

The blast wave is enormous, lights up the park, knocks Judd flat, sends a wall of flaming shrapnel across the sky.

•

Thud.

'Oh!' Lola clutches the right side of her stomach. She looks at Corey, then her bloodied hand, horrified and confused. 'What is that?'

The pain comes quickly and she collapses. Corey catches her before she hits the ground.

Judd pulls himself into a sitting position and watches the cockpit burn. The grief hits him like a sucker punch. He puts his head in his hands. He didn't say it. He didn't tell her he loved her.

He should have told her.

'Dry your eyes. I'm not dead yet.'

Judd looks up.

Severson appears out of the haze.

'Sev!' Judd bounces to his feet. 'Where's Rhonda?'

'Right here.' Rhonda leads a large crowd of dazed but relieved passengers and crew. Judd's relief is as overwhelming as the grief had been a moment before.

She runs to him and they embrace, hold each other tight. He pulls back and studies her soot-smeared face. 'Welcome to LA.'

She smiles and gestures to the jet's burning fuselage. 'Sorry I'm late, parking was a bitch.' He laughs and she takes him in. 'Thanks for finding me the runway.'

'Anytime.'

'I'm guessing that big explosion was the bomb Severson didn't tell me about?'

He nods. 'Yeah, long story.'

She pulls him close, looks at him with nothing but affection. 'I love you, baby.'

'Wow. You've gone the full lovey-dovey twice in one day.'

'And I'm gonna keep doing it from now on.'

'Fine by me – and I love you too.' They kiss – and the passengers break into a round of applause. Rhonda and Judd part, embarrassed.

Severson leads the applause and addresses the crowd. 'Ladies and gentlemen, I give you our captain, the woman who just landed an airliner without engine power in the middle of a tourist attraction and saved every one of our arses, the one and only, Ms Rhonda Jacolby!' He sweeps a hand towards her and the applause morphs into a cheer. Severson grins. 'And, yes, I taught her everything she knows.'

Rhonda nods to him and mouths: 'Thank you.'

He returns it. 'Anytime, Nagatha.'

Twenty-five metres away Lola lies on the grass. Corey kneels beside her, studies the pencil-sized shard of metal that protrudes from the right side of her stomach just above her hip. 'I'm going to pull it out now.'

'That sounds *really* painful.'

'You ready?'

Not really but do it anyway!'

He gently takes hold of the shard. She muffles a scream.

'Okay. On three.'

She nods. 'On three.'

'One —' He pulls out the shard.

She screams: 'What happened to *three*?'

'It's better if you don't expect it.'

Her eyelids flutter.

'Stay with me.'

Her face is grey.

'Lola! Are you staying with me?'

She is not. She passes out.

Spike barks.

'No, taking off my shirt will not make her wake up.'

'Lola.' Corey lightly slaps her cheek. 'Lola.' She's limp in his arms. He feels sick to his stomach. 'Lola, wake up.' She doesn't. He inspects the wound.

Spike barks.

'Yes, thank you for pointing out I'm not a doctor. But I need to stop the bleeding —'

'Who are you talking to?'

Caught, Corey looks at Lola as her eyes blink open. 'I'm, well, I um . . .'

'It's your dog, isn't it? You're talking to your dog.'

Corey takes a moment, then nods.

'You know what he's saying?'

He nods again.

'Why didn't you tell me this?'

'Most girls think it's crazy.'

'I'm not most girls.'

'I noticed.'

She winces, looks at her wound. 'Man, it hurts like a *mutha*. I mean, *seriously*.'

'It's not that deep, but we have to stop the bleeding. We need a bandage to put some pressure on it.' He stops, thinks, then realises what he must do. He pulls off his T-shirt.

Spike barks.

'Shut it.'

'What did he say?'

'"I see you've finally got your shirt off."' He's been telling me to do it for weeks, thought it'd make you like me.'

Lola can't help but check out his cut physique as he rips the T-shirt, still damp from the tar pit, into one long strip and binds it around her torso, makes sure the material presses firmly against the wound. 'That should do it until we get you to a doc.'

She nods stoically.

'I'm glad you're okay.'

'Thanks to you.'

'You helped me too. Anybody would have done the same thing.'

She smiles through the pain. 'You know, they really wouldn't.' She looks him in the eyes. 'I'm having a thought, which I'm turning into an idea.'

'Oh, yeah? What is it?'

She pushes herself up and kisses him on the mouth, hard and fast.

He's genuinely surprised. 'But – aren't you with Scott?'

'Not any more. Remember when I said other people wouldn't do what you did? I was talking about Scott.'

'Really? I did not get that *at all*. I think I told you I'm not great with subtext.'

'Then let me lay it out. In a crisis situation you see a person's true nature. I saw his and it was awful. And then I saw yours, and it was – breathtaking. It literally took my breath away. And now I'm worried I've screwed up any chance of . . . us.'

'Well, yeah, you kind of did.'

She deflates. 'I know, and I'm so pissed off about that.'

He looks at her. 'You let me do that whole thing, with the dancing and the moonlight and the beach and you didn't tell me you had a boyfriend. It was bloody embarrassing.'

'Of course it was. And I'm an *idiot*. But I did it because I like being with you. If you could just – do you think you could forget about it? Because I think this works. You and me. It works.'

He rubs his face and turns away and she can see he doesn't agree. Gee, she *royally* screwed this up. She can't think of anything to say – but she can think of something to sing, so begins in a low, husky timbre: 'Baby come back . . . '

She sings the song for a moment and then trails off when it doesn't have the positive effect she was hoping for.

He studies her. 'You know, I've always thought she *should* come back in that song.'

'Really?'

'Yeah. He seems to be genuinely apologetic, and he went to the trouble of writing a great song.'

'So you think she should give him a second chance?'

'Well, if the roles were reversed and he hadn't told her the truth about, say – how he could understand his dog, for example, or maybe he'd landed his helicopter in the middle of nowhere and told her to get out —'

'And she'd been really pissed off about it.'

'Exactly. Then maybe, you know, considering all that, they could call it even.'

'Maybe they could.' She rises up and kisses him again – and he's not surprised by it this time. They part and their eyes meet. She touches his face. 'You know you don't need to protect me, or try to save me, right? I'm not your mother.'

He nods.

'I'd like you to tell me about her, though. About what happened.'

'I will.'

'Good. You can start now if you'd like.'

Corey regards her for a moment, then begins: 'Well, her name was Roberta . . . '

EPILOGUE

Cement dust swirls around the room.

Whack. Corey slams a heavy mallet into a brick wall. *Whack.* Another lands right next to it, swung by Judd this time. Rubble falls to the floor and is scooped up in a shovel, which Rhonda deposits into a large green garbage bin. Lola picks up the next load with her shovel and the process begins again.

All wearing dust masks and work clothes, they're in the living room of the house on Sepulveda which Lola inherited from her grandfather. It was partially damaged on 7/27, when a motorcycle ploughed through the wall they're presently demolishing, so Lola decided to extend the hole and install a panoramic window to overlook the front garden.

Like her grandfather's house, greater Los Angeles is being rebuilt too, though three months after the events of 7/27, progress is glacial. Lola had heard the damage is even worse than the Northridge quake in 1994, the final price of the clean-up and reconstruction estimated at over one and a half trillion dollars. The good news is that the death toll, though still a staggering 1867, was less than first feared.

Whack. Lola takes in Corey as he swings the mallet again. The Aussie volunteered to do the renovation and it's going really well. He's very good with his hands, in a number of ways, which she's happily finding out, and knocking down walls is one of them.

They're taking the relationship slow but it feels right to her, like nothing she's experienced before. He's a man – actually he's a *bloke* – and she couldn't be happier about that.

Whack. Corey thumps his mallet into the wall again. So the trip to the Florida Keys has been put on the backburner indefinitely. His relationship with Lola is hitting its stride so there is no way he's going to leave LA. They have a great time together and he's as happy as he's ever been. He's even talked to her about his mother, which has been a difficult but positive experience. His only concern is what he's going to do with himself after this reno is done. Should he start a chopper-for-hire business? Apart from the fact there are already a bazillion guys in LA doing just that, he's been flying his whole life. He'd like to try something different for a while. He just doesn't know what it is.

On the plus side, Spike likes Lola and Lola likes Spike. She doesn't seem to give two hoots that he talks to his dog. He tries to keep it to a minimum around her mates and work colleagues, but no one appears to give a stuff. That's one of the great things he's found about the entertainment business in Los Angeles. Eccentricity, and by eccentricity he means outright craziness, is not shunned here, but celebrated – especially if you're successful and making people money.

Rhonda scoops up a load of rubble and drops it into the bin. The landing, though not a success in the 'did you save the aircraft?' department, was a big success in the 'did everyone live?' department. There were a few minor injuries – some cuts and bruises, and one guy broke a finger – but that was it. Not only did it burnish her already impressive reputation, but it snapped her out of her Orion simulator funk. She has yet to perfect it, but the experience of flying and landing the 737 had changed her thinking enough so that she now felt comfortable improvising when things went south.

She has Severson to thank for that. As usual, he came out of the whole thing smelling like roses. His impromptu post-crash speech was filmed by one of the grateful passengers on a mobile phone, uploaded to YouTube and has been now been viewed over fifty-seven million times. With his increased profile, he has been tapped to lead the Mars mission's crew selection committee. Having been happy to say previously that a decision was 'above his pay scale' so he could shirk responsibility, Severson now finds himself *at* that higher pay scale – with the extraordinary responsibility of deciding who will be the first human being to set foot on the red planet.

Since 7/27, she's been going the lovey-dovey with Judd often and unprompted. She now understood the simplest thing, which her father never did: tell the people you love how you feel, every day, because you never know when the cabin will suffer an explosive decompression.

Whack. Judd swings his mallet again and dislodges another chunk of the wall. Once he'd passed the counteragent to the federal authorities they'd synthesised and distributed it. The petroleum companies began adding it to their supplies five weeks after 7/27, though it was another month before people felt completely comfortable about driving or flying again, particularly in Southern California, where winds and weather had spread the virus widely. With its fifteen-year half-life, the counteragent would be in use for the foreseeable future.

If anyone stopped to ruminate on the planet's reliance on fossil fuels, it certainly wasn't obvious to Judd. People were just happy to get back to business as usual. So Zac Bunsen had caused a great deal of heartache and almost destroyed the city, but had failed to change much of anything.

If Judd and Corey had been famous previously, they were bona fide superstars now. Even before the *Atlantis* 4 movie started shooting, Twentieth Century Fox signed them for a sequel based on their adventures on 7/27. There's no title yet but Judd is leaning towards *Ignition*, the studio likes *7/27* and Corey thinks *Combustion* could be a goer.

Principal photography on the *Atlantis* 4 movie is slated to begin next week. The announcement, which brought them to LA in the first place, was rescheduled for next Monday. That's why Judd and Rhonda are in town – and how Corey lassoed them into helping with the reno.

Ding dong. The doorbell rings.

Lola pulls the dust mask down around her neck. 'I'll get it.' She moves through the house and opens the front door.

On the stoop stands Scott Ford, movie star, the Blue Cyclone, looking sheepish. Lola regards him blankly. 'What?'

'I just – I came to apologise. Your assistant told me where you were.'

'Well, I will kick his arse for that. I'm taking the week. No work.'

'This isn't about work. This is – I've been trying to contact you for three months. You didn't return my calls or texts or anything.'

She stares at him. 'Gee, I wonder why.'

'Look, I was hoping we could have lunch and talk about it —'

'You went sailing while I was trapped under a beam in a building. There's nothing to talk about.'

'I'm sure we could find something, sweetness.' He leans in, lightly touches her forearm, smiles his four-billion-dollar smile.

Her tone remains even. 'Get your goddamn hand off me.'

He removes it. 'There must be some way I can walk this back?'

'There really isn't. But there is a way you can stop me telling the world what happened.'

Scott's smile vanishes. Instantly. 'You wouldn't.'

'Really?'

He studies her, realises she would. 'What do you want?'

'Three times in the near future I will call on you with various projects from my clients. They'll be quality projects and you will say yes to starring in each one of them. You will make each movie for fifty per cent of your current quote because you "love it so much" – and you will do it with a smile.'

He looks at her, clearly chilled and excited in equal measure. 'You are the devil.'

'If that means I own your arse, then yes, yes, I am.'

'Lola, is there a vacuum cleaner somewhere? There's so much bloody dust . . . ' Corey rounds the corner, his dust mask around his neck too.

Scott sees him and gets very excited. 'Oh, man. Corey Purchase! I just finished your *LA Times* profile. What you did on 7/27 was *amazing*. You saved the city – the world, really.'

'Oh, no.' Corey waves it off. 'You'd have done the same thing, mate.'

Lola looks at Scott, her expression inscrutable. 'Yeah, you would have, wouldn't you? If you hadn't gone sailing?'

He ignores her. 'So, how do you guys know each other?'

'Corey's my boyfriend.'

Suddenly Scott's very uncomfortable. 'Oh. Right.'

Lola isn't. 'Actually, Corey has an excellent movie concept he's working on at the moment. A zombie-vampire mashup.' She grins at Scott. 'We should set up a meeting.'

Scott forces a grin right back. 'Sounds great.'

'I'm sure it will be.'

Scott jabs a thumb over his shoulder. 'I should get . . . '

Lola nods. 'Yeah, you should.'

Scott holds out a hand to Corey. 'Really great to meet you.'

Corey shakes it. 'Pleasure's all mine, mate. What was your name again?'

Scott keeps shaking, crestfallen. 'Scott. Scott Ford.'

'Oh! Sorry. Didn't recognise you without your tights.'

Scott pivots and leaves. Lola closes the door behind him. 'Ba-bye.'

Corey watches him go. 'Well, he seems pleasant enough.'

'He's a complete wuss, but he'll be perfect for *Zompire*.'

'Yeah?'

'Yeah, and I have a feeling he's going to love it. You should write it up.'

Corey takes this in, intrigued by the idea. The movie had completely slipped his mind since 7/27. 'Maybe I will.' Maybe *that's* what he'll do after the reno.

They move back into the living room, where Judd reaches into the wall cavity. 'There's something in here – I can't quite – my arm's not quite long enough.'

Spike barks. He also wears a dust mask.

Corey suppresses a smile, but everyone sees it.

Judd's not amused. 'Ha ha. What did he say?'

'Nothing.'

Lola leans in and Corey whispers it to her. She laughs.

Judd sees it. 'Yeah, yeah, very funny – oh, got it!' He pulls out a wide, flat, circular tin. 'What is this?'

Rhonda knows. 'A film can. Looks like 16mm.' She turns to Lola. 'Is it your grandfather's?'

'Don't know. Never seen it before.'

Corey gets excited. 'Maybe it's a home movie.'

Judd brushes dust off the can. 'Why would a home movie be bricked into a wall?'

'Maybe it's not very good.'

Lola takes the tin from Judd. 'Only one way to find out. I saw a projector around here somewhere. Think it's in the garage.'

Lola threads the film onto an old Elmo film projector. She follows the diagram on the side of the machine and after a little trial and error gets it right. On the opposite side of the room Corey and Judd finish clearing up the last of the debris.

'Here goes.' Lola flicks the switch and the projector clatters to life. Rhonda pulls the faded curtains across the window and the far wall is illuminated. All that's projected is white film leader marked with a series of random letters and numbers in black felt tip marker.

Corey whispers to Judd: 'No wonder it was cemented into the wall.'

Rhonda turns to Lola. 'So what did your grandpa do?'

'Worked for the government. Something in the Department of Agriculture, I think. He never really talked about it.'

The white film leader ends and an image is projected on the wall. It's in black and white and there is no sound. They all watch it.

Lola takes in a sharp breath. 'What the hell is this?'

Corey's eyes don't leave the image, his words slow and surprised. 'I don't think it's a home movie.'

Lola frowns in confusion. 'I don't think it is either.'

Rhonda takes a sharp breath. 'What the hell *is* this?'

Judd steps forward to get a closer look, to make sure his eyes aren't playing tricks on him.

They're not.

Stunned, Judd turns to his friends. 'Did we just find proof the moon landings were *faked*?'

THE END

ACKNOWLEDGEMENTS

First, I must thank my super agent, Selwa Anthony. As always, without your tireless effort this book would not have seen the light of day. I could not be more grateful for your guidance and support. Also, a big thanks to Linda Anthony and Drew Keys.

To Belinda Byrne, thank you for making the publication experience so enjoyable. I truly value our friendship. Also, a big thanks to Caro Cooper, Clementine Edwards, Chantelle Sturt and the whole gang at Penguin.

Thank you to my family, Gus, Vicky, David, Janelle and Ian for your love and encouragement.

To Robert Connolly, Mark Lazarus, Siobhan Hannan, Tony McNamara, Malla Nunn and Andrew Jeffery, thank you for your continued support and insight.

Special thanks to Prue Jeffery, Robert Patterson, Michael King, Yvette, Isabelle and Chloe Azzam, David and Steph Griffiths, Rose and Eric Campbell, Tony and Denise Parker, Kiff and Francesca Newby, Louise and Joe Tawfik, and James Bradley.

Finally, to my wife and best friend Georgie, and our remarkable daughter Holly. I am so lucky to have you in my life. This book is for you.

Read on for a sneak peek at

QUICK

by

STEVE WORLAND

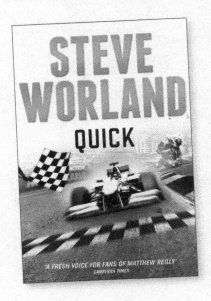

PROLOGUE

A tenth of a second.

It's no time at all.

A finger snap.

An eye blink.

But in motorsport it's the difference between winning and losing.

Between champion and also ran.

Between life and death.

The red light disappears and Billy Hotchkiss stamps on the accelerator.

The five-litre V8 thunders as the Autobarn Holden Commodore launches off the Mount Panorama pit straight. Billy knows the beginning of a V8 Supercar race is the best opportunity to move up the grid if qualifying didn't go to plan — and his hadn't gone to plan. In yesterday's shootout for starting positions a light sprinkle of rain at the top of the mountain turned the track slippery halfway through his lap and he ended up fourth on the grid.

Bam. The big V8 slams into the 7500 rev limit.

Clunk. Billy thumps the lever forward on the sequential gearbox and his Holden leaps forward. To the right Garth Tander's Holden Racing Team machine bogs down horribly. Billy cruises past and he's third before he reaches the end of the pit straight and takes the sharp left turn at Hell Corner.

There's not too much understeer from the Commodore as he feeds in the power and carries momentum up Mountain Straight, over eleven hundred metres up a steep gradient. Two cars are ahead. Craig Lowndes' Vodafone Racing Falcon leads Mark 'Frosty' Winterbottom from Ford Performance Racing.

Billy can't let them skip away. They will never be as close as they are right now so he must make the most of this moment if he wants to lead this race by the end of lap one. More people watch the start than any point until the chequered flag falls, which is a thousand kilometres and one hundred and sixty-one laps away. Anything could happen over the next six hours: his car could have a mechanical failure or his co-driver could have an accident. What he does have control over is making sure he leads every lap while he's behind the wheel. He's only just turned nineteen but the motor racing world thinks he might be *quick*, that ephemeral quality only the great ones posses, so it's his responsibility to show them they're right. He knows his team won't want him taking stupid risks but then they'll love the visibility for their sponsors if his car leads at the end of lap one. Of course he can't *win* the race on the first lap but he just might be able to build himself a reputation, which would help his cause when he attempts the jump from V8 Supercars to Formula One, his ultimate goal.

Clunk. He ratchets the gear lever forward again, pulls sixth gear doing two hundred and fifty kilometres an hour, Sir Isaac Newton prohibiting his Supercar from traveling any quicker up the steep incline. He's not catching the two cars ahead but then they're not drawing away either. He knows Lowndes and Frosty won't just give him first place.

I will need to take it.

As he crests the rise at the end of Mountain Straight Billy draws beside Frosty's Falcon. Billy's only met Frosty once and liked the guy, though he would like him even more if he wasn't drifting wide as they take Griffiths Bend —

Thump. The right corner of Billy's front bumper connects with the left corner of Frosty's rear bumper. It has little effect on Billy's Commodore but sets the Ford's tail wagging. Frosty takes his sweet time to get it under control and loses precious tenths in the process.

Billy sweeps past and now he's second. He falls in behind Lowndes' Falcon as they slow to ninety and take the tight left turn into The Cutting. Billy carries good speed but there's little room to pass through here so he cools his jets and wait for the right moment.

Line astern, the Ford and the Holden sweep towards the top of the mountain, past Reid Park, then down to 'metal grate', which is, unsurprisingly, a metal drainage grate at the right shoulder of the roadway, then on to Sulman Park, then McPhillamy Park, tyres scrubbing as the gentle left turn tightens, then tightens again. Over the thunder of twenty-seven V8 engines kicking out six hundred and fifty horsepower a piece he can hear a roar lift from the crowd that lines the track to the right.

Woh. The steering goes light in Billy's hands as his Commodore crests Skyline, the highest part of the circuit at eight hundred and sixty-two metres above sea level. He momentarily takes in a panoramic view of the surrounding countryside then plunges into the Esses.

Down and down and down, cold brakes squeal as he turns left then right then left again, the giant wing on the boot of Lowndes' Vodafone Falcon bobbing and weaving just a metre in front of Billy's radiator grill. There's no way past.

This is not the moment.

Clank clank clank. Down to second gear and ninety kilometres an hour as Billy turns hard right and drops the Holden into The Dipper, the V8 whining as he uses the engine to brake the fourteen hundred kilogram race car.

Christ, it's so bloody steep.

Down and down and down. The sedan reaches the bottom of The Dipper and settles.

Clunk clunk clunk. Up to fifth gear and one seventy along the short straight, then down the box again. On the brakes deep and hard as he takes the sharp left turn at Forest Elbow at a leisurely eight-three kays. Lowndes is still just a meter ahead but not giving anything away. The corner seems to take an age.

Smooth and clean, smooth and clean.

Out of the corner he gets on the power smooth and clean, without any wheel spin, and shoots down Conrod Straight. At almost two kilometres it's the longest, fastest section of racetrack in this great southern land.

The speed builds fast as he pumps the gear lever: third, fourth, fifth, sixth – two sixty, two seventy kilometres an hour, the speed builds, two hundred and eighty kilometres an hour, still builds, two eighty-five. It's like space and time have warped, the engine revs pinned to 7500 in sixth. Lowndes Falcon is still just a metre ahead. He's not pulling away. Billy can get him under braking as they exit The Chase. He's sure of it.

Two hundred and ninety-seven kilometres an hour.

The Chase approaches. It's a slight kink to the right then a short straight, then a hard left-hander. Billy will need to be the last of the brakers to pass the defending champion. He'll drive up the left side then own the corner with track position. Lowndes won't want to turn in on him and risk a collision on the first lap. He's too smart for that.

Billy's Commodore touches three hundred kilometres an hour as The Chase arrives. The road bends right and Billy dabs the brake, wipes off twenty klicks. As the left turn approaches, Lowndes Falcon stays to the centre of the track, gives Billy just enough racing room.

This is his moment.

Don't-brake-yet-don't-brake-yet-don't-brake-yet.

Billy waits — and waits — then throws out the anchors and clanks down the gears, aims the Commodore up the left side of the Lowndes Falcon. He draws level, but the race car's tiny change of direction coupled with a slight nosedive from the heavy braking unsettles the rear of the vehicle and the back drifts to the edge of the track — then over it and onto the grass.

That's all it takes.

The left back wheel digs into the soft surface and the tail flicks around and spears the Supercar across the track.

Time slows.

'Christ.' Billy tries to catch it but it's over as soon as it begins. Traveling at two hundred kilometres an hour, the giant sedan pirouettes, tyres smoking as rubber grinds on bitumen.

Billy watches Craig Lowndes yank the steering wheel left to avoid the sliding Supercar and round the corner. As the Falcon ducks out of the way Billy glimpses the metal snake of race cars that winds up Conrod Straight.

He can still save this.

He just needs to hit the kitty litter nose first. The kitty litter is a sand trap designed to slow vehicles if they leave the track at The Chase. It works best if a vehicle enters nose first. Billy wrenches the steering wheel, tries to get the nose around.

It doesn't work.

Time speeds up.

Traveling one hundred and eighty kilometres an hour, the Commodore slides off the racetrack and hits the kitty litter side on.

Crunch. He can hear sand blast against the underside of the vehicle.

He can still save this.

If he can slide the car *across* the kitty litter to where the sand meets the grass then he'll be able to drive around the edge of trap and rejoin the race. He just has to hope the wheels don't dig into the sand and flip the car —

The wheels dig into the sand and flip the car.

'Oh Jesus.'

He can no longer save this.

He's now a passenger on the way to the scene of the accident. The Commodore flicks up and rolls violently, kicks up a wall of sand with each revolution. Billy holds on for dear life, can only wait for it to end. Metal tears and glass shatters as the six hundred thousand dollar vehicle sheds wheels and panels and wings — and keeps rolling.

Craaack.

What the hell was that?

Centrifugal force wrenches the V8 from beneath the Commodore's chassis. The engine makes a break for freedom, cartwheels across the kitty litter spewing oil and water and gasoline —

Whump. It bursts into flames, lights a wall of fire across the sand. Billy catches a glimpse of it as the Commodore keeps rolling. Nine times, ten times, over and over and over. It feels like he's being dumped by a tidal wave. Without the weight of the engine the chassis seems to pick up speed as it rotates —

Thump. It stops dead.

A moment passes.

Shaken, Billy blinks twice, takes a breath and does a quick inventory of limbs. They're all attached and in working order. He can't believe he escaped such a monster shunt without so much as a scratch. The car is right side up but the nose points towards the heavens at a steep angle. Through a tear in the floor Billy can see the front of the chassis is balanced on one of the wheels.

V8s rumble close by. He looks back. What remains of his Commodore is perched at the edge of the kitty litter near the exit of The Chase. That metal snake of cars whip past on the track just a metre behind.

Creeeeak.

'Oh damn.' The wrecked Commodore shudders, slips off the wheel and rolls backwards onto the track. Billy pumps the brake pedal to stop it.

Nothing happens.

Clank. A car in the metal snake clips the Commodore's rear quarter panel and spins the vehicle across the track —

Bam. The last car in the snake T-bones the Commodore's driver's door.

Billy's world turns dark.

There is nothing but pain.

A tenth of a second.

It's really no time at all.

A finger snap.

An eye blink.

But in motorsport it's the difference between winning and losing.

Between champion and also ran.

Between life and death.

Sunday, 12th October 2008.

Craig Lowndes wins the Bathurst 1000 with co-driver Jamie Whincup in a Vodafone Ford Falcon. Billy Hotchkiss' Autobarn Commodore is destroyed on the first lap when it is hit by a back-marker at the exit of The Chase.

The back-marker escapes injury.

Billy does not.

He breaks his back, his pelvis, his left shoulder and both legs.

He spends a year in physical therapy.

He never drives a race car again.

SIX YEARS LATER

1

With landing gear raised, the single-engined Beechcraft 19 descends from the clear blue sky.

Billy Hotchkiss pilots the aircraft. He doesn't look that different from the fresh-faced kid who tried and failed to lead the first lap of Bathurst back in 2008. He's still tall and lean with a cheeky grin. The only visible change in his appearance are the pair of long, thin vertical scars above his left eyebrow, where his helmet shattered and sliced into his forehead.

Beside him sits his flight instructor, Ernie Jenkins, thinning hair, happy face, sixty if he's a day. 'So we're cleared to land.'

Billy nods, his expression a portrait of concentration. 'Okay, cleared to land.'

Stick and pedals, stick and pedals.

'I can do this. Stick and pedals.'

Ernie nods. 'So, what do we need to think about?'

Billy scans the instruments of the tiny aircraft, his mind turning. 'Well, we have a crosswind. It's . . . it's about eight knots.'

'Okay. That's good. Are you all lined up?'

Billy looks out the aircraft's windscreen. 'Runway thirty-five at Essendon Airport is directly ahead. Big tanks to the right, hangars to the left. All lined up.'

'Beautiful. Okay, what else?'

Billy glances at the instruments once more. 'Airspeed is correct. Altitude is . . . correct. I just need to take it on in.'

'Sure, but is there anything else?'

Billy racks his brain, glances at his instructor with a concerned smile. 'I don't know, what am I forgetting?'

'What do we land on?'

'The runway.'

'Yes, and what lands on the runway?'

'The plane.'

'What part of the plane?'

Billy's confused. 'The undercarriage?'

'And what else is that called?'

Billy stares at him blankly for a moment, then: 'Oh Christ, the bloody landing gear!' He flips a lever. The landing gear lowers with a hum then locks with a clunk below them.

Ernie smiles. 'There you go.'

Billy is mortified. 'Ohmigod.'

'Happens to everyone once. Just make sure it doesn't happen twice. Now just take us on in, nice and gentle.'

Billy nods, works the stick and rudder and eases the little Beechcraft down.

Chirp. He settles the plane on the tarmac nice and gentle, just like Ernie asked. This is Billy's third flying lesson so he's pleased with how quickly he's picked it up, though that's the only thing that's pleased him. He hoped flying would give him something approaching the adrenaline rush he felt when he raced, the adrenaline rush he missed so much, but no, flying was like doing maths with a chance of engine failure. It was exacting rather than exciting and there was always the chance you could plummet out of the sky, which might be worth it if it was more exciting, which it wasn't. Through the lessons Billy realised that what he loves is speed when it's up close and personal. That's what gives him the rush. In the air he could be doing one hundred knots or three hundred and it all felt the same because there were so few reference points. But on the ground you felt everything because the road is right beneath you and it's one big reference point.

Billy angles the Beechcraft towards the hangars as Ernie pipes up: 'So, another couple of flights like today and you'll be ready for a solo, as long as you remember to lower the landing gear.'

Ernie smiles at this and Billy forces a grin in return. He's going to have to break the bad news to the old codger sooner or later so he may as well lay it on him now: 'Ernie, about that . . .'

The sun is out and a cool breeze eases along Collins Street in Melbourne. Traffic is light for a Saturday morning.

A Kenworth semi-trailer truck, without a trailer, trundles along the roadway, the towering skyscrapers reflected in its cherry-red paint job and heavily tinted windows. Inside, three people sit along the front bench seat. They wear dark-grey jumpsuits and racing helmets with visors raised. The person wearing the yellow helmet with wide green stripes is behind the wheel. 'Can anyone see it?'

The person wearing the red helmet with thin silver stripes nods and points out the windscreen. 'There. About two hundred metres ahead.'

The person wearing the black helmet with the red, yellow and blue stripes glances in the side mirror. 'We're clear behind.'

Mister Yellow nods and presses the accelerator. The giant turbo diesel spools up and the truck gains speed, surges towards the set of traffic lights ahead. Fifteen metres away the light turns from green to amber.

Red puts a hand on Yellow's arm. 'We don't want to have an accident before we get there.'

'Of course.' Yellow nods and hits the brakes. The truck eases to a stop, right on the line. Traffic sweeps across the road before them.

Red reaches into a backpack, pulls out three nine-millimetre Glock pistols, keeps one and passes the others to Yellow and Black. 'They're loaded and the safeties are on. Do not fire unless there's no other option.'

They both nod, then Yellow looks up at the set of traffic lights and waits for the green.

Ernie accepted the news with good-hearted disappointment. From the sound of it Billy figured that Ernie had had plenty of students who had taken a couple of lessons before realising flying wasn't their bag, so he didn't take it personally.

Billy shifts in the seat. Since his prang at Bathurst, sitting on hard surfaces for long periods, and long meant more than about three minutes, had become a bit of a chore. His lower back starts to sing, he gets pins and needles in his right thigh and his left foot cramps. Even so, he has no cause for complaint. For the first week after the accident the doctors were sure they would need to amputate *both* his legs, so the occasional bout of pins and needles and the odd cramp seem like the deal of the century in comparison.

He's seated on a wooden bench by the front window of an old building that had been gentrified and turned into a McDonald's. He's here because he loves the hotcakes at Maccas. *Looooves* them. But he only allows himself one serving per week so he doesn't chunk up. After he's eaten this week's helping he plans to meet up with some mates to watch the Formula One qualifying at Albert Park, which will include a V8 Supercar race as a curtain raiser.

He's been looking forward to it for months.

That's strange.

Through the window he catches sight of a red semi-trailer truck that waits at the lights. It's a big one, an oversized version with a sleeper behind the cabin. Apart from the fact it's rare to see a big rig without a trailer attached, and in the middle of the city no less, what surprises him is the fact that its windscreen has what looks like dark tint applied to it. He's aware of this because he's a proud member of the Victorian Police Force. He has worked a lot of traffic duty and ticketed a number of people, mostly young guys, for driving cars with tint that is too dark.

Billy picked up the idea of joining the force during his yearlong recuperation following his prang at Bathurst. His physical therapist had once been a cop and talked up the idea. Billy never imagined himself as anything but a race car driver but when that door slammed shut he needed to find a job that would hold his attention. To his surprise being a police officer did just that.

He pulls his gaze from the red truck and looks at the hotcakes, then glances back at the truck. It isn't just his imagination, is it? That windscreen is definitely tinted and that is illegal.

The traffic light changes, there's a blast of smoke from the truck's exhaust stack and it rolls on.

Time to make a decision.

What do I do?

'Christ.' He stands and strides out to the footpath, pulls on his Detroit Tigers cap and Ray Ban aviators. Why, exactly, is he doing this? On his day off? Chasing up some bozo with illegal window tint? It doesn't make sense and yet here he is, abandoning an incredibly tasty breakfast so he can write a vehicle defect ticket.

Why?

Well, technically it's the 'broken windows theory' of policing, which states that law enforcement officers should always prosecute petty crimes, seemingly little things like graffiti and littering and broken taillights, otherwise the criminals will graduate to more serious crimes over time. The New York Police Department used it to great effect during the 1990s to cut the city's crime rate. But Billy knows what he's doing is not just about enacting a theory of law and order.

It's about the adrenaline rush.

Since the accident he has rarely been unable to find it. Nothing came close to motor racing, as he just learned with those pricey flying lessons. He experimented with jet skis and skydiving and rock climbing and a bunch of other 'xtreme' pursuits, but they didn't include the two most important elements for him: they weren't competitive and they didn't involve cars. He just loved bloody cars, had loved them since he was knee high to his father's Falcon GTHO. Of course, he could have raced privately, but he barely had enough dough to cover his rent so that wasn't going to happen. Motor racing was, even at the most junior of levels, eye-wateringly expensive. Luckily for him his job as a cop occasionally gave him the buzz he was looking for. It had the competitive element, the 'will I or won't I catch this bad guy', and it often involved driving a high-powered vehicle of some description.

The other thing he liked about being a cop, which he hadn't even considered before he applied to the academy, was 'being of service'. Sure, you couldn't always help everyone, but aiding people in need did leave him with a great feeling. It made him think about all the other things he could do, beyond what was happening in this city, or even Australia. What about the people who didn't have running water, or adequate housing? He wondered if he shouldn't take his next vacation somewhere he might be able to do something useful.

Billy breaks into a jog, his eyes locked on the red truck as it continues along Collins Street. It's in the far lane, about twenty metres ahead. He'll wait for it to stop at the next set of lights then make his way over to the driver, flash his badge and see what's what. As he moves closer he notices a sticker on the cab's rear window that reads Rentco. It's the name of a large truck rental company that his Dad sometimes used to ferry cars and equipment to interstate races back in Billy's motor racing days.

Why would a truck rental company put illegal tint on the windscreen? The answer is they wouldn't. Whoever's driving it did. And why would they do that? So they won't be easily seen. And why don't they want to be easily seen? Well that's the $64 000 question, isn't it? Suddenly leaving the hotcakes uneaten doesn't feel so crazy after all. He instinctively reaches under his jacket to check his holstered Glock — and realises it's not there because today is his day off.

Bugger.

'We have company.' Black's eyes are locked on the right side-view mirror as he takes in a young man who moves along the footpath and follows the truck.

'What does that mean?'

'It means there's a guy following us down the street.'

'Are you sure?' Yellow turns, looks out the rear window.

'It's the guy in the dark denim jacket.'

Yellow nods. 'I see him.'

'He's looking at us, right?'

'Who knows? He's wearing sunglasses.'

Black turns to Yellow: 'We should abort.'

Yellow's helmet shakes. 'No can do.'

'What if he's a cop?'

'Then we deal with it.'

Red points out the windscreen. 'There it is.'

'Okay. Here we go.' They flip their helmet visors down as Yellow mashes the accelerator to the floor.

The turbo diesel barks and the truck pulls away.

'Christ.' Billy takes off after it. He sprints hard and instantly his lower back starts to throb from the jarring impact of his heels on the pavement. He ignores it, as he always does, and promises himself a couple of Panadeine later, which he will forget to take.

In spite of its size, the truck nimbly swerves through the traffic and Billy can't help but think that whoever's driving knows what he's doing. It gains speed quickly, now half a block ahead. 'Where the hell is it going?' Billy cranes his neck — then sees where.

Yellow's eyes don't leave the road in front. 'That guy still on us?'

Black glances back. 'Yes, and now he's running.'

Red looks through the rear window at the guy as he shrinks into the distance behind them. 'Yeah, good luck with that buddy!' Red turns to Black. 'Guess you were right about him.'

Black gets no joy from being correct. 'I don't feel good about this.'

'You never feel good about anything. Now everybody hold on.' Yellow yanks the wheel and the big rig cuts sharply across the road —

Crunch. It clips the rear of a Mini and knocks it aside like a child's toy, mounts the footpath and bowls over a parked Vespa motor scooter. The truck shudders to a halt, its rear wheels five metres in front of a hulking Brinks armoured car.

Yellow turns to the others. 'You know what to do. Don't get dead.'

Black pushes open the passenger door and leaps to the roadway, Red right behind. Pistols raised, they sprint to the rear of the truck. Black grabs two thick, metal chains coiled around the fifth wheel coupling, the flat metal circle a trailer would be hitched to. Both chains have a large hook attached to the end. Black moves to the front of the armoured car as Red covers him —

A security guard, fifty if he's a day, steps out from the right rear of the armoured car and double-takes. He's genuinely shocked to see the two helmeted individuals. 'Oh crap.' He reaches for the gun on his hip.

Red steps forward, raises the pistol. 'Face down on the ground, hands behind your head.'

The guard doesn't need to be asked twice. He drops to the footpath.

Black crouches, crawls under the front of the armoured car, reaches into the right wheel well and *clank*, attaches one of the hooks to the suspension's right control arm, then slides across to the left wheel well and *clank*, attaches the second hook to the left control arm. He slithers out from beneath the vehicle and finds his feet as Red directs a second security guard to lie face down on the footpath too.

Black and Red turn to the remaining security guard. He's a kid, can't be more than twenty-one, who sits behind the steering wheel in the cabin. He makes sure both front doors are locked.

Red raps his pistol on the windscreen: 'Out!'

The kid shakes his head, his expression one of petrified resolve. Red knows that firing at the bulletproof windscreen won't do any good so there's no use wasting time. Instead Red points at the guy,

'You'll want to get soon enough.' Red gestures to Yellow with a thumps up sign.

Yellow sees it through the truck's rear window and steps on the gas. The turbo diesel barks and the prime mover surges forward. The metal chains attached to the truck's fifth wheel uncoil.

Twang. The chains pull tight and jolt the armoured car forward. Its handbrake is engaged so the wheels don't turn but it's dragged along the street anyway.

The truck's five hundred and twenty horsepower Cummings engine strains under the load as it hauls the armoured car forward in a long, screeching, slow motion skid. Black runs to the truck's passenger door, yanks it open and climbs in as Red vaults onto the truck's rear section and grabs the back of the cabin for balance.

The truck picks up speed. The armoured car's tyres grind and rip on the bitumen, trail an acrid grey smoke as it is dragged along Collins Street. Red scans the roadway, searches for the guy who was following them earlier. There doesn't seem to be any sign of him – oh, there he is.

He sprints after them, a phone to his ear.

In the truck's cabin Yellow keeps the accelerator flat to the floor, the speedometer touching fifty-five kilometres an hour. Their destination is just a short tour across town. It shouldn't take more than three minutes to reach the large, empty garage they rented for today.

A siren echoes across the soundscape. Black looks through the windscreen and is unhappy to see blue and red flashing lights in the distance. 'Police.'

Yellow nods. 'I have it under control.'

'I told you I had a bad feeling about this.'

'Reminding me of that doesn't help.'

Black glances at the speedometer. 'We won't outrun them doing fifty-five.'

'Really? Thanks for stating the obvious. I would never have worked that out on my own.'

Yellow and Black see the Commodore police cruiser swerve through the traffic towards them. It's only a few seconds away.

Black's voice vibrates with concern: 'What are we going to do?'

'You're going to stop whining and I'm going to do *this*.' Yellow pulls on the steering wheel.

The truck tips into a sharp turn and its left front left wheel lifts off the roadway.

'Jeeze!' Behind the cabin Red realises they're pulling a giant U-turn and holds on tight. The armoured car is yanked into the U-turn as well and momentarily mounts the footpath —

Crunch. It obliterates a post box then is hauled back across the roadway in a giant, screeching arc, tyres burning from unrelenting friction —

Boom. The right side front wheel gives up the ghost and detonates in a spray of flaming rubber —

Boom. The right side rear tyre blows next and the metal wheel rims dig into the road. The armoured car flips over and hangs in the air for an impossibly long moment —

Slam. It thumps on to its right side and the windscreen pops out.

The truck finishes its U-turn and drives along the opposite side of the road. Red watches the police cruiser roar straight towards them as the armoured car swings around to complete its U-turn —

Wham. It spanks the side of the cruiser and knocks it across the road —

Smash. The cruiser is launched through the window of a

Priceline pharmacy and comes to a dead stop, lights still flashing, siren still blaring.

Yellow watches it in the side-view mirror then turns to Black with grin. 'Told you I had it under control.' Yellow floors the accelerator and the truck picks up speed. 'That's more like it. That thing's easier to tow when it's on its side.' The truck touches sixty-five, then seventy kilometres an hour. 'Okay, we can't make it to location A so we head for location B.'

Black nods, realises making that the U-turn has changed their plans. Unfortunately location B is a lot further away.

Billy stops running as the truck head back towards him on the side of the road. It still tows the armoured car now on its side and sprays the street with a shower of orange sparks. He had called for backup. Unfortunately the police cruiser that arrived had just been hurled through a shop window.

There's movement in the armoured car's cabin. Billy's eyes flick to a terrified security guard who climbs out through the hole where the windscreen used to be.

'What the hell?' Billy needs to help that guy. He turns, scans his surroundings — and twenty metres up the street sees a way he can do it.

Red watches the Security Guard clamber onto the side of the armoured car. Why's he doing that? Surely it's safer *inside* the cabin.

Bet he wishes he got out when he had the chance.

Vroom. A black flash swerves across the roadway and speeds towards the armoured car.

Is that a Vespa? Yes, it's a black Vespa, the same one the truck knocked over earlier, and it's being ridden by that guy who was following them earlier.

The odd thing about Billy's Bathurst near-death accident at Bathurst is that he didn't lose his mojo afterwards. In fact the *opposite* happened. He now has *too much* mojo. Instead of realising that life is a precious blessing that must be treasured, he went the other way and now thinks nothing can kill him, or at least it would take a lot more than rolling a car eighteen times at two hundred kilometres an hour. That's why he's so good at his job. He is, by any real measure, fearless.

Which is why he gives the Vespa full throttle and swerves through traffic towards the armoured car. The scooter's little engine sounds like a sewing machine on crack but hopefully has enough power for what he's about to do. It had been knocked over by the truck but was still in working condition and only took a moment to hot wire.

Vroom. Billy swerves around a Corolla, then a Hyundai, and homes in on the armoured car. The sound of it scraping across the bitumen sets his teeth on edge.

Clang. The truck clips a vehicle —

'Christ!' A Subaru spins towards him. He works the Vespa's handlebars and swerves around the wreck. 'That was close —'

Bam. A tyre bounces through the wall of sparks and clips Billy's shoulder.

Ahhh. It doesn't hit him that hard, but it's hard enough to make the Vespa wobble. Violently. It's called a tank-slapper in the bike riding world and it's a bastard to recover from. The scooter bucks and weaves like an unbroken stallion, tries to turf him off. He holds on tight, works the brakes, wipes off some pace and recovers his balance.

'Man!' Instead of being chastened by the experience it only *confirms* that he's hard to kill him. He watches the armoured car drift left across the roadway, picks his moment, guns the bike down its right side and ploughs through the wall of sparks. He can feel the pricks of heat on his face and hands as he searches for the security guard —

There. He's balanced on the side of the bonnet and clutches the windscreen's frame with an expression of abject terror. It would appear that the full extent of his plan was to climb out onto the bonnet. Now that he's there he doesn't seem to know what to do next.

Billy pulls up beside him and shouts over the roaring wind and the scraping metal. 'Get on!'

The security guard looks from where he's crouched on the bonnet, to the scooter, which is a metre away, then back to the bonnet. He shakes his head.

Billy can't believe it. 'Are you kidding me? Get on!'

'I can't.'

'What do you mean you can't? It's a whole lot better down here than up there.'

'I'm scared.'

From the rear of the truck Red watches the security guard and the guy on the Vespa have what appears to be an argument.

What the hell could they fighting about?

Then the penny drops. The security guard doesn't want to get off the truck. First he didn't want to get out of the truck and now he doesn't want to get onto the bike. 'What a dickhead.' Red really wants him to get off. It'll save them the trouble of dealing with him later.

Billy shouts at the security guard: 'Why are we even having this conversation? Get on!'

'What if we have an accident?'

'You're on top of an armoured car being dragged through the city on its side. You're already having an accident!'

The security guard is still unsure.

'We're not going to have an accident. Okay?'

The security guard takes this in – then nods reluctantly. 'Okay.'

'Okay. Good. Now do it.'

The security guard steels himself, slides across the bonnet, reaches out with his right foot, hooks it over the bike, then slump-drops onto the seat behind Billy. He looks back at the guard. 'See? No problem —'

The armoured car abruptly lurches right.

Thump. It slams into Billy's leg. It doesn't hurt but it sends the Vespa into another violent tank-slapper. Billy slows the bike as best he can but can't stop the gyrations. 'We're having an accident!'

'What?! But you just said —!' The security guard doesn't finish the sentence because the Vespa bucks them both off. Billy knows the landing is going to hurt but he's equally concerned by the fact that he's wearing his favourite Levi 501s. He's owned them for a decade without once ripping them but now he's about to feed them to the bitumen.

Wham. He lands on his left thigh and it hurts more than he could have imagined. He can feel the blacktop burn through the denim as he slides towards a line of cars parked by the side of the road, the spinning Vespa to his right, the screaming security guard to his left.

One of the parked cars pulls out, a white Honda Jazz, and Billy realises he's about to slide *under* the Japanese econobox. He raises his feet, lines them up with the bumper bar and grits his teeth —

Thunk. His Blundstone boots thump into the bumper bar – and the Honda lurches to a halt. The security guard clunks into the next

car along as the Vespa spins to a stop nearby, its engine still bur-
bling. Billy drags himself to his feet as the Honda drives around him
and peels off without even a 'you okay?'

Billy's right thigh stings from a nasty road rash and his palms and
elbows are skinned and bleeding, but he's not feeling pain because
the adrenaline is pumping. The pain, he knows, will come later, it
always comes later, but for now the adrenaline is in charge.

He turns and helps the security guard to his feet, who then studies his own skinned hands and elbows, then looks at Billy gratefully.
'You saved my life.'

'You're welcome.' Billy turns, locks eyes on the truck as it tows
the armoured car up the street, sees there's a guy wearing a red helmet standing behind the cabin with, Billy is sure, a pistol in hand.

What does he do now?

He quickly realises he doesn't *have* to do anything. He already
called for backup *and* saved this grateful security guard, he could
just walk back to Maccas, clean up these cuts and grazes in the
restroom and order another plate of hotcakes. But, for good or bad,
that's just not in his nature. He wants to stop the people currently
dragging an armoured car down the middle of his city before they
really hurt someone – and, just as importantly, he wants to ride this
adrenaline rush for as long as he can.

He glances at the Vespa. It's *really* dinged up but the engine still
runs and neither of the tyres are flat. He picks it up and throws a leg
over the seat.

The security guard watches him, both confused and surprised.
'What are you doing?'

'I'm gonna catch those pricks.' Billy revs the engine and screeches
off, the rear tyre smoking the whole way.

Yellow glances at Black. 'How's it looking?'

Black studies the right side-view mirror. 'The guy on the Vespa is gone. Apart from that, no problems.'

Yellow nods then scans the roadway. 'Location B is close — damn.' Flashing lights in the distance. The Police. *Again. Two* cruisers this time. They speed towards the truck, five hundred metres away and closing. 'Looks like it's going to be Location C.' He takes in a set of traffic lights ahead and points the truck towards them —

Boom. It ploughs into the narrow gap between a BMW and a Toyota, swats them aside then turns hard left down another road.

'Yowza!' Tyres screech as Red holds on tight, watches the wrecked vehicles spin away as the armoured car swings out on the chain behind —

Clang. It sideswipes a street sign, knocks it flat —

Clung. It glances off a traffic light junction box then shimmies back into the middle of the road.

Billy sees the truck make the turn and immediately knows what he must do. He swerves the Vespa hard left and plunged into a narrow street that runs parallel to the road the truck turned down. He guns the little engine, then turns hard right down an even narrower lane. It's clear of traffic —

An older gentleman hobbles onto a zebra crossing to the right.

Woh! Billy swerves around him.

The old bloke raises a fist. 'Ass clown!'

And quite right, he should be annoyed, that was too close. Billy shouts back at him. 'Sorry —!'

A van backs out of a driveway to the left.

Woh! Billy swerves around it.

Jeezelouise.

He rides on, takes a deep breath, focuses on the intersection ahead. He doesn't have a plan so much as a general idea of what he wants to achieve. He just needs to be careful of that guy wearing the red helmet who's perched behind the truck's cabin.

Billy reaches the intersection and sees the truck thunder along the road from the right. It's near.

Crunch. The armoured car sideswipes a taxi. It thumps onto the footpath and narrowly misses a group of teenagers.

Christ that was close.

Billy grits his teeth. He needs to stop these pricks before they kill someone. He guns the Vespa and shoots straight towards the truck's cabin, pulls up beside it. He can just make out someone wearing a black helmet through the tinted passenger window. He looks straight ahead and doesn't appear to notice Billy.

Billy glances back, can see no sign of the red helmeted guy, then takes in the truck's large cylinder-shaped petrol tank beside him. That'll work nicely. He grabs hold of it, clicks the Vespa's gearbox into neutral, then wedges the right side of the scooter's handlebars between the bodywork and the tank so the bike freewheels along beside the truck.

He places his right foot on the petrol tank's step, grabs the handle on the side of the cabin and levers himself up. He presses his body flat against the bodywork, hands splayed for maximum surface contact, then shuffles towards the rear of the cabin. The moment he reaches it he'll need to subdue Mister Red. The upside is that he has the element of surprise on his side. The downside is that he has no weapon if the Mister Red isn't easily surprised.

He reaches the rear of the cabin and looks back. He can see where the metal chains that drag the armoured car are looped around the fifth wheel but he can see no sign of the bloke —

Mister Red rises from behind the fifth wheel, a nine millimetre pistol in hand.

'Oh shit —'

Bam. He fires as Billy swings back to the side of the cabin.

Thud. The bullet thumps into the bodywork.

So much for the element of surprise. Now what?

A flash of sunlight off a windscreen to the right. Billy pivots towards it.

Oh no.

A tram thunders straight towards the truck — and Billy. Its wheels lock up and squeal as the stunned driver attempts an emergency stop.

The tram slows.

It's going to miss the truck —

But it won't miss the armoured car.

This is going to be bad.

Wham. The tram slams into the rear of the armoured car.

Smash. The tram's front windscreen detonates in a shower of glass. The armoured car shudders, then continues on its way —

Twang. The impact sends a giant tremor along the steel chains and vibrates the truck like a giant tuning fork —

Billy is jerked sideways. He watches Mister Red throw out his gun hand to steady himself against the fifth wheel —

Clank. He misses and knocks the weapon from his hand.

The truck shudders again.

Woh! Billy overbalances and drops to the roadway below —

Hey! He catches hold of one of the chains, the steel caps toes of his Blundstone boots dragging along the roadway. He hangs on for dear life, the chain creaking in his palms, which now scream with a special kind of pain, the gravel rash not enjoying contact with bare metal.

He pushes it from his mind and looks up at Mister Red. On his knees, he reaches down into the chassis of the truck to retrieve the gun he dropped. It's balanced on a support beam just below. His fingers touch it but he can't quite grab it.

Good. Billy needs to move his arse before Mister Red gets hold of it. He glances back at the armoured car. It's about five metres away.

Can I get to it along this chain?

The truck's engine note changes as the driver drops down a gear. He's using the engine to brake and the vehicle slows. Unfortunately no one informed the armoured car about the braking situation so it continues at its current pace and slides directly towards Billy. It's going to crush him against the back of the truck —

Clang. The armoured car slams into the back of the truck as Billy swings out of its way, grabs the armoured car's bonnet and climbs on. How ironic. He took all that time to talk the security guard off this thing and now he's thrilled to be on it.

Billy levers himself up, grabs onto the windscreen's pillar then looks back at Mister Red. The guy's still trying to snag that bloody pistol. Billy's eyes are drawn to his helmet and for the first time he realises it has white markings on it as well. There's something familiar about it. Come to think of it the helmet on the guy sitting in the passenger seat was familiar too. It was black with coloured markings. Billy looks through the rear window of the cabin at the guy driving the truck. He also wears a helmet, yellow with strips around it. He's sure he's seen that before as well.

The truck's engine barks and the vehicle picks up speed again, thunders beneath an overpass, its exhaust note reverberating off the cement surface above.

Mister Red rises and finds his feet, the pistol in his right hand.

Oh bugger.

Well, that's that then. Billy realises any chance of bringing these guys to justice is over. He now needs to find a way out of this situation before he gets himself shot. He could just step off the armoured car and drop to the roadway below, take his chances with the landing, but he'd prefer not. Four months in traction is enough for one lifetime. Unfortunately it looks like his only option.

The truck clears the overpass and takes a tight turn. The armoured car swings out —

Crunch. It mounts the footpath and flattens a small tree, then another, keeps swinging until Billy realises he just might have found another option.

Red aims his pistol at the guy as he climbs to the top of the armoured car. Yep, it's the same fella who ran after the truck, the one who commandeered the Vespa and saved that moron of a security guard. The guy looks like he has some nasty road burns, his jeans ripped and torn, his hands and arms bloody. Red studies him, intrigued. 'Who the hell is this guy?'

Actually it doesn't matter because he's about to bite the big one.

Red raises the weapon, aims it and squeezes the trigger —

The guy takes three long, fast steps then jumps off the armoured car. He hangs in the air, arms windmilling, legs pumping like he's riding an invisible bicycle.

Red tracks his trajectory with the pistol, finger tight on the trigger. It's a shame to kill the guy. He kept on coming until he was all out of options then made the ballsiest escape Red could have imagined. Still, he stuck his nose in where it didn't belong and that couldn't be tolerated.

Red pulls the trigger.

Billy sails through the air —

Bam. 'Ahhh.' He feels a sharp sting on his left shoulder. It hurts like hell but that's not what worries him. It's the Yarra River in front of him that's the real concern. The downside of having spent his youth driving around racetracks is that he never learned how to swim. Not the Aussie crawl, not breaststroke, not even bloody dog paddle. So why he's now decided to jump into a large body of water can only be put down to a serious lack of options. Fortunately, there's a wooden walkway beside the river.

Woh! He clears it by the width of a cigarette paper – and grabs it with his left hand as he plunges into the Yarra's icy brown depths. He jolts to a stop as the water stings his gravel rash. He quickly rises to the surface, looks at the shoulder and realises it's a bullet wound. It's minor in the scheme of things, just a graze really, but still, that prick just shot him.

Billy turns and watches the truck drag the armoured car across the wrought-iron arch of Queens Bridge, catches sight of the red hel-meted bastard standing at the rear.

That's it.

Billy knows why that red helmet looks so familiar. He can't believe it took so long to work out. It's the same helmet as the one Formula One World Champion Michael Schumacher wore during his years driving for Ferrari.